MARYLAND
WRITERS'
ASSOCIATION

The Maryland Writers' Association (MWA) is a voluntary, not-for-profit organization dedicated to supporting the art, business, and craft of writing in all its forms. The MWA strives to:
- Bring together aspiring, emerging, and established writers of all genres and disciplines;
- Serve as an information and networking resource;
- Help members make contacts that lead to publication;
- Encourage writers to reach their full potential, and;
- Promote writing within Maryland communities.

In keeping with the MWA's mission, a national novel contest was held in 2014. The submitted excerpt from *The Last Government Girl* won against forty novel entries and is published here in full. We are grateful to all the judges who participated in evaluating the submissions:
Lalita Noronha, MWA President
Holly Morse-Ellington, MWA Vice President
Brandi Dawn Henderson
Shenan Prestwich

A special thanks to the judge of our finalists:
Dean Bartoli Smith

We'd also like to thank Apprentice House Press for this partnership with the MWA contest. The MWA couldn't achieve its goals for its members without such a supportive community of writers, editors, and publishers.

The Last Government Girl

The Last Government Girl

Ellen Herbert

Apprentice House
Loyola University Maryland
Baltimore, Maryland

This book is a work of fiction. Names, characters, places, and incidents either are the products of the author's imagination or are used fictitiously.

First Edition

Printed in the United States of America

Hardcover ISBN: 978-1-62720-086-8
Paperback ISBN: 978-1-62720-087-5
E-book ISBN: 978-1-62720-088-2

Design by Apprentice House

Published by Apprentice House

Apprentice House
Loyola University Maryland
4501 N. Charles Street
Baltimore, MD 21210
410.617.5265 • 410.617.2198 (fax)
www.ApprenticeHouse.com

info@ApprenticeHouse.com

In memory of my mother,
Helen Smith Klarpp,
a government girl

1

The town of Saltville lay wedged between the Blue Ridge and Allegheny Mountains in a valley not green, but gray. A sea of hungry salt marshes hid below the surface, sometimes sucking down miner's shacks, any structure foolish enough to be built on the flats. Things of value must be set up high, the company store, the train station, and the two-story houses with roofs of tin.

In front of one such house, a young woman named Eddie, short for Edwina, stood inside the boxwood hedge beneath a star-tossed sky. She held her breath. She waited for wonderful.

No light burned in the house behind her. Upstairs, her twin sisters in their double bed, content in their double life, tied rags in each other's hair, so they would have curls for school tomorrow. They needed no light. They read each other's heads like Braille. Across the hall, Mama lay terrified, sinking like shacks on the marsh. Behind the house, the garage sat dark and empty, its doors flung wide. Dad, a night supervisor, was at work mining salt.

Eddie heard the 9:13's long shrill whistle, her favorite night music. She breathed its delicious coal smoke and scorched iron smell, as it sped past to cities she had only read about. "Washington, Washington, Washington," she whispered like a prayer.

Next came the best part: the dining car. Golden light spilled from its windows. The diners' happy faces passed in a blur. How did she know they were happy? They must be. They were going somewhere.

If she stayed here, she would sink like her mother. She vowed to leave by summer. There was a war on and office workers needed in Washington.

2

In that gray in-between when night has slipped away and dawn waits on the doorsill, Vernon Lanier found the girl on the towpath beside the C&O Canal. She lay stomach down, her head to one side, her skirt hiked up, showing her thighs. Lines had been drawn on the backs of her bare legs to look as if she wore seamed stockings.

"Miss?" His own voice startled him. "Miss?"

She didn't move. Her coal black hair had unraveled from the roll that wreathed her head. A high heel dangled off one foot, her other foot bare, her sole pink as the inside of a seashell.

A well of sorrow rose in Vernon. What had brought her to this place? But he knew, oh he knew. He was young once, full of sap and desperate to be alone with Bess.

He knelt beside her, dampness seeping into the knees of his overalls. Around him, the world went silent, even the doves hushed, and the skin on the back of his neck prickled. He brought his fingertip to her face. Her skin felt cold and firm and dead.

He leapt to his feet. He could not help her. He picked up her baby blue coat lying nearby and read its label: *This garment was sewn with love for Doris R. Reynolds by her mother.* He covered Doris in her coat made with love.

From the towpath something glinted. He dug out a piece of jewelry, two joined silver bars, familiar somehow. High boy voices sounded behind him. Probably kids going fishing, but he wasn't waiting to find out.

He dropped the pin in his pocket, flung his feed sack over his shoulder, and took off, splashing through swampy woods a few hundred yards until he reached the Potomac, the river he loved like a friend. Here it was wide, studded with rocks, its current treacherous. Fog rose from it as if the river were breathing heavy.

He skittered along its shore and scrambled up the embankment to the Chain Bridge.

While he felt awful about Doris, he wished he hadn't walked so close to her on the towpath, its dirt soft from recent rain. Mud had seeped into the bottoms of his work boots. He'd pushed tacks through their soles to keep from slipping when he shingled the roofs of tempos on the National Mall. He'd taken the tacks out, but tiny holes remained. His soles were like fingerprints. They identified him.

Just as the sun pushed up from the horizon, he ran onto the bridge.

"What's your hurry, mister?" called a fisherman, his hat stuck with lures, fishing line angled into the rapids. "Seen you running hell bent for leather upriver."

Vernon tugged his cap low. No sense giving this man a better look. The police liked to find some tramp to haul in and charge. While Vernon might look like a tramp, he was just a mountain man come down the Potomac to work for the war effort.

"Catch anything?" Vernon tried to sound casual.

"Grandpappy catfish long as your arm."

Fishermen and their lies, not that Vernon would challenge him.

Usually he took the towpath to Great Falls, Maryland, but today he needed to travel far from the canal. Soon police would be swarming around Doris. He listened for a siren. None came.

Once over the bridge on the Virginia side, he felt eyes watching him. He kept looking over his shoulder. He walked fast, not quite a run but almost.

The sun had climbed into the blue dome when an engine revved behind him.

A delivery truck was barreling downhill toward him. The road's shoulder narrowed here. He had nowhere to go.

The engine drowned all sounds. White metal filled his vision. He stood paralyzed, heart kicking at his chest. He was going to die. When the truck's bumper was almost upon him, he leapt the guardrail, tumbling downhill through soft weeds. A sycamore's red trunk stopped him. Dazed, he opened his eyes and stared into the sycamore's bare branches, scratching at the sky.

"Hey buddy," a man called from the road. "You all right?"

"I reckon." Vernon patted the tree trunk in thanks and crawled up. The man offered his hand over the guardrail. Vernon hesitated. Was this the driver who almost hit him?

Vernon let the man haul him onto the road. "Your brakes give out?"

"We weren't the ones tried to run you over." He was a bald man in overalls dirty as Vernon's. "Never seen a man fly till you went over into that ravine."

Vernon heard the mountains in his voice and accepted the bandana he offered. "Thanks." He wiped blood from his chin. His arms were scratched up good, too.

A horn honked. An empty chicken truck idled ahead. The driver and another man sat in the cab. "We're headed the other side of Martinsville," the man said. "Where you going?"

"Going home," Vernon said. "Not far over the West Virginia line."

"Then hop aboard, brother."

Vernon grabbed his sack and climbed into the truck bed among empty chicken cages. Once they started moving, feathers flew like a snow storm. While his body ached from his tumble, cool wind blew sense into him. With tires and so much else rationed, a lot of vehicles on the road were unsafe. That delivery truck's brakes probably gave out, and the driver was too scared to come back and check on Vernon.

Returning home usually cheered him, but not this time. In his mind's eye, he saw Doris's neck with its red burns the width of a man's belt and her frightened eyes. She was murdered only a few hundred yards from the abandoned lockkeeper's cottage, where he had slept last night. She must have screamed, but he didn't hear her.

He took the twin silver bars from his pocket. Captain's bars. Did the pin belong to her killer? It might be a clue. He wished he could put it back. It was wrong for him to take it. He vowed to find a way to make this right.

A little before midnight, his wife, Bess, in her nubby beige bathrobe opened the door. "Welcome, Vernon. Bet you're hungry. Got stew and biscuits right ready for you."

All that was home rushed at him. "Glad to be back, Bess." Once he finished eating, they sat on the sofa, where he told Bess about finding Doris.

"She was probably drunk and sleeping it off." Bess's tone was sharp. "Don't go back to sin city, Vernon. Plenty of jobs right here. Farms need laborers, and there's the new Pet Milk plant in Shepherdstown."

He sighed. How quickly they slid into their old argument. They sat side-by-side, their shoulders touching, but not their hearts or minds.

"I'm a roofer, Bess, and needed in Washington." He lowered his voice. "Laugh if you want, but our foreman Red tells us we're fighting Hitler one shingle at a time." By day's end when Vernon's back felt permanently bent, Red's words made him stand straighter.

Bess turned to him. "I worry, Vernon. You shouldn't stay in a place where no one knows you. What if you go sleepwalking again?"

He sandwiched her face between his hands and kissed her hard, hoping to ignite the white hot flame that once burned between them.

She pushed him away as usual. "You're almost fifty, Vernon. Act your age."

Aching for what they'd once had, he sat back, rolled a cigarette, and lit it.

He wouldn't argue about Washington, but he wanted her to understand about the girl. "She wasn't drunk, Bess. Girls like her are coming from all over the country to work for government agencies." He tugged smoke deep into his lungs. "They do office jobs to free up men to go fight in the war."

The world was involved in a great struggle, and he had taken a side. The military wouldn't accept him, but he found a way to do his part. He had roofed acres of government buildings and would roof acres more.

Bess hugged her bathrobe tighter. "Don't kid yourself, Vernon. These gals come to Washington to get away from their folks and go wild, not because they're patriotic. And that gal you found was a floozy who got right what she deserved."

"You're wrong, Bess. She was no floozy. She's what they call a government girl."

3

Sunday, May 28, 1944
Saltville, Virginia

"Sir, why haven't we left yet?" Eddie asked the conductor, who hurried down the aisle without answering.

The world awaited 300 miles north in Washington, D.C. Eddie felt its pull, a force strong as gravity. What was the hold up? Why were they still here?

Rachel sat next to the window in an emerald dress drenched in sunlight, her curly black hair tamed into victory rolls on top, the rest of her hair cascading down her back. "The longer the train stays here, the more time Papa has to change his mind."

Their reflections, overlapping in the glass, were a study in contrasts. Eddie, a head taller, was a lanky, green-eyed blonde, while Rachel had curves in all the right places with eyes the color of chestnuts that turned anthracite hard when she got angry. But beneath their surfaces, they were alike. Eddie sensed Rachel's heart thudding in time with her own. They wanted to be gone, gone, gone.

Together, their fathers watched them from the depot platform. Their shadows reached downhill to the train as if to hold their daughters in Saltville.

The rest of their lives depended on the next few moments. Had the train broken down? Would they be forced to stay?

Too much tension, *Sturm und Drang* in German, Eddie's college minor. At one time, German had comforted her, but that was before Hitler. Now she seldom spoke her grandmother's language, except to Rachel.

"Don't look at your father," she told Rachel. "If we look, we turn into salt like Lot's wife and get stuck in Saltville forever."

An old joke between them, but Rachel didn't smile. Instead, she rubbed her silver heart-shaped locket, "go, go, go," her incantation.

Out the edge of her eye, Eddie saw that the shorter shadow on the platform disappear, and she tensed. "Rachel, I think your father's coming down to the train."

Rachel linked her arm through Eddie's. "I'm going with you, no matter what he says."

"Of course," Eddie said as if she was certain.

Months ago, Rachel told Eddie about her nightmares the Nazis had invaded Saltville and were coming for her because she was Jewish. Eddie had promised to hide her on Smith land so deep in the mountains no one would ever find her.

Yet at this moment, Eddie wasn't sure she could protect Rachel from her father, Moses Margolis, owner of Margolis Department Store, a powerful man in Saltville. If he'd changed his mind about Rachel working in Washington, she would have to get off the train.

A knock on the glass startled them. "Lower the window, Rachel," Mr. Margolis called. His voice carried as if he was on the loudspeaker at his store calling for a clerk to come to house-wares.

Rachel fiddled with the window latch. "Sorry Papa, it won't budge."

"Call me tonight. Understand? Tonight. Reverse the charges. I need to know you arrived safely. Do you still have the paper I gave you?"

Rachel took an envelope from her alligator purse and pressed it to the glass.

"Our cousin's address and phone number," he said. "And his factory's address. I told him you would come for Shabbat so——"

The train let out a shrill whistle and chuffed forward, slowly then faster, faster. The most beautiful sound Eddie had ever heard. Rachel's face opened in an astonished grin, her dimples deep with delight. Mr. Margolis yelled more instructions lost in the noise and smoke.

Once they left him behind, they hugged hard, silenced by joy. In one swift motion, they peeled off their gloves, unpinned their hats, and smoothed each other's hair. Like monkeys, Eddie thought, deliriously happy monkeys.

Rachel ripped the envelope in two and was about to rip further.

"Don't." Eddie grabbed the pieces, still large enough to read. "You're going to have to visit your cousin eventually."

"I'm tired of being under Papa's thumb. And I wish we didn't have to stay with your aunt. The last thing we need is some old biddy watching and reporting on what we do."

"True." But the only way Eddie convinced her father to let her go was to agree that she and Rachel would live on Georgia Avenue with his stepsister, Viola Trundle.

Aunt Viola was living up to her reputation as a cheapskate. In her letter, she informed Eddie she would charge each girl ten dollars a month for the room they would share and insisted they send her a month's rent in advance. And for housing government girls, Aunt Viola would get extra ration coupons from the Office of Price Administration.

"Hide me," Rachel said. "I want to change shoes."

Eddie held her sweater wide like a curtain, so no one could see Rachel reach under her dress and tug down her woolen hose. Rachel pushed off her saddle shoes and slipped on white anklets and high heels, sexy ones she'd used all her shoe coupons to buy.

"Hello, ladies." A dark-eyed soldier leaned over them. "How would you two like to have cocktails with us in the club car?" The blond soldier behind him said, "I second that."

Ah, temptations already, liquor and men. Eddie laughed inside. This train, the Crescent out of New Orleans, was packed with military men traveling north from bases all over the South. Able-bodied men had been scarce in southwest Virginia. Under her father's gaze, Eddie had ignored the men aboard, but at this moment, she felt as if she'd landed in a candy factory.

Still she said, "No, thank you." She needed to sit and feel the miles grow between her and Saltville. This was the greatest day of her life. Even when she went to college, she didn't leave home. She went to Emory and Henry seven miles from Saltville. While life on campus was another world, every night she hurried to board the bus, relieved when they rounded the corner into town and she saw their house was still standing, that Mama hadn't set it on fire.

"Is there a piano in the club car?" Rachel asked Private Dark Eyes.

"Yep, there is." He winked. "What's your favorite song, honey?"

"Rachel." Eddie had promised Mr. Margolis she would look after Rachel, a recent graduate of Saltville High, where Eddie had been a teacher. Because a friendship between a teacher and student wasn't allowed, they had kept theirs a secret.

"You're barking up the wrong trees with them two," a female voice called behind them. "They're snooty as all get out."

"Says who?" Rachel got on her knees and turned backward to look into the seat behind them. Eddie rose to see who was speaking.

"Pearl Ballou, that's who. Remember me, Miss Smith?" Pearl sat in near darkness, her window shade pulled down. A kerchief covered her hair and obscured her face.

At the sight of her former student, Eddie groaned inside. "Hello Pearl. Where are you traveling to?" Pearl, a bony redhead, had been in Eddie's remedial English class last fall until she dropped out because she was pregnant. Pregnancy was also not allowed at Saltville High.

"To Washington City." Pearl lifted her chin. "Gonna be a government girl."

Eddie wondered who was caring for Pearl's baby, not that this was any of her business. "We're going there, too, Pearl. We took the Department of the Army's test two months ago at the bank. I don't recall seeing you there."

Pearl's expression soured. "You always did put a lot of store in tests, Miss Smith. Not ever body has to take one. If I need testing, they'll do it when I git up there."

Eddie had learned not to trust anything Pearl said, but Pearl was no longer her student—hurrah. No need to argue. "We're not in school anymore, Pearl. Call me, Eddie."

"Okay, Eddie." When Pearl untied the kerchief, her faded blouse rode up showing a thick cloth pouch tied around her middle. What was it?

And where had Pearl gotten the money for a train ticket to Washington? Eddie remembered Pearl sneaking into the pool in summer and into Saltville's movie theater through the exit door. At school, she ate from other students' lunch pails. Pearl had been raised by a bootlegger uncle who never gave her anything except his daughter's hand-me-downs. Eddie felt sorry for her.

But if Pearl had sneaked onto the train, she was about to get caught.

"Ladies," the conductor gestured to Rachel and Eddie, "sit in your seats. Ticket, please," he said to Pearl.

Eddie listened intently. His ticket punch clicked, meaning Pearl had a ticket.

After he punched their tickets, Rachel said, "I'm making one of your dreams come true this evening, Eddie. I'm treating you to dinner in the dining car."

Eddie had told Rachel about her nights spent watching trains, longing to be on the inside, looking out the dining car's window. "Thank you," she said and felt the pull of tears.

"Don't cry, Bubula." Rachel's dimples appeared. "Our real lives started…" she checked her watch, "seventeen minutes ago. Nothing but blue skies ahead for us."

She lowered the window, so they could feel the wind in their faces.

For fun, they played a word game Eddie had made up. "*Aufregend*," Eddie said and waited for Rachel to give her a synonym in German. Rachel had been Eddie's only advanced German student. While Eddie helped Rachel write in German and translate Goethe, Rachel taught Eddie some Yiddish, a language akin to German, but more fun.

Once a silver twilight descended, Rachel said, "Our reservation is for six. Let's go."

Eddie turned in her seat. "Pearl, I brought fried chicken for our dinner. Since we're eating in the dining car, I hate for this to go to waste." She offered the box over the seat.

"Happy to oblige, Eddie." Pearl brought the box to her nose. "Saltville folks say your mama's a right good cook."

Eddie let this pass. Her mother was in the asylum at Kingsport again.

Months before the rest of the family knew, Eddie sensed Mama's mood turning blue. She tasted it in her mother's heavy biscuits and felt it in the buttons she broke in the wringer washing machine. By the time Mama did nothing but rock on the porch, sometimes in her nightgown, all of Saltville knew. At the asylum, she would be given electric shock treatments that left her hollow-eyed but eventually more like her former self when she would return home, and the whole cycle began again.

Only this time, Eddie wouldn't be there. The idea left her shaky with relief and fear.

In the dining car, a colored waiter in an elegant burgundy uniform showed them to a table covered with a white tablecloth, decorated by a single rose in a bud vase. The splendor of it all rushed at her. This was a day of firsts.

The car was filled with well-dressed diners, their voices rising in a pleasant babble accompanied by the silvery clink of knives and forks. The light above their table shone down as if they were on stage.

"Here I am on the inside looking out," Eddie whispered. "My *luftschloss* come true."

"*Our* sky castle, you mean." Rachel adjusted the green ribbon holding back her long hair. "We did it, Bubula. We left Saltville." Rachel shook salt from the shaker onto her palm and tossed it over her shoulder.

Eddie did the same. After the waiter brought their dinner, Eddie said, "To us, Schatzi." They touched glasses of lemonade and sipped.

"You look like Veronica Lake." Rachel lowered her voice. "Here we are Veronica and Elizabeth Taylor dining together. I hope some snoopy photographer doesn't spoil things by snapping our picture for *Photoplay.*" She tilted her head, posing.

Eddie giggled in a way she hadn't since girlhood, taking in her reflection in the window. She had released her thick blonde hair from its roll, and it fell into a perfect page boy. "We're the only women in here not wearing hats." She wanted to be modern, not improper.

"And the only women under forty." Rachel rolled her eyes. "I meant to ask Pearl if she would be working for the Department of the Army, too."

Eddie cut into her chicken pie, steam escaping its crust. "Rachel, I need to warn you about Pearl." She set her fork down. "I doubt she has a job in Washington."

Rachel arched an eyebrow. "Why don't you ever trust people, Eddie?" Her voice had an edge. "Pearl wouldn't say she had a job in Washington if she didn't."

"Yes, she would. When Pearl was my student, I caught her in plenty of lies. And she was impossible to teach." Pearl had made jokes behind Eddie's back, which got the other students laughing at their nervous young teacher.

Rachel leaned forward, her fingers rubbing her locket. One side of the heart contained Eddie's photo, the other Rachel's mother, who died four years ago. "You say you don't want to be judgmental like your father. So don't be." Rachel's voice gentled. "You've hurried through life, Eddie, finishing high school when there were only eleven grades, going through college in the wartime accelerated program. You're only twenty. Slow down, have fun, and stop doubting everyone."

Her words fell on fertile ground. Eddie was tired of being a mother to her seventeen-year-old twin sisters, a housekeeper for her father, and worst of all, her mother's caretaker.

"You're right. Off with mean Miss Smith, schoolmarm." Eddie scrunched her features and pretended to toss away a mask. "From now on, I'm Eddie Smith sunny government girl."

"That's the spirit." Rachel hummed along with music drifting from the club car. "Let's join them once we finish."

In the packed club car, the soldiers, sailors, and marines around the piano made room for them. They were singing a Rachel favorite, a silly song about mares and does eating oats.

To Eddie's surprise, Pearl stood on the opposite side of the piano, singing, her pointed chin lifted, bliss on her freckled elf face. Eddie's embroidered blue sweater was buttoned over Pearl's blouse. Rachel gave Eddie a pointed look and glanced down at Pearl's feet. Pearl wore the saddle shoes Rachel had kicked off.

Pearl glanced from Eddie to Rachel, as if she was afraid they would take their things. Eddie tried out a sunny, no-worry smile. After all, Pearl would be going her own way once they got to Washington. And good luck to her.

Pearl came from a family of notorious bootleggers, who lived far out in the woods so their stills wouldn't be discovered. Pearl must need to escape Saltville, too.

Pearl shifted to stand next to Rachel, who rested an arm on Pearl's shoulder and joined in the chorus. Eddie added her voice to theirs, and the three stood together singing as if they were the Andrews Sisters.

"A blonde, a brunette, and a redhead," a soldier said. "I must be in heaven."

With darkness pressing at the windows, they sang the miles away, really belting out Cole Porter's, "Don't Fence Me In," their escape from Saltville anthem.

As they sang, "I'll be seeing you in all those old familiar places..." Rachel's smile slipped. Eddie knew Rachel still grieved her mother. They both mourned their mothers, though Eddie's was still alive.

When a waiter presented them with a tray of Coca-Colas, Eddie looked around for who ever had sent them. Food and drinks were expensive on the train.

A blond officer, tanned and broad-shouldered, sat smoking at a nearby table. On his uniform collar, twin silver bars. He raised his glass of amber liquid to her questioning eyes. She lifted her bottle and mouthed *thank you.*

They were singing about swinging on a star, carrying moonbeams in a jar when the conductor called, "Union Station, Washington, D.C., fifteen minutes."

The singers let out a collective groan. The journey was over too soon. Eddie feared the whole summer would pass like their journey, and they'd be on their way back to Saltville and their old lives. The idea filled her with *verzagen,* despair.

Before leaving the club car, she glanced around to the man at the table. He crooked his finger at her, his battleship gray eyes hypnotic. Without a conscious decision to do so, she changed course and threaded her way through the crowd to him.

He set down his cigarette with its long worm of ash and pushed a small leather-bound notebook and an expensive fountain pen across the table to her. "Your name and telephone number, please, Miss."

Her insides turned to jelly, a reminder she was not the wunderkind Saltville folks said she was. She was a fraud. People always remarked on her maturity, her intelligence, but she was no valedictorian when it came to men.

In her best penmanship, she wrote what he'd asked.

On her way back to her seat, in a vestibule between cars, the Washington Monument appeared in a rain-flecked window. "Hello Washington," she whispered and placed her palm on the glass as if to embrace this city she loved already.

Yet cold dread crept up her spine, and she shivered at a danger she couldn't name. Washington must have its salt flats, too, dangers that could suck you under. And unlike Saltville, she didn't know where these were.

Beside Rachel again, she said, "I've become a floozy already. I gave my name and phone number to a man I don't know."

"You mean the handsome Marine Corps captain, who only had eyes for you?" Rachel winked. "If you didn't give him your number, how would you see him again?"

4

Washington, D.C.

Special Agent Jessup Lindsay weeded the squash vines. He was too anxious to do anything else. On the last Sunday of every month since January, a government girl's body had been found. And today was the last Sunday in May.

Let it not happen again, let it not happen, he repeated to himself.

Around him in the victory garden, dusk folded into night. The light was fading. If he wasn't careful, he would pull out a vine instead of a weed.

No lights burned from the back of the three-story house on Georgia Avenue, where their landlady, Mrs. Trundle, lived. Behind her house was the bungalow, little bigger than a henhouse, but he and Alonso called it home and paid Mrs. Trundle, a war profiteer if ever there was one, a whopping thirty-five dollars a month for it and for the garage. At first, their bungalow hadn't even been livable. Alonso, who Mrs. Trundle referred to as "your nigra manservant," had screened its windows and run a wire from the house for electricity.

Mrs. Trundle's back porch light came on. Jess straightened, dread coursing through him. This could be it.

Footsteps pounded down the porch steps. "Jess, Jess," Bert, Mrs. Trundle's adult son, called. Tall and stocky, Bert stood on the path in khaki trousers with Civil Defense pins attached to his shirt like military insignia.

Jess wiped his hand on his dark trousers and walked down the garden row. Bert's eyes searched Jess's for what…disapproval, scorn about his rigged uniform. Jess understood. Men not in uniform felt they owed folks an explanation.

Bert said, "Agent Friedlander's on the phone for you."

Jess's heart tightened like a fist. Their boss calling on Sunday night meant only one thing. He looked up at the window above the garage, where Alonso stood, his palm lifted to Jess. Alonso knew, too.

Jess pivoted and ran to the house.

"Wait up, Jess," Bert called. At the back porch, Bert reached around Jess to open the screen door as if Jess, who had only one arm, was helpless.

Jess, accustomed to people overdoing assistance, refused to take offense.

On a cabinet door in the kitchen, a calendar listed Bert's Civil Defense meetings as well as the dinners of fried spam and canned peaches Mrs. Trundle had planned for them.

Bert stopped at the sink to wash his hands. He was a clean man, who appropriately enough worked for a laundry.

Jess strode into the hall, floorboards creaking under him, the smell of mothballs and furniture polish strong in the humid air. At the telephone table tucked beneath the staircase, he lifted the receiver. "Jessup Lindsay," he said. Wedging the receiver between his shoulder and cheek, he motioned for Bert to give him privacy.

His hands red from washing, Bert pushed open the parlor door. Swing music spilled from the radio, the happy round notes of Benny Goodman's clarinet.

Jess took the pad from his pocket and wrote. "Okay Fred," he told Agent Friedlander. "We're on our way."

As soon as he hung up, squat Mrs. Trundle appeared in the parlor door, her face lifted to him, her white hair pulled into a bun so tight it made her eyes slant. She'd been eavesdropping. Again.

Mrs. Trundle considered this narrow strip of land on Georgia Avenue, the house, their bungalow behind it, and the garage fronting the alley, her kingdom, where she ruled like a tyrant. She believed everything that happened here was her business. He would never have rented from the busybody if they hadn't been desperate for a place to live in crowded DC.

"Mr. Lindsay, I'm worried about my niece and her friend taking the streetcar late with their luggage." She smoothed her dress over her big pillow of a bosom. "After you finish your business for the Bureau, would you kindly fetch them from Union Station?"

"No, Mrs. Trundle, I won't. My car is strictly for government use. Sorry." More polite than he felt. "The young ladies ought to take a taxi."

A red dot bloomed in each pale cheek. "Well, I never…"

He rushed back, feeling a twinge of guilt for refusing to pick up her government girls, not that they were in danger, not together.

Inside the bungalow, he grabbed his badge, hat, and jacket.

From the garage, their Packard's engine pierced the neighborhood's quiet.

He sprinted down the path to the alley, the air sugared with honeysuckle. Thick vines climbed the garage's brick wall and the wooden archway over the path, forming a leafy tunnel. Something shone among the vines: an electric wire.

Alonso backed the Packard out. Jess slid in beside him. On the seat between them was Alonso's beloved camera, big as a toddler in its case.

Two barefoot colored boys came running, closed the garage doors, and locked them with the padlock. Alonso paid the boys to watch the garage and alert him if anyone tried to break in. Gas was so precious thieves siphoned it from vehicles all over the city.

The boys stood at attention and saluted. "At ease, men," Alonso called with a salute of his own.

They rolled down the narrow alley between grim two-story tenements. This was the other Washington, Negro Washington. Alleyways like this lay tucked away all over the city. Behind a white neighborhood was a Negro one. The newspapers called the alleyways *the secret city.*

Jess noticed cardboard stars taped in some tenement windows, signifying these families had a member fighting in the war. Patriotism existed here, where running water, indoor plumbing, and electricity didn't.

From several windows, oil lamps gave off soft glows, but from the window closest to the garage, an electric bulb came on, lighting the alley like a beacon.

Jess stared at that bright window. "Ruth's waving at you, Al."

Without turning his head, Alonso touched his fedora's brim to her.

"What happens when Mrs. Trundle discovers you're sending electricity from her house to Ruth's?" Jess asked.

"Let there be light," Alonso said, a smile in his voice. "Don't worry, Jess. Mrs. Trundle never comes out here."

Women with babies in their laps and elderly men sat on stoops, fanning themselves. Someone played a spiritual on a harmonica. Voices sang along softly. Men rolling dice moved out of the way to let their sedan pass. Standing with hands on hips, the dice players glared at Alonso, a mulatto.

Jess rubbed the notch in his chin. "No wonder Ruth brings you collards and cornbread all the time."

"Ruth needed better light to study. She wants to become a government girl, but I doubt that's going to happen."

"Why not? This war's opening up opportunities for everyone. Only in wartime would the FBI hire a one-armed man."

"They hired the famous Alabama detective, Jessup Lindsay. And you forced them to take me."

Jess took in Alonso's profile, so like his own. "Brother, I let Fred know I never solved anything without you, that you and me are two crackers from the same cracker barrel."

The corners of Alonso's mouth lifted at the word *brother* for they were half-brothers, not that anything between them felt divided. On his own, Jess couldn't cuff a suspect, but Alonso could. They worked like a pair of hands and traveled from job-to-job. This one with the FBI was temporary. Once they solved this case, they'd be on their way. Unless they didn't solve it quickly enough for Director Hoover and were fired.

Alonso braked at the street. "Where was her body found, Jess?"

"Arlington National Cemetery." Jess took the map from the glove compartment. "Know where that is?" They had been on the job a month now and were still learning Washington.

"Sure. Put the map away." Alonso stuck his arm out the window, signaling a left turn.

They took Georgia Avenue, which became 7th Street, through the city. Whenever their motor car crossed streetcar tracks, Alonso reached over to steady his camera.

"He's right on schedule," Alonso said, a catch in his voice.

Jess understood how his brother felt. They hadn't found the killer yet. A young woman died tonight because they had failed to find this killer, and for that they grieved.

"Oh, yes," said Jess. "He's punctual and ritualistic."

Everywhere, streets were brightly lit, and sidewalks filled with uniforms, Navy whites and jaunty sailor hats, marines and army in summertime khaki. A long line waited to get into the Apex Movie Theater on 14th Street to see *Double Indemnity.*

"It's after 10:00 on a Sunday night, but this city's still having a Saturday night party." Jess scanned the faces in the crowd. Was the killer among them? "Only the party guests keep changing."

This was the strangest case they had ever worked. They hadn't found a single witness who remembered the victim when she disappeared, much less the man at her side.

Alonso stopped at a light. "According to that Bureau report, 15,000 servicemen from military bases a bus or train ride away pour into Washington every weekend."

"That's like having 15,000 suspects."

MPs, their whistles shrill, ran toward a crowd of sailors fighting with some soldiers.

Alonso pulled out from the light and steered around a telegram boy pedaling fast on his bicycle. The government sent telegrams to the families of servicemen wounded, missing in action, or killed. This boy would deliver bad news to some family tonight.

"You suppose if we questioned all 15,000 every weekend, we'd find him?" Jess sighed. "Which reminds me. We've got a few cells of servicemen to question after this is done tonight. The officer on duty blamed the heat for the rise in assaults on women." He heard his own discouragement.

"Sometime soon we're going to catch a break."

A police siren wailed in the distance.

"Hope you're right, Al. Most of these servicemen aren't stateside long enough to kill anyone. And we both know these kinds of killings are the hardest to solve because the victim doesn't know her killer."

Jess went over his notes in his head. They were overlooking something. "If government girls are so khaki wacky, how come they can't distinguish one uniform from another?"

The first victim told her roommates she'd met a Naval officer in Lafayette Park, but the second government girl, whose body was found in Rock Creek Park, wrote in her diary she met a handsome Marine at the USO. Were any of these the man the girls went off with? The man who wrapped his belt around their necks and squeezed the life out of them?

"I tested Ruth and Miss Minnie with those photographs." Alonso nodded at the windshield. "They got all the branches of the service right as well as each man's rank. What do you make of that?"

Jess considered. "Well, Ruth and her mother have lived in Washington a long time, so they've been around the military, and Miss Minnie works in a laundry, cleaning and mending uniforms. Whereas most government girls are new to the city, like these two coming to live at Mrs. Trundle's tonight. Maybe they'll allow us to test them."

They passed the Lincoln Memorial covered in darkness. Couples walked up its marble steps hand-in-hand. The memorial, kept dark at night as a conservation measure, had become a lovers' lane. Couples went there to kiss and pet.

But the killer found even more remote places to leave his victim's body.

They drove between the twin statues of muscular men on horseback flanking the Memorial Bridge and crossed the Potomac. Reflected light from the bridge's equidistant lamps flickered in the dark water.

"This river is a common thread in all the murders," Jess said. "Every place a woman's body has been found is near the Potomac, including the Rock Creek that flows from the Potomac."

"So you reckon the killer lives near the river?"

"It's a possibility. Maybe he brings the woman to his house, where he kills her then puts her in his car and leaves her close to the Potomac."

"That's a lot of traveling about, "Alonso said. "He's taking the chance of being seen."

Jess agreed. "But he hasn't been seen yet. We need to find a native Washingtonian, if there is such a person, to ask about the area. Where would the killer live to be able to do all that in secret? Where is the murder scene?" When they found that, they would find the killer.

The dark hills of Arlington National Cemetery rose in front of them. Lightning splintered the night sky. Once over the bridge, they entered the state of Virginia.

"This is Park Police territory, right?" Alonso asked.

"Yep." Jurisdiction was confusing here. The first two murders took place in Washington City, the third on the C&O Canal, and the fourth at Theodore Roosevelt Island, both under the Park Police.

They traveled partway around a circle until they turned right, crossed a cobblestone forecourt, and stopped outside large, wrought iron gates. A maroon Oldsmobile and a battered truck were parked to their right.

Emerging from the motor car, a curly-haired young man in Clark Kent glasses rushed Jess's side of the Packard. "You're the Bureau's man," he said and held out an identification card. "I'm Thad Graham, *Washington Herald.* What's going on up there? Somebody murdered in the cemetery?"

Jess heard Mississippi in his accent and smiled in spite of himself. Thad was like them, a Southerner a long way from home.

"Get back, you," a Park Policeman yelled and chased the reporter away, then came to Jess's window.

Jess showed him his Bureau ID. The policeman opened the gates and leaned in. "They're way up near the Confederate Memorial. Follow the signs. Sorry 'bout them newsies. They showed up right behind the DC police."

Once Alonso put the car in first, another man leaped in front of them and took a photograph through the windshield, his flashbulb blinding them.

Alonso braked hard, rocking them forward and back. The car stalled. "That's one photographer who near about got himself run over."

Jess blinked, adjusting his eyes. "Hope Thad Graham figures out what's going on here." The Bureau insisted on keeping a lid on the murders, so as not to discourage young women from coming to Washington to work. "Whatever you do, don't talk to the press," Fred had told them. "That comes from the highest level. Keep these murders quiet."

But in other cases, Jess and Alonso had gotten help from the public. Witnesses came forward. Someone might have seen something here in DC—the city was too crowded not to—but nothing had been reported.

With these murders, they were on their own and worse, government girls like the ones coming to live with Mrs. Trundle were unaware of the danger. These young women believed Washington was safe and that men in uniform were heroes, never suspecting one of their heroes was a killer.

5

"Stay close," Eddie told Rachel.

Union Station's covered platform overflowed with people shouting to be heard. Thunder rumbled overhead. Pandemonium reigned.

With her pulse in her throat, Eddie couldn't stop looking around. She was finally, finally, finally here.

"Never been in a city before." Pearl squeezed Eddie's forearm. "I'm so scared."

Eddie patted Pearl's hand. "I feel like a country mouse, too." The city's vastness loomed around her. *Mut*, she told herself, courage.

They stood beside their stacked luggage. Rachel had two suitcases in addition to her compact case and hat box. Eddie's giant suitcase, so heavy she could barely lift it, contained her typewriter and her beloved German-English dictionary.

How would they find their way with all their baggage?

Eddie noticed Pearl carried only a feed sack. Her curiosity pricked, she said, "By the way, Pearl, where are you staying in Washington?"

Pearl didn't answer.

Rachel took hold of Pearl's shoulders. "Where are you billeted, Pearl?"

"Same as you two, with Eddie's aunt." Pearl's grip on Eddie tightened. "Don't leave me, please."

"Of course, we won't," Rachel told her.

Eddie didn't believe Pearl, but it was almost midnight, too late to argue. They had to find Aunt Viola's house and get ready for tomorrow, their first day working for the government.

Rachel summoned a porter to help with their suitcases. Rachel had traveled to Washington before, even to New York City with her father on buying trips for their department store. She had seen the world and it showed.

They helped the wiry cinnamon-colored man load their things onto a cart. "Coming through," he called and pushed the cart. The crowd parted. He led them onto an elevator.

Upstairs in the lobby, Eddie craned her neck to take in the gorgeous vaulted ceiling and arched doorways. She felt as if they had joined a huge party. The lobby pulsed with young women, other soon-to-be government girls, who wore their skirts short, long and in-between, and spoke English with strange accents. Few wore hats, none had on gloves. They were modern women, and Eddie felt kinship with them. They had come to Washington to be typists, file clerks, secretaries, but they were soldiers in this war as much as men in uniforms.

The porter stacked their suitcases beside a revolving door and accepted the tip Rachel gave him. "Can we get a taxi out there?" Rachel pointed to the portico.

"Yes, Ma'am." He touched his cap's bill. "But tonight there are too many folks and not enough taxicabs. One of you needs to stand in that line and wait. Sorry I…"

"Rachel, look." Eddie pointed to a sign above the crowd that read **Miss Rachel Margolis**. Eddie started toward the sign when Rachel pulled her back.

"Papa must have called our cousin and asked for someone to meet us." Rachel bit her bottom lip. "I want nothing to do with whoever it is."

"Bless your father for sending someone to take us to Aunt Viola's."

The sign moved closer, held by a young man in starched overalls.

"Please, I have money for a taxi." Rachel squeezed Eddie's hand.

Eddie understood. They wanted to be independent.

Outside a crowd jostled for taxis. "Rachel, look at me." When their eyes met, Eddie said, "If we have to wait for a taxi, we might be here for hours, and we need to report to the Pentagon by 9:00 tomorrow morning."

Rachel huffed, brought her hair over her shoulders, and made her way through the crowd toward the man with the sign. After Eddie told Pearl to wait beside the door and watch their things, she followed.

"Whoever you are, please put that sign away," Rachel said to the man. "It's embarrassing."

"You must be Rachel." The man folded the sign and slipped it under his arm. "I'm Dan Wozniak. I work for your cousin, Mr. Meyer Rosen."

Dan, tall and barrel-chested, had sullen cupid bow lips, a thick curtain of lashes above small dark eyes that focused on Rachel. In that way he was like most men for Rachel was head-turning gorgeous. Even in this huge crowd of young women, she stood out.

"Mr. Rosen sent me to take you and your friend to Georgia Avenue."

"Do you have identification?" Rachel crossed her arms over her chest.

From his wallet, he took his driver's license and handed it to her. "But since you've never heard of me, there's this, too." He pointed to the patch on his pocket, where a long- stemmed red rose and the words, Rose Clothing, were stitched.

"If he knows your name and that we're staying on Georgia Avenue, Mr. Rosen must have sent him," Eddie said to Rachel. To Dan, Eddie asked, "Doesn't your factory make uniforms for the military?"

"Right. Rose is the second largest military uniform supplier on the East Coast." This said with pride.

"Okay, I guess you are who you say you are." Rachel pointed to their pile of luggage. "Those are our things."

They walked to the revolving door, where Eddie introduced everyone.

Pearl said, "Howdy, Dan."

Dan rolled his eyes. "Okay, Rubes. Get your suitcases. Let's go."

"You mean you're not going to carry our things?" Rachel's face turned fiery.

"That's not how it works in DC these days, Princess. I'm betting most of this luggage is yours." He thrust a thumb at their things. "You brought it, you carry it."

Eddie sighed. She was accustomed to dealing with difficult people like her mother, her father, even her students. "If we each take two bags, we can make it in one trip."

"Okay, Eddie. It's a deal." Dan took her heavy suitcase.

"I guess chivalry isn't dead after all." Rachel's flush receded.

"Dead as a doornail in this town," Dan said. "We got a factory full of gals doing men's work. Women don't need knights in shining armor anymore."

"Lucky," Rachel told him, "since all the knights are Over There and we women are left with the schlubs."

Eddie swallowed a laugh, hoping Dan wouldn't get insulted and leave them.

He lowered his lashes halfway, his expression sly. "The fewer guys here, the more gals I gotta fight off, and I got the scars to prove it. I'd like to show them to you sometime." He winked at Rachel before he went through the revolving door.

Under a low muddy sky, they lugged their things down the sidewalk behind him. In front of Union Station, an artillery gun was pointed upward, a reminder of the enemy.

Dan stopped beside a white truck, which resembled a milkman's van, and opened its back, lined with canvas floor to ceiling. He jumped in. "Pass 'em up here."

Once everything was loaded, Dan leapt down, and Pearl hoisted herself into the back. "I'll ride in here."

Before Eddie could protest, Dan said, "No, you won't, Red." He took Pearl's hand and helped her back onto the pavement. In the process, he stroked her bottom. Pearl's grin went wide as a hammock, and she winked at him.

Eddie and Rachel exchanged a look of disgust.

"Nothing rides in back, except uniforms," Dan said. "We all got to squeeze in the truck's cab, cozy-like." He lowered the door, which rumbled like soft thunder.

Eddie and Rachel let Pearl get in next to Dan. Rachel whispered to Eddie, "My cousin's employee is a real peach."

"Dummkopf," Eddie said. *Stupid head.* Often German words sounded like what they meant as did Yiddish. Saying them released emotion.

Pearl scooted close to Dan on the bench seat, Eddie and Rachel beside her.

Dan maneuvered his way through taxis and cars, coming so close to a brightly lit streetcar, Eddie had to close her eyes. They pulled up to a red light on North Capitol Street lined with turreted row houses that reminded Eddie of a block-long castle. She drank in the city, trying to remember street names and storefronts. Once she knew Washington, she would feel as if she belonged. How she wanted to belong.

Soon he turned onto Georgia Avenue, where houses appeared behind picket fences and the aroma of baking bread wafted. A bakery was nearby. He stopped in front of a narrow yellow three-story. A streetlight lit the patch of front lawn planted with staked tomatoes and peppers, a victory garden.

Rachel opened the passenger door, and they spilled onto the sidewalk.

Three men emerged from the vine-covered porch. One of them ran down the sidewalk and opened the gate. "Hey there, Edwina, I'm your cousin, Bert." He was a big florid man with a handsome face, his parted hair shiny with Vitalis, wearing some sort of uniform. He threw his arms around her and squeezed so hard he lifted her off her feet. "I'm so glad you and your friend have come to live with us."

Warmed by his welcome, Eddie took his hand, which felt rough to the touch. Bert, a decade older than Eddie, had been described by her dad as a strange overgrown mama's boy. As usual, her father's judgment was too harsh.

She introduced her cousin to Rachel and Pearl.

Bert said, "And these men here are from Rose Clothing, waiting for a ride back to Silver Spring."

"I'm Luca," the shorter one told them. "And this is my friend, Tony."

Luca, a short freckled redhead, was almost Pearl's *doppelganger*. Slender Tony had dark good looks, but wore his shyness like armor, his eyes meeting only Luca's.

Dan emerged from the truck, a cigarette dangling from his mouth like a movie gangster.

"Hey, Dan," Luca said. "Remember you said you'd give us a ride if we met you here?"

"Sure, cutters. How else you gonna get back to work?"

Luca turned to them. "See, we're cloth cutters at Rose Clothing, and Dan's our boss."

"First, give me a hand here," Dan said to the men and lifted the truck's backdoor. "These hillbilly gals brought everything they own from Southwest Virginia."

Once their things were on the porch, Dan gave Rachel a letter. "This is from Mrs. Rosen. They expect you next Friday night for Shabbat. I'll pick you up here at 7:30."

Frowning, Rachel took the letter. "But what if I don't want…"

"The Rosens remember you from when you were little." He dropped his cigarette on the sidewalk and pressed his toe into it. "They're swell, you'll see."

He turned to Luca and Tony. "Let's go, cutters. The midnight shift calls." He went down the walk and through the gate toward his truck, Tony in his wake.

"Wait a minute, boss," Luca yelled and drew Pearl aside. "May I have your telephone number, Pearl? Sure would like to show you Washington." He offered her a pen and a matchbook.

Matches reminded Eddie of her mother, who sometimes set fires. She needed to send a list of things her sisters must do before Mama returned home. At the top of the list: *hide the matches*.

"All righty." Pearl smiled at Luca and handed the matchbook to Bert. "Could you write your telephone number?" Grinning, Bert wrote and passed it back to Luca.

This exchange was wartime and romantic. Everyone wanted to live their own version of *Casablanca*.

Dan eased the truck away from the curb and honked. Luca ran and got aboard.

"Okay, Eddie." Bert gestured to the house. They followed him onto the porch. "Mama's in the parlor waiting for ya'll." He opened the front door and stood back.

Eddie hesitated. This was what she dreaded.

6

Arlington Cemetery's narrow road wound uphill. Oaks lined the way, throwing nets of shadow over them. As they passed rows of white tombstones like troops on parade, Jess felt a familiar burning in his chest. He would never become immune to murder, the ultimate violation.

Lowering his head, he prayed, *yea though I walk through the valley of the shadow of death, I will fear no evil...* Alonso's hands tightened on the wheel, knuckles rising beneath the skin. Jess sensed him sharing the dark sensation that gripped them whenever they met the murder victim.

Alonso parked behind the DC police car. "Of course, Ray K. got here first."

"It's not a race," Jess said, "but I bet he had his siren on through the city."

Their nemesis, Detective Kaminski, Ray K. as he liked to be called, of the Metropolitan Police of the District of Columbia or MPD, unintentionally brought humor to places where there was none.

Short and wide as a garden shed, Ray K. strutted toward them in a double-breasted jacket, its buttons straining to contain him. His driver, a young beat cop, leaned against the black-and-white. Chin in the air, the driver blew smoke into the starless sky.

"Need help getting out, Jess?" Ray K. straightened and looked over the hood at Alonso. "Get lost driving here, Al? Finding your way in the big city can be confusing for 'Bama boys."

This was Ray's favorite theme: that Jess and Alonso were ignoramuses, hopelessly out of their depths in DC. Jess had begun to fear Ray was right.

Pulling his kit from under the seat, Jess slung its strap over his shoulder and pushed open the car door forcing Ray to step back onto the grass.

Jess rushed at him, grabbed his tie, and yanked him forward. "Your siren brought the press to the gates."

Immediately Jess was ashamed of himself. He was six inches taller and at least ten years younger than the DC detective.

His aggression got the attention of the beat cop, who started around the black-and-white as if to protect his boss. Alonso blocked his way.

Ray K. motioned for the uniform to back off. The man had his pride. He was a rescuer not one in need of rescue.

"Careful with my favorite tie, 'Bama." He shoved Jess back. "For your information, our siren was not on. Sometimes reporters wait outside the station and tail us." He smoothed his tie back into his jacket. "In this town, we call it a free press. Maybe they don't have such a thing in Alabama."

Because the first two government girls' bodies had been found in Washington City, Ray K. and his partner had been assigned the cases. After the third murder, the Bureau was called in. Of course, they were all supposed to be working this together, but police detectives were like dogs. They marked their territory and didn't welcome encroachers. Ray K. resented Jess on sight, although he pretended to be cooperative.

What Ray didn't know was that on almost all their previous cases, there had been at least one local dick like him to deal with.

"I need to be sure Thad Graham found out about the murdered young woman by following you here," Jess said. "Also it looked like his photographer came in another vehicle. Why did they drive here separately?"

"You talk to the press and J. Edgar's going to hit you with his hammer," Ray K. said. "I know Thad. I'll talk to him for you." Ray's wandering left eye truly wandered tonight, leaving most of his eyeball white. "This way, boys," he said as if they were scouts in his troop.

The three walked toward the police lamps, bright in the cemetery's vast darkness. Alonso carried his camera snug under his arm.

"This is the oldest part of the cemetery, where the Union's Civil War dead are buried." Ray K. brought both eyes into alignment to direct his gaze. "But I doubt they let Johnny Rebs like you in here, Jess."

"Lucky I'm not looking for a burial place right now." Part of his outburst with Ray stemmed from his frustration with the investigation.

Jess introduced himself and Alonso to the two Park Policemen standing uphill from the girl's body, their cigarettes glowing in the dark. Men smoked in the presence of death. It was the one thing they could do when they were afraid that didn't make them look afraid.

A young Park Policeman in dusty riding boots stood back from the group, holding the reins of his horse, a quiet neighing presence.

With all of them walking around in the dark, no telling what evidence had been trampled. "Pick up your cigarette butts, fellas," Jess called and stepped into the brightness the circle of lamps made.

The girl lay on her side, one arm stretched over the grassy grave as if to caress it. Her body appeared posed. Jess studied her from various angles. Like the others, she was dark-haired pretty, a little plump, further proof these weren't random murders. The killer selected his victims, all of whom looked so much alike they could have been related.

Jess crouched beside her. She wore a knee-length skirt and a jacket too warm for the weather. The edge of her right sleeve was stained purple probably from a typewriter ribbon. And this time there were no lines drawn up the backs of her legs.

"Another government girl out for a good time." Ray K. stood uphill from Jess. "You think she'd have better sense than go off with a fella she didn't know from Adam's house- cat."

"Too late for a lecture, Ray K." Jess's gaze stayed with the girl.

Not that Jess didn't see Ray's point. The war encouraged folks to act as if each day was their last. The nearness of death breathed on all of them, making life brighter, more vivid. This girl had taken a risk in moving to Washington and an even greater risk when she went away with a man she didn't know, but her killer must have been in uniform, so she trusted him.

From his kit, Jess took out a stiff rubber glove. Without a word between them, Alonso set his camera down and tugged the glove up Jess's arm.

Jess crouched beside the girl her pupils large with surprise, red spots caused by broken capillaries dotted her face, her mouth open as if to scream. Three things struck him, the first that her lipstick wasn't smeared. Thelma Sykes, the government girl murdered in April, also had perfectly applied lipstick.

He put his hand on her forehead, closed his eyes, and imagined the terror she felt in those moments before she died, when she realized what was happening, but couldn't stop it.

How he wished the dead could speak. In some ways they did. Instead of words they left signs. He studied her fingernails, unbroken without skin or dirt beneath them. Why hadn't she struggled?

Alonso screwed a flashbulb in his camera and sent Jess a glance he read like a telegram.

"You best blinker your horse," Jess called. The policeman led his horse away.

Because they had come out of the Deep South, where Jim Crow ruled, they had developed a system. Alonso never told a white person what to do. Conversely, when they dealt with coloreds, Alonso took the lead, and Jess kept quiet. That way they avoided the unnecessary complications brought on by race relations, as bad in Washington as anywhere else they'd been.

Jess dreamed of a place in America without the color bar, where he and his brother didn't have to hide their bond of blood.

The camera flashed from the foot of the grave, turning night to day. Alonso made his way around the dead girl, hat tilted back on his head to make room for the big camera covering his face. A flashbulb exploded with each snap.

The Park Policemen and the groundskeeper, Mr. Novak, an elderly man with a great shock of white hair, averted their eyes, but stood in place, as if stunned by what had happened on their watch.

The medical examiner, Dr. Lee, a slender Chinaman, joined the group with a nod to Jess. He stayed in the shadows, clutching his bag, until Alonso finished.

Jess led Mr. Novak away from the rest and asked, "What time did you find her?"

"It was almost dark when I look for clippers." Mr. Novak pointed to shrubs on a nearby ridge. "I trim there yesterday and leave clippers, if not maybe she not found for long long time." He rubbed his eyes, some of his white eyebrows as long as cat's whiskers.

Dressed in a stained shirt and ragged trousers, the man smelled of physical labor under a hot sun. Jess knew that sour odor. He and Alonso had picked cotton in Alabama heat from dawn to dusk on their father's land.

Jess squatted beneath a linden tree, using the flat of his thigh to write in his notebook. "Does the cemetery keep a record of the cars and trucks that come through its gates?"

"No record." The old man sat cross-legged before him. His hands reached around, tugging at the grass. "Only me and Marek here, six days a week. We trade off Sundays."

"Did you see any cars or trucks parked along here today?"

"No. Today I work in Spanish American War, far from roads. I see no cars, no trucks, no one."

"If you see a vehicle, do you check whether it has a right to be here?" As soon as Jess asked, he knew the answer.

"No." Mr. Novak shook his head. "Is only me and Marek."

Jess leaned against the linden's trunk, feeling as if he'd absorbed some of the man's exhaustion. "Okay, Mr. Novak." They stood. Jess gave him his card. "If you think of anything that might help us find the person who did this, call me, please. And would you ask Marek to do the same?"

"Ya, I tell Marek." He pocketed the card. "Terrible sad this young lady…"

"Yes." Jess meandered through nearby tombstones, where he made a discovery. "Any of ya'll put a lady's pocketbook back here?" he called to the men.

"No, sir," the Park Policeman in charge called back. "We didn't touch anything."

Jess picked up the pocketbook by its handle so as not to disturb any fingerprints. He took it into the light, squatted, opened it, and went through the wallet. It contained a government ID from the Pentagon with the dead girl's photograph and name, Kaye Krieger, as well as her address in

Alexandria, Virginia. The address appeared to be a house. Was it possible she was a native?

The other murdered government girls came from all over the country, so it fell to local police departments to inform their next-of-kin. A dreadful, but necessary duty he'd done before. But with the government girls' murders, they got no closer to the victim than the friend she had traveled here with. They talked to the girl's roommates, co-workers, boss, but government girls were strangers to the city, often strangers to each other, strangers surrounded by strangers.

Inside her purse was a half-smoked pack of Kools and a new matchbook from the Palace Royale Ballroom, a dance place on H Street. Jess opened it. Not one match had been struck. Had she been at the Palace Royale tonight? Is that where she met her killer?

"Pretty gals give them matchbooks out downtown," Ray K. said, looking over Jess's shoulder. "Got one myself even though I never went inside the place."

Jess didn't care how many matchbooks were given out. The Palace Royale would be their next stop. He put her ID in his pocket. They'd show it to the manager, employees, and patrons. If she was there earlier, maybe someone remembered her and possibly could identify the man at her side.

He searched the purse's lining, but could find no lipstick. Where was it?

While lipstick was precious to women, metal was critical to the war effort. Women saved the metal tube their lipstick came in and bought colored refills at stores like Woolworth's or G.C. Murphy's.

Dr. Lee cleared his throat.

"Ready?" Jess looked up at the doctor's serious unblinking eyes magnified by thick glasses. Dr. Lee dropped his chin in a polite nod.

Jess put the contents of Karen Krieger's pocketbook back, placed the pocketbook in a paper evidence bag to be turned over to the Bureau's Identification Department, and stepped from light into darkness.

"Mind if I'm in on this?" Ray K. asked Jess.

Jess said, "Come along." Ray K. could make things difficult if he felt left out. And they needed good relations with the MPD.

"This time is different," Dr. Lee said to them.

The three walked up a graveled path to a copse of maples at the cemetery's edge. The slice of moon slipped from the clouds. Wind rustled the leaves, the smell of rain in the air.

"Manual strangulation, no belt," Dr. Lee said. "There is a thumb-size bruise right here." He brought his thumb to the notch at the base of his throat.

Ray K. said, "Maybe she wasn't killed by the same guy."

Jess hated the idea there were two killers. Still he wondered why no belt. Did a branch of the service have a beltless uniform? He and Alonso had studied uniforms since they got here, yet he couldn't recall one like that. But it was important the killer's pattern had changed. They needed to stop focusing on how the murders were similar and study their differences.

Away from the lights and group around the girl's body, moonlight shone on the backs of the tombstones, sending blanket-sized shadows over the dead. Why did he bring her here? Was it significant that this was the oldest part of the cemetery, or that it was near the memorial to the Confederate dead? Maybe he thought her body wouldn't be found for days.

"Did he do her like he did the others…you know?" Ray tugged on his cigarette, its red glow pulsing.

The other girls had been sodomized after death.

Dr. Lee looked from Ray K. to Jess. "I will know for certain after the post mortem."

"Any idea when she died?" Jess asked.

Dr. Lee pushed his glasses up on the bridge of his nose and left his finger there, holding the glasses in place. "With asphyxiation victims, it is difficult to pinpoint, but because of today's heat, rigor is already present. I would guess maybe three, four hours ago."

Jess slapped his thigh. "Daylight? He left her body here in daylight?"

Ray said. "Cemetery's locked at sunset. He drove up here and dropped her off."

Drivers had to have special permits to buy gasoline. The Office of Price Administration had instituted a tiered system of rationing depending on the driver's occupation. In Washington, getting a permit wasn't difficult. Most of the men, who worked in the offices with the murdered girls, had both a permit to buy gasoline and a vehicle. Yet they also had alibis, which Jess and Alonso had verified.

"He must be subduing the woman some way... Could he have given her a barbiturate, maybe in her drink?" Jess asked Dr. Lee. "Her tongue was stained purple as if she'd drunk grape soda or wine."

"Yes. I also see purple tongue." Dr. Lee was nodding. "These days, barbiturates are almost as common as aspirin. Doctors prescribe them for anyone having trouble sleeping. And because of the war, that is many people. I will test the contents of her stomach for a barbiturate."

Jess felt a tingling in his chest, a sensation he got when he was onto something. A barbiturate might lead to a prescription with a name on it.

As they walked back to the girl's body, one of the Park Police watching them nudged the policeman beside him. With the moonlight behind Jess, they could see he was missing an arm. Jess imagined one saying to the other, "The Bureau must be hard up these days."

Yet his stump had become a badge of honor, albeit an unmerited one. No one asked how he'd lost it. Folks assumed it had happened in the war, which made him feel guilty. More than anything, he wanted to fight for his country as the men whose graves surrounded him had done.

"Wait a minute, fellas," Jess called to the ambulance crew taking her body away.

He lifted the blanket and studied Kaye's face, wishing he had a woman with him to tell him what she thought. The lipstick though freshly applied went above her lip line. With the tracing paper from his kit, he blotted her lips.

"More photographs?" Alonso asked him.

"Please, and get her blouse or whatever it's called." Jess stepped away.

Beneath her jacket, she wore a low-necked top made of thin cotton that showed off her ample breasts. Thelma Sykes had worn a similar one.

Alonso snapped some photographs.

"It's called a peasant blouse," Ray K. said behind Jess, "like Jane Russell wears in them movie posters. Some call it cheap, others think it's sexy. You must not have a woman in your life, or you'd know about such things."

Nothing like getting women's fashion tips from Ray K. Still Jess took out his notebook, crouched, and wrote *peasant blouse* and the actress's name.

The men on the hillside watched the ambulance bear Kaye Krieger's body away, its red taillights disappearing down the hill, united in a moment none would forget.

After the ambulance went through the gates at the bottom of the hill, Thad Graham's car pulled out behind it and followed across the Memorial Bridge.

Ambulance chasers: Jess had thought the term referred to lawyers. He didn't know a newspaper would pay a reporter to sit outside police headquarters, hoping for something to happen. Ray K. was right about him. He had a lot to learn about Washington.

After everyone left, Jess asked Alonso. "See any footprints?"

"Not in this thick grass. Wish I had."

They had been given a photograph of a shoe print found near the woman's body on the C&O Canal. The shoe had tiny holes in the soles like hobnail boots, except the pattern of holes was irregular. They were making the rounds of construction crews talking to roofers, who sometimes put tacks through their soles to keep secure as they climbed.

Rain began to fall in drops large as coins.

They ran to the car. Once inside, Alonso turned to Jess and said. "Again, she was missing her right shoe."

"His souvenir."

7

Eddie took a deep breath and stepped into Aunt Viola's parlor.

The small warm room crowded in at her, its frilly curtains, crocheted doilies everywhere, a mantle of tiny ceramic poodles, beady eyes aglow. The smell of all things old, lavender, talcum powder and dust, hung in the air.

Eddie hated small spaces. Sweat rolled down the furrow of her spine. She felt Rachel, Bert, and Pearl standing behind her, too many for this room.

In the corner, Aunt Viola filled an armchair. Her feet in flat slippers rested on an ottoman, a potentate's pose. A glossy wooden Mission Bell radio sat on the table beside her, its dials fingertip close.

"Aunt Viola." Eddie crossed the room and kissed the old goat's powdery cheek. She never liked the woman and knew the feeling was mutual.

"Well, Edwina, you're finally here. Go over yonder to the lamp and let me get a better look at you."

Eddie sighed and stepped into the arc of light. Rachel watched with sympathy, while Pearl stayed in the doorway looking as if she might run away.

Aunt Viola put on glasses that hung from a chain around her neck. With eyes reduced to slits, she studied Eddie. "Turn 'round, Edwina. Still a tall skinny gal, aren't ya? You could a knocked me over with a feather when your daddy wrote that you got picked runner-up for Miss Saltville, but you're a sight prettier than you used to be."

"Thank you kindly, Aunt Viola." Who needed detractors when you had relatives like her aunt?

"And that one with the long curly hair must be Miss Rachel Margolis. Come closer, honey. I won't bite." Aunt Viola sat straighter. Her aunt loved money and those who had it like Rachel. In her letter, Aunt Viola wrote how proud she would be to have the Margolis Department Store heiress living under her roof.

"Good evening, Mrs. Trundle." Rachel's voice was bright. Eddie had warned her about Aunt Viola.

"Course, I can see why you won Miss Saltville over Edwina. You're really beautiful, Rachel, a beautiful little Jewess."

Cringing, Eddie covered her mouth, but she could tell Rachel was taking it in stride.

"Thank you, Ma'am." Rachel curtsied. Eddie rolled her eyes.

Aunt Viola looked beyond Rachel. "But who the dickens is that other girl?"

"Aunt Viola, this is Pearl." Eddie extended her arm to Pearl, who came forward, smoothing her faded skirt. "She's billeted with you, too. Pearl is from just outside Saltville."

"They didn't mention a third girl." Her chins folded like an accordion.

Pearl set her feed sack in front of Aunt Viola, who eyed it with derision. "I think I've got my letter right in here, Miz Trundle." Pearl untied the end of the sack and peered in.

"I don't need to be reading a letter this late in the evening. But I do need to know who's living in my house. What's your last name, girl?"

Pearl stared at Aunt Viola. Eddie held her breath, afraid of her aunt's reaction. The mantle clock's ticks divided the silence.

"Speak up, girl."

Pearl bowed her head. "Ballou," she said, her voice breaking over the syllables.

Something inside Eddie broke as well. She understood what Pearl was feeling: shame. Pearl had a baby out of wedlock, and, worse, Pearl came from a notorious family, which meant she had to assume their sins as well.

That's the way Saltville worked.

"Ballou?" Aunt Viola's fleshy chins shook. "All Ballous are moonshiners. Ever body knows that."

"You bring any moonshine with you, Pearl?" Bert called from the doorway.

"Albert Trundle, close that door and don't ever say the word moonshine, you hear?"

"Yes, Ma'am."

Why would a grown man like Bert allow his mother to speak to him in such a way? Those who lived at home remained children. Eddie ought to know. Living under her father's roof, she'd assumed the responsibilities of an adult without any of the freedom.

Aunt Viola lumbered to her feet her head flung so far back Eddie looked into the dark caves of her nostrils. Not a pretty sight. "Edwina, how dare you bring a Ballou into my house?"

Pearl's eyes filled with tears, before she lowered her head and snuffled.

Eddie's hands shook. She longed to grab her aunt and shake her. "I brought Pearl because she was assigned to stay here." She placed her hand on Pearl's waist and felt Pearl's pouch. "Don't be mean to Pearl. She's my friend."

Pearl couldn't help being born into a family of bootleggers any more than Eddie could help being crazy Mrs. Smith's daughter.

"She's my friend, too." Rachel strode to Pearl's side. "If you don't want Pearl here, we'll take a taxi to a hotel tonight and find another place to live tomorrow."

Over Pearl's head, Eddie exchanged a glance with Rachel, her eyes luminous with righteousness. They stood united against Aunt Viola's injustice, even though Pearl had probably lied about her government job and thus had lied about being billeted here.

"Please don't leave, Rachel." Aunt Viola collapsed into her chair. "Edwina knows how I get when I'm tired." She spoke only to Rachel as if her nastiness was Eddie's fault. "Welcome to my house, girls." She raised her hands, her fingers stubby as link sausages. "Bert will show ya'll upstairs to your room, but you're going to have to bunk up together since there's only a double bed and a twin."

Rachel was out the door, Eddie close behind when Aunt Viola said, "And Pearl, I need ten dollars from you now for your first month's rent."

"All righty, ma'am." Pearl turned from Aunt Viola, lifted her blouse, and opened the pouch around her waist.

Lamplight fell on Pearl's wad of money, more money than Eddie had ever seen. Where had Pearl gotten it? Unease came over Eddie. She couldn't think of any way Pearl had come by that money legitimately.

As Pearl flipped through the bills, a new smell was released into the room. It was the odor of alcohol, moonshine. Or was Eddie imagining this?

Pearl pulled out two damp tens, covered the pouch with her blouse, and turned to offer the bills to her aunt. "This here's for two months, Miz Trundle."

Aunt Viola smoothed the bills and smiled at Pearl for the first time. "Thank you, Pearl."

Her aunt loved money, even moonshine money.

8

"Where did you get that money in your pouch?" Eddie asked Pearl when they were alone.

Water gurgled through the pipes. Rachel was in the bathroom taking a bath.

Eddie stood behind Pearl, who sat on the stool in front of the dressing table, pinning her hair into victory rolls. Her bony shoulders moved like bird's wings.

"Earned it," Pearl said, her hand went to the pouch, now under her ragged night gown.

"I don't believe you, Pearl. Tell me the truth or get dressed and leave here now."

The money frightened Eddie. Why had she stood up for Pearl? She wasn't thinking straight. She rubbed her eyes and yawned. This was the longest day of her life. For the last week she'd been so excited about coming to Washington, she had barely slept and now she was exhausted.

Pearl leapt to her feet and gripped Eddie's arm. "Promise not to tell?"

Eddie sighed. She shouldn't agree, but she said, "All right."

Pearl leaned closer. "Found near about five hundred dollars in a Mason jar buried in the roots of a river birch."

Eddie got dizzy. "Five hundred dollars is a fortune." She pried Pearl's hand from her arm. "You know who that money belongs to, Pearl."

"Don't be a scaredy cat." Pearl wore the smug expression Eddie had so disliked in the classroom. "I left bills around the outside of the jar and filled the middle with tore up pages from the *Sears and Roebuck*. Uncle Alton don't even know it's gone."

Alton Ballou: his name sent a shiver between Eddie's shoulders.

Government revenuers, who went onto his land to arrest him, were never seen again. And the local newspaper editor knew better than to mention the bootlegger's name in connection with their disappearance. Even Saltville's sheriff steered clear of Alton Ballou.

"What will he do when he finds out his money is gone?" Eddie could barely get the words out.

"This here's moonshine money, so he can't go to the law." Pearl patted her pouch. "Admit it, Eddie. It's the perfect crime. Even a hard grading teacher like you would have to give me an A."

"Give you an A for what, Pearl?" Rachel entered rosy from her bath, her white terrycloth bathrobe tied around her.

"Aw, Eddie and me were just funning with each other." Pearl went to the double bed and pulled down the bedspread.

They had decided since Eddie was tallest she would sleep in the long twin bed. An arrangement Eddie found familiar, yet lonely. This was how the bedroom she shared with the twins was set up.

Rachel said, "Your turn to take a bath, Pearl."

"Eddie, go 'head and have yours." Pearl sent her a conspiratorial look. "I don't need a bath. Took a good one in the stream a few weeks ago."

Rachel's eyes widened. She and Pearl were to share the same bed.

Eddie felt a twinge of *schadenfreude*. Rachel had grown up in a grand house with all the modern conveniences. Let her learn how the poor lived, many without indoor plumbing. In households where hygiene was a priority, a metal tub came out on Saturdays, which was filled with water heated on the coal stove. Each member bathed, usually in the same water. That's how the Smiths had done it before Eddie's father got promoted to night supervisor at the mine, and they could afford a bathroom.

"Come on, Pearl. I'll let you use my special bubble bath." Rachel took a bottle of pink liquid from her compact case. "It'll be fun."

"I don't fancy getting wet at night." But Pearl let Rachel lead her to the bathroom.

Eddie lay on her twin bed and tried not the think about Pearl's money stolen from the most dangerous man in Saltville. Her heart pulsed in her throat, her body tight with fear. She doubted she would sleep.

Through the wall, she heard Rachel say, "Start with your face, Pearl. Here's a washrag. Let me put soap on it. Now go down around your ears and neck…"

Rain drummed on the tin roof, reminding Eddie of home. Sometime during the bathing lesson, she fell asleep, still in her clothes.

A little before dawn, she woke, not knowing where she was, her mind dark with nightmare images. Large man hands had wrapped electric cord around her neck sending shock waves through her. She sat up, tense with raw terror. Was Mama getting her shock treatment at this moment?

Eddie watched the sunrise turn the sky pale pink and calmed.

Once Bert finished washing up, she hurried to the bathroom. The tub was so filthy she decided to take a sponge bath at the sink. After she washed and dressed, she went to the bed where Rachel and Pearl lay sleeping like tangled kittens.

"Time to get up." She angled the lamp's light in their faces.

Rachel blinked awake. "Our first day as government girls." She sprang up, climbed over the footboard, and threw on her bathrobe. "I'll be ready in a snap."

"Turn off that durn light." Pearl rolled across the bed and back to sleep.

Eddie, in the smart beige suit she'd bought at Margolis Department Store, fixed her hair and makeup in front of the dressing table mirror.

Rachel returned, dressed in a similar suit of navy gabardine, and put her hair in victory rolls. All the while she called to Pearl. She went to the bed and shook her. "Get up, Pearl. We need to catch the streetcar in half an hour."

Pearl pushed up against the headboard, the sheet held to her chest. "I need to tell ya'll something." She looked from Rachel to Eddie, her eyes shiny with tears. "I don't have a job yet. But I'm fixing to get one today. I swear."

Rachel shot Eddie a look of apology then rounded on Pearl. "Why did you lie to us?"

"Sorry, Rachel. More than anything, I want to be a government girl like you and Eddie." Pearl snuffled. "See I run away from Saltville after Uncle Alton give my baby Billy to his married daughter who lives in Chilhowie." Pearl covered her face and sobbed.

She was good at turning on the waterworks, Eddie thought and regretted being hard-heartedness, but she would always be a skeptic.

"You poor thing." Rachel stroked her hair. "But Eddie and I have to go now or we'll be late." Rachel faced the mirror and applied lipstick.

Eddie stuck a hatpin in the crown of her picture hat. Like proper young ladies, they were back in hats and short white cotton gloves for their first day.

"Before ya'll go, I need to ask a favor." Pearl spoke in a calm voice, no more tears.

They turned, impatient to leave.

"Don't tell anybody I'm here in Washington. If Uncle Alton finds out where I am, he'll come hurt me bad."

"Why would he do that?" Rachel said.

Pearl's hand slid under her pillow and touched what was hidden there. "Because he's the meanest bootlegger there is."

"That's why you had the shade down on the train, isn't it?" Eddie said. "You didn't want anyone to see you leave Saltville."

Pearl gave her Cheshire cat grin.

"I'm going to grab us some toast to eat on the way to the streetcar stop." Rachel waved to Pearl and went downstairs.

Holding the door handle, Eddie said, "I assure you, Pearl, someone at the depot saw you. You can't keep a secret in Saltville. Your uncle will find out where you are." With that she shut the door.

What a mistake she had made insisting Pearl stay on Georgia Avenue. She had invited *achtung,* danger.

"I'm not hungry," she told Rachel downstairs.

The knot in her stomach remained as she and Rachel crowded onto the streetcar. They made their way down the aisle and held onto straps that hung from the ceiling, crammed in with other government girls. Rachel was talking, but it was as if she was speaking underwater. Eddie heard only the roar of fear rising inside.

She had wanted to leave Saltville behind, but instead she brought the worst of it with her, its lawlessness, its violence.

She resolved to make Pearl move out this afternoon. She would help Pearl find somewhere else to live. Aunt Viola had been right. Better not get involved with bootleggers or their kin. Pearl had stolen a fortune from her uncle. He would come for his money and would hurt anyone in his way, including all those who lived with Pearl on Georgia Avenue. *Achtung.*

Eddie bent to watch Washington slide past the streetcar's windows, but her mind traveled three hundred miles southwest to Saltville, certain this city wasn't far enough away from the evil reach of Alton Ballou.

9

Tuesday, June 6, 1944
Washington, D.C.

Vernon slipped down in the steamy water. What a luxury to take a bath anytime he wanted, even before five in the morning. And he needed a bath to wash away his dream of Doris. Every night she came to him, begging him to help her. But she was dead. What could he do about that?

His Doris dreams were the only fly in the buttermilk his life had become.

Even though his reflection was distorted in the shiny faucet, he could make out his wide pie-eating grin. He couldn't believe his luck. He was staying on the top floor of a beautiful row house for free, and all because of the rain. Rain had pelted Washington since he arrived Friday night. May it rain and rain.

When he showed up on G Street at District Construction Saturday morning, Red told him they had enough roofers for the tempos on the Mall right now.

"Don't give me that hangdog look, Vernon. I got a special friend whose roof is leaking. You'll thank me for this one." Red winked and handed him the address of a widow woman on 14th Street.

Mrs. Frazier turned out to be a wasp-waisted buxom blonde, who opened the front door in a flowered dressing gown that wasn't closed completely. Vernon feasted his eyes on her in the spacious foyer.

"Most of our pots and pans are set out in the attic to collect leaks, Mr. Lanier." She spoke in a honeyed Southern drawl. "But, I'm afraid the rain is winning this war." She pressed her palm to his chest, sending a quiver through his body. "Please say you can help me."

Vernon strapped on his tool belt and went out an attic window onto Mrs. Frazier's mansard roof. Even in rain, he loved walking a roof and looking over the city. He felt at home in the sky.

A few tugs of his hammer's claw, and he found the problem. He ended up sending Jeremiah, the elderly colored man who worked for Mrs. Frazier, to the hardware store for boards, while he got to work taking up the rotten ones.

"You poor man," Mrs. Frazier said to him at nightfall. She'd come up to the attic with a mug of tea for him. She and Vernon sat on wooden boxes and faced each other. Around them, rain pinged in pots and buckets.

He accepted the tea and told her the extent of the damages. "It's a big job, Ma'am." Okay, he was exaggerating. It would be tough for a lone man, not that he wanted another roofer's help here. "But I'll get her done for you." Holding his mug in his palm, he lifted the warm liquid to his lips and gulped. No sipping for him. Nothing ever tasted so sweet.

"That's great news, Vernon. Why don't you just stay here?" she said. "I've got plenty of room on the third floor, and after the roof is fixed, there are lots of little jobs like doors that stick and kitchen cabinets that need painting. Jeremiah's a dear, but he's not handy like you."

Vernon didn't need convincing. He almost ran to his boarding house in Georgetown to pick up the feed sack stuffed with his things and tell his landlady he wouldn't be returning.

Only on his way back, he remembered the silver captain's bars, which he'd wrapped in a cloth scrap and tucked in the bottom of the sack. Thoughts of that pin made his load heavier. He carried the murdered girl's memory wherever he went. *Go away, Doris. Leave me please.*

Someone knocked at the bathroom door. Vernon stirred in the water.

The door creaked open. "Hope you don't mind, Vernon, but I thought you might like some lavender shampoo." Mrs. Frazier entered, wearing that same dressing gown, barely closed now.

Vernon drew his knees to his chest. She could see him naked through the water.

"Oh relax, Vernon." Her hands pressed on his shoulders. "Would you like for me to wash your hair?" Her voice came from behind him.

"Yes, Ma'am. I'd appreciate it." He sunk into the water and stretched his legs. Let her see what she'd done to him.

She giggled, got a towel, positioned it on the floor behind his head, and knelt. Her fingers massaged his scalp. The steamy room filled with the sweetness of lavender and the sound of his breathing.

He didn't kid himself, though. Mrs. Frazier ran a house of ill repute, and the young ladies who entertained gentlemen downstairs in the evening weren't really her nieces. But whenever Bess's voice sounded in his head, he cut her off like a spigot. He'd been living the sweet life here on 14th Street for two days and did not want it to end.

After his bath, Mrs. Frazier wrapped him in a big cotton towel and led him to his bedroom, where he sprawled across the bed and watched her. She opened her silky dressing gown, dropped her drawers, and presented her big soft breasts to him. He held them and suckled their brown tips until she climbed on top of him and rode him into the dawn.

"Thy rod it comforts me," she whispered in his ear, giggling. "Can you tell my daddy was a preacher?" After they were done filling up with each other, they shared the rolled cigarette on his bedside table before she curled next to him and slept.

He lay back against the pillow. Through the blinds, fingers of sunlight reached across the flowered bedspread. He didn't know when he'd been this happy. Yes, he did. It was before he and Bess married, when he imagined they would have a lifetime of such bliss.

The rain stopped at last, and he was sorry for it. That rain had blessed him.

Jeremiah had left his wet boots on newspaper beside the door. From here he read the headline: **Government Girl Murdered in Arlington Cemetery**. Carefully he got to his feet without disturbing Mrs. Frazier, and crept to the newspaper. He picked it up and returned to her warm nakedness.

The paper was dated Tuesday, May 30. On the bottom front page of

The Washington Herald was a photograph of the murdered girl taken from her high school yearbook. She could have been Doris. Her dark eyes sent a quiver through him as if Doris was speaking to him.

The story continued on page six with another photograph of two men taken through a car windshield. A colored man named Alonso Crooms was driving. The other man was identified as Jessup Lindsay, a special agent with the FBI. According to the story, Jessup Lindsay was a famous detective, who'd caught the Dothan child killer and went on to solve murders all over the South. The reporter couldn't confirm what Lindsay was doing in Washington City, but the reader could make an accurate guess. This girl's murder wasn't the first, and Jessup Lindsay was trying to find the killer before he killed again.

This idea sent Vernon's heart thumping: *before he killed again.* He knew what he had to do.

10

Vernon walked around the circle, where the statue of General Thomas on horseback watched over the junction of Massachusetts and Vermont Avenues. Steam drifted up from asphalt the color of licorice. The general and his horse were pointed in the direction Vernon was headed.

A young boy selling newspapers called, "Troops in France, our troops in France." Vernon bought a *Washington Post,* whose headline read: ALLIES LAND IN FRANCE, WIPE OUT BIG AIR BASES. Before he could read more, the streetcar approached, its bell clanging.

Onboard everyone was excited about D-Day. Strangers talked to each other like friends. In his "Fireside Chats," the President kept saying they were all in this war together, and today his words felt true.

"This is what everyone's been waiting for," Vernon said to the elderly man beside him in a suit that smelled of mothballs.

The man gave a sad smile. "Our men landed on those beaches, but at an awful cost, I'm afraid."

Vernon patted his shoulder. "I take your meaning." Many American boys must have died already. He sent out a prayer for the troops. "What does the D in D-Day stand for?"

"Wondered that myself," the man said. "I know they landed in a place called Normandy." Tears in his voice. "The Germans were dug in and waiting…"

Vernon closed his eyes. He'd never seen the ocean, but he went to picture shows and could imagine the dark swells, boats opening up in the water and from the shore that awful mechanical rattle of machine guns, death in the salty air.

The Justice Department took up an entire block. He marveled at its roofs that went on forever, as he walked around the five-story marble mountain. It fronted Tenth Street and Constitution Avenue. Its deep windows reminded him of watching eyes.

His hand dug in his pocket, and he touched the silver bars. She would stop haunting him once he did this. Of that he was certain.

But it wasn't going to be easy giving the pin to Agent Jessup Lindsay.

Could he march into the huge lobby, hand the pin to the man behind the desk, and tell him to give it to Jessup Lindsay?

The troops rode those boats onto the beach and jumped out, knowing the Krauts were dug in, guns pointed. If they could do such a brave thing, why was he scared to go into the FBI building? It's not like anyone was going to shoot him, but he might get arrested. He had stolen evidence from a murder and left Doris on the towpath. He might even be accused of killing her.

But for his peace of mind, he had to give the pin to Agent Lindsay. Maybe he could mail it to him, but what if the pin got lost in the mail? No, he had to do this right. He had to put the pin into the man's hand.

He crossed Constitution and bought a peach from a street vendor set up in front of the National Gallery of Art.

"Which side of that building is the entrance to the Bureau of Investigation?" he asked.

"This side." The swarthy man grinned showing a gold tooth. "Want to see a real G-Man?" He winked and pretended to shoot a Tommy gun.

Vernon remained solemn. This was no laughing matter. He was here to dispel a ghost.

He kept his vigil in front of the Justice Department, walking back and forth. A little after six o'clock, people poured out. Government girls emerged in twos and threes. In their pale summer dresses the color of flowers, they almost floated down the street toward the streetcar stops on Pennsylvania

Avenue.

He was about to give up when Alonso Crooms emerged from the building. Vernon recognized him because he was over six feet with skin about as light as a colored man's could be. And he wore the gray fedora he had on in the newspaper photograph. He crossed to the vendor Vernon had bought from and filled a bag with peaches.

Vernon followed him across the street and around the building to the streetcar stop. A block away, the streetcar clanged its arrival.

"Al," a man called from the crowd. The man was Jessup Lindsay. He was a little shorter than Alonso with wavy brown hair. Both men had the same notched chin and large wide-set eyes. Lindsay's left arm was a shriveled pale thing that ended a little above his elbow. Vernon hadn't expected a famous detective to have only one arm.

Both were dressed in dark cotton trousers, white short-sleeve shirts, and dark ties, the same as most of the men coming out of the Justice Department.

The streetcar approached clickety-clack, clickety-clack the steady ring of its bell a warning to government girls and messenger boys on swerving motorbikes to stop crossing its path.

Alonso ran for it, so did Vernon, who got on behind him and stayed close.

In Washington City, coloreds could ride anywhere they wanted on buses or streetcars, but once they crossed into Virginia, they had to move to the back. Vernon had learned about Jim Crow laws once he got here.

Folks crammed on. Vernon held to the strap overhead, swaying with the crowd.

When they passed the Bond Bread plant near Florida Avenue and the yeasty aroma of bread filled the air, Vernon closed his eyes and was transported home. He imagined biting into one of Bess's fluffy biscuits.

He loved his wife, yet today he'd sinned with another woman and didn't feel bad about it. He had become a true sinner, who enjoyed his sin and hoped to repeat it soon.

At the stop after Florida, Jessup and Alonso got off. The pair met beside the curb. Vernon got off, too, hanging back so they wouldn't know he was following.

He wasn't sure how to give the pin to Agent Lindsay. He couldn't just walk up to him on the street. He wished he'd brought pencil, paper, and an envelope so he could tell him when and where he found the pin. And slip it all into his mailbox.

Alonso Crooms and Jessup Lindsay turned off Georgia onto V Street and went up an alley. Vernon watched from behind a smelly compost heap.

The alley was lined with brick tenements where coloreds lived. Wealthy Negroes, doctors and lawyers, lived on what was called the Gold Coast, middle and upper 16th Street Northwest. Vernon had roofed one of their mansions. Bess couldn't believe when he told her how these colored folks had colored servants of their own.

Alonso and Jessup stopped beside a water pump between the shacks and washed some peaches. Alonso handed one to Jessup who took a big bite. Peach juice dribbled down his chin. With his handkerchief, Alonso wiped Jessup's face. Most men wouldn't appreciate another man wiping their face, but Jessup just nodded and continued to eat.

Three barefoot colored boys stopped throwing a ball and ran to them. Alonso gave the boys peaches and made them wash the fruit before they ate.

The men walked a little further down the alley and opened an iron gate that whined shut behind them. The boys went back to playing baseball, and Vernon crept from his hiding place to their gate. He was looking into the backyard with its huge garden when someone grabbed his arm and pulled it behind his back.

"Why you following us?" a voice asked.

The gate opened, and Vernon was pushed through. Jessup Lindsay opened a door beside the garage. Alonso Crooms forced Vernon up a narrow set of stairs, dark as night. "I'm right behind you, so don't try anything." Alonso let Vernon's arm go. Vernon stumbled. Alonso helped him up. "Watch your step."

Vernon entered the room over the garage. A sweet odor filled the air, so sweet it made his stomach roil. The only light came from the small window facing the alley.

"Don't look around," Alonso said.

But Vernon already had. A huge photograph of Doris stared at him from the back wall. Her dead eyes bored into him. His knees gave way and he slumped to the floor.

11

Pausing on the stairs, Rachel turned back to Eddie. "I notice Captain Silver Spoon didn't pick you up here, so don't give my date the third degree, please."

"Silver Spoon's too upper crusty to come to Georgia Avenue." Eddie brought her index finger to the tip of her nose and pushed it up. "I met him and his Yale pals at a restaurant, where he acted more interested in his friends than in me."

Rachel rolled her eyes. "Mrs. Trundle even asked my date about his family in Mississippi."

Eddie flushed with *fremdschamen,* vicarious embarrassment. Aunt Viola acted as if their ancestors had come over on the Mayflower when they were really hardscrabble mountainfolk.

"You said Bert knows this guy, right?" Eddie worried about Rachel going out with a man she met on the streetcar this afternoon. Of course, Eddie had met Silver Spoon on the train. Gone were the days when a woman and man needed a proper introduction.

"Mr. Berman, Bert's employer, is also Thad's landlord." Rachel held the parlor door for Eddie.

A reedy young man with unruly sandy blond hair and black glasses got to his feet. "Hello, there." His features swam into place, eyes dark as onyx, snub nose, easy smile, too easy. Thad Graham didn't look unhappy trapped in Aunt Viola's web, and Eddie found that odd.

When Rachel introduced them, Eddie shook his hand and felt the writing callous on his middle finger and the roughness of his palm. Thad hadn't always been an office worker.

Eddie said, "I'm surprised a reporter isn't still at work on such an auspicious day."

All day she'd longed to telephone her father to talk about D-Day. Beginning with that December when they listened to the news bulletin that Pearl Harbor had been bombed, they'd been on a journey. It wasn't over yet, but maybe what had happened on those French beaches brought the end nearer.

"Right you are, Eddie. The whole newsroom is buzzing with D-Day, but my beat's local, what's happening right here in Washington." He had a sweet southern drawl.

"You mean crime?" Eddie said.

"Edwina, don't you start. I forbid that kind of talk in my parlor." Aunt Viola flapped a large paper fan *Jones Funeral Home* printed over a blazing sunset on one side, sunrise on the other, not a subtle metaphor. "Ya'll sit and stop treating my parlor like Union Station."

"Beg pardon, Ma'am." Thad sank into his cushioned armchair, while Rachel crouched in a nearby chair like a runner waiting for the start of her race.

Palms folded on his lap, Thad said, "So how long has the G-man lived out back, Ma'am?"

Bert spoke up from the sofa. "Mama, Jess doesn't want us discussing them."

Aunt Viola shot Bert a look. Seldom did her son correct her. "I want Thad to know I'm doing my part for the war."

But Eddie's alarm bells went off. After the big deal her aunt made about not introducing Jessup Lindsay to her and Rachel, Eddie had found and read the article about him in *The Washington Herald,* Thad's employer.

"You wrote the article about Special Agent Lindsay, didn't you?" Eddie was guessing.

"You're pretty sharp, Eddie." Thad showed nice white teeth. "Rachel tells me you're a writer, too."

Thad was pretty sharp, too. "Not really." Eddie wasn't sure about him. Had his meeting Rachel really been by chance? Eddie imagined Rachel telling her to stop distrusting everyone. If people were more trustworthy, maybe she could.

"Last winter Eddie won a poetry competition with a beautiful poem about Saltville. It was published in *The Atlantic Monthly* magazine." Rachel traded a sideways glance with Thad, a look full of sparks.

"Sure would like to read it, Eddie," Thad said.

"Of course." Eddie couldn't deny he was cute. And if he had an ulterior motive for meeting Rachel, maybe he didn't any longer. Thad Graham appeared smitten.

"I never heard of that magazine," Aunt Viola said. "This here's my favorite." She reached into her magazine stand and pulled out *Photoplay*, a dark-haired young actress on the cover.

Bert craned forward and snapped his fingers. "That's who you look like, Rachel. Elizabeth Taylor."

They all agreed, except for Rachel, her face pink with delight. She thanked Bert. Eddie knew Rachel did her best to look like the actress.

"That reminds me, Thad." Rachel stood, purse wedged under her arm. "Hadn't we better be going if we want to make the next showing of *Suspicion*? It's almost six-thirty."

Thad sighed as if reluctant to leave.

"Thank you so much for the candied pecans, Thad." Aunt Viola patted the box beside her radio. "You're so sweet to bring 'em to me."

Thad took Aunt Viola's hand as if she was royalty. "I do believe this is the coolest, most pleasant parlor in all Washington City, Ma'am. I hope I may visit you again."

He knew who had the loose lips in this house.

"Please do, Thad. You're always welcome. Too many young-uns don't have your nice manners."

Rachel got Thad out the front door. Eddie and Bert followed. From the porch, they watched Thad walk Rachel toward a maroon-colored car. His hand edged up her back.

"Is he trustworthy?" Eddie asked her cousin.

"I reckon. He rents the Berman's basement, but with them gone for the summer, he has the run of their whole house and the plant. Sometimes he borrows a truck if he's low on gasoline, and he's always showing up with laundry he wants done right away."

"So the laundry plant is near the Berman's house?"

"Yup." Bert leaned against the porch post, looking dog-tired. He delivered laundry for Berman's then worked weekends for Jones Funeral Home on 16th Street. His dream was to get his funeral director license. Their grandfather had been an embalmer, so funerals were in their blood.

Eddie noticed that Bert's ankles looked swollen. She guessed this was from his hemophilia, not that he complained. She put her hand on his shoulder. "I hope you don't have to work tonight."

"'Afraid, so, Cuz. Got to grab a sandwich before I head out." He turned his gaze to the street. "Uh-oh, here comes trouble."

Pearl approached their gate, a large shopping bag in each hand.

Pearl had promised to move out as soon as she got a job. The problem was she couldn't get hired, even in Washington where employers were desperate for workers.

"See you later, Eddie." Bert went inside. He had avoided Pearl ever since she went to his room late one night and offered to rub his back. Shocked at how forward she was, he sent her away and told Eddie about it.

Eddie went down the sidewalk and helped Pearl with her bags. What had she bought now? Pearl so enjoyed having money for the first time in her life.

"Rachel introduced me to her date, Thad." Pearl said. "He's a real dreamboat."

"Uh-huh." Eddie held the door. "How's your job-hunting?"

Tonight Eddie was going to give Pearl an ultimatum. Pearl either moved out or Eddie would tell Bert about the stolen money. He had a right to know since the money threatened everyone living here.

"I got real good news, Eddie." Pearl winked.

Eddie didn't get her hopes up. Pearl kept telling them she was close to getting hired at different government agencies, but when Eddie went through Pearl's dresser drawer, she found copies of failed tests for typing, record-keeping, even filing. How could Pearl not know the alphabet?

Okay, so Eddie was a snoop, but she had to be with Pearl, who seldom told the truth.

Aunt Viola turned down the radio. "Hey, Pearl girl. Come in and show me what you bought."

As Pearl had transformed from ragged hillbilly to city girl with plenty of money, Aunt Viola had warmed to her. Eddie enjoyed observing people do an about-face, as her aunt had done about Pearl. Yet why didn't Aunt Viola or Rachel wonder where Pearl's money came from?

Pearl went in the parlor and took out a cotton dress from a Hecht Company bag. "Rachel showed me colors partial to redheads like me. This here's peach."

Yes, Pearl was a quick learner when it came to fashion and makeup. Rachel had an unerring sense of color and style, which she taught to Pearl and Eddie.

Eddie sat at the telephone table and listened to Aunt Viola rhapsodize about the dress. Her aunt was such a *faulpelz*. She did nothing all day, except listen to radio soap operas, keeping the radio's volume high to hear over the fan's whir.

Ruth trudged downstairs in her housekeeper's apron, her forehead bunched. When she saw Eddie, her mask of indifference dropped, and she whispered, "Tomorrow."

"You're ready." Eddie squeezed Ruth's hand before Ruth went down the hall to the kitchen.

Last week Eddie ran into Ruth at the Mt. Pleasant Library, where Ruth had not been friendly. Why should she be? Ever since Ruth graduated from high school last year, she'd worked for Aunt Viola, which would turn anyone sour.

After Eddie discovered Ruth was studying for the Civil Service test, Eddie found books for her. Since then, she and Ruth had met at the library to go over sample tests. Intelligent Ruth deserved better than cleaning and cooking here six days a week.

In the parlor, Aunt Viola told Pearl, "Model it for me later, honey, once *Bachelor's Children* is over."

Eddie helped take Pearl's bags upstairs. Once she closed the door behind them, she said, "Pearl, you promised to move out as soon as you found a job, but…"

"You hit the nail on the head." Pearl perched on the dressing table's bench. "I'm about to get hired as a switchboard operator trainee for the War Department."

Eddie sat on her bed, her back against the wall and studied Pearl's watery blue eyes that looked straight at Eddie. She had read that when people tell a lie their gazes shift, which must be where the adjective shifty came from.

But at the moment Pearl held Eddie's gaze.

"So you'll be working at the Pentagon?" The Pentagon was in Virginia, which would make a great excuse for Pearl to move out in order to live closer to her job.

"Not so fast. To get the job, I need your help." She sauntered over to Eddie. "Since you was my high school English teacher, I put your name and our telephone number on the paper. You have to give me a real good reference."

Eddie scooted forward on the bed. "But you got Ds in my class before you dropped out. How can I give you a good reference?"

"You want me to move out, don't you?" Pearl grabbed the scarf around Eddie's neck and yanked her forward. "I'm not going anywhere unless you…"

Eddie shoved Pearl back and stood. "How dare you threaten me." If Pearl had been a man instead of a pipsqueak woman, she might have been as violent as her uncle.

"Sorry Eddie." Pearl reached up and straightened Eddie's scarf.

"Don't touch me." Eddie swatted her hands away.

Pearl said, "I want to be a government girl so bad…"

So bad she refused to apply for jobs that weren't with the government, which Eddie had suggested. Pearl said she hadn't come all the way to Washington to work just anywhere.

Downstairs the telephone rang.

"That's probably Mrs. Shelton, the switchboard supervisor. She told me she'd call around seven. Pretty please, Eddie. Give me a good reference."

Eddie went down the steps, not sure what she would say. She hated to lie, but Pearl needed to leave Georgia Avenue. Still, she had never believed the ends justified the means.

She picked up the receiver, listened to the voice, and swallowed hard. "I'm sorry. You must have the wrong number." She set the receiver back in its cradle.

"That was quick," Pearl said when Eddie returned to the room. "What did you tell her?"

"That wasn't your supervisor, Pearl. That was a man with a mountain accent, who asked for you, Pearl Ballou."

12

"Drink, please." Jess nodded to the glass of water on the small table in front of this mountain of a man.

He straightened in the chair, lifted the glass in big calloused hands, a working man's hands, and sipped. His coarse hair streaked with gray was combed straight back from his forehead, and he was deeply tanned from working outside. A wedding band width of pale skin encircled his ring finger. Why he had stopped wearing his ring?

Wafting from him was the smell of sweat and lavender, huge purple fields of it. Not that it was easy to smell anything in here with the sink area cordoned off for Alonso's dark room. The almond-like smell from the potassium cyanide's fixing bath permeated. Jess had become so used to the smell, it barely registered.

"What happened to me?" the man asked Jess, who sat opposite.

"Fainted. Keep your eyes straight ahead, so you don't do it again."

Jess hated for him to see their case map, but they couldn't take him to their bungalow, it being so close to the house. "What's your name, and why were you following us?"

"Vernon, Vernon Lanier." Vernon crossed one leg over the other, hunched, and brought his hands to the back of his head as if to protect it. He showed them his ID card from District Construction.

"We're not going to hurt you, Mr. Lanier." Jess took his own badge from his pocket and showed Vernon. "We work for the Bureau of Investigation." He angled the lamp's light on Vernon's long horsey face. "But we need some straight answers, or we'll have to take you down to DC police headquarters."

"I know who you are. You're Jessup Lindsay and Alonso Crooms. Seen your picture in the paper. That's why I followed you."

Jess exchanged a glance with Alonso, who gave a frustrated shake of his head.

Ever since Thad Graham's story about them appeared in *The Herald*, their office phone hadn't stopped ringing. Mothers who didn't receive their weekly letters from their daughters feared they'd been murdered. Police from the Maryland and Virginia suburbs demanded to be filled in on the details. How many girls had been murdered, and where? Why hadn't they been informed?

And a few crazies called to confess. Still they had to be checked out, every call a waste of time.

Jess even got grief from Mrs. Trundle, who insisted he take his supper in the kitchen with Alonso from now on. "I can't have my niece and Miss Margolis associating with someone who does your kind of work, Mr. Lindsay."

Ruth had given Alonso a copy of their newspaper photograph in which she'd outlined their faces with their identical jaws and cleft chins. She also drew round Tojo glasses on both of them. A broad hint they looked alike.

"Jess, look at this." Alonso pointed to the sole of Vernon's boots.

Jess got up to see. Vernon tried to set his foot down, but Alonso held on.

Vernon's shoe had tiny holes in the sole.

Jess's pulse kicked up a notch. Although the towpath murder happened before they came on the job, they were given the evidence collected. An item of special interest: the photograph of a footprint. That photograph was on the back wall attached by colored string to the location of the government girl's body found on the C&O Canal.

Jess grabbed Vernon's hand. "There's tar under your fingernails. You're a roofer."

"That's not against the law." Vernon tried to get up from his chair, but

Alonso brought his hands to the man's broad shoulders and kept him seated. "I didn't kill her. If that's what you're thinking."

"Okay." Jess sat, reached in his shirt pocket, and pulled out a pad. "Tell us why your footprints were found near her body, Mr. Lanier."

Vernon told them about sleeping in the abandoned lockkeeper's house. "She must've screamed, but I didn't hear her." He was trembling. "I feel her eyes on me now. Could you take her photograph down?"

Jess raised an eyebrow at Alonso. Vernon was strange, but he was their first real lead. Five dead women, all kinds of crazy clues, but this man was the closest they had to a witness.

"Sure, Mr. Lanier." Alonso sent Jess a look. "I'll take it down."

They would test Vernon. Jess would make sure Vernon didn't look behind him.

Alonso had blown up photographs of the five girls' faces, their eyes open, their faces startled in that last moment of life. Five death masks. The photographs were tacked to the back wall alongside a huge map of the Washington area marked with the murder locations, the Georgetown Reservoir, the Rock Creek Park, the C&O Canal, Roosevelt Island, and Arlington Cemetery. Clues printed on paper were attached to the various locations by colored string.

Alonso climbed the step ladder and covered the entire wall with a sheet. He got down and returned to the desk. "Is that better?" he asked Vernon.

"Now Doris is looking at me through a veil…" Vernon's voice broke. "I feel her eyes…"

Alonso and Jess exchanged a startled glance. "How do you know her name?" Jess almost shouted.

Vernon could have read it in the newspaper. Thad Graham had done his research and dug up all the girls' names. Ray K. says the reporter has a source within the MPD, but Jess suspected that source might be Ray himself.

"Her name was in her coat," Vernon said.

"Did you cover her in her coat?"

"I did." Vernon nodded.

Jess pounded the desk a moment in frustration, then wrote in his notebook.

A killer, who covered his victim, meant the killer felt regret, even shame for what he had done. Doris Reynolds was the only victim who had been covered. This killer had no regret or shame.

"By covering her, you disturbed a crime scene, Vernon. That's illegal. Police need to see the body in situ."

Vernon kept his head lowered. "I can hardly get my breath with her eyes on me."

Alonso went to the case map, took all the girls' photographs down, and stacked them between large pieces of cardboard for safekeeping. He left the sheet over the maps and clues and put the stack of photographs under the camp bed.

Jess watched Vernon to make sure he didn't look around. Could Vernon tell her photograph was no longer on the wall?

Alonso returned and said, "How's that, sir?"

Vernon lifted his head and inhaled. "Thank you, Alonso."

Maybe Vernon had that sixth sense. What some called intuition, but was so much more.

Vernon rose partway from his chair. "This is for you." From his pocket, he pulled out something small. "Found it on the path near her. I shouldn't have taken it. That was wrong of me. Forgive me." He gave it to Jess, sighed, and slumped in the chair.

Jess examined the twin silver bars. On the back were two prongs. "It attaches to the uniform's collar with these." Jess brought the bars to his own collar to show Alonso.

"Captain's bars." Alonso extended his hand. Jess gave him the insignia. "Brackets attach to the prongs and hold them in place."

"If she ripped the bars off, the uniform would have a ragged collar, right?" Jess looked at Alonso, who said, "Couldn't be worn again."

Jess wrote in his notebook. The captain would have to be Army or Marines since a Navy captain was a high rank and would be older than their killer, or so they had decided. How many uniforms was a captain allotted? Did the officer have to account for the loss of a shirt? Was it easy to order another?

Alonso stood behind Vernon and took their father's gold watch from his pocket, signaling what he wanted to try. Jess set his palm on the desk, his fingers spread wide, gesturing they needed to lower the tension first.

Alonso stepped over to the desk. "Would you gentlemen care for a cool drink?" he asked with a slight bow.

How easily Al switched into his manservant role.

"Sounds good to me," Jess said. "How about you, Mr. Lanier?"

Suspicious, Vernon looked from Jess to Alonso and back again before he dropped his chin in a slow nod. "I would appreciate it."

"May we call you Vernon?" Jess sat back. When Vernon said sure, Jess told him their first names. "Where you from Vernon?"

"I hale from a little place called Frog Hollow between Harpers Ferry and Shepherdstown."

"I thought I recognized West Virginia in your voice."

"Yep, I'm a mountain man. My pap worked the mines. Died in a cave-in. Myself, I like high airy places, mountains and rooftops." He slumped in the chair. "Mind if I smoke?"

"Go 'head." A cigarette would relax him.

Vernon took out a pack of rolling papers and a grimy leather pouch. How steady his hand was as he filled the paper with golden brown tobacco from his pouch. He lit up and took a long drag, his eyes closing with pleasure. Jess set a saucer in front of him to be used as an ashtray.

The clink of bottles sounded. Alonso placed three soda pops on the table, grape, cherry, and orange. The bottles were dewy from the refrigerator they'd bought and hid from Mrs. Trundle, who complained about her electric bill.

With his pocket knife, Alonso popped their tops. "Choose your poison, Mr. Vernon."

Vernon took the cherry, brought it to his lips, and almost guzzled the whole thing in one gulp. He wiped his mouth with the back of his hand. "You going to arrest me for taking the pin?"

"No." Jess sipped his grape soda. "Tell us about that night and morning again."

Vernon went back over everything.

Jess leaned across the table and looked into Vernon's gray ghost eyes.

"The mind can be like a crowded cupboard, Vernon. Sometimes things get stored in its darkest reaches, things we don't even know are there."

Alonso cut the lamp, while Jess studied the man's strong face.

Vernon's eyes fixed on Jess, while his hand reached for the pop bottle he set on the floor beside him. He finished off the soda, set it back, and took another drag on his cigarette, depositing its ash in the saucer.

Jess marveled at how two-handed people juggled items. "Vernon, do you understand what I'm saying?"

Vernon dropped his chin in a deep nod. "You're talking about things we know, but don't know we know."

"Exactly," Jess said, "even if it sounds like a riddle." If ever there was a candidate for Al's technique, it was Vernon Lanier. "Bear with us a minute, Vernon." Jess got up from his chair and went to stand beside Vernon.

Alonso sat in Jess's place. "This isn't going to hurt, Mr. Vernon." Alonso produced the railroad watch from his pocket. Actually it was their father's watch, which Alonso carried. Jess disliked anything heavy in his pocket. One-armed, he was unbalanced enough.

"I want you to relax and keep your eyes on this here watch." He dangled it by its chain a few inches in front of Vernon's eyes. "Don't look away now. Stay with the watch, stay with it." He kept repeating, his voice going lower.

For a few minutes, Vernon's eyelids fluttered, the refrigerator's hum the only sound in the room.

"Your eyes feel heavy, heavy. Let them close let them sink into their sockets."

Vernon's eyes closed. Jess had to fight to keep his own eyes open. His brother's soft voice always lulled him.

Alonso said, "Go back to that night in March. You're asleep in the lock-keeper's cottage. You're lying on the stone floor, sleeping, but something almost awakens you. What do you hear?"

Vernon was silent for a long moment. "I'm so tired." He speaks in a whisper. "I have a crick in my neck. I roll my head and hear soft thunder, once, twice." Vernon slumped forward and flinched. "A roar and white metal comes at me…"

Voices from the alley interrupted. Ruth was explaining about the time difference between here and Europe. "Our Jasper is already in France, Mama." Ruth was talking about her brother in the Army.

"Lord Jesus, keep him safe," Miss Minnie said.

Vernon shook his head like he had water in his ears. "I was dead asleep. What did you do to me?"

Alonso stood. "I was helping you remember that night." He got the *Farmer's Almanac* from the bookshelf and checked the date.

Jess sat, wrote *soft thunder* in his notebook then flipped through his pages of notes. "You said you heard soft thunder in your sleep that night. Twice you heard it."

Vernon looked surprised. "I don't remember thunder."

"According to the *Almanac* the night of March 25th was clear and cool," Alonso said, "with a full moon."

"Yep. That's what the police report says, too." Jess studied Vernon who shrugged. "Then you said there was a roar and white metal came at you."

Vernon brought his thumb and index finger to either side of his mouth and wiped. "That happened the next day, after I found her." He told them about a white delivery truck whose brakes must have given out and almost hit him on the way home.

Jess and Alonso exchanged a puzzled look. Maybe the killer followed Vernon and tried to run him over. "You say a man appeared and helped you back on the road?"

"He was in a chicken truck heading to West Virginia. Nice fellas. They rode me almost all the way home."

"Is it possible that chicken truck was the one that tried to run you over?"

Lowering his eyes, Vernon said, "I travelled in the back, so I never seen the front of the chicken truck, but I don't believe they were one and the same."

"Do you remember the license number of the truck that tried to run you over?"

Vernon closed his eyes. "Don't believe it had a front plate."

"How long a time was it between you finding the girl's body and almost getting hit by the truck?"

"Maybe half an hour."

Jess said, "Describe the truck."

"Well, it was white and smaller than the chicken truck. And when it picked up speed, it rattled like the exhaust pipe was loose. And it still had its chrome bumper."

He said this because the War Productions Board encouraged drivers to hand in their bumpers for scrap metal. "What kind of things might this truck have carried?"

Vernon made a face. "Bread, laundry, newspapers, maybe even milk...I don't know."

Jess stuck his pencil behind his ear and sat back. "When it comes to murder, I don't believe in coincidences, Vernon. You find a young woman dead and a little while later a truck tries to run you over."

"I see what you mean." Vernon scrubbed his bristly jaw. "But I don't know why he would want to do that."

"Tell me about every person you saw after you found her body."

"Nobody except a fisherman I passed on the bridge, but it was misty. I didn't see him too good." Vernon closed his eyes tight. "One thing, though. He told me he caught a big catfish, but he didn't have a bucket, so where'd he put his fish?"

Alonso picked up his orange soda from the desk. "He didn't catch a catfish from the bridge," he said. "Catfish are bottom feeders. You fish them in shallows."

"Describe this fisherman."

Vernon closed his eyes. "He wore an old canvas hat stuck with lures pulled low on his head. That's all I remember."

Jess wrote this in his notebook.

Vernon stood. "Look, I gave you the pin. Now I've got to get back..."

"So you work for District Construction?" Jess stood as well and faced him.

"Uh-huh." Vernon's eyes skated from Jess's.

He was lying, something he wasn't good at. "Give me your address in case we need to talk to you again."

"2010 Prospect, Georgetown. It's a rooming house."

Jess sat and wrote it, noticing how Vernon had touched his left ring finger, where he'd once worn a wedding ring. His lies had to do with a woman, probably not his wife.

Alonso said, "The smell from that rendering plant in Georgetown must keep you up nights."

"Amen to that. You don't want no breezes off the water." His eyes avoided theirs.

But Jess didn't smell the rendering plant's stink on Vernon's clothes.

"We'll let you go, Vernon. But first we need to fingerprint you. We can do it here or take you downtown. It's your choice."

Vernon dropped back in the chair.

Jess got the ink pad and papers from his kit. With a rag, Alonso wiped and dried Vernon's hands, inked his fingers, and pressed each fingertip to paper.

Vernon lifted his hand and stared at his inky fingers, his expression grim. No one enjoyed being fingerprinted. "I didn't kill her." He looked from Jess to Alonso.

In the movies, Vernon would be cast as the crazed killer because of his size, his wild gray hair, and deep set eyes, but Jess couldn't see a government girl going off with him. Still he had to make sure the man had no criminal record, not here in Washington or in West Virginia.

"Here you go, Mr. Vernon. Use this to clean them." Alonso gave him the rag and a bottle of rubbing alcohol. "I take a picture of every witness," Alonso told him and moved around the room turning on all the lamps for brightness.

"Right," Jess said. Since there'd been no other witnesses, what Al said was true.

Vernon perked up and stood. "Haven't been photographed in years." He dug a comb from his pocket, strode to the little mirror on the wall, and primped. Jess almost laughed.

Alonso positioned Vernon closer to the window and snapped his picture, the flashbulb going off like a brilliant dying sun.

Vernon stood blinking. "Sure would like to see what your camera says I look like." A wide grin opened his face. "Been told I'm a lovely man." He gave a pleasured laugh.

"I'll make a copy for you," Alonso said. "Come by Friday evening long about this time, and I'll give it to you."

Great idea. That way they could talk to Vernon again.

"All right." Vernon's grin stayed fixed. "I'll come through that back gate and knock downstairs."

Jess and Alonso followed Vernon into the alley. Past the gate, Jess clapped his hand on Vernon's shoulder. "Vernon, if you think of anything else, you don't wait 'til Friday." He handed Vernon his card. "Call us."

Vernon stuck the card in his shirt pocket, lifted his hand in farewell, and strolled off down the alley. Jess and Alonso watched him.

"I best go separate Vernon's truth from his lies," Alonso said. Once Vernon turned the corner, he slipped away, following the roofer.

Almost at the end of the alley, little boys were having a shoot-out with their fingers and sticks as guns. One of them yelled at Alonso, "Got the jump on you." Alonso clutched his heart as if he'd been shot before he rounded the corner.

13

Jess turned to go back to their bungalow when he heard the clatter of typewriter keys coming from Ruth's house. He stepped onto her stoop and knocked. The electric bulb in their back room went off before Ruth opened the door.

"Hello." He tried to remove his hat when he realized he had left it in the room over the garage. "Just checking to see if Miss Minnie has finished our laundry?"

"Come on in, Mr. Jess," Miss Minnie called from inside the dark room. Ruth looked as if she would prefer him to wait on the stoop.

Inside he took in the smell of collard greens cooked in fat back drifting from their kitchen. His mouth watered. The aroma made him homesick for Alabama, but he didn't comment on the food because Miss Minnie often fed Alonso. She was a generous lady, but couldn't be expected to feed every Southern transplant in the neighborhood.

A stiff green velvet sofa sat high and proud on glossy wooden legs in the middle of the front room, a yellow wedding ring quilt covering it for protection. How many stacks of laundry and cooked meals for the Trundles had gone into buying it? A shelf filled with books, mostly tattered paperbacks, took up one wall. On the table in the next room beneath the dangling light bulb sat an old Remington typewriter.

Ruth followed his gaze. "Miss Smith loaned me that typewriter so I could practice." Her words rushed. For good reasons, coloreds didn't trust whites. Ruth was afraid he would think she had stolen it.

In a short time, Miss Smith had gotten to know Ruth, who usually kept herself apart from white folks. How had Miss Smith done what he had not been able to? Ruth still didn't trust him even though she and Alonso were close.

"I'm a one-handed typist, so I don't know your accuracy," Jess said to Ruth, "but listening to you type, I'd say you're at least fifty words a minute."

She pushed the carriage release, took the paper out, and brought the sheet to him. *Now is the time for all good men to come to the aide of their country...*

"Perfect," he said.

Miss Minnie, a tiny woman with grizzly white hair around her face and an eyelid that drooped, came in holding two big boxes tied with string. "Here you go, Mr. Jess."

"Thank you, Ma'am. You don't know how much we need these." He took the box, set it on the floor beside his feet, and handed her a dollar.

"Got any change, Mr. Jess? You only owe me fifty-five cents."

"Keep it, Miss Minnie. I'm grateful to you for doing it. You know how difficult it is to get clothes washed in this city? Your employer, Berman's, refuses to accept new customers except ones in the military." Jess glanced at Ruth. "And besides typewriter paper is expensive."

A light came into Miss Minnie's face as she looked at her daughter. "She wants a job typing for the Veteran's Administration. My Jasper can fight in France, but colored girls aren't going to become government girls."

"But they do, Miss Minnie. There's that new dormitory for Negro government girls over on Third and U. Ruth has a good chance."

"I'm not letting my baby live in no dormitory."

"Mama." Ruth groaned and shot Jess a *look what you started* glance.

He'd given Miss Minnie another worry. He said goodnight and turned to leave when a jar near Miss Minnie's old Singer sewing machine caught his eye.

"What have you got here?" He picked up the jar filled with brass military buttons, insignias, even single silver bars designating the rank of lieutenant.

"Those come off uniforms at the laundry. We collect them, then when a uniform needs a button or a sergeant's patch, I sew 'em on."

He felt as if the breath had been knocked out of him. Just when he thought they had a strong clue, the captain's bars Vernon found, it proved worthless. Jess moved the glittery jar side-to-side to see all it contained.

Then he understood. If a man had the right insignia with the right uniform, he could be in any branch of the service. He drifted back to their bungalow, light-headed with the idea. Maybe the government girls had been right about the uniform and rank of the man they met. The killer could be impersonating an officer. So where could a man get access to different uniforms?

No sooner did he unlock the door and set the laundry on his desk when he heard rustling in the garden. A shadow moved between the rows of corn. He grabbed his gun from the desk drawer and went outside.

14

Eddie saw a long shadow on the path and crouched in the garden.

A tall man holding something above his head moved sideways through the rows of string frames thick with pea vines. Light from a window fell on what the man was holding: a gun. Its metal gave off a sinister glint.

Her thudding heart drowned other sounds. He came closer, closer. So close she could grab his ankle. This must be the man who had called and asked for Pearl. *Zugzwang*: she had to do something. Should she bring him down and try to grab his gun? Or did this work only in movies?

This man wasn't Alton Ballou, who she'd seen only once and from the back in Margolis Department Store. She had been with her father in the men's department when a rough booming voice drew their attention. Two salesmen quaked before a mountain of a man, who had sugar bowl handle ears and a bald head fringed in yellow fluff.

Although not Alton Ballou, this man could be someone the bootlegger had sent to get his money. He could be a hired killer.

She made herself as small as possible and got ready to pounce. Her whole body throbbed with fear until the yellow porch light came on, illuminating the man: Jessup Lindsay.

She let out a long sigh, which drew his gaze.

He gave her a lopsided grin and slipped his gun into his jacket pocket.

"Miss Smith, what are you…"

She brought her finger to her lips and shushed him.

"Who's out there?" Aunt Viola called from the back porch.

Eddie reached up, grabbed Agent Lindsay's hand, and pulled him down so he crouched beside her. A bold move.

She took in his angular face and blistering blue eyes fixed on her. She had surprised him. Good. As her fear dissipated, she relaxed and took in the luscious loamy smell of growing things surrounding them. How she loved a vegetable garden.

The strangeness of their situation, hiding from her aunt in the peas, made her giddy. When Jessup Lindsay wobbled in his squat, she grabbed his stump of an arm and steadied him. Holding him there felt so intimate. She wondered how he'd lost his arm.

His soft black pupils widened, more surprise. "Except for nurses, no woman has ever touched me there," he whispered. "You're disarming me, Miss Smith."

She smiled at his pun, but said nothing for fear her aunt would hear.

Aunt Viola turned off the light and closed and bolted the door.

"Great," Eddie said. "I'm either going to have to go in the front door and face her wrath or shimmy up the drainpipe to our bedroom."

One of Aunt Viola's many rules was that the girls didn't use the back door, ever. Eddy wasn't sure whether Aunt Viola was trying to protect them from Jess Lindsay or from Atlanta Alley where the colored people lived.

Still she and Jess remained crouched between the string frames.

"So what are we doing here, Miss Smith?"

She tugged a pea pod off a vine and popped it in her mouth. "I'm getting something fresh to eat." After that scary telephone call earlier, she'd been unable to eat dinner. She picked another pea pod and offered it to him. "And you're playing Gene Autry. Thanks for not shooting me."

"You're as welcome as the flowers in May." He put the pod in his mouth, chewed, and swallowed. "Good, even raw."

"Raw is best." She fed him another, this time putting it on his tongue. She smelled grape soda on his breath.

"Wouldn't it be simpler to ask your aunt to serve peas for dinner?"

"As a detective, Agent Lindsay, you ought to know Aunt Viola serves us only what she can buy with our ration coupons, like spam and other canned goods. While she sells these delicious early peas to the Italian man who runs the vegetable market on U Street."

"That lady is sharp with money." He blinked and hunkered down. "No offense."

Eddie rolled her eyes. "She's an awful skinflint."

He acknowledged this with a quick nod. "By the way, are you hungry?"

"Starved." She popped another pea pod into her mouth.

"Keep low." He took her hand and led her past the chubby scarecrow in an old straw hat. They turned right at the end of the row and moved between the high wooden fence and the marigold border planted to keep insects away. On the stone path, they walked beneath a sweet honeysuckle arch. He opened the gate beside the garage.

She stepped into the alley, where she heard the clatter of her own ancient typewriter, a sound she loved. Ruth must be practicing.

"This way, Miss Smith. You're perfectly safe here. Nothing to be afraid of."

"What do you think is going to frighten me, Agent Lindsay?"

"Alley life is a part of Washington most white folks...don't see."

"As a high school teacher, I'm not easily frightened." What a lie. Every time the doorbell rang, she held her breath afraid the caller might be Alton Ballou, as if the ruthless bootlegger would ring a doorbell before entering.

"I didn't mean to offend you." He pulled a leaf from her hair. "Would you mind calling me Jess?"

"If you'll call me Eddie."

In the alley women and children crowded around an elderly man cutting a watermelon sunk in a washtub of ice. "This here's a D-Day party," Miss Minnie called from her neighbor's stoop. "You're welcome to watermelon."

"Thank you," Eddie called and wondered why Aunt Viola hadn't held a similar party. Odd that living on Georgia Avenue with her aunt, Eddie felt further from the war than she had in Saltville. There folks talked of nothing else because most had sons or husbands away in the fighting.

She and Jess walked over to the watermelon man. "Melon for the lady and the G-Man." He handed them juicy wedges.

Jess thanked him and told Eddie, "We need to hurry. Before it closes."

They ate the sweet melon, while striding to the end of the alley, where they tossed their rinds over a picket fence into the compost heap. That was one thing Washington and Saltville had in common: every patch of ground was a victory garden.

"This way." On the sidewalk, he pivoted toward the neighborhood shops. Near the busy corner of Georgia and Florida Avenues sat a Peoples Drug lit with neon lights that declared WE ALWAYS SELL THE BEST.

They crossed the street and went inside. Customers, mostly women, crowded the aisles, shopping. At the lunch counter, a few people sat on stools, hunched over their plates.

A tired-looking waitress wiped the counter, her hairnet slightly askew over curly brown hair. "Miss Mildred," Jess said to her, "I know it's late, but could we have some BLTs, French fries and sodas?"

She straightened and rolled her eyes at Jess. "Got any bacon left, Lloyd?" she called to the small gray-haired colored man scraping the grill. "We got us a hungry detective and his friend." She winked at Eddie.

"Always." Lloyd waved his spatula like a scepter and threw a rasher of bacon on the grill. The aroma made Eddie's stomach gurgle. Someone had cut out the newspaper photograph of Jess and Alonso Crooms and taped it to the long mirror behind the counter.

Jess led her to a booth, where they took seats opposite each other. A ceiling fan stirred warm air above them.

"Jess, everyone knows who you are. I read the article about you, too." She reached across with a paper napkin and removed a watermelon seed stuck to his cheek. "How does it feel to be famous?"

Beneath his tanned face, he paled. "Like a fraud." His eyes dropped to his hand, palm up on the tabletop. "That newspaper story made me sound like Sherlock Holmes, but I'm starting to think Alonso and I got lucky in solving other cases. We're hayseeds out of our depth here in Washington."

"I understand." A need to comfort Jess rose in her, so palpable she could taste it. She reached across the table and put her hand on top of his.

"S'cuse me, Lovebirds." Mildred set down her tray of Coca-colas and plates of food. With a wink, she gave Jess an extra sandwich in a paper bag.

"You got a great memory, Miss Mildred." He slipped the bag into his other pocket, the one that didn't contain his gun.

After she walked away, he said, "Alonso missed his spam dinner tonight, too."

"So Alonso's your driver and your crime photographer?" They ate and sipped their sodas.

He said, "I believe folks in this city would starve if not for Peoples lunch counters."

Okay, so he didn't want to talk about Alonso Crooms. She dipped a French fry in the pool of ketchup he'd squeezed onto his plate. "Jess, you've got the deepest Southern accent I've ever heard."

"Guilty as charged. I was born in Abbeville, Alabama, a town so small I'm sure you never heard of it."

"I'm from a small town, too, and will have to return there in the fall to teach at Saltville High, but for now I'm thrilled to be here."

"You look too young to teach high school."

"I'll be twenty-one in September." An important birthday because it meant she could be free of her father if she had the will to break away. *If she had the will.*

She sat up straighter and brushed the sides of her face, sticky with watermelon juice. She didn't want to imagine how unkempt she looked after crawling around in the garden. "Since my high school had only eleven grades, I graduated when I was sixteen and went through Emory and Henry College in an accelerated war-time program. At the end of May, I finished my first year of teaching."

"That's impressive, Eddie." His gaze remained on her.

"Thanks," she said. Her name on his lips sounded like thick warm molasses. She could listen to him say it all night.

"Your aunt told me you were valedictorian of your high school and college classes. You must be quite a scholar."

"Not really, Jess. I just work hard. I'm surprised Aunt Viola credits me for anything."

"Time for us to go home," Mildred called from the counter. "You kids stay as long as you like, but when you go, put your dishes in the sink, or we'll send the law after you."

Lloyd hooted at this.

Jess got up and paid her. Everyone else in the counter section had left.

"I don't have any money with me, Jess," Eddie said when he sat back down. "Is it all right if I pay you when we get back?" This wasn't a date. He shouldn't be expected to pay for her.

"My treat, Eddie." He sipped his soda. "What do you teach at Saltville High?"

"English, mostly grammar, letter-writing, literature, Beowulf to Shakespeare. And I have one small class of German." Very small, consisting of one wonderful student.

"German? Is that what you're doing here? Translating for the Department of the Army?" His words rose in excitement.

"I wish. I signed an agreement to keep what I do secret, but telling an FBI agent I do menial clerical work isn't divulging anything." Her job wasn't the challenge she'd expected.

She worked in a large hot room filled with rows of women at desks busy doing something they couldn't discuss. She combed through records of men wounded or killed on Anzio beachhead and enumerated the various types of injuries suffered. Sad, mind-numbing work, but she forced herself to think of each record as a man who had fought for this country.

"I assure you there's a lot of routine in what we do, too," Jess said.

"You're looking for a killer. That's not routine."

He paused and studied her as if assessing her for…what?

"We've looked up every man remotely connected with a victim and checked his gasoline permit through the Office of Price Administration. That's tedious." His voice lowered to a whisper. "We assume a government girl wouldn't go off with a total stranger."

Eddie leaned forward. "You're wrong. Government girls adore men in uniform and would go with anyone wearing one. To them, a man's uniform makes him trustworthy. The only enemies are Over There, Hitler, Hirohito."

She recalled the ant-aircraft guns scattered over the city, pointed skyward. Most thought the enemy was out there, but her enemy was truly homegrown, from Saltville, Virginia.

"I believe you." Jess nodded. "In our past cases, finding the intersection of motive, means, and opportunity has eventually led us to the killer." He scrubbed his jaw. He was in need of a shave. "Of course, with this killer, the motive…"

Still leaning forward, every nerve ending in her body attuned to him, she said the word he couldn't say. "Sexual," she said, "His motive is sexual." She noted how he colored. "I picked that up from the newspaper, not that it was stated directly."

"This is all secret, Eddie. You understand that?"

"Yes, of course." She looked directly into his eyes, so blue you expected clouds to float across them. "*The Herald* has published a series of stories about the murdered government girls. There've been five murders, right?"

Jess nodded slowly. "A certain reporter is doing his research and making a name for himself."

Jess sounded bitter. Should she tell him Thad Graham was asking about him tonight, that this barbarian was truly at Jess's gate?

A female voice over a loudspeaker announced the drugstore would be closing in ten minutes. They got up and took their plates and glasses around the counter, where Eddie washed and rinsed, and Jess dried with a dishtowel and put them away. Eddie watched how he managed one-handed.

"When do you have to be back?" he asked out on the sidewalk. "We could take a walk or a streetcar ride. Have you been out to Cabin John on the streetcar?" She shook her head. "It's beautiful out there. I like to ride a streetcar to the end of the line, then go to the other side of the street and take it back again. That way, I learn the city."

"Sounds wonderful, Jess." She didn't want her time with him to end. "My roommates will be back soon and might alert Aunt Viola that I'm not in our room."

At that moment, Pearl, her boy friend, Luca, and his friend Tony came around the corner.

"Please. Let's avoid them." Eddie took Jess's arm and turned him, so they faced a window of stationery goods.

The three passed behind them, their reflections moving across the glass.

Tony and Luca walked on either side of Pearl in her new peach dress. Luca reached over and tickled Pearl under the chin. She giggled and stroked Tony's back, a sneaky maneuver.

"Your roommate looks like she's having fun," Jess said to Eddie's reflection.

"Oh, yes." After that phone call, Eddie tried to convince Pearl to move out right away. Pearl refused, saying she felt safe with them on Georgia Avenue.

"You look worried about her." Jess studied Eddie.

"I'm worried about what I did for her. She needed a reference for a switchboard operator job with the War Department. She gave her supervisor my name because I'd been her English teacher..."

Eddie had lied about Pearl's grades, even lied about her high school graduation. Anything to help her get this job, so she would leave Georgia Avenue.

"You gave her a better reference than she deserved. Don't worry. They were probably just checking to make sure Pearl is who she says she is and not some Axis spy."

Eddie let his words buoy her. Pearl and her stolen money had weighed Eddie down like stones in her pockets. For this moment she felt lighter than she had since she arrived in Washington.

Jess said, "I guess we better get back then before they spill the beans?"

"Okay." Not that she was ready to part from him.

Pearl and the rest turned onto Georgia Avenue, making their way through a group of sailors, round white hats angled on their heads. They followed from a safe distance. Eddie took hold of Jess' half arm.

"Eddie, something I've wondered about...why isn't your cousin Bert in the service?"

Ah, this was a family secret she could not divulge. She swallowed hard. "He's 4-F, because of a medical condition." Bert had a mild form of hemophilia, an inherited disease. Women were its carriers, and the disease manifested itself in males. So Aunt Viola, a carrier through her mother, had passed hemophilia to Bert, which encouraged her to smother him.

"Lucky for your aunt he doesn't have to serve. I'm not sure she could do without him." They turned the corner. "Eddie, there's something I want to ask you. Feel free to say no."

They stopped four houses away from Aunt Viola's, in the shadow of a spreading poplar.

Was he going to ask her out? She hoped so. "Okay."

"I need a journal article translated. The Bureau has a German translator, but he's swamped. He's had this article for weeks."

Disappointed, she raked her fingers through her hair. "Sure. I'd be glad to, Jess."

"Before you say yes, you need to know what the article's about and who wrote it." A crease appeared between his eyebrows and his eyes turned steely. "The author is a Berlin detective named Ernst Gennat. And it's a grisly subject, serial murderers. You might not want to read such material."

"*Serienmorder*," she said. "Is Detective Gennat a Nazi?"

"No. Somehow he managed to stay out of politics. And he died in 1939…"

"Will this article help you find the killer?" Eddie asked.

"Maybe. I need all the help I can get. And I'll pay you to translate."

She placed her hand on his chest, her palm opened over his heart. His modesty emboldened her. "I don't want to be paid, Jess. I'll do it gladly and quickly." She didn't care if she sounded eager. She was eager and interested in Jess Lindsay and his work.

They agreed to meet at Peoples tomorrow after work, so he could give her the journal. "Oh, and Eddie, Washington is wonderful, but dangerous. I know you're not afraid of anything, but please be careful. Never go off alone with a man you don't know."

She felt the corners of her mouth lift. "You mean the way I went off with you?"

At that moment, a dark Oldsmobile pulled up in front of Mrs. Trundle's.

"That's Rachel. Tonight's her first date with the newspaper man, Thad Graham, who wrote the stories about the murdered government girls."

Jess's jaw tensed. "How did Rachel meet him?"

Rachel opened her car door, but Thad pulled her back inside, across the seat.

"On the streetcar. He stood up and let her have his seat. You're thinking he might have met her on purpose in order to get information about you, right?"

Jess looked straight into her eyes. People always talked about looking someone in the eyes, but seldom did anyone actually do it. She felt as if he was really seeing her.

"I'm thinking you ought to be a detective, Eddie." He broke their stare. "And that Thad Graham has a knack for being in the right place at the right time."

Her body was suffused in warmth: *you ought to be a detective.* She hadn't known what she wanted to be until this moment: a detective. All her life she'd been a snoop, a reader of clues, her mother's moods, her father's anger. She had been accused of not minding her own business, of being too curious, neither a compliment in Saltville, but good qualities for a detective.

"I'll find out what he asks about you, not that she knows much to tell him."

"Thanks. I'd appreciate that." Jess took her hand. "Eddie, I've really enjoyed this evening."

"Me, too. *Auf wiedersehen,* Jess," she said and walked toward the house.

Rachel didn't see her and sprang from the car ahead. With a stack of newspapers under her arm, she ran into the house. The newspapers weren't a new development. Rachel had been reading newspapers from all over the country ever since she visited her cousins, Meyer and Sarah Rosen.

Thad drove off without walking Rachel to her door, which wasn't in keeping with the polite young man he'd presented himself to be to Aunt Viola.

When Eddie opened the picket fence and stepped onto the sidewalk, Bert came down the porch steps toward her. "Saw you with Jess Lindsay, but that's our secret, Cuz."

They walked to the porch. "Since Mama thinks you're in your room, I'll go into the parlor and distract her so you can sneak upstairs."

"Thanks," she whispered. "I think you're swell, Cousin Bert."

His eyes blinked at the compliment.

Eddie tiptoed up the stairs, listening to her aunt chastise Bert about something.

Why did Bert let his mother treat him like a child? Eddie's father treated her the same way. When she graduated from Emory and Henry, he wouldn't sign for her to go into the WAVES. He said only a certain kind of woman went into the military.

Eddie had been convinced that once she had a college degree, her father would treat her like an adult. But even with a BA, she remained a child, whose life was not her own.

Both she and Bert had parents who held onto their children so tightly they almost strangled the life out of them.

15

Wednesday, June 7, 1944

A tiny click woke Eddie. Rachel stood as if in a trance at the dark window, her filmy nightgown billowing in the breeze. She was opening and shutting her locket.

Eddie checked her wristwatch, three AM., got out of bed, and came to Rachel's side. "Did you have a bad dream?"

Rachel hadn't been her sunny self since that first Friday night she visited the Rosens in Maryland. When Eddie asked what was bothering her, Rachel said she couldn't talk about it. Yet in Saltville they'd shared every detail of their lives. Now secrets divided them.

Often Eddie's mother had set her index finger on her chest, over her heart, and said, "Lock your secrets here, Eddie. Never let them out." Eddie came to believe Mama's locked-away secrets were what sent her to the asylum.

Rachel whispered, "I feel like there's someone in the garden watching us."

Eddie saw a glint of metal through the cornrows. "Me, too."

The man in the garden could be Alton Ballou. She shivered and tugged Rachel back from the window.

Jess's bungalow was dark, but she was certain he would come if he heard a commotion. His nearness gave her comfort.

She and Rachel sat cross-legged on her bed. From the double bed across the room, Pearl mumbled in her sleep.

Rachel said, "Recently I've thought someone was following me, not that it bothers me. I like to imagine whoever's out there is my guardian angel, protecting me." She gave a sad laugh. "My *schtzengel*. Of course, I wonder why I'm the only Jew in the world with a guardian angel. The ones in Europe could certainly use one."

"That's why you're buying all those newspapers, isn't it?"

She nodded slowly, her eyes moist. "Now I know why Papa stopped bringing newspapers home. When they arrived in the mail from Washington, New York, he would hole up in his office reading." Her voice cracked. "Then he burned them as if that would make what was happening go away."

"You're cold." Rachel's arms were covered in gooseflesh.

"Eddie, you read about what was going on, but you didn't tell me."

"Your father thought with your mother's death and the nightmares you had…"

Rachel's long fingernails dug into Eddie's arm. "Didn't he know I would find out?" Her voice was barely a whisper. "But my eyes are open now. The Jews are being slaughtered. Genocide, that's what's going on. They're trying to wipe us off the face of the earth."

"Genocide," Eddie repeated. She had never heard the word spoken before.

"Thad's going to take me to the *Herald's* archives tomorrow night, so I can read about this from the beginning with the Nuremberg Laws. At the Rosen's, I met some garment workers from France. They talked about how their relatives have been rounded up and sent East…" She convulsed in a shudder.

"Let's get under the covers." Eddie pulled down the sheet and lay with her back pressed to the wall.

Rachel got into the bed with her back to Eddie. "Treat me like a grownup, Eddie. Don't keep secrets from me."

"You're right…" Eddie started to tell her about Pearl's stolen money, but hesitated. Rachel had enough to worry about, besides Eddie had promised Pearl she wouldn't tell.

She changed the subject. "Did you have a good time with Thad?"

"Oh yes. He's had such a difficult life. His mother died in a fire when he was thirteen. He tried to rescue her and was given an award for bravery. And he got through Princeton by working for the town newspaper."

"He sounds remarkable."

"He is." Rachel meshed fingers with Eddie. "Last time I was at the Rosens, Sarah opened my locket, saw your photograph, and said she'd like to meet you. I promised I'd bring you Friday night. Please say you'll come."

"But I'm not..." The Rosens held some sort of religious ceremony. Whatever they did couldn't be worse than a Southern Baptist revival, where she'd spent many nights with Mama. "Of course, I'll come."

"Good. And that way I won't have to ride alone with Dan Wozniak. I never want to do that again. On the way home last Friday, he took me to some lover's lane."

"He has his nerve. I could tell the night we met him he was full of himself. Being a factory boss has gone to his head."

Rachel let out a sharp sigh. "I admit I'd had a little too much wine, and Dan had been so sweet. I kissed him first. Everything was okay until he tried to unbutton my dress, and I slapped him. At one point he even put his hands around my neck, as if he might strangle me." She paused. "Oh, maybe I'm exaggerating."

Eddie brought her arms around her. "Considering Dan works for your cousin, I'm shocked he would do that. I'd like to kick him where it hurts, the schmuck."

Rachel giggled and rolled to face Eddie, her voice barely audible. "Before we got home, he apologized and said Tony told him Pearl was a sharecropper." Filthy slang that meant a girl was promiscuous. "Dan said he figured I was like her, but I told him off and stuck up for Pearl."

"Good for you."

"Pearl's like a wounded little bird. She's had it really rough being raised by that bootlegger uncle."

"No matter what Dan Wozniak heard about Pearl, he was a complete jerk to act that way toward you. You need to tell your cousin Sarah about him."

"I know, but Sarah and Meyer adore Dan. They're childless, and he's like the son they never had. I don't want to tattle on him, but I don't want to be alone with him, either. And somehow I have to let Sarah know."

16

Jess stood before Kurt's open door. "Knock, knock."

Even though this entire floor was designated top secret, a restricted area, Kurt never shut his door, except when he left his office, if he ever left his office. To Jess, Kurt had admitted he was claustrophobic and was forced to work in a room so small he could stretch his arms and touch the file cabinets surrounding him. That's why he left the door open.

This afternoon Kurt's tiny space felt roasting hot. Jess was glad he and Alonso's office was in the subbasement. Alonso, the only Negro working for the Bureau who wasn't a janitor, joked that they were placed in the subbasement along with the cleaning supplies. Whatever the reason, their subterranean office, little bigger than a closet, was a cool closet.

"Come on in, Jess." Kurt tugged off his thick glasses and rubbed his eyes.

From atop the corner cabinet, a rotating fan blew hot air around, fluttering papers on his desk. The room smelled rank, a combination of body odor, onions, and fried spam sandwiches. There was no space for another chair, so Jess stood in the doorway.

In a short-sleeved shirt, sweat ringing his underarms, pale, pudgy Kurt balanced his chin on his palm. "Sorry I didn't get to your article. I really want to read it myself." He ducked his head, his close-cropped blond hair beaded in sweat, and scrambled through some desk drawers. "Ernst Gennat may be the most famous policeman who ever lived. My grandpapa, also a policeman, actually met him once in…" Hesitating, he straightened, holding the journal in his hand.

Jess knew Kurt was about to say some place in Germany. Kurt's last name was Bauer, but he told Jess he had wanted to change it to Bower because of America's animosity toward German Americans. Still the Bureau was fortunate to have an almost native speaker like Kurt to run the Bureau's translation unit, which was swamped with top secret work.

Kurt handed the journal to Jess. "So who's this translator you've found?"

Jess tucked it under his arm. "A young college graduate named Eddie Smith."

"Well, let me know how he does with it. If he's any good, we can rush a security clearance through and hire him."

Jess waved the journal at Kurt and left, realizing he'd failed to mention that Eddie wasn't a "he."

Eddie: she was all he could think about. The way she'd taken hold of his half-arm in the garden, the flash in her beautiful grape green eyes when she told him she wasn't afraid. He had to keep reminding himself he was one-armed and almost ten years older. However much he wished he were, he was not beautiful Eddie's Prince Charming.

He ran down the marble staircase with the journal, wanting to put it into Eddie's hands. Or maybe he just wanted to see her. He'd watched her get off the streetcar this morning on Pennsylvania Avenue, her streaky blonde hair easy to pick out in the crowd.

His mind was so full of her, he slid down a few steps. He should have been holding the banister. Without an arm, he was unbalanced and needed to be careful. Eddie had unbalanced him, too.

You've got a killer to catch, he told himself. . . It was the tenth day since Kaye Krieger's murder. They had eighteen days left to find the killer before he struck again. No time to get dreamy over a woman.

In the late afternoon the hottest time of the day, Agent Fred Friedlander sat behind his desk, going over their interviews with Kaye Krieger's roommates.

Fred was a tall man, balding on top with large ears that stuck straight out. He often turned his head as if he were picking up sounds no one else could hear. What tickled Jess and Alonso was that he smoked a Sherlock Holmes pipe, a meerschaum, which he stuffed with tobacco as he read. His pipe was almost a prop since he rarely lit it. He said his wife didn't approve of smoking.

Fred and his Mrs. lived across Georgia Avenue from Mrs. Trundle. Fred had helped Jess and Alonso get their place with her. "I sense Viola might not be an easy woman to deal with," was Fred's understated warning about their landlady.

Fred looked up from the end of Jess's report that stated they were no closer to finding the killer. "You need to get a little perspective here, Jess." Fred had an odd singsong accent completely foreign to Jess, yet pleasant, even reassuring.

Jess and Alonso sat in front of him in two leather chairs that absorbed heat, true hot seats. Jess sweated profusely whenever he had to sit here. Out the window the National Gallery's majestic dome gleamed in the afternoon light. He imagined walking its cool rooms with Eddie at his side.

He shook off his daydream. "What perspective should I have?"

"You two have barely been on the job a month yet," their boss said. "And now the murders are out in the open, thanks to this spunky *Washington Herald* reporter." He looked from Jess to Alonso and back again. "Our little secret…" He drew his shoulders toward his ears and spoke in a low voice, "I'm glad the press got hold of it. The public will help us, you'll see. If not for the newspaper story, this roofer wouldn't have come forward."

Jess agreed. "And now that government girls know about the murders, they'll be more cautious about going off with a stranger." Alonso nodded at Jess's words.

Fred shook his finger at them. "Oh you two are a pair of naïve Southern boys. This won't stop these girls from taking wild chances. I assure you."

Fred sounded like Ray K.

Maybe he and Al were too naïve. But they'd taken on the case of murdered prostitutes and solved it. The problem there had been that few people cared about the prostitutes' deaths. "Good riddance," many citizens of New Orleans' French quarter had told them.

Fred put his pipe in its stand, brought his hands together, his index fingers forming a steeple. "So even though this roofer lied to you, you still don't think he had anything to do with the murders?"

"I'm not eliminating him. Sometimes this kind of killer will contact the police and pretend to be helpful. But Vernon Lanier is almost fifty and unkempt. A government girl wouldn't go off with him." Jess stroked the cleft in his chin with his thumb. "I think he lied because he's married and is living in a whorehouse."

"Yeah, I would lie about that, too." Fred laughed and picked up a pen. "Give me the address of the place. I should probably pass it along to DC Vice."

"Couldn't we keep the place to ourselves? We want to talk to the roofer again, and he won't be cooperative if the house where he's living gets raided." Jess chafed at being part of this huge bureaucracy. He didn't like surrendering information they'd uncovered to other authorities, especially when their investigation could be affected. "We're not the morality police, right?"

Fred leaned forward. "Don't let our director hear you say that." His face opened in a grin, showing the space between his two front teeth. "We are the morality police in this town."

"Take a look at this, Sir." Alonso handed a photograph to Fred.

When Fred had first contacted Jess about working for the Bureau, Jess had written him the truth he'd always wanted to tell someone. *I work with a partner, Alonso Crooms, a Negro, and my half brother.* Jess also wrote that Alonso had never gotten the credit he deserved in solving their cases, and that he, Jess, wouldn't come to Washington without him. Alonso had to be offered a job with the Bureau as well. To all this, Agent Friedlander, originally from Minnesota, had agreed.

Fred studied the photograph. Alonso had taken it in daylight and from a distance of a man entering the townhouse. "Oh, I see what you mean." The man was a well-known Congressman, the ranking Republican on the Judiciary committee. A well-dressed colored man held the door open for the Congressman.

"May I have the negative of this photograph, Alonso?"

Alonso had anticipated this. He gave Fred an envelope. "So this is the only copy?" Fred shook the envelope.

"Yes, sir."

"Good work, Alonso, but let's not get distracted by this." He put the photograph and envelope containing the negative into a file. "So how are the clerks doing with the lists from the pharmacies?"

This was the bright spot in their investigation. Dr. Lee had found barbiturates in Kaye Krieger's stomach.

Jess leaned forward. "Even looking at men only between the ages of nineteen to forty, there are hundreds. We're going through them, checking their employers, trying to find a connection between one of them and a victim."

"I can get you more men to go through the lists."

"We need to do this checking ourselves." Jess looked at Alonso. "We also need to go through police records for pharmacies that were robbed. The barbiturates could have been stolen. Or the killer could be using someone else's prescription."

Alonso sat straighter. After their first meeting, Fred insisted Alonso speak directly to him. "I won't allow Jess to be your intermediary. I don't care what your past protocol has been. I need to hear from both of you."

"We got a call from a man named Marek," Alonso said, "a groundskeeper at Arlington Cemetery. He remembers seeing a white truck parked in their public lot several days before the murder. We're thinking the killer might have been checking out the place."

17

In Peoples Drugstore, Eddie waved to Jess from the booth they'd shared the night before. "I ordered this cream soda for you," she said when he sat opposite. "It's grape." She remembered his purple tongue from last night.

"Thank you." He took a long sip and whispered, "We're sitting in our spot."

"No. Our spot is between the pea vines."

"That's right." His eyes crinkled when he smiled. "Did you make it past your aunt last night without being discovered?"

"With Bert's help, I did."

Government girls just off work crowded the drugstore's cosmetics aisles. In the mirror that flanked the lunch counter, Eddie saw Alonso across the store talking to the elderly man who worked at the camera supplies counter.

"This is it." Jess handed her a thick journal covered in brown paper. "I bookmarked the article. Alonso was afraid I might arouse suspicion if someone noticed me carrying around a German journal, so he made a cover for it."

She opened it and read aloud, "Kriminalistische Monatshefte 1931. I'm glad I brought my trusty German/English dictionary from Saltville. I can't wait to get to work on this."

"Say the article's name again. I like to hear your German."

She repeated it. "German reminds me of my great grandmother, who was born in Berlin and never learned much English. She spent her last years living with my grandmother in Abingdon, Virginia. I lived with them in the summer…"

"Hello there." Rachel stood beside their booth, Pearl at her side. Eddie introduced Jess to them. Pearl said, "I always wanted to sit next to a G-Man."

"Now's your chance." He scooted over.

"Miz Trundle's on the warpath." Pearl set her elbows on the table and leaned forward. "Told us we'd have to git our own dinners tonight."

"Ruth quit her job with your aunt." Dimples creased Rachel's face. "Mrs. Trundle said it should be against the law for Ruth to leave her. I told her it's a free country, which appeared to be news to her."

Again Eddie felt *fremdschamen* about Aunt Viola, who hadn't been raised with servants. Where did she get her to-the-manor-born attitude? She didn't even tend her own garden. Colored women from the alley did it with the understanding they could pick and eat what they wanted.

"You find out who kilt those government girls?" Pearl asked Jess.

Jess stared at Pearl. "What color is your lipstick?"

Strange question, Eddie thought, but noticed Pearl wore a mauve color better suited for her complexion than the red Tangee she used to wear.

"It's called azalea blossom," Pearl said. "Rachel says it's a good color for redheads."

Ruth, in a neat sky blue dress and small stylish hat, hurried down the lunch counter aisle, a smiling Alonso in her wake. Ruth looked radiant as a bride. "Eddie? Guess what?" She was almost jumping with excitement. Eddie had never seen her so animated. "I got the job typing for the Veterans Administration. I'm a government girl. I start tomorrow."

"Congratulations." Eddie stood and hugged Ruth. "I knew you'd get it."

People all over the drugstore, including Lloyd and Mildred behind the counter, turned to stare. Was it against Jim Crow laws for them to hug?

"Thanks for warning me about the recommendation," Ruth whispered. "Mr. Bert let me give his name, so Personnel called him at Berman's Laundry and he told them I walked on water." She smiled with her whole face, and when she did she was so pretty. "I walk on water."

Looking over Ruth's shoulder, Eddie saw a familiar face peering in the drugstore's crowded window.

Rachel saw her, too. "Yente alert," she said to Eddie.

"Oh, no." Eddie turned to those in the booth as well as Ruth, especially Ruth. "All of you, stay right here. I'll head her off." She snapped up Jess's journal and her bag and ran out.

18

"Edwina, you're just who I'm looking for." Aunt Viola grabbed her arm and leaned on her. "This has been the awfulest day in creation. And that Bert is nowhere to be found when I need him."

Her aunt wore no hat or gloves. Strands of her snow white hair had come loose from her bun and hung lifeless around her face. On her feet were her worn blue bedroom shoes. She must have run out of the house. But whatever the emergency, her aunt hadn't left her pocketbook behind. It dangled from her wrist.

"Your son helps you all the time, Aunt Viola. You know he does deliveries some evenings." Eddie turned her aunt away from Peoples and walked her to the corner. The last thing Eddie wanted was for Aunt Viola to confront Ruth in the drugstore.

At the light they crossed the street. Leafy trees lining Georgia Avenue swayed in the warm breeze. People passed, hurrying home to dinner.

"You don't know what a comfort it is to have kin nearby." Aunt Viola stroked Eddie's arm, her voice quivery.

Was this change in Aunt Viola a result of Ruth quitting her job?

"Good evening, Ladies." Jess came abreast of them and tipped his hat. "Are ya'll out for a stroll?"

Aunt Viola grabbed Jess's arm like she was drowning. "Mr. Lindsay, you're just who I want to see."

They paused beneath an arching mimosa, its fuzzy pink blossoms floating in the air. Aunt Viola introduced Jess to Eddie. Both kept straight faces.

"I've heard so much about you, Mr. Lindsay." Eddie felt silly pretending, but what else could she do?

"Likewise," Jess said, his lashes fluttering. "Please call me Jess."

When she told him to call her Eddie, Aunt Viola snorted. "She wants to be modern, calling herself Eddie, but her name is Edwina. She's named for Edwin, our daddy. See me and Edwina's daddy had different mamas. My people are from Marion, Virginia. I'm related to…" She walked between them, talking ancestry, holding tight to their arms.

"Hey there, Wanda," she called to Agent Friedlander's wife, who was watering her tomatoes.

At the house, Eddie asked her, "Did you leave the house without closing the front door?" The gate opened with a whine.

Ignoring Eddie, Aunt Viola said to Jess, "I'm just talking up a blue streak, aren't I?"

"Are you feeling all right, Aunt Viola?" Maybe she had suffered a stroke. They walked her down the sidewalk to the shady porch, the sun's last rays gilding the leaves.

"I'm fine, Edwina. He didn't hurt me or nothing, but I knew he wasn't a meter man when I opened the door. I could tell by the color of his overalls. Washington Power men wear green."

"Who didn't hurt you, Mrs. Trundle?" Jess helped her into the parlor, where she collapsed in her chair and put her feet up.

The noisy window fan sent warm air across the room.

"Start from the beginning, Aunt Viola. When did this man knock on the door?"

Aunt Viola raised her face to Eddie, her expression shifting to irritation. "Edwina, I'm truly parched. Would you get me a tall iced tea with some crushed mint leaves in it? The mint is in the garden. And bring a glass for Mr. Lindsay, too." She flicked her stubby fingers at Eddie before motioning for Jess to sit on the sofa. "I need to speak to Mr. Lindsay in private."

So she had been dismissed. Before making her aunt's tea, she went upstairs to put away her bag and Jess's journal.

She opened the bedroom door, and a hulk of a man sprang at her, shoving her against the wall with a thud. She was knocked breathless.

"Ah," she gasped. She tried to scream, but no sound came out. She felt as if she'd entered a nightmare.

The man held a hunting knife to her throat. Her eyes focused on its serrated silver edge. *Achtung.* She took in his unwashed smell and fought to keep upright.

"Girlie, don't make no noise, lest you want to get gutted like a rabbit." His words came with brown spittle, a chaw of tobacco wedged between his gum and cheek. He spoke with a Smoky Mountains accent, the same as hers.

Gritting her teeth, she willed herself calm. She had no doubt he would slit her throat if she called for Jess, who might not hear her over the parlor fan.

Mut, she told herself, *mut.* "All right, Mr. Ballou."

His body, pressed against hers, slackened. "I ain't Mr. Ballou, and don't never say his name, girlie. Never."

"Sorry." She knew he wasn't Alton Ballou. Why had she called him that?

"Where does Pearl keep that money she stole?"

In the dressing table mirror, Eddie saw their room had been torn apart, both mattresses on the floor. Drawers and closets were emptied with loose powder sprinkled everywhere. Even Rachel's African violets on the window sill had been uprooted and thrown on the floor.

He brought the knife to her throat again. "Where's that money, girlie?"

At first, Pearl had kept it under her pillow, but she must have moved it. Eddie didn't know where it was, but she knew better than to say so.

"Hear the man talking downstairs?" she whispered, forcing herself to look into the hard dark kernels of his eyes. Beneath Aunt Viola's high squeals, Jess's voice was a low murmur.

"I ain't scared of no city fellow."

"Sure, but this one is an agent with the Federal Bureau of Investigation."

He stepped back, still holding the knife in front of her. "A Revenuer?" He sheathed his knife and shoved her to the floor. Her head hit the edge of the overturned night table.

The man thundered downstairs. She struggled to her feet and to the landing.

"Hey, you," Jess yelled from the foyer. "Stop!"

Both he and Eddie took off after the man, who vaulted over the front fence and ran across the street in front of a clanging streetcar. A few seconds later, and the man from Saltville would have been run over.

Eddie and Jess had to wait to cross after the streetcar passed.

The sidewalk was crowded with workers, but the man wasn't among them. They went through the crowd asking people if they'd seen a large man in overalls. Eddie could still smell his unwashed odor.

"Did he get on the streetcar?" Jess asked.

"I doubt it," Eddie said.

"Your aunt told me he was long gone. I shouldn't have believed her. I should have searched the house." His face paled in anger.

"Calm down. You didn't know. She's confused, to say the least."

As they walked back to the house, Eddie told him what had happened and about the stolen money. It felt good to tell him. She didn't care about breaking her promise to Pearl.

Jess said, "He could have killed you while I sat listening to your aunt tell me the plot to some radio show." He brought his arm around Eddie. "I ought to have protected you. I let you down. I'm sorry."

They sat side-by-side on the porch swing. "Don't be silly," she said. "We'll protect each other."

He took her palm and kissed it. This was so unexpected, so delightful. Eddie felt her breath catch in her throat. "Jess," she said his name just to say it. "Jess."

Eventually they went inside and up the stairs so she could show him the damage.

"I told your aunt we had to call the police, but she refused. She doesn't want her neighbors to know." He leaned against the door frame.

"I don't care about her pride or whatever it is. We live here, too." She paused to take in their reflections in the mirror across the room. She liked the way they looked together.

"Mr. Lindsay, Mr. Lindsay," Aunt Viola called. "I hear ya'll talking up there. What's going on?"

Eddie and Jess came downstairs and found Aunt Viola waiting by the telephone table.

"How dare you take Mr. Lindsay to your bedroom, Edwina?" Aunt Viola yelled. "What kind of house do you think this is?" Her head flung back, nostrils flaring, the Aunt Viola she knew had returned.

"Mr. Lindsay was looking at the damage done by your intruder. We're calling the police."

"No, you're…" Aunt Viola said just as the telephone rang. She grabbed the receiver. "Trundle residence." She swallowed. "Yes, he's here, Fred. Nice to hear your voice. Oh, all right, just a moment."

"Your boss." She handed the telephone to Jess. "Yankees are so rude," she hissed to Eddie. "Now go get my sweet tea."

Jess wedged the receiver between his neck and shoulder, took the pencil and pad from his pocket, and wrote something. "We're on our way." Jess hung up.

By the set of his jaw, his mouth a tight line, Eddie knew another government girl had been murdered. According to the newspaper stories, each murder had occurred the last week of the month, but this was only the beginning of June.

Bert unlocked the front door and stepped inside. He wrote starched beige overalls with Berman Cleaners embroidered on the breast pocket. He always looked so tidy, even in the heat.

"Hello everyone. What's going on?"

"Oh Bert, you're just who I was looking for." His mother wrapped her arms around him and buried her face in his chest. "This has been the awfulest day." She told him about Ruth quitting as if that was the worst thing that had happened.

"I have to go," Jess whispered to Eddie. "I wish I didn't, but…"

"Go," Eddie said. "I understand."

Jess and Eddie followed Bert to the kitchen. While Bert washed his hands thoroughly, Jess told him about the intruder. "Call the police and keep the doors locked until they get here. I doubt the man will come back tonight, but you never know."

Looking stunned, Bert nodded at Jess's words.

"Follow me, Eddie," Jess said. They took the path through the garden, shadowy in twilight. "Wait here," he said at the door of his bungalow.

When he came out, he held his jacket over his arm and under it, his gun in its holster. "This is my Colt .38." He showed her. "It's loaded with its safety on. Have you ever fired a gun before?"

"Yes. My father taught me."

"Good. I want you to keep my gun tonight."

"No, Jess. You must take it." She helped him put the holster over his left shoulder and under his half arm. She secured the holster with buckles over his chest. That way, he could draw with his right hand.

He faced her again. "I'd feel better if you had it."

"I wouldn't," she said. "A gun might be dangerous in my hands tonight. I'm going to have a showdown with Pearl."

19

"Montrose Park," Jess told Alonso in the car.

At the end of the alley, Alonso extended his arm, bending at the elbow to signal a right onto Florida Avenue. "Check the map, Jess. I believe it's near Dumbarton Oaks."

Jess studied the map. "You're right. We're looking for Q Street and Dumbarton Bridge over the Rock Creek." Jess pulled out a calendar. "If this is him, he's changed his pattern. It's only been eighteen days since Kaye Krieger's body was found in Arlington Cemetery."

"If this is him," Alonso said.

The long dusk had almost deepened to night when Alonso pulled into a parking space on crowded R Street in front of Oak Hill Cemetery. Jess took his crime kit, Alonso his camera and they hurried down the sidewalk.

They passed an ambulance, an idling fire truck, and cars parked nose-to-tail. Revolving red lights from black and whites raked the neighborhood.

"It's the G-Man," called Thad's chubby photographer. "My name's Clay." Like Thad, Clay had a thick Mississippi accent. Grinning, he blocked the sidewalk long enough to snap their picture.

Jess and Alonso blinked at the flash, but barely broke their stride.

From a pale green Victorian mansion the other side of R Street, people congregated on the brightly lit veranda, the women in glittery evening gowns, men in black tie. Many held champagne flutes and puffed on cigarettes in long holders. Chatting to each other, the party-goers gestured at the bystanders and police as if they were here for their amusement.

Rich folks: their world remained mostly untouched by the war. On the contrary, many saw the war as an opportunity and came to Washington to sell whatever their factories manufactured to the government, usually to the military. Jess would enjoy seeing a fireman turn a hose on these on the veranda and wash away their smugness.

He was angry about what had happened to Eddie in her bedroom and angry because he'd failed to find this killer before he killed again. And he had the same foolish hope he always had when they approached the murder scene. Maybe someone had made a mistake, maybe no one had been killed, that they'd been called in error.

Alonso put his palm on Jess's back. Ever since the night Jess had almost bled to death in the back of a pickup truck with his head in his brother's lap, his mangled arm in a tourniquet at his side, Alonso had known what Jess was thinking. Their telepathy sometimes went the other way, so that Jess knew Alonso's mind, but lately Alonso had become more opaque.

They followed a high boxwood hedge to the park's entrance and went through a large wrought iron gate shaped like a keyhole. Beyond the trees lay a meadow of high grass, where bats flew out of a giant fir like bits of black paper tossed across the sky.

They headed for the crowd and joined the ambulance crew ready with their stretcher. Jess waved his badge and called, "Bureau of Investigation."

These were police, Park Police as well as MPD, including Ray K. Several raised their hands in greeting, but no one spoke, the opposite of the gay veranda crowd. Huge lamps illuminating the area had been set out, so it was brighter than day. A cricket choir and all manner of chirping rose from the meadow grass.

All of them were gathered in a semi-circle at the base of a majestic white oak, maybe seventy-five feet high, its stout trunk supporting the great horizontal spread of its branches.

Under the tree, a young blonde woman in a rose petal pink evening dress lay curled almost as if she was asleep. Her fingers were splayed over her stomach, and the soles of her feet were dirty. Gray tree bark was lodged between the second and third toes of her right foot. Had she fallen from the tree?

In her flowing dress and matching pink hair ribbon, she could have stepped from the pages of *Alice in Wonderland* except this Alice looked as if she'd broken her neck.

Her white strappy sandals were closer to the tree, one on top of the other. Their soles held the impressions of her feet. Jess stared at them. Both her shoes were here. She was blonde not a brunette. Montrose Park was crowded with people unlike the deserted locations their killer found. These details didn't jibe with the government girl murders.

Jess exchanged a glance with Alonso, who pursed his lips and gave a slow shake of his head. Most likely this wasn't their killer's victim, and for a moment Jess' spirits lifted. A lifting he quashed, ashamed of himself. This *lovely* girl died on a *lovely* summer evening, nothing uplifting about it.

A breeze stirred the oak's long branches and parted the meadow's tall grass like hair. A night bird screeched from the park's deep darkness.

Jess knelt beside the girl.

Blood from her head had seeped onto a pile of white oak leaves, shaped like children's hands. Her face was twisted to the side, her chocolate brown eyes opened, one door knob cheekbone pressed into a gnarled tree root. And her unpainted lips turned up in a smile as if she saw something she liked.

Once Jess stood and stepped back, he motioned with his hand for the others to do likewise.

Alonso took his camera, screwed in the flashbulb, pushed his hat back on his head, and made his way around her body. The group blinked as the first flash went off.

Ray K. stormed over. "Are you going to be called every time something happens to a government girl in this city?"

"I believe so. Hope to give you as much assistance as you've given us." Jess kept his tone mild, without too much sarcasm. "Who found her body?"

"That fellow over there." Ray gestured to a small man, sitting on a stone bench near the entrance, his elbows on his knees, head in his hands.

Walking Jess over to the man, Ray said, "You aren't still angry that I brought the press to Arlington Cemetery, are ya?"

In Jess's report, he'd had to say how the press found out about the murder. The Bureau then squawked to the MPD's chief-of-police about Ray.

"No. Of course not," Jess said. "You couldn't stop the reporter from following you."

Pausing on the sidewalk, Jess noticed that the white oak stood directly across the street from the party on the veranda. You wouldn't have to climb too high to see over the boxwood hedge to the veranda and first floor.

Jess introduced himself to the man on the bench and showed his badge. "Are you the one who found the girl?" Jess and Ray K. sat on either side of him.

"No. Jack, our seven-year-old, was playing with a ball and came back to tell us he saw a princess fly through the air, that I needed to come see. I thought he was making it up. After I saw her on the ground, I found a Park Policeman. My son and wife are waiting on the street. I didn't want our boy to know the princess is dead."

Jess nodded. "Had you seen the girl earlier?" Jess was thinking the girl might have wandered over from the party since she was dressed for it.

"We think we did. We were sitting on a blanket eating our sandwiches when my wife saw someone come through the park's gate. My wife said something like, looks like their party's moving over here. I turned to see a girl in a pink dress running around that." He pointed to a large sundial that rose from the middle of an overgrown bed of flowering heather, their purple heads tilting in the breeze.

"So she left that party to climb a tree?" Ray K. said to Jess on their return to her body. "These government girls are hard to figure out."

Dr. Lee stood beside the body. The ambulance crew lifted the girl onto a stretcher. Dr. Lee tilted his head. Ray K. and Jess followed him away from the crowd to a stand of white birches, their black markings on white bark resembling eyes.

"Her neck is broken cleanly" Dr. Lee said. "She must have fallen from the tree." They turned to the oak and looked into its wide branches.

Jess took a flashlight from his kit and ran its circle of light over the trunk. Halfway up a book bag hung on a broken branch. Eddie carried a similar bag. He pushed thoughts of her away and stayed focused.

"Could someone carefully climb up and get that bag?" Jess called to the police, keeping his light trained on the bag.

"Yes, sir," a young Park Policeman said with enthusiasm. He plopped on the ground, tugged off his high boots, ran to the tree, and grabbed the lowest branch. He pulled himself up. How had she done that in her long dress?

"Wait, Jim," another Park Police called to the climber, stood below, and offered up a coil of rope with a hook on the end.

Jim balanced on the branch, tied the rope around his waist, and flung the rope's other end over a high sturdy branch. He took hold of the rope, testing that the branch he'd snagged would hold his weight. Then he climbed one branch to the next, hugging the trunk. If he lost his footing or if a branch broke under him, he would stay attached to the tree.

All faces lifted to watch him.

"So it was an accident?" Jess asked Dr. Lee, his eyes on Jim.

As a homicide detective, he liked the word accident even when the accident resulted in death. It meant there was no ill intent, no crime.

"Or suicide. I think when I do the post mortem, I'll find this girl is… was pregnant." Dr. Lee dropped his chin a moment. "Maybe four or five months pregnant." Ray let out a whistle. "I will telephone you both tomorrow to inform you." Dr. Lee walked beside Ray K., both following the stretcher with her body.

That's why the girl had been holding her stomach. She was protecting the child inside, which didn't sound like suicide. Nor did the fact that she left her bag high in the tree. Would someone intent on killing herself care what happened to her bag?

Jess squatted and made notes of all this. He would discuss these points with Dr. Lee tomorrow. A terrible accident, meaning a ruling of death by misadventure, would be easier on her family than a verdict of suicide.

Jim, the climber, presented the girl's bag to Jess, who thanked him. "It's a good climbing tree," he said, "the way the branches are spaced."

"Would you hold the bag a second?" Jess didn't reprimand Jim for getting his fingerprints on the bag. It's not like he could have climbed the tree in gloves. Still Jess took his rubber glove from his kit.

Alonso appeared and helped Jess put the glove on and open her bag.

According to her Department of the Army Identification, she was Amelia Eisner, nineteen years old. Jess studied her determined expression. He'd begun to feel responsible for all government girls, as if he could keep them safe until this war was over, so they could go home. Of course, some like Eddie didn't want to go home, but Amelia had no choice. She was going home.

She had two opened letters postmarked from Baltimore. Jess scanned one and discovered Dr. Lee was right. Amelia was pregnant, and she'd told her mother, who urged her to come home, so they could take care of her and the baby. The letter was warm and loving, and for that Jess was grateful. Also in her bag was a packet of photographs developed by Peoples Drugstore.

"Let's go through these," he told Alonso.

They took her snapshots to a bench beneath a streetlamp and sat. Jess held each with his gloved hand, so Alonso could see. The one on top was of Amelia herself sitting at an outdoor café with a man much older than she. The man's arm draped over her shoulder. Her features, lifted in happiness, were focused on him, while he squinted at the camera or perhaps at the photographer, his features tense as if he didn't want his picture taken. The other photographs were of Amelia with two girls in a messy bedroom, and more with these same girls in swim suits at a rooftop pool, maybe here in Washington.

Jess put Amelia Eisner's purse and its contents in a paper evidence bag, all except for the photograph of Amelia and the older man, which he slipped into his pocket.

"Good evening, Agent Lindsay, Mr. Alonso Crooms." Thad Graham, in a striped tie and starched white shirt, stood before them, smiling. He offered Jess his hand.

Fred had told them that Bureau agents needed to keep their distance from reporters, but rudeness wasn't in Jess's nature. He stood and shook the man's hand. In many ways, Thad had done them a great favor by breaking the story.

Thad turned and offered his hand to Alonso as well, a little unusual for a white Southerner. Jess appreciated that Thad did so.

With his fingers hooked in the leather loops of his suspenders, he stepped back and stuck out his chest. "I'm the fellow who made ya'll famous."

Jess and Alonso stared at the cocky young newspaperman. Behind Thad, Clay leaned against the streetlamp, blowing perfect smoke rings upward.

"So in gratitude, I know ya'll will tell me what's going on here."

"Sorry, Thad." Jess grinned. "No comment." Jess tilted his head at Alonso, then turned toward Thad. "Does *the Herald* pay you to sit outside the police station on Sundays and follow black-and-whites?"

"No, Sir. I did that on my own initiative." His cockiness was gone.

"Was your photographer with you outside the police station?"

Thad gave a slight shake of his head. "No, after I saw something going on at the Cemetery, I went and called Clay from a telephone booth."

Thad followed them over to Ray K. Jess handed Ray the evidence bag. "I feel certain this is your case, Ray. I kept a photograph that I'll return to you later." Jess leaned in and whispered. "A letter in her bag confirms Dr. Lee's suspicion."

Ray K. placed his hand on Jess's forearm. "Gotcha."

It was their first moment of real cooperation. May it not be their last, Jess hoped.

Thad peppered Ray with questions. Warming to the attention, Ray straightened his tie, buttoned his jacket, and told the reporter it appeared the girl climbed the tree and fell. "The coroner's verdict isn't in yet, but I believe it was a terrible accident."

Thad's face fell in disappointment. He had wanted another murder. Murders sold newspapers. The idea made Jess sick. Clay snapped a picture of the tree.

"So you sure no one pushed her?" Thad asked. "What's her name?"

Thad had done his research, found all the murdered government girls, and written stories about them. He wrote well, Jess would give him that. Jess had studied Thad's stories with the idea that the reporter might have found something they'd overlooked.

"We're not releasing the young lady's name yet," Ray K. told Thad. "Got to notify her next of kin."

"But why did she climb the tree in an evening gown?" The reporter's gaze swept Ray K. and Jess. Both ignored his question.

"Ray K., Alonso and I thought we would go across the street and ask some questions if you don't mind," Jess said. "According to that witness, the victim may have come from the party being held there." Ray already knew this.

"Have fun." Ray shook a cigarette out of a pack and lit it. "Let me know what you find out."

20

As they crossed R Street, Alonso flashed Jess a grin. Thad and Clay were fast on their heels, exactly what Jess had wanted.

Another man appeared and called that he was from *the Washington Post*. Jess heard him say, "Hey Thad, is this another murdered government girl?"

At his callous tone, Jess winced. These city reporters were a cynical lot.

A wrought iron fence surrounded the stately Victorian. Jess opened its gate and closed it behind them. "Ya'll better stay here," Jess told the newsmen behind him.

The veranda was dark and empty now, the guests gathered in a huge melon-colored dining room. A chandelier hovered over the table, all visible from the street. Jess rang the doorbell.

No one in the dining room appeared to notice the bell, but the porch light came on.

A pretty colored maid in a black uniform with a frilly white apron and frilly white cap to match opened the door and stepped out. In her uniform, she looked right out of central casting.

"May I help you?" she said.

Many Washington folks wore uniforms, not just those in the military. And these uniforms denoted what the wearers did and for whom. This young woman, her shoulders stooped with fatigue, must work for a most particular person who wanted everyone ordered and in his or her place.

Alonso took over. "Good evening, Ma'am." He tipped his hat. "We're from the Justice Department's Bureau of Investigation." Al showed her his identification as a Bureau employee, which he was uncommonly proud of.

After she studied his ID, she looked back at his face, brightened a little, and stood straighter.

Jess handed the photograph to Alonso, who said, "Do you recall seeing this woman at the party tonight?" He gave her the photograph.

She cradled the photograph in her pink palm and lifted it to the porch light. "Yes, sir. I believe I do." She looked harder. "I'm sure I do."

An older white woman in a shiny black evening dress hurried out to them, her dress rustling as she walked. "What's this all about?" Dressed in black with a beak nose, she reminded Jess of a crow.

"These men…gentlemen are from the Justice Department, and…"

"You go on inside, Darla, and cut out the porch light. I'll handle this." The woman turned to Jess. "Whatever this is about, can't it wait 'til morning? I'm Hortense Strickland. This is my house. We're in the middle of an important dinner party." Her gaze traveled from Jess to Alonso and returned to Jess. "The Secretary of the Army is here having dinner, right now." She spoke in a low voice that let them know they ought to be impressed.

Jess's turn to talk. "No, Mrs. Strickland, our business cannot wait. We're in the middle of a murder investigation."

He introduced himself and showed his badge, which she studied, even turning it over as if it might be fake.

"Mrs. Strickland, a young woman died right across the street from your house tonight. Some witnesses saw her leaving your house, your party." He was twisting the facts, but he wanted her attention.

"Oh, my Lord." A lacy handkerchief appeared from somewhere, which she used to cover her mouth. "That's so terrible. Please come sit in the summer porch, so we can talk."

She glanced over her shoulder at the men gathered on the other side of her fence. There were four reporters now and at least as many photographers. These newspapermen were like crows, too, the way they multiplied.

"Hey Miz Strickland, how do you know the dead girl?" Thad called.

"How about a smile, Hortense?" a photographer called and snapped a picture.

"Please make them leave," Mrs. Strickland told Jess. "They are the rudest bunch in this town, and that's saying something."

"Sorry, Mrs. Strickland. They've got a right to be here. It's called a free press." Jess stole Ray K.'s line.

He followed her to the other side of the veranda and into a screened-in porch with a sofa and chairs. From the dining room, talk and laugher floated into the night.

Mrs. Strickland flinched when more flashes went off from the sidewalk. They were taking photographs of her house. She sat in a porch rocker, while Jess took a seat on the sofa across from her. Alonso stationed himself at the screened door, his feet wide, hands behind his back like a guard.

"Was this young woman one of your guests?" Jess showed her the photograph and watched her face. Jess could tell by her expression she recognized both the girl and the man at her side. Out came the handkerchief and she covered her mouth as if she didn't want to say.

"Mrs. Strickland?"

"I don't know the girl's name, but she came here to drop off some papers to…" she pointed at the man in the photograph. "To Jones Davidson, her boss. She caused quite a stir. Apparently she thought she could just stay at the party as if she was invited. When Jones informed her she would have to leave, she acted real ugly." Strickland rolled her eyes. "Some of these government girls are…"

Jess raised his hand. He would hear no criticism of government girls, certainly not from this woman. "Is Mr. Davidson still here?"

"Yes, but I can't interrupt his dinner. Like I said, this dinner party is more than it appears. We're involved in the war effort, and …"

Jess got up. "Alonso, would you go into the dining room, find Mr. Jones Davidson, and bring him here."

"Yes, Sir." Alonso produced his handcuffs. He always kept them handy. "Want me to cuff him, Boss?"

Jess almost laughed. How he wished this bigwig was their man, wished they could arrest him. Mr. Davidson was certainly a bad guy, but probably not their bad guy.

"Oh, no." Mrs. Strickland sprang from her rocker, leaving it creaking back and forth.

Maybe she was imagining the photograph of Mr. Davidson frog marched out of her house, hands cuffed behind him. "I will ask Mr. Davidson if he wouldn't mind coming outside to speak to you. Wait right here. Both of you."

When Mrs. Strickland passed the front of the veranda, someone took another photograph of her, making her cry out as if she'd been struck.

Jess and Alonso watched her hurry inside then they traded places. Alonso sat behind Jess, who stood with his coat open, his gun in its holster visible. The reporters left the front of the house and came around to the side, calling questions to them over the fence, which they ignored.

The big white oak looked back at Jess from the park. Why had Amelia climbed so high? She could have seen into the veranda from that first limb. Maybe she wanted a chance to look down on this party of bigwigs the way they'd looked down on her.

Mr. Davidson came out, his footsteps hurried against the porch's floor-boards. "Sir, how do you know the dead girl?" Thad called to him. "Mr. Davidson, sir?"

Jones Davidson, tall and lean with thinning gray hair, gave Jess an affable smile. "Perhaps we should go into the living room where we'll have more privacy." When a flashbulb went off, Mr. Davidson covered his face with his hands.

"No, thanks." Jess didn't want privacy. He took out his badge and handed it to the Under Secretary of the Army. "Alonso, please show Mr. Davidson your identification from the Bureau."

With Thad and his colleagues looking on, Jess wanted to slow this process down for maximum embarrassment. This might be the only punishment Jones Davidson ever received.

"Keep your ID." Mr. Davidson waved Alonso's away. "Please tell me what this is about."

"Does this young woman work for you?" Jess showed him the photograph of him and Amelia together.

His smile faded. "Yes, she does." He crossed his arms over his chest. "Look here, Agent Lindsay. I'm a busy man. Whatever Miss Eisner, Amy, has said or done is not my…"

"Amelia Eisner is dead." Jess paused to let that sink in.

Mr. Davidson covered his mouth, a favorite gesture with this crowd. His pale face went paler. "Oh, no." He blinked hard as if to keep back tears, but Jess didn't buy his grief.

*That man you work for ought to answer for what he's done, but I suppose he won't, what with the war and all…*Amelia's mother had written. Jess wished all government girls had a mother like Amelia's, one they told their most intimate secrets to.

"We're investigating her death, and we need to ask you some questions about your relationship with her."

"What do you mean my relationship with her? I was her boss." He hissed in a low voice. "What are you insinuating? I'm married. My wife is in the dining room right this moment waiting for me to return."

Jess noticed the man never asked how Amelia Eisner died. Did he know? Had he been on the veranda to see her fall and decided his troubles with her were over? "Well, don't let us stop you from returning to your wife."

They had nothing on this man. Jess brought the reporters over here. That's the best he could do. It was up to Thad and his lot to ferret out the story.

Jones Davidson visibly relaxed.

"I wanted to inform you of her death and let you know an autopsy is being done on her right now."

"Oh, dear Lord." Mr. Davison slumped against a post and rubbed his temples. "That girl was nothing but trouble from the start."

"The District police will notify her parents. I'm sure her parents would appreciate a call from you, her boss, tomorrow." Let them give it to him. "Good-night, Mr. Davidson."

Jess and Alonso walked toward the front porch steps.

Mr. Davidson followed. "Agent Lindsay?"

Jess looked over his shoulder at the man.

"May I have that photo of Amy and me? Just as a memento."

"Not on your life," Jess said, and he and Alonso walked off down the sidewalk, this time leaving the gate open behind them.

21

"Pearl knows why the man from Saltville came here." Eddie sat on her bed, holding the ice pack Bert had made for her. A lump had risen on her forehead from her collision with the table when the Saltville thug threw her to the floor.

"You do?" Rachel asked Pearl. She and Pearl had been cleaning the room. They'd gotten everything back as it had been and were sweeping the floor.

Pearl emptied the dustpan into a trash can and turned to shoot Eddie a glare. "You promised you wouldn't tell, Eddie." Her words a snarl.

"And you promised your uncle wouldn't come for his money. You had committed the perfect crime, remember?"

Pearl slumped on the dressing table bench, head in her hands. Eddie knew what was coming. Pearl would cry and carry-on to garner Rachel's sympathy. Eddie had become immune to Pearl's drama.

Rachel sent Eddie a disappointed look. "I thought we weren't going to keep any more secrets from each other."

Eddie remembered her father's words about only being as good as your word.

Pearl said, "Once Uncle Alton knowed my baby Billy wasn't no redhead like me, he give Billy to his daughter, who lives in Chilhowie. A redheaded stepchild is what they call me, but my Billy is blonde as a haystack like Uncle

Alton."

Rachel sent Eddie a startled look. Did Pearl mean her uncle was the baby's father? Rachel's dark eyebrows swam in her forehead. She was shocked, Eddie not so much.

Pearl's eyes were glassy. "I miss my baby boy." She shook with sobs.

Rachel crossed the room, her eyes bright as anthracite, hard slow-burning coal that will keep the cold away all night. From her dresser drawer, she got an embroidered handkerchief, returned, and gave it to Pearl.

Crouching in front of her, she asked, "So you took money from your uncle?"

"He always said he kept it in a bank but he didn't mean the Bank of Saltville. He meant the river bank." Grinning Pearl blinked back tears. "After a storm, I seen something shiny under a birch. Dug a Mason jar out from between the roots and inside was his treasure."

Eddie said, "Maybe there's a way you could give back what you haven't . . ."

"No!" Pearl leapt to her feet and pounded her fist into her palm. "I'm not given back a nickel. He owed me that money for taking my baby, for never giving me anything my whole life. He owed me."

"So your uncle sent a thug here to get his money." Rachel gestured at Eddie. "And Eddie had to face down the thug, and in the process got hurt."

Eddie knew she deserved what she got. After all she'd known about the money since the night they arrived.

"Could have been worse," Pearl whispered. "Them fellas that work for Uncle Alton would slit a man's throat quick as look at 'em."

Twin red spots appeared in Rachel's cheeks, and her hand went to her neck as if to protect it. She understood what Eddie had feared. All of them were in danger.

"That's not comforting, Pearl," Eddie said, exhausted from all that had happened. Still she doubted she could sleep. Every time she closed her eyes, she felt the tickle of the man's blade against her skin.

"You know what, Pearl?" Rachel said. "This isn't our affair. This is between you and your uncle. For our safety and for yours, you need to leave Georgia Avenue right away."

"Yes," Eddie said, sitting up.

Pearl snatched Rachel's hand. "I thought we was friends, Rachel. You been the nicest friend I ever had. You taught me more than I ever learnt in school." Pearl's eyes cut to Eddie. "Important things like how to dress, how to put on makeup…"

Eddie gave an exasperated laugh. Too bad she had tried to teach Pearl useless language skills like spelling, punctuation, diagramming sentences. Okay, well maybe diagramming was useless.

Rachel took her hand back. "We are friends, Pearl, but that doesn't change the fact that you need to find a new place to live. Don't you see? Your uncle must have tracked you here because of us. We're from Saltville. Anyone in town could have told your uncle we're living with Eddie's aunt."

"I been looking to move for a while, but I can't find anywhere."

"Then don't look in Washington City," Eddie said. The ice in the ice pack had melted and was dripping. She set it in the basin beside her bed. "You said eventually you'll be working at the Pentagon. Why not look for a place in Virginia?"

"Right," Rachel said. "Ask the girls you're training with if they need a roommate. And we'll ask everyone we know." Rachel nodded at Eddie. "Check your personnel office's bulletin board. We'll even help you pack and move your things."

22

Thursday, June 8, 1944

Late in the afternoon, Jess and Alonso were called into Fred's office. He gestured for them to sit in those leather chairs that pulsed with heat. Jess could tell by the way his boss fidgeted with his pipe, he was upset.

They'd spent the morning going over the murder site on the C&O Canal and tracing Vernon Lanier's route home until that truck almost ran him over. The killer must have been parked at a lot adjacent to the canal or somewhere on the wooded ridge overlooking the bridge, an area called the Palisades.

They kept coming back to the question: what had Vernon Lanier seen to make the killer try to run him over?

Fred put down his unlit pipe. "A Mrs. Strickland called my boss late last night and complained that Agent Jess Lindsay interrupted her dinner party." He gave his gap-toothed grin and passed a soiled handkerchief over his damp forehead and bald head. The fierce humidity made his office feel like a steam bath.

"I thought she would complain." Jess got out his own handkerchief and blessed Miss Minnie, who had ironed it into neat squares. He loved that fresh laundered smell, one of life's little pleasures.

"He laughed off your interrupting her dinner party, but her other complaint got more attention. She said you led reporters to her house."

Fred opened a copy of *the Post's* "Metro" section and pointed to the photo of Mrs. Strickland on her veranda. The headline read *Guest Falls to her Death*.

Fred thumped the newspaper. "They weren't happy about this." Jess scanned the article, which didn't mention the government girl's name, but gave a brief biography of Mrs. Strickland, an industrialist's widow, Connecticut native, and well-known Washington socialite. The story gave little information. The *Post* came out in the morning and clearly didn't want to get scooped, so they printed this accurate article without stating what had happened at Montrose Park.

"But not this one." Fred opened a copy of *The Washington Herald* and handed it to Jess.

He and Alonso bent their heads and read the article written by Thad Graham. Jess admired journalists, especially ones who wrote as well as Thad. His article appeared on the front page and focused on the government girl Amelia Eisner of Baltimore, Maryland, a guest at Mrs. Strickland's, who left her party, climbed a tree in Montrose Park, and fell to her death. The story stated that earlier in the evening Amelia had arrived at Mrs. Strickland's party to deliver some important papers to her boss, Under Secretary of the Army Jones Davidson. According to an unnamed guest, the girl and her boss got into a loud argument. "They caused quite a stir before the young lady left."

Later in the piece, Amelia Eisner's brother was quoted as saying, "I don't know why Amy climbed that tree, but she always was a tomboy." A small photograph of the white oak went along with the article as if to implicate the tree.

Thad had gotten it right again.

Fred said, "The end is what concerns me."

Alonso turned to page three, where the last paragraph stated that after the girl's death, Special Agent Jessup Lindsay went to Mrs. Strickland's house and questioned Under Secretary of the Army Jones Davidson. *Agent Lindsay is investigating the government girl murders that have taken place since January here in the Washington, DC area.* The reader was left with the impression that Jones Davidson was a murder suspect.

"Are we going to hear from Mr. Davidson next?" Fred tugged at his collar.

Jess stroked the cleft in his chin. "I doubt it. I just got a call from Dr. Lee." Jess explained about the girl's pregnancy and the letter from her mother in her bag. He showed Fred the photograph he'd taken from her purse.

Fred studied the photograph. "May I keep this?"

"Sure." Jess shrugged. "Ray K. has the photograph's negative. This morning he talked to Amelia Eisner's roommates, who told him Amelia was in love with her boss and expecting his child."

Fred stared at the photo. "Poor girl. This is what happens when chickens are sent to work with wolves. Still I doubt we'll get a complaint from Jones Davidson. I hope he loses his job." He fiddled with his pipe. "So has Dr. Lee ruled on her death?"

"This evening Ray K. and I are meeting with Dr. Lee to go over the PM report. It's clearly an accident. I doubt there'll be an inquest."

"Okay. But remember stay away from the press, right? Let Ray K. be their pal."

Nodding, Alonso and Jess got up, ready to be dismissed. Fred looked at Alonso, who'd been silent throughout.

"Jess told those newsmen no comment. They saw us going over to Mrs. Strickland's." Alonso shrugged. "We couldn't stop them from following."

"I understand. Just remember you two aren't in Alabama anymore. Maybe reporters down there are respectful, but the ones here would stomp on their grandmother for a story. So watch out when they swarm. And all this is a distraction." He swept his hand back and forth. "Stay focused on your murders."

Eddie was standing outside the Justice Department in a pale pink suit, the skirt of which came a little above her knees. The color reminded Jess of Amelia Eisner's dress, and he shook off the comparison. Eddie wore beige high heels that made her long legs look even longer.

"Hello," Jess called, delighted to see her. "Are you waiting for me?" At the idea, happiness flooded him.

Her face lit up in a smile that traveled all the way to her emerald eyes.

"How was your day, Jess?"

Her voice was like music. "It's looking up now."

Alonso passed, tipped his hat to Eddie, and called, "See ya," to Jess.

From the other side of the building, the streetcar's bell dinged, announcing its arrival. Alonso ran for it.

"You look lovely," Jess told Eddie when he stood beside her. "Do you always dress up for work?"

The sun pressed down on them like a giant thumb, their shadows pooling at their feet. There were hours of daylight left. First, he would take her with him to the morgue. After his meeting with Dr. Lee, they could have dinner at an outdoor café and maybe take a streetcar ride.

"I never dress like this," she said. "Tonight I have a date for dinner, so I brought clothes with me. These high heels are Rachel's and a little small for me, and the suit is hers too, the skirt a little short."

This stung him: she had a date.

"Oh," was all he could say. She was a beautiful young woman, who, of course, had a date.

"I brought you the first pages I translated from your article." She handed him some folded papers. "I didn't have time to type them up, but I tried to write neatly so you could start reading." Her voice raised an octave, her face animated. "This policeman Gennat investigated and apprehended several men who murdered for deep-seated psychological reasons."

"Do you have time to sit and talk about it?" Jess pictured them on a shady bench behind the National Gallery. He slipped the papers in his jacket pocket.

She looked at her watch. "Not really, Jess. Sorry."

"Where are you meeting your date?" Jealousy coursed through him.

"A hotel called the Hay-Adams. It's across the street from the White House."

Jess whistled. "That's very fancy. I wish I was taking you there."

She held his good arm, and they walked around the building toward the streetcar stop. "I'd prefer to be with you, Jess. My date is a Marine I met on the train coming here. He called me a while back. He's heading overseas, so I didn't think it was right to cancel…"

I'd prefer to be with you buoyed him. "I understand." He patted his pocket. "Well, thanks for doing this. I'll read it right away."

"I should have the rest done for you this weekend. As soon as I do, I'll knock on your door."

"Please do." He imagined her in the classroom, the eager girl with her hand up, ready to give the teacher the correct answer. "You don't know how much I appreciate it."

Another streetcar tolled its bell. "I better catch this one," she said. "Bye, Jess." She squeezed his hand.

He watched her disappear into the crowd boarding the streetcar and was filled with apprehension. She was meeting a Marine, most likely an officer since he was taking her to the Hay-Adams for dinner. He could be a captain, who'd had his bars ripped off his uniform. He could be their captain, the killer.

Jess closed his eyes and saw a man taking his belt from its loops and lashing it around Eddie's neck. The image left him so dizzy he had to sit down on the curb. His thoughts about this guy were wild speculation, he knew, driven by jealousy, but somewhere in this city the killer was searching for his next victim.

Only seventeen days were left in the month until he killed again. Jess felt this certainty deep in his bones. He had to find him before he killed again.

When he calmed, he got to his feet, bought some grapes from the vendor, and ate them as he walked to North Capitol Street and the morgue.

23

Eddie got off the streetcar in front of Lafayette Square and paused to take in the view of the White House across the street. To think the Roosevelt's lived within those walls. This was something she would write about to her father and sisters.

She still thrilled at living in this beautiful city, but she was late, couldn't dawdle.

A small crowd stood beneath the Hay-Adams' shady portico.

She tried to make her way through, but a plush rope had been strung across the entrance, where men in the hotel's burgundy uniforms stood guard.

"I'm meeting someone for dinner," Eddie told a hedgehog of a man with stiff reddish hair and gold braids dangling from his epaulettes.

"Have to wait, miss. A certain famous guest is arriving." His bushy eyebrows twitched for emphasis.

Eddie was about to argue when a limousine pulled up. The crowd stirred.

A young girl with blonde pigtails thick as paint brushes turned to Eddie. In a breathy voice, she said, "Lindy, Lindy." Her eyes squeezed shut in ecstasy. The girl stood beside a blond matron in hat and gloves, certainly her mother.

Charles Lindbergh was no hero to Eddie, and she wondered if he still admired the Nazis. He'd been a leader in America First, an organization bent on keeping America out of the war, but the attack on Pearl Harbor silenced the group.

The doorman opened the limousine, and the tall aviator unfolded from the back seat. Okay, so he was blond and boyishly handsome.

"Welcome to Washington, Lindy," a woman called. With a squeal, the pigtailed girl pushed ahead of Eddie and thrust an autograph book at him. Photographers snapped his picture, while reporters called out questions, some not so polite. Eddie blessed the rude free press.

Lindbergh ignored all the adults and signed the girl's book, making a nice photograph for tomorrow's paper as well as good publicity for a man on the wrong side of everything important in the world.

"I'd like to throw a rotten tomato at him," Eddie said, her thoughts becoming words.

The matron beside her appeared shocked. "What would your mother say about your rudeness, young lady?"

Eddie hated when people brought up mothers, but she kept quiet. Discretion is the better part of valor, she told herself, even though the line was spoken by Falstaff, one of Shakespeare's greatest cowards.

After Lindy's grand entrance, the little people were allowed inside the hotel.

Eddie crossed the wood-paneled lobby and entered the Lafayette Dining Room, where a chill enveloped her. It was air-conditioned! How lovely after the scorching heat. The large understated room with its sea of white table-cloths and tall linen-curtained windows had a simple grace. This was where the important people came to meet and eat. So what was she doing here?

"I'm meeting Captain Richardson," she told the man at the door, who summoned a waiter.

"This way, miss." She followed the waiter to a table in the corner.

"Here's my Hillbilly." Austin stood, a little unsteady on his feet, and kissed her on the lips, not what she had expected.

"Hi Silver Spoon," she said. They'd nicknamed each other the first time they went out.

Still, she wondered what they were doing together. Austin came from a long line of Yale men. His father was a New York City banker, while hers had an eighth grade education and worked nights as a supervisor in the salt mine. They didn't match, but Rachel had declared him a dreamboat, and he had orders to ship out to the Pacific, so Eddie had accepted his invitations.

But friendships should never be based on charity. Wouldn't he laugh if he knew she considered going out with him charity?

He pulled her chair out for her. "What would you like to drink?" he asked. "A Tom Collins?"

This was the drink she'd ordered before when they were together. She didn't really drink, just sipped and let the ice cubes melt. "Looks like you've gotten a head start."

He summoned the waiter, ordered one for her, and a double scotch on the rocks for himself.

Their table had only two place settings. "Isn't Peter or any of your other friends joining us?" It dawned on her they'd always been a group before, never alone.

He gave her a deep look. "Tonight's just you and me, Hillbilly."

She didn't like the sound of that. "Isn't it exciting about Normandy?" she asked. "Or maybe you'd rather not talk about the war since you'll be in the thick of it soon."

"That's where you're wrong, Hillbilly. I got a reprieve." He reached across the space between them and took her hand. "I've been made a general's adjutant, which means I'll remain at the Pentagon. That's why we're celebrating."

"Congratulations." Most men wanted to be in combat.

"Tonight is our real beginning. I want to talk about us."

Where was this coming from? The first time they went out, he warned her not to get designs on him. She'd made him laugh by telling him she didn't like him that much anyway.

"There is no *us*, Austin. Remember how we laughed about silly wartime romances after seeing *To Have and Have Not*"?

He scooted his chair closer. "That's before you got under my skin, Hillbilly," he said in his best Humphrey Bogart. He brought his hand to her face, and she was afraid he was going to kiss her again. She wished she hadn't come.

The waiter appeared. Austin ordered steak frites for both of them. "You'll love it. I promise." Along with the steak, he ordered a bottle of red wine.

When they were alone again, he pushed a pink box with a jewelry store's name on it across the table at her. "I picked this up for you today."

"That's kind, but I can't accept it." She pushed the box back across the tablecloth. "We don't know each other well enough."

"Don't be a stick-in-the-mud schoolmarm, Eddie. In case you haven't figured it out, I'm fairly well off. This is just a small token." He opened the box to reveal a gold necklace with a tiny gold train dangling from it.

She smiled in spite of herself. "It's adorable."

"May I put it on you?" He leaned closer.

She turned in her chair and let him fasten it around her neck. She touched the little train and remembered her ride here. "Thank you."

While they ate their delicious thin steak with shoestring potatoes, he poured the wine and insisted she drink, so she did. He drank two glasses to her every one.

After dinner, with his head drooping like a limp flower on a stem, and his eyes half-closed, he said. "Sorry, but I'm not feeling too well." His words slurred.

"Let's go for a walk and get some coffee."

She was a little light-headed from the wine, but he was so drunk he could barely stand. She put her bag over her shoulder and let him lean on her. That's the way they left the dining room for the crowded lobby.

Austin covered his mouth. "Might be sick, Eddie. Help me to my room, 209."

They took the stairs one slow step at a time. Eddie was afraid if she let go he'd fall. At his room, she took the key and opened the door.

She barely closed it behind them when he pinned her against the door, and his hands reached up her skirt. "Oh Eddie, I want you badly."

He was no longer limp—anywhere. What a fool she'd been. And the silence hit her. Only a few moments ago they'd been surrounded by people.

She shoved at his shoulders. "Back off, Captain."

But he was stronger. He grabbed the strap on her book bag and slung her across the room. She landed on the bed, but scrambled to sit on its side.

Only yesterday, she'd been confronted by the Saltville thug. And like her confrontation with the thug, she knew she wasn't going to win in hand-to-hand combat with Austin, even though she longed to fight him.

She took a deep breath and forced herself to calm.

"Slow down, Austin. Let's enjoy this. We have all night." To prove her point, she set her book bag down and kicked off her heels. She couldn't run in them anyway.

He grinned at her. "That's more like it." He was beside her, his hand under her blouse.

"Is that cold champagne?" A bottle was sunk in a silver bucket of melting ice on a stand beside the bed.

He grinned. "Want some?"

He could never resist booze. She imagined the red-faced angry drunk he would become later in life, and for all his fancy Yale education, nothing would stop its progression. Observing Saltville's slice of mankind had taught her about people.

"Please," she said, her pulse throbbing in her ears.

She wanted home, Saltville, her father. She was so homesick, *heimwehkrank*. Like Dorothy in *The Wizard of Oz*, she wished she could click her heels together—*there's no place like home, there's no place like home*—and be back safe inside the boxwood hedge.

"All right," he said. "While I pop the cork, do a hillbilly striptease for me." He went to the ice bucket. "Start with your skirt and panties."

Forcing a smile, she stood and unbuttoned her short jacket. Her face, torso, arms, and hands poured sweat as if her body were raining.

He lifted the bottle out of the ice and took it to the drinks trolley across the room. The further away he got the better, but he was fast and could pounce at any moment.

She estimated the distance between herself and the door. Fortunately the door wasn't locked from the inside. Not yet. She leaned over and picked up her heels as if she was going to slip them on.

All the while she swayed her hips. He snapped on the radio and smoky jazz filled the room. When he returned to the drinks trolley and began to untwist the wire around the bottle's cork, his attention concentrated, she saw her chance.

Over the music, people's voices carried. They were in the hall, nearby and that gave her courage, *mut*.

She ran to the door. Austin dropped the bottle with a crack, cursed, and came at her. She got the door open. He slammed it shut, so hard the wall shook. He brought his hands around her neck, and a terrible idea exploded in her brain: what if he was the killer Jess was looking for?

He yelped when she scraped the spiky high heel along his jaw line. If she could have, she would have stabbed him in the throat.

He said, "You little hellcat."

"What's going on in there?" a man called from the hallway.

Her life was at stake. She opened her mouth to scream, but Austin covered it. Then he looked down. Blood had pooled around his foot. He had stepped on glass from the broken champagne bottle.

She stomped on his hurt foot as hard as she could.

"Owwwww!" He stumbled backward.

She pushed him further, opened the door, and stepped into the hall.

"Are you all right, Miss?" a bellhop asked. He was pushing a cart of luggage.

Eddie nodded but couldn't speak. She slipped on her heels and walked down the hall. Not until she got out on the street did she let her emotions go. She ripped off her shoes and ran. She was going home, not to Georgia Avenue, but to Saltville and safety.

24

"I would like to discuss these murders with you," Jess told Dr. Lee after Ray K. and the other police had left. Jess sat in front of Dr. Lee's desk in his bright cold basement office. The morgue had air conditioning, which had impressed the police at their meeting.

Of course the dead had to be kept cold, and the hum of refrigerators filled the chilled air. Dr. Lee's office felt like a different climate. Jess' arms were pebbled in goose-bumps, and his stump throbbed with the cold.

"Come have dinner with me now, Jess." Dr. Lee stood and took off his white lab coat. Beneath it he had on a worn brown sweater, patches on the elbows. "Unless you have other plans."

"No. I'd be glad to. Thank you." He followed Dr. Lee upstairs, and out into bright 7:00 twilight, night's coolness still a long way off.

For once, the wall of heat that hit him felt good after the morgue's deep freeze.

In his beige Ford, Dr. Lee crept through the city, barely going the speed limit. On H Street a Chinaman waved to Dr. Lee and signaled him into a parking lot.

Jess said, "Looks like you're known around here."

"Oh, yes. They know me well, Jess. I am a creature of habit and have never learned the fine art of parallel parking like your associate, Alonso

Crooms." He gave a deep throaty laugh. It was the first time Jess had ever heard him joke.

H Street was crowded with people, mostly couples in a long line outside a black tiled restaurant, the tile so shiny they could see themselves reflected in it. The neon sign high above the entrance read China Doll, written in large cursive letters. Below its name was another sign in Chinese characters.

Because of the waiting crowd, Jess was about to suggest they try somewhere else when the maitre d' appeared and came to them. "Good evening, Dr. Lee." The man bowed. "Follow me, please."

He ushered them inside a modern dining room with Formica-topped tables and booths against the wall. Another waiter showed them to a booth in back. A ceiling fan breezed overhead.

The menu was immense and confusing. Jess looked through it. The dishes were in Chinese with English translations.

"Have you ever eaten Chinese food before?" Dr. Lee asked.

"No. I'm a real Alabama hayseed." He lifted his face from the menu.

"May I order for you, then?"

"Please. I would appreciate that."

What followed was the best meal Jess had eaten since he got to Washington. He took out his little notebook, asked what each dish was, and wrote it down, starting with the delicious sweet and sour soup.

"I would like to bring a young lady here," he said.

At the end of the meal, Jess felt he could talk business. "As I've told you before, we're frustrated with our progress in finding this murderer. We're still following up on the idea that the killer is giving his victim a drink containing a barbiturate." He took out the pages Eddie had given him. "This is a translation of an article by a German policeman, who solved some cases he called serial murders by considering the psyche of the murderer."

Dr. Lee was nodding. "Yes. That makes sense to me. There is a ritualistic quality to the murders of these government girls." He lowered his voice, not that it was necessary in the noisy China Doll. "The girl is always strangled and violated sexually yet her hair, her makeup, is undisturbed, and her clothes are in good order. This killer is tidy, neat. Usually women raped and murdered are bruised terribly, torn skin, ripped fingernails, bloodied hair.

You know what I mean."

Jess did know and nodded. He'd watched many autopsies because much could be learned from them. The prostitute murders in New Orleans were especially gruesome, since the killer tortured them, his way of punishing them for their occupation.

Not that he watched autopsies easily. Come to think of it, he had wondered why a man would go through medical school and end up working only on the dead. He would have to know Dr. Lee better to ask him such an impertinent question.

"Do you know a psychiatrist or psychologist who specializes in criminal behavior?"

"I do." Dr. Lee poured Jess more tea from a tiny white pitcher. "He works at St. Elizabeth's, the federal hospital for the insane."

The long twilight was fading to night, not that it made much difference on bright Seventh Street. Jess sat at the streetcar's window, scanning the crowd on the sidewalk when a running woman caught his attention, her blonde hair flying, a pink jacket under one arm: Eddie.

He jumped up and yanked the bell. When nothing happened, he held onto the bell.

"No need for all that, Sir," the driver yelled.

Everyone in the car turned to Jess. He would have leapt out an open window if he could have.

"Folks, remember I stop only at assigned stops," the prissy driver said into his microphone. "We're not a taxi service."

When Jess got off, he passed a line of people waiting to get into *Arsenic and Old Lace*. Eddie wasn't among them. By not looking where he was going, he almost ran into a huge freestanding poster outside the Bijou Theatre showing Cary Grant with some actress slung over his shoulder, both of them grinning.

Up ahead at the corner, through a clot of sailors, he saw her pink skirt. "Eddie," he called. She paused and looked around.

He ran and caught up with her, both of them breathing heavy. He looked down and saw she was barefoot, her high heels in one hand, her eyes bright with tears. "I stepped on a lit cigarette butt a block or so back that made me want to scream."

"Come sit down." He led her into a small outdoor seating area, where a table had just been vacated.

"Jess, I don't want to talk." She lowered her head so her chin almost fit into the notch at the base of her throat.

He reached across the small round table and brought a finger to her neck, where a ridge cut her skin. "You're bleeding." He handed her his handkerchief.

She touched her neck. "Let me use a paper napkin." She daubed at her neck.

"Did he do this to you?" His mind sprang to his killer.

"It's not what you think, Jess." Her grape green eyes flashed at him. "This is a result of my own stupidity."

"Eddie, you're not a stupid woman." He took her hand. "Far from it."

"When it comes to men," she said, "I'm an idiot."

25

Eddie sat on the bench, her back to the weathered boards of Jess's bungalow, her aching feet pressed into the soft mossy ground. She lifted the Coca-cola to her lips and sipped, letting its cold sweetness slide down her throat. How wonderful to be in the dark and away from people. And like Jess said, the Coca-Cola might settle her stomach.

On their long walk back to Mrs. Trundle's, she'd vomited her fancy Hay-Adams' steak dinner beneath a tree in a little park somewhere off Seventh Street. Jess had held her hair back, even as some older Rosie the Riveter types passed and made nasty remarks about drunken government girls, how factory gals like them could hold their liquor.

"Okay. See if this doesn't make you feel better." Jess set a small washtub on the grass in front of her. She slipped her feet into the tub's cold water.

"I feel as if I've died and gone to heaven." She wiggled her toes in the water. Her feet had swollen from walking back barefoot, but Rachel's tight high heels would have hurt more. It was crazy of her to borrow them in the first place.

Jess sat down at the other end of the bench, his chin tilted toward the sickle of a moon and stars sprinkled across the night sky. "Sitting here, I feel like I'm out in the country, except the city lights make the stars less distinct."

Eddie appreciated the way Jess hadn't asked what happened earlier at the

Hay-Adams. Or why she was running down the street like a crazy woman.

"I like the crickets, the creak and groan of the streetcar, even that crazy owl hooting from somewhere close by, but I could do without the rooster that wakes us at dawn, even on Sundays."

"That's Clarence. He's a Rhode Island Red, owned and loved by my boss's wife, who was raised on a farm in Minnesota." She heard the smile in his voice.

The bench faced the back of the garage and the part of the victory garden where vegetables in need of partial shade grew, lettuce, beets, cauliflower. A skinny scarecrow stood in the middle of the plants. Were birds really fooled by these silly effigies? A thick row of marigolds bordered the garden. Their ferny smell scented the air.

They sat in silence until she said, "Austin, the man I was with tonight, was drunk when I met him in the Hay-Adams' dining room. Or rather he was acting drunk. I ought to have gotten up and walked out right then, but I hate to make a scene. After dinner, I helped him to his room because I thought he needed help." She shook her head.

Jess, sensing where this was going, said, "I'd like to knock this guy on his keister."

She touched her neck that still hurt. "I ripped off the necklace he gave me, threw it at him, and left. I'm naïve and stupid." In truth, she didn't recall how she lost the necklace. "I only regret leaving my book bag with my German-English dictionary in it. My grandmother gave me that dictionary before my freshman year at Emory and Henry."

He reached across the bench and touched her hand. "At least you didn't lose something you can't get back."

She withdrew her hand. Did he mean what she thought he meant?

"Sorry, Eddie. I put that badly." He choked on his words. "I didn't mean what it sounded like, I didn't mean your..."

"Virginity?" She smiled at how embarrassed he sounded. "How do you know I'm a virgin?" She had never talked to a man the way she talked to Jess. She felt an odd combination of comfort and edginess when she was with him.

"I meant we could get you another dictionary."

"Answer my question, Agent."

He cleared his throat and whispered, "I assume you're a virgin, but it doesn't matter to me if you're not."

She let his words linger in the soft air. "For the record, I am." She was falling, falling, falling, for him. "So, Jess, what did you lose you couldn't get back?"

"My arm, of course. I'm told it won't ever grow back."

"How did it happen?" She wiggled her toes in the water.

"Papa bought a new mechanized gin. I was only twelve, but I thought I was the smartest person in Henry County, Alabama. I was supervising some of the colored workers when seeds clogged... but maybe you don't need to hear the gore..."

"I want to know all about you. Go on."

"I stuck my hand in to unclog it. Folks were yelling at me not to, but I wouldn't listen. We had a quota of cotton to process, and I was determined to make that quota, to show Papa I was ready to run the business." He paused and lifted his half arm. "I ought to apologize to my stump every day for what I did."

"So the machine came on while your arm was inside?"

"Yes, Ma'am. Mr. Smarty Pants forgot to turn the blame thing off. That's what folks were trying to tell me. Some older folks are suspicious of all things electrical. I came to appreciate their point-of-view."

"Where was your father when this happened?"

"That's a mystery we never solved. Papa wandered away a lot. He liked whiskey, gambling, and baseball, not necessarily in that order. Wherever he was, he wasn't there. Lucky for me, Alonso was. He put a tourniquet around my arm and got me to the hospital. If not, I would have bled to death..." He turned to face her. She felt his steely blue gaze. "And I wouldn't be sitting here with you."

She lifted her feet from the water and scooted down the bench to him until their sides touched. She brought her hand to his face. He leaned in and put his lips to hers, and she sunk into their kiss. Somewhere deep inside her, a door opened.

For the first time in her life, she understood desire. His bed was on the other side of the wall. She imagined them lying in it, touching each other in their secret places.

His right arm came around her and pulled her closer. She brought her hand to his half arm and placed her palm against his stump. He moaned.

A shadow fell over them. Moonlight glinted off a blade.

26

"Who's there?" Jess called and put himself between Eddie and danger.

"Just me, Jess." Alonso came from the side of the bungalow, holding his dark room scissors, not a knife. "That red-headed girl's in the room over the garage. She's lying in the camp bed and refuses to leave."

Jess understood Alonso's concern. Alonso never wanted to be alone with a white woman. That's how black men got lynched.

"Okay." Jess took Eddie's hand. She had to come with him. He wasn't leaving her alone in the dark.

They followed Alonso to the garage and up the steps. Alonso turned on a floor lamp and angled it toward the figure on the bed.

Pearl buried her face in the pillow. "Put out that light, please."

"Pearl?" Eddie stepped closer.

Jess said, "You can't be up here, Pearl." His eyes went to the back wall, where Alonso had covered their case map with a sheet.

The room smelled like almonds, which meant Alonso was developing film when he discovered her.

Pearl lifted her face. Her left eye was swollen shut, her lip cut, and blood was drying in her hair. "I couldn't go to the house and let Mrs. Trundle see me."

"Oh Pearl." Eddie sprang across the room to the sink, where she wet a clean rag. She brought it to the camp bed, knelt beside Pearl, and washed the blood from her forehead and mouth.

Alonso brought a grape soda from the refrigerator. The bottle smoked with cold. "Miss Pearl, think you could drink this?"

"Thank you, Alonso." She scooted up in bed, her back to the wall.

He popped the bottle's cap with his pocket knife and handed it to her. She took a long sip. "My stars that's good."

"What happened, Pearl?" Eddie brought an old ladder back chair beside the bed and sat.

"That thug set on me and attacked me." Pearl dropped her face, bunching the bed sheet up over her bent knees.

"Where did this happen?" Jess asked.

"He was on the streetcar when I got on after work. I didn't know it at the time, but he was behind me. Soon as I got off on Georgia Avenue, he grabbed me 'round the waist and took me to a dark warehouse..." She brought her hand to her swollen face. "Don't make me leave ya'll, Eddie. Please say I can stay a little longer."

Eddie swallowed. "Of course," she said. "Sure. You must stay until you heal."

Jess was angry with Bert for not calling the police yesterday when this man broke into the house. His mother didn't want the police called, so Bert went along with her. Bert needed to quit being such a mama's boy.

"You say this warehouse where he took you is close?" Alonso gave Pearl a pencil and a sheet of paper on which he'd drawn a simple map of the streets around the streetcar stop. "Mark where that warehouse is."

"How much money did you take from your uncle?" Jess asked.

"Almost five hundred dollars," Pearl said.

Jess whistled. This was a fortune to anyone, but to a bootlegger from Appalachia it might be several years of profit. "You must have money left you can return to him. Maybe if..."

"No!" Pearl sat straighter. "I'm not giving him back a red cent. I need that money for a fresh start. I'm going to get fired from switchboard operating if I can't talk better, so I'm taking elocution lessons."

Jess understood about the speech lessons. Where Eddie had a charming twinge of an accent, Pearl wasn't always easy to understand.

"Did the man have a gun?" Jess asked.

Pearl shook her head. "Had a knife in his boot, though. That's how he drugged me to the warehouse. Said he'd cut me if I yelped."

"What did he look like?" Alonso asked.

"Big as a bear, bald as a cue ball, wearin' stinky overalls."

"Sounds like the same man I found in our bedroom."

"Whether we manage to chase this man off or not, you're going to have to promise to report your assault to the police, so they'll have it on record," Jess said to Pearl, who nodded. "Wait here with her," Jess told Eddie. "And lock the door behind us."

Alonso took the map Pearl had marked.

They went to the bungalow, where Jess slipped on his gun in its holster, and Alonso got his handcuffs and his knife. Alonso was hooking Jess's holster across his chest when a form appeared in the doorway. The two men started until they saw the person was Eddie.

"Listen," she whispered through the screen. "Don't either of you endanger your life for Pearl." She looked from Jess to Alonso and back again. "If she wasn't so greedy, she'd return the money she hasn't spent. Her uncle is a dangerous man, a criminal."

Jess grinned at Alonso, who nodded. "If we can flash my badge and scare this fellow we will, but we won't tussle with him."

Still barefooted, Eddie walked them to the gate. There she hugged Jess and set her hand on Alonso's back. "Be careful."

She took the steps up to the garage, where she found Pearl at the window that overlooked the alley, a satisfied grin on her bruised face, a grin that vanished when Eddie appeared. Pearl had been watching Jess and Alonso go down the alley.

"You're good at manipulating others, Pearl." Eddie led her back to the camp bed. "You've gotten all of us to do your bidding, but if any harm comes to either of those men tonight, you are leaving this house at dawn."

27

Jess and Alonso found a small warehouse off Euclid Street. Was this the one Pearl told them about?

Jess wasn't sure what they were getting into. "This isn't an empty warehouse," he whispered.

They'd driven by here before. At daybreak, the place hummed with older Italian men loading their vendor carts with fruits and vegetables. The men pushed these carts all over the city and sold their produce until nightfall. The company could be owned by the Mafia.

Alonso shone his flashlight on the warehouse's side door. It was padlocked.

"Cake," Alonso whispered and got out his picks.

Jess held the flashlight on the padlock, and in quick order, Alonso opened the lock and the door.

Vendor carts were crammed inside, and the place smelled of overripe fruit. In the dusty silence someone snored. They followed the sound making their way around the carts.

On a pallet in the left back corner, they found a big slumbering bald man, his sleep so sound he didn't wake when they stood over him.

Even the meanest galoot could look peaceful asleep. This one was shirt-less, his bare chest a thick rug of hair. Pearl was right. He did resemble a bear.

A bear that could use a good bath.

Beside his pallet was an almost empty bottle of colorless liquid. Alonso lifted it, smelled, and nodded to Jess. The man had enjoyed his own product before going to sleep. Alonso searched the feed sack beside his pallet, found a Bowie knife in its sheath, and stuck it in his pocket

When the man rolled on his side, Al squatted and cuffed him, so fast the man didn't have time to react. "What the hell?" he shouted, his voice groggy. He leapt to his feet and found a gun pointed at him.

"Don't move, Mr. Moonshine," Jess said. Alonso flashed Jess's badge at the man. "Federal Bureau of Investigation."

Those words worked. The man crumpled to the floor as if Jess had shot him. "Oh Lordy, revenuers got me."

Revenuers were with the Treasury Department, but the bear could believe what he wanted. Jess squatted in front of the man. "Did you beat up a young woman by the name of Pearl Ballou?"

The man blinked at Jess as if all this might be a nightmare he would wake from.

"You best answer the agent," Alonso said, still standing over him.

The man nodded. "See she stole…"

"Don't want to hear about it." Jess shook his gun at the man. "Tell you what. At first light, you're going to get on a train back to Saltville, Virginia and tell Mr. Alton Ballou to leave Pearl alone. If he can't do that, he's going to hear from us. Got it?"

The bear nodded.

"Now stand up," Alonso told him. The man did. "Even when you think you're not being watched, you are. We'll know if you don't do what we told ya."

"He don't want no trouble with the Feds," he said.

Next came the scary part, the part that would show if the man meant what he said. Alonso looked at Jess, who nodded. Alonso unlocked the man's handcuffs. Jess kept his gun trained on the man.

"Move back against that wall," Alonso said.

A smear of moonlight from a high window shone on the man. "Put yer hands high, keep 'em up, and don't move."

Now they had to get away from him and leave this place the way they came in. As they eased around the wooden carts, they kept their eyes on the man, whose hands stayed in the air, his large shadow covering the wall.

At the door, Alonso placed the man's knife on an overturned cart, put the padlock back in place, and locked up.

"Time will tell," Jess said, and they made their way home, imitating the snorty snores of the Saltville bear.

28

Friday, June 9, 1944

Jess slung a tie around his collar. "Some days Clarence doesn't know when to quit," he said to Alonso. Even though the sun had been up for an hour, Clarence was still crowing from their boss's backyard across Georgia Avenue.

Outside their bungalow, dew shone on the grass. How Jess missed the Alabama cotton fields early in the morning. An earthy smell that made him feel the world was being created anew.

"Likes the sound of his voice." Alonso stood before the mirror above the wash basin, shaving.

Jess looked at Eddie's window and recollected her at the door last night, barefoot, disheveled, and lovely. He liked her hesitancy and her certainty, how she'd tried to dissuade them from finding Pearl's attacker, but accepted when she couldn't change their minds.

Alonso turned to him. "You dressing up for this psychiatrist?"

They were going to St. Elizabeth's to talk with Dr. Kushner, a referral they'd gotten from Dr. Lee. "My tie tip you off?"

After their father died, they found seven silk ties hanging in his closet. They buried him in one and divided the others, three each. This blue silk was the pick of the litter, or so Jess believed, and he wore it whenever he wanted to impress, something Al teased him about.

"On our way there, we need to stop at a fancy hotel called the Hay-Adams right across from the White House."

"Turn 'tward me." Alonso looped and knotted Jess's tie.

"Thanks, Al." Jess anchored the tie to his shirt with his New Orleans Police Department tie clip, a gift from the police department, and walked to the mirror to admire their work. "And before you ask, I admit this first stop has nothing to do with our investigation. We're going to pay an early morning visit to a certain Marine captain, who got fresh with Eddie last night."

"Sounds like fun."

Alonso parked near Lafayette Park, where servicemen were still stretched out on benches. These warm nights they slept in parks and green spaces all over town. Perky USO girls were walking among them, handing out cups of coffee and fried doughnuts.

Jess's mouth watered since they'd skipped breakfast at Mrs. Trundle's.

They walked between the hotel's fancy columns onto its sunlit portico.

The doorman, a stout white man in a fancy uniform, gold braid dangling from his shoulders, gave Alonso a penetrating stare, as if to say only a nervy Negro would try and enter the Hay-Adams by the front door.

Jess was about to pull out his badge, when Alonso nodded to the man and indicated with a lift of his briefcase that he was with this white man, just a servant carrying his master's briefcase. That was all right, then. The doorman tipped his hat.

Jess stepped into the lobby, laughing inside. Wouldn't that doorman be surprised to know the briefcase belonged to Alonso? Al carried it with him because he fretted about someone breaking into their car and taking it. Today it contained photos and information about the murdered government girls for Dr. Kushner.

The Hay-Adams' lobby glowed in wood paneling and wainscoting. A giant arrangement of pink roses sat beside the front desk. The hotel's gleam and polish told those who entered that even a war couldn't diminish this hotel's standard of excellence.

Jess took out his badge and offered it across the counter to the elderly concierge, a pale man with a pencil colored mustache, so thin it looked drawn on.

The man studied it. "Federal Bureau of Investigation?" He looked up and studied Jess's face as well, as if looking for a match.

"I need the room number of a man named Austin Richardson."

The concierge cleared his throat. "It's against our policy to give out our guests' room numbers, but…" The man looked back at Jess's badge and lowered his head to a book behind the counter. "Captain Richardson is in room 209." He spoke in a voice barely above a whisper. "Now may I make a request of you?"

"All right," Jess said.

The man leaned across the counter. "If you arrest him, could you take him out the back staircase, so as not to upset our other guests?"

"You bet," Jess said.

At Captain Richardson's room, Alonso banged on the door. Someone stirred behind it. "At least we won't have to crawl around dirty wooden carts to get to this man," Alonso said.

Jess got his drift. What they were doing now wasn't so different from last night, and neither had anything to do with their case.

A tall blond man, as shirtless and hairy as the Saltville bear, opened the door, but that's where their similarities ended. Jess took in the Captain's muscled arms, admiring their symmetry, mussed blond hair and movie star handsome face. His chiseled Aryan features might get him the part of a Nazi officer in a war movie.

"I'm Special Agent Jessup Lindsay." His badge cupped in his palm, he brought it close to the man's face. "Are you Captain Austin Richardson, United States Marine Corps?"

"Yes." He swallowed hard and stepped back.

Like the Saltville bear, the captain reeked of alcohol, but he had indulged in something fancier than moonshine. Across the hall, a man in Navy whites opened his door and stared at them.

"You'd better come in," the Captain said in almost a whisper. "What's this all about?"

Alonso and Jess stood just inside the door, the Captain not far away.

With the sun streaming in the room's windows, Jess took in the scratches around the man's eyes and deep cuts along his jaw-line. Eddie had struggled with him more than she'd let on. She played down what happened between them. This man could have raped her.

Jess's hand curled into a fist, and he wanted to hurt him.

Instead he said, "Did you lure a young woman named Edwina Smith to your room last night?"

"Lure? Is that what she said?" The Captain forced a smile and batted long blonde lashes at them. "Maybe she lured me."

Alonso took out his handcuffs. Their twin circles made shadows on the hardwood floor.

The Captain's smile faded as his eyes focused on the silver handcuffs.

His accent was Northeastern. Eddie said he worked at the Pentagon, a general's adjutant, the kind of job one got by having the right connections.

"Did Eddie turn me into the FBI?" He swallowed hard.

The room reeked of alcohol. And the Captain's left foot was bandaged. Had Eddie done that?

"Just answer my question, Captain Richardson."

With the handcuffs jangling, Alonso walked around the room. He was looking for Eddie's book bag. That's the real reason they came. Al stopped beside a sofa against the wall. The bag lay on the coffee table.

"Okay, I brought her up here." Just as Alonso grabbed Eddie's bag, the Captain turned and snapped his fingers. "Wait. I know what this is about. I found a German-English dictionary in her bag." He paled and ambled to the unmade bed, where he collapsed, his fingers kneading his scalp. "Dear God, tell me she's not a spy."

Jess and Alonso exchanged a look. Al had warned Jess that if he carried that article in German around with him, folks would think he was a spy.

"And I thought she was just a pretty hillbilly." Captain Richardson looked at them.

"We need to take her bag and its contents, Captain."

"I put everything back in it, but stupidly I looked through her dictionary, so my fingerprints are on it."

"We'll keep that in mind."

Alonso was already at the door, the book bag's long strap slung over his chest the way Eddie wore it.

The captain's jacket hung on the back of the chair across the room. Its twin silver bars glinted in the sunlight. An idea came to Jess, who believed in serendipity. Sometimes in an investigation you got lucky.

"Captain, where were you the night of May 21st?" Jess took his notebook from his pocket.

Alonso came back from the door, his shadow falling over the Captain, who rubbed his bristly jaw. "That was a Sunday night, and I was on a train coming north from New Orleans. It was the night I met Eddie. Why do you ask?"

Eddie had told Jess she met this guy on the train coming here, and she arrived on the night the last government girl, Kaye Krieger, was murdered.

"Good day, Captain."

Before Jess got to the door, the Captain sprang across the room and tugged on Jess' empty sleeve. "Will this go on my record? That I was involved with a German spy? I'm starting an important job, a position vital to the war, if you know what I mean. So I can't afford for anything like…?"

This made Jess smile. Why did so many people in Washington consider themselves vital to the war? Jess was tempted to tell the Captain that he was in deep trouble.

Alonso had his hand on the door handle, a signal they'd wasted enough time here.

Jess cleared his throat. "I didn't say Miss Smith was a spy. Nor am I responsible for what goes on your record, but I will say you messed with the wrong woman last night. Be more respectful of women, especially our government girls. They're serving this country, too, and very vital to the war effort."

Before turning the ignition in the car, Alonso looked at him. "They're going to make you the patron saint of government girls."

Jess laughed then hit the dash. "Damn it, Al. I wish I could protect them. For a moment up there, I thought he might be our man."

"Yeah, I know. In a flash, your eyes turned big as saucers."

"Lily Regis, Donna Gerber, Doris Reynolds, Thelma Sykes, Kaye Krieger. I wake thinking about those young women who died too soon. I feel the killer's breath on our necks. Every day brings us closer to his next murder. We've got only sixteen days until…"

"I know. The last thing I think about before going to sleep is that another day has passed, and we didn't find him. Let's get breakfast and start working our plan at the same time."

They sat in the window at the new Florida Avenue Grill and ordered breakfast from a surly middle-aged colored man. He stared at the horrifying photograph of Doris Reynolds, the third girl murdered. Quickly Alonso turned the photograph over.

"You po-lice?" the waiter asked. His skin color might be called high yellow like Alonso's. His stare wasn't friendly.

The Florida Grill, Negro-owned, was one of the few places that served both colors. At 7:30 in the morning, it was crowded with white cabbies, who worked up an appetite on the night shift driving all over the city. In quick order, the restaurant had become known for its breakfast, and the aroma of frying bacon and country ham in the air was enough to make a hungry man weep.

"No," Alonso said to the waiter, "not exactly."

The waiter set plates in front of them, watching them, his forehead bunched, clearly not pleased with Alonso's answer. He could wait all day as far as Jess was concerned, who tucked into his eggs, grits, and homemade biscuits.

Opening a fluffy biscuit, Jess lowered his face to inhale its sweet steam.

"Well, either you are or you ain't po-lice. Which is it?" He brought over a pot of coffee and refilled their cups.

Alonso wiped his mouth with a napkin. "We work for the Justice Department, Bureau of Investigation." Alonso showed him his ID. Jess knew he enjoyed doing this.

The waiter read his ID card and gave it back. "Justice De-partment, huh? Brother, you sound like a cracker same as me. What you do at the Bureau of Investigation?"

Since colored folks were Al's territory, Jess ate and listened.

"I'm a photographer, and I drive this here cracker around." Al gestured with his fork to Jess.

The comment struck Jess as funny. He laughed so hard, he coughed. The table of noisy cabbies quieted and turned to stare. The waiter brought Jess more water to sip so he'd stop coughing.

By the time they stood to leave, the waiter named Macy and Alonso had traded what part of the South they were from. Macy was from the mountains of western Georgia.

"Macy, looks like you know a lot of folks in this town," Alonso said, a toothpick in his mouth. "You ever hear anything said about the murders of these government girls?"

They were going to the community for help, and the Florida Grill was their first port-of-call.

"You the fellas looking for the killer, aren't you?" Grinning, he shook a finger at them.

Alonso gave him their card with their phone number on it and told him to call if he heard any gossip about the murders.

They went to a table of cab drivers. This time, Jess showed his ID. At the sight of it, a few men looked like they wanted to leave. Jess raised his hand palm out to calm them. "If any of ya'll are asked to take a couple some place far like to the C&O Canal or Arlington Cemetery, would you alert your dispatcher and have them call us? Or if you see anything suspicious." Alonso passed out their cards to the men. "And pass the word to other drivers."

This afternoon they would visit all the taxi dispatch offices and ask the dispatchers the same thing. They doubted the killer used taxis, but taxi drivers were all over the city at all hours. They believed the killer took the woman somewhere, killed her then left her body near the Potomac. All that driving might attract a cabbie's attention.

29

"Washington City's divided into four quadrants," Alonzo said. They were traveling Alabama Avenue. "This here is Anacostia in the Southeast quadrant."

St. Elizabeth's Hospital sat high on bluffs above the confluence of the Potomac and Anacostia Rivers. St. E.'s operated as the only federal mental health facility. Half its patients were civilly committed, the other half criminal, those who'd been found criminally insane by the court.

But which was which? They saw people milling around under the trees, all wearing white. How could you tell staff from patients?

"The colored men must be staff," Alonso said, reading Jess's mind.

"No. St. E.'s takes Negro patients. In fact, the famous psychiatrist Carl Jung did a study here with them to see if their race affected their mental health."

Alonso stopped on the path. "If their race affected their... mental... health?" He could barely get the words out for laughing. "White-hooded men chasing you with a noose might affect a fellow's mental health." He set down his briefcase and wiped his eyes with the backs of his hands.

"I take your point." Jess didn't laugh.

He and Alonso had witnessed a mob scene in Alabama, where the lynching of a colored man was treated like a county fair. White families brought picnic dinners.

About the Klan, their father often said any man who had to cover his face to do something was doing the wrong thing. And his dying wish had been for Alonso to take his tiny inheritance and leave the South forever. Al, who never did exactly what Papa told him, went west to string electrical wire across the prairies, but returned.

Jess paused to look down the hill. "Odd, too, that one of the few places where whites and Negroes mix is an insane asylum."

Alonso lifted his face and squinted. He formed a rectangle with his hands and looked through as if he was taking a photo. "Mysterious-looking building."

Crenellation around the top of the building made it look like a castle. Windows peeked through dense ivy that covered the exterior. A square tower jutted from the front, rising five stories with French windows opening onto balconies on the higher stories.

"We're early," Jess said to Alonso. "Go get your camera and take some photographs."

"I'll do it afterward."

"The light, the shadows will be different then. That's what you always tell me."

Alonso pivoted and sprinted back down the path for his camera.

"Come see my view," Dr. Sheldon Kushner told them in his office on the fourth floor, the huge windows opened to the warm breeze. They stood on either side of the doctor and admired the green hillside that sloped down to the dark rivers far below.

Dr. Kushner had welcomed them like honored guests, serving them iced tea and cookies. Although the Bureau had strict rules about accepting food and drink while they were working, they took what Dr. Kushner offered. Not to do so would be rude.

Once they were seated again, he said, "I've worked with prisons and courts all my professional life, but you two are the first detectives to come to me to help catch a killer." He lifted his teacup and sipped. He told them earlier that hot drinks made him feel cooler, a belief that made Jess wonder about Dr. Kushner's sanity. "I like the idea of being on the other side of a crime." He looked from Jess to Alonso. "Thank you."

He was a pale small man in his fifties, wearing an open-collared white shirt and loose trousers held up with sagging braces. Entirely forgettable in appearance, but his face became animated when he spoke, and he possessed a cheerfulness that belied his profession. Treating the criminally insane couldn't be that enjoyable, but he made it seem so.

"We'd like some guidance from you about the man we're looking for." Jess tried to juggle his glass and a cookie. Dr. Kushner read his unease and set a small table beside his arm. "His characteristics, motivation, that kind of thing. A template for the kind of man who could commit these murders?"

The doctor was back behind his desk again. "But what about these poor girls?" Dr. Kushner raised the folder of photographs and copy of their notes Alonso had given him. "They're the known in this equation. Do they have anything in common?"

"Well, their appearance is so similar they could be from the same family." Alonso spoke up even though Dr. Kushner was white. The doctor had a way about him that encouraged talk. "They're dark-haired, a little on the plump side, dressed..." he paused and looked to Jess. Alonso didn't like to comment on white women's sexuality.

Jess picked up his thread. "Some might say, they're dressed provocatively in low-necked blouses or snug sweaters. Yet, they're well-groomed. Their lipstick isn't even disturbed when we find them."

"Interesting." Dr. Kushner wrote something down. "Good. And what is it in their background that encourages them to go with this man?"

Jess thought a moment. "All their supervisors said they were hard-workers, dedicated, patriotic. Kaye Krieger's boss told us Kaye saw her file clerk job as a higher calling because of the war."

"So you think the killer is in the military?"

"No," Jess said. "We believe he dresses in different uniforms." This idea had been hatching ever since he picked up Miss Minnie's jar of military buttons and insignias. "We need to look at men who have access to different uniforms."

"Yes," Alonso whispered. "Yes." His dark eyes flashed at Jess. They had discussed this for a while, but today seeing the people dressed in white on the hillside and not knowing patients from staff had encouraged it.

"So the government girl would go with the killer because of his uniform, khaki wacky, as they say." Dr. Kushner smiled. "Do you realize how many slang terms we have for the insane? Crazy, bonkers, nuts, loony..."

Alonso and Jess found themselves adding to his list. The doctor had a way of wandering off, but whatever the magic in his office, Jess knew they'd made a breakthrough about the uniforms. Who had easy access to a variety of military uniforms? Laundries, dry cleaners, uniform makers and wholesalers.

"How are you feeling about the case?" Dr. Kushner asked.

Jess and Alonso exchanged a glance. "If we don't find him before he kills again, we're going to blame ourselves." Jess closed his eyes. Was Dr. Kushner trying to treat them?

Alonso nodded at this.

"Don't just nod at what your half-brother says, Alonso. Tell me in your own words."

Jess and Alonso exchanged a glance.

"Stop talking without words." Dr. Kushner patted his desk. "It's rude."

"How do you know we're related?" Alonso asked.

"Fred," Jess whispered although he couldn't imagine Fred calling Dr. Kushner and telling him this. Besides Fred had let them know he thought visiting Dr. Kushner was a fool's errand, no matter what Ernst Gennat advised.

"I don't know this Fred." The doctor took off his glasses and turned them to show their thickness. "I'm nearly blind without these, but with them I see well enough to notice the shape of your faces, the way you rub that notch in your chin at the same time. Alonso's skin is light colored. I'm betting same father different mothers."

"You ought to be a detective," Jess said.

"I am in a way, except my cases don't get solved." His face sagged at these words, and he drained his teacup. "I'm thinking the uniform is key to your investigation. Maybe this man longs to be in the military. Maybe he's tried to get in and was turned down."

Jess took all this down in his notebook. This was another line of inquiry. The various military branches had lists of men turned down for physical or mental reasons.

Before they left, Dr. Kushner promised to write "a template" of the killer from the information they'd brought him. "I'll send it by messenger before we escape to Maine. If you ever want to talk about the case or about anything else, please call me, either of you." He gave them his card.

30

Eddie sat on the porch swing, reading the message delivered to her at work that day. The envelope was addressed to Mr. Eddie Smith. Mr. Bauer of the Bureau of Investigation wrote: *please come to my office at 7:30 AM Monday to talk about doing translation work.*

"Does this mean you're leaving us, Miss Smith?" Mrs. Abercrombie, Eddie's snoopy supervisor, had asked. The message was sent in a sealed envelope, so Mrs. Abercrombie had to be guessing at its contents.

"I think there's been some mistake," Eddie told her, hoping with all her heart there had not been. After filing medical reports for a week, she wanted to run to the Justice Department right now and beg Mr. Bauer to take her on.

She would tell no one about the interview, except Jess. And Rachel, and solicit her help in getting the right ensemble together to meet Mr. Bauer. Everyone knew Director Hoover was particular about how those who worked for him dressed.

She folded the message and returned it to her pocketbook.

Leaning back, she swung through watery light filtered through the morning glory vines that covered this end of the porch like a leafy wall. She loved sitting here alone. Finding solitude in Washington was difficult.

Not that the porch was quiet. Aunt Viola was listening to *Bachelor's*

Children, the radio's volume high, the audience's laughter spilling from the parlor windows.

A truck's brakes wheezed to a stop in front, its muffler rattling. Eddie slid from the swing. From the truck's sound, she knew this was Bert in his laundry truck, not Dan Wozniak.

Bert got out carrying several boxes of laundry, dry cleaning covered in a white paper sleeve slung over his shoulder. Eddie went down the sidewalk and opened the gate for him.

He was dressed in his beige starched Berman Laundry overalls, his hair glistening with Vitalis. And he was limping a little.

"How do you manage to stay immaculate in this heat?" she asked.

"We've got a shower at the laundry plant. It's my home away from home. I wash up there every spare moment. You know how I love water."

"I do." Her cousin worked for the right place. He was a clean man. "Let me help." She took one of the boxes tied with string.

"Thanks, Cuz. Just set it on the porch. Mama's going to be happy to have her things washed and ironed. She's having a hard time managing without Ruth."

Managing might be easier if Aunt Viola got off her duff and did something, but Eddie didn't voice this. Whenever anyone criticized his mother, a hurt look came over Bert. He was a good son, if too much of what the Germans called "a slipper hero," a *pantoffelheld.*

"I'm impressed that you gave Ruth a wonderful reference, even though you knew how difficult it would be for you and your mother. That's admirable, Bert."

"It was the right thing to do. Ruth is a smart young lady and deserved better than cleaning up after us."

"Sit a while, Bert." Eddie went to the pitcher she'd brought out and poured Bert a glass of water. "This was cold not long ago."

Bert hung his dry cleaning on a hook under the porch eaves and eased himself down on the swing. The swing sloped under his weight. "Thanks, Eddie." He took the glass and sipped.

She positioned a wicker chair across from him. "Put your foot up there."

"Don't go spoiling me, Cuz."

In a low voice, she asked, "How did you hurt your ankle?" It looked swollen. She had never mentioned his hemophilia before.

"Usually a fellow rides with me and takes deliveries into buildings, but his wife had a baby last night, so I told him to stay at the hospital." He unlaced his shoe and rolled his ankle around.

"Wait right here. I'll go get some ice to put on your swelling."

He touched her arm. "Don't. It'll upset Mama."

She was about to protest when he said, ""How's Pearl?" He rubbed his hands, which were so rough they made a scratching sound.

"She says she feels better," Eddie said, "but her bruises have turned egg-plant color. Thanks for all you did last night, Bert."

He had helped sneak Pearl upstairs past eagle-eyed Aunt Viola. Then he walked Rachel to the nearest telephone booth, so she could call Pearl's supervisor and say Pearl had an accident and couldn't come to work today. They had called from the pay phone out of Aunt Viola's earshot.

Yes, Pearl had them all working for her. Because Pearl had been a poor student, Eddie had underestimated her. Pearl excelled at manipulating others.

He studied his hands. "I hate to say this, but once Pearl gets better…"

"I know. She needs to find a new place to live."

"Yes. I don't want Mama here alone in case that man from Saltville comes back."

"You're protective of her."

He gave a little nod. "I feel the same about you and Rachel, so I hope ya'll aren't riding out to the Rosens with Dan Wozniak."

"I'm afraid we are. He's picking us up in his delivery truck. Why?"

Bert leaned forward, dug a handkerchief from his back pocket, and wiped his forehead. "I reckon ya'll be all right together, but the night Tony and Luca waited here for a ride, Tony said Dan wasn't trustworthy around women."

"Tony's a real gossip, but what he said about Dan doesn't surprise me. Don't worry. Rachel and I can take Dan on if we have to." Eddie nodded to Bert's drying cleaning bag. "What did you have dry cleaned?"

"My old funeral suit. Saturdays are the only day Jones Funeral Parlor has enough men to give the dead a nice ceremony. We're burying four folks tomorrow. I'm going out there this evening to help get their bodies ready."

"Do you embalm them?" Their grandfather, Edwin Smith, had been an embalmer, and burying people a family occupation.

"I help any way I can, Eddie. The dead deserve my best efforts"

A honk out front. "Excuse me, Bert." Eddie went inside and called upstairs, "Rachel, he's here."

Her face damp with sweat, Aunt Viola waddled to the parlor door. "Who's that out yonder honking like my house is some kind of drive-in restaurant?"

For once, Eddie agreed with her aunt. Dan Wozniak had no manners.

Before she could apologize, Rachel came downstairs. "Sorry, Mrs. Trundle. The driver works for my cousin. I've told him not to honk, but…"

"Now don't fret about it, Rachel honey," Aunt Viola said. "I know it's not your fault. Ya'll have a nice time." To Aunt Viola, Rachel could do no wrong.

On the sidewalk, they found Bert, hands on his hips, talking to Dan through the truck's open window.

Bert stepped away from the van, and in a low voice said to Eddie, "Don't worry about Pearl. I'll make a little something for her to eat and take it to her." He opened the truck's door, closed it once they'd gotten in, and sent Dan a pointed look before he walked back to the house.

Bert must have put Dan on notice.

"Hey, Rachel." Dan winked at her. "You're looking spiffy."

"Eddie, you remember Dan Wozniak." Rachel smoothed the skirt of her mauve cotton dress, its wide belt cinching in her narrow waist. She had lost weight since they arrived.

Eddie arranged her skirt as well. "Hello, Dan. Thank you for giving us a ride." Her words correct, but cold. After the way he had treated Rachel, she wanted nothing to do with him.

"Hi ya, Eddie." Dan pulled away from the curb and hung a U-turn, heading for the DC/ Maryland line. "So the fuddy-duddy in overalls is your cousin?"

"Bert's our friend," Rachel said, "and a real gentleman. You should take lessons from him, Dan."

"Ah, don't bust my chops, Princess. I've looked forward to seeing you all week. Swell news about D-Day, huh?"

Eddie kept a stony silence as city gave way to suburbs then rolling country in a place called Silver Spring, Maryland. She didn't feel like making small talk with Dan Wozniak. Rachel said only enough to be polite. The tension became thick inside the cab.

Dan stopped trying to get a conversation going and drove. They were silent for half an hour. Once they traveled around a bend, Dan said, "There she is."

Eddie heard his pride, just as she had the night he met them at Union Station.

The rambling Victorian painted robin's egg blue sat on the hump of a hill, its turrets rising into the pearl gray sky. Wisteria vines climbed its gingerbread fretwork.

Eddie was surprised to see cows on the front lawn. Two women herded them toward the barn's open doors.

"Is this a farm?" Eddie asked Rachel.

Dan chimed in. "You bet. We call it Rosenville, since the factory is right down that road."

He took the winding drive to the front door, where Eddie got out.

Behind her, Dan grabbed Rachel's hand and said something to her. She shook him off and joined Eddie on the veranda, lined with white wicker rockers and glorious ferns hanging from the ceiling.

No one sat on the porch, yet voices could be heard from all directions. The place hummed with activity.

A tall, slender woman, her jet black hair brushed back, opened the front door and stepped out. She was dressed in Katherine Hepburn pants and a thin sleeveless shirt, but she had the kind of looks—high cheek bones, aquiline nose—that made her simple outfit elegant.

After she hugged Rachel, Rachel said, "Sarah, this is my best friend in the world, Edwina Smith. Everyone calls her Eddie."

"Eddie." Mrs. Rosen extended her hand. "I'm Sarah Rosen. Welcome to our home. Would you like the penny tour?"

"Yes, thanks Mrs. Rosen."

"Don't make me feel ancient. Call me Sarah, Eddie. I insist." Sarah picked up a small basket containing a pair of shears. "This way."

Sarah was younger than Eddie had expected and possessed the kind of looks called handsome, striking. Her English was spoken with a hint of a French accent, elegant as well.

Eddie and Rachel accompanied her around the veranda to the back yard, passing the kitchen, where women were cooking and calling to each other in a polyglot of French, German, and Yiddish. The smell of cinnamon wafted.

In the back, a garden extended as far as the eye could see. Eddie stood on the porch steps. "This is the biggest victory garden I've ever seen."

"Can you believe all this used to be nothing but rolling lawn?" Sarah stepped down to a stone path. "We can't afford to waste land like that now. We grow enough vegetables to feed our whole community."

They walked past zinnias in a rainbow of colors, heads of green lettuce, rows of staked tomatoes perfectly equidistant like marching soldiers. The garden's loamy aroma reminded her of home. And brought memories of planting, weeding, and picking in their garden, work she'd enjoyed.

Her mother had returned from the asylum now. The family was in what Eddie had thought of as their *honeymoon* period. The twins had written that Mama was cured this time. Eddie remembered when she had believed that.

In shoulder-high corn, they stopped at the approach of a small young woman, her skin nut brown and freckled from the sun, her hair covered in a blue kerchief.

"Hi Dominique," Rachel said.

"Bonjour," Dominique said with a shy smile and added something else in French.

A dark cloud passed over Sarah's face, and she spoke to Dominique in fast French. Eddie picked up Sarah's reproach.

Dominique's smile vanished and she flushed as if she'd been slapped. "Yes yes, pardon, pardon." She nodded. Under her arm was a large basket of ruffled bib lettuce, onions, and plump ripe tomatoes.

"We will see you soon, yes?" Sarah's sweetness returned.

After Dominique passed, Sarah said, "Some refugees don't work hard enough to learn English. Maybe they think after the war they will go back to their old lives in Europe." She shook her head. "So why bother learning this new language? They find other French people and speak only French. Our rule here is English only."

Eddie recalled the women in the kitchen speaking French.

"Maybe speaking her language comforts Dominique," Rachel said.

"Yes, of course." Sarah stopped beside a patch of herbs, bent, and cut some curly parsley and basil, releasing its pungent aroma. "But their old lives are gone. The sooner they accept that, the better off they'll be."

Their old lives are gone. How could anyone accept that? Eddie had no idea what Europe would be like after the war. But surely these refugees or displaced persons, as the newspapers called them, could find their place again and rebuild the communities they left.

"When did Dominique come from France?" Eddie asked. With German U-Boats swarming the Atlantic, it was dangerous traveling to the U. S.

"She left in '39, but could only get into the Dominican Republic." Sarah focused on Eddie. "America's immigration laws keep Jews out." Fury in her voice. "Because Dominique had worked in our Lyon factory, eventually we were able to get her a visa and arrange for her to come here."

Behind them, the sun in splashes of pink and gold sank on the horizon, its colors brilliant as if to make up for the darkness soon to come.

On the way back to the house, Sarah said, "Before Hitler came to power, Meyer and I weren't particularly religious. In fact, I was agnostic I guess, but after bringing all these Jews here, we have Shabbat every Friday evening."

Eddie said, "I read that the orthodox don't do any work between sunset Friday to sunset Saturday. Is that correct?"

Rachel's dimples dented her face. "Studying up on us, eh?"

"Because we must defeat Hitler, we cannot afford to be so observant. Our factory down that road," Sarah extended her arm, "is open every day of the week." Sarah stopped on the path and looked from Rachel to Eddie. "We will not close until the Axis surrenders."

Impressed, Eddie said, "Good for you."

Jess and Alonso were also working non-stop to catch a killer. These ideas fused in Eddie's mind. What if the government girl killings were an act of sabotage? An attempt to weaken morale. Was that too far-fetched? She would mention this idea to Jess tomorrow.

31

Windows on three sides made the Rosen's immense dining room feel cool. The evening breeze lifted the gauzy curtains like ghosts. Large framed photographs covered the walls.

Eddie inspected a photograph of Eleanor Roosevelt with Sarah Rosen at her side. Eddie was amazed. Mrs. Rosen was important. In another, Sarah in a crowd of people all in formal dress stood with a smiling man in rimless glasses.

"I recognize him from the newspapers," Eddie said to Sarah. "That's Secretary Morgenthau."

"Yes," Sarah said. "The photograph is recent, taken after the announcement of the War Refugee Board. My husband was appointed to that board."

"And speak of the devil." Meyer Rosen, gray-haired and trim, joined them. He was at least twenty years older than Sarah and three inches shorter. What had brought this unlikely pair together? A question Eddie would save for Rachel.

Mr. Rosen hugged Rachel and shook Eddie's hand. "So glad you could come, Eddie. Rachel has told us wonderful things about you. Not twenty-one yet, and you're already a college graduate. So impressive."

Blood rushed to Eddie's face and her tongue swelled so that all she could do was beam at him. His words made her feel like the Saltville wunderkind again.

When they were seated around the long dining table, Eddie counted more than thirty people. All were young like Dominique, a few couples with children on their laps. Rachel told Eddie that most lived here in the house with the Rosens or in cottages on their property.

Some worked at the clothing factory, others on the farm, and according to Rachel they came from all over occupied Europe. English spoken with foreign accents swirled around them.

Sarah sat at the head of the table with Eddie to her right, while Mr. Rosen was seated at the far end with Rachel. Eddie noticed that Dan Wozniak had managed to sit across from Rachel, his gaze fixed on her.

Meyer Rosen stood. A young man handed him a lit candle. The people around the table bowed their heads. Mr. Rosen tried to light the candles in a holder, but because of the breeze, they wouldn't stay lit. Another man got up and closed the nearest windows.

Mr. Rosen cupped his hands behind each candle, lit them, and said, "Blessed are You, Lord our God, King of the universe, who has sanctified us with His commandments and commanded us to light the Shabbat candles."

After he sat, food in large bowls was passed, salads, home-made bread, and tender beef in broth, everything fresh and delicious.

Dan Wozniak continued to stare at Rachel, who ignored him. Eddie imagined Dan's hands around Rachel's neck. Rachel with her long dark hair and pale smooth skin resembled the other murdered government girls, except Rachel was beautiful.

Eddie had seen the victims' photographs the night she stayed with Pearl in the room above the garage. Once Pearl fell asleep, Eddie went to the mysterious back wall covered by a sheet. Lifting it, she studied what lay beneath, photos, a map of the Washington area, and clues. *Has access to a vehicle, car, hearse, or truck.* Dan Wozniak did. An odd clue: *vehicle makes a sound like "soft thunder."*

The night Dan picked them up at Union Station she had thought his truck's large back door rattled like *soft thunder* when he closed it. But more importantly Rachel said Dan had tried to choke her. Maybe Rachel was lucky to escape with her life. Could Dan be the government girl killer?

Eddie's pulse revved. She would pass his name to Jess.

At that moment Dan laughed at something Rachel said, and he looked like any normal young man with a crush.

Eddie's dislike of Dan stemmed from her biases: his lack of respect for women and his use of slang, an English teacher prejudice.

Two women to Eddie's right were speaking in hushed German about the D-Day invasion. The older woman wondered where the most casualties had occurred. Eddie couldn't resist.

"*Der Strand war genannte Omaha*," Eddie said to them.

"*Danke*," answered the one who'd asked and repeated, "O-ma-ha."

Eddie switched to English. "I think Omaha is an Indian word. It's also the capital of the state of Nebraska." Miss Smith, the schoolmarm, was back.

Sarah, whose attention had been elsewhere, focused on Eddie. "You speak German?" Surprise on her face.

"I studied it in college. My great-grandmother came here from Berlin at the turn of the century."

Sarah nodded. "For what the Germans are doing to my people, I will never ever forgive." Her voice bitter. "I hope when they lose the war, their whole country is turned into one big potato field."

Around the table, people stopped to listen and nod in agreement.

"But, Sarah, remember what Confucius said." Mr. Rosen spoke loud enough for all to hear. "When you seek revenge, you must dig two graves. The Nazis will be punished, but…"

"They have dug many more than two," a handsome boy interrupted, a trace of moustache like iron filings on his upper lip.

Sarah clapped her hands. "No war talk at dinner, please, ladies and gentlemen. It is not good for digestion. We practice polite English."

The whole table went silent. What a censor Sarah Rosen was. She and Aunt Viola had little in common, except how both wanted to rule her kingdom. Which must mean a lot happened here Sarah Rosen knew nothing about, just as they kept Aunt Viola in the dark on Georgia Avenue.

"My mother came to this country as a young woman from a little Polish *shtetl* called Kielce," Mr. Rosen addressed everyone again, smiling now. "And oh how Mama struggled to learn this American English. But she would always say to us, speak Polish you can go back to Kielce but speak English and you can go to California."

Rachel and Eddie laughed, and a moment later the others laughed, as if it took them a moment to understand that what Mr. Rosen had said was funny. That's the problem with a language not your own. Irony and humor are often missed.

"No work for guests," Mr. Rosen told Eddie after dinner, when she lifted a dirty platter to take into the kitchen. "Come rock with an old man."

Sarah had taken Rachel upstairs. Maybe Rachel would tell Sarah about Dan.

Eddie and Meyer Rosen sat in cushioned wicker rockers on the veranda. Light from the house fell over the back of his head and shoulders like a shawl. On the lawn, fireflies rose in the darkness and blinked. Crickets sang from the grass.

"I love to sit here this time of the day." He rocked back and forth.

One of the young women came out with a tray of thick pound cake slices. Mr. Rosen waved a slice away, but Eddie took hers, cut it and put the bite in her mouth, savoring.

"This tastes the way we used to make it with a pound of flour, a pound of butter, a pound of sugar."

He stopped rocking. "We adhere strictly to government rationing, Eddie, and buy nothing off the black market. We keep bees for honey, so that's where the sweetness comes from."

She wanted to clarify that she'd meant it only as a compliment. But she stayed silent. After running his factory all day, Mr. Rosen deserved some peace.

He closed his eyes, his large blue-veined hands resting on the arms of the chair, and rocked again. "D-Day, that's all everyone talks about. One of my foremen wanted to start planning for our return to ready-to-wear." He smiled at Eddie. "As if the Axis is about to surrender because we landed on those beaches."

"Everyone's been waiting for the invasion for so long. We want to believe the end will come soon. But the Nazis may fight to the last man, especially if they know our plans for their country."

"So if you were in charge, Eddie, those plans would be top secret, eh?"

She realized her impertinence. "Sorry for going on, Mr. Rosen. I'm just a girl from Saltville, Virginia, who sometimes thinks she's smarter than she really is."

"Give yourself more credit, Eddie. I think you're plenty smart and right about revenge. There's a long German word about not being able to deal with the past…"

"Vergangenheitsbewaeltigung," she said.

"That's a mouthful. But let that be their fate. Generations of Germans to come will have to deal with…"

Rachel appeared with a big canvas bag. "Clothes for both of us, beautiful clothes." She hugged the bag, delighted. "Sarah's sewn them from remnants she had lying around."

Eddie wondered why she and Rachel should get beautiful clothes with all the displaced refugees living here. Like most government girls, she and Rachel needed clothes. Maybe she'd be able to put together a professional-looking outfit to go to the Bureau of Investigation on Monday.

Sarah appeared with a small suitcase.

Mr. Rosen stood and extended his arm toward her. "Oh, Sarah's an amazing dress designer. That's how we met. She was working as a seamstress in Paris, and I was dazzled by her beauty, her talent."

Sarah brought her arm around him, too, her hand caressing his face. "Hush, you old flatterer. You make me blush."

Eddie savored their affection as she had their pound cake, both sweet and light. They loved each other, an overflowing love that gathered others around them. They'd built a community here from the wreckage of occupied Europe.

Dan pulled up front in the truck. Eddie didn't want to ride with him. Why hadn't Rachel told Sarah what happened last week?

Sarah walked down the steps to Dan. "You're not driving the girls back, Dan." The way she said this let Eddie know Rachel had told her. Good. "Meyer has a meeting in the morning, so we're staying in town tonight. We're taking Rachel and Eddie back."

"But I don't mind…" Dan started, but Sarah waved for him to move on.

"Goodnight, Dan," Mr. Rosen called.

Through the window, Dan sent Rachel a smoldering look and crept down the driveway.

A large black car pulled up. The young man, who'd driven it, got out, took the Rosen's suitcase, and put it in the trunk. Then Sarah Rosen got behind the wheel. This amazed Eddie. Her father would never have allowed himself to be driven anywhere by a woman.

Before Mr. Rosen got in the front, he opened the back door and said, "Hop aboard, Government Girls."

32

Vernon walked down the alley.

In front of the tenement doorway closest to the Jess's gate, colored folks crowded around, some in chairs, others on blankets spread around the stoop, all quiet and still, listening to *Amos 'n' Andy*. A long electric cord snaked out the window. Like the honored guest, a radio sat in the middle of the group on a small table.

Vernon liked Amos and Andy, too. The show featured two colored fellows from Georgia who come to Chicago for a better life with only four ham and cheese sandwiches and twenty-four dollars between them. At something one of the characters said, the group erupted in laughter.

The stingy streetlight fell over Vernon. He tipped his cap to them.

Several adults nodded, but one little boy, nestled in his mama's lap, let out a squeal and buried his face in her bosom. Vernon understood. The huge bruise that covered one side of his face made him look like the boogie man.

The gate whined shut behind him, and he knocked on the garage door. No one answered.

Where were the G-Men? Had another government girl been murdered? At the idea he got queasy.

Light glowed from the little squat bungalow up the path and more lights in the house beyond. He was about to head that way when the garage door opened.

"Hello, Mr. Vernon," Alonso said. "Please, come upstairs." Alonso wore a sleeveless undershirt and stained pants with suspenders, working man's clothes like his own.

In this city of fancy pants men carrying umbrellas, Vernon felt kinship with working men. "Evening, Alonso."

As soon as Vernon stood in the dusty room, Doris's eyes fell on him. She still came to him in his dreams. He had decided she wanted him to help the G-Men find her killer.

"Please have a seat, Sir," Alonso said, "while I fetch your photograph."

"You developing pictures back there?" Vernon took in the scent of almonds, which he'd smelled here before.

"Yes, Sir." Alonso went behind the tarp that separated the sink area from the rest of the room and said, "Jess, Mr. Vernon is here."

When he came back, he brought a bottle of Nesbitt's soda. "While your photograph dries, would you care for something cool to drink?"

"Appreciate it, Alonso." Vernon took the bottle. "You got a telephone back there?"

"C&P finally came and put a regular telephone in our bungalow." Alonso popped the bottle's cap with an opener attached to the side if the table and handed the smoking cold soda to Vernon. "I ran a tin can telephone between here and the bungalow. Works good."

Jess appeared in a white open-collared shirt and shook Vernon's hand.

"We'd given up on you this evening, Vernon," Jess said and studied Vernon's face.

Vernon's finger worried at the soda bottle's label. "I roof till near 'bout dark every day now, even Sundays."

"Roofing is hard work, dangerous too by the looks of you." Jess sat across from him and brought out his notebook.

"Yeah." Vernon brought his hand above his bruise. "Slid down some shingles." His eyes skittered away from Jess's.

Jess sighed. "Vernon, you're a terrible liar. What happened to you?"

Vernon didn't appreciate being called a liar. "Give me my photograph, so I can be on my way."

With his palm, Jess patted the air, a signal for Vernon to calm. "You lied to us when we talked to you before. Lied about where you live, and now you're lying about what happened to your face. We need the truth from you."

Vernon dropped his head his long gray-streaked brown hair falling forward. "Alonso," he said. "Could you take Doris's photograph down? I feel her eyes on my back. Can't hardly get my breath when she looks at me like that."

Alonso went to the case map, lifted the sheet, and pulled the thumbtacks out of the photograph of Doris Reynolds. He put her picture between cardboard and slid it under the camp bed.

Vernon straightened and took an audible breath. "Thanks. That's better."

Alonso pulled up a chair, and both he and Jess stared at him.

"The truth, Vernon?" Jess said.

"Oh right, well." He placed his big rough hands on the table. The white skin around his ring finger had disappeared, browned by the sun. He looked from Jess to Alonso. "I'm married, see, but my wife is back in Frog Hollow. Here I'm living with…" He paused as if wondering how much he had to say. "A lady I think the world of." He refused to call Rickey any of the ugly names the world might call her. She was his fantasy come to life, and yes, he was in love with her and knew how hopeless his love was.

"Good, Vernon. Now about your face?"

Vernon dropped his head, searching for something to tell them. "I remember something from the morning beside the canal, something I forgot to tell you. About Doris."

"All right."

Vernon closed his eyes. "She was lying on her stomach on the towpath, her head to one side, her skirt hiked up a little in back." He squeezed his eyes tight. "Even though it was March and cold at night, she didn't wear socks or stockings. Her legs were bare except for black lines drawn up the backs." He looked into Jess's eyes. "Girls do that to make people think they have on hose."

"Yes." Jess frowned. "We know this, Vernon."

"Thing is those lines on her legs were perfect. And after what happened to her, you'd think they'd be smudged, but they weren't. I figure he drew them on her after..."

Jess wrote in his notebook.

"May I have my photograph now, please? Need to get home." Saturday nights were busy at Mrs. Frazier's. He would climb the fire escape in the alley to his room, avoiding *their guests* as Rickey called the men who came.

Did some of those men want his Rickey instead of one of the young girls? That's what worried him most. When he had asked Rickey about this, she'd laughed and said he flattered her.

Alonso went to the area where he did his developing and came back with his photograph.

Vernon's face opened in a wide grin. "Who is that wild mountain man?" That's what Rickey called him, *my wild mountain man*. She didn't even mind his bruised face, said it gave him more character. For a moment, he studied what the camera said he looked like before getting up to leave.

"Let me put it in cardboard to protect it." Alonso wrapped the photograph on the desk in back and handed it to Vernon.

"Well, thanks for this." He lifted the photograph by the twine tied around it.

"Wait, Vernon." In a low voice, Jess said, "Lilly Regis, Donna Gerber, Doris Reynolds, Thelma Sykes, Kaye Krieger."

"Who are they?" Vernon said, but he knew. He remembered their names from the newspaper articles.

Alonso went to the camp bed, took out a different photograph, and showed it to Vernon. "This is Doris from her high school yearbook."

It was a huge black-and-white in which Doris wore a white blouse with a corsage.

She looked so happy, so young. He wanted to pivot and run, but he didn't. "Okay, okay. I'll tell ya'll about this." He pointed to his face. "But it has nothing to do with the murders. And I hate to talk about it."

Alonso and Jess leaned against the wall, expectant.

"I was dead asleep one night in my bedroom on the third floor when I got up and fell down the stairs."

"That's it?" Jess straightened. "You fell down the stairs?"

"Yep." Vernon nodded slowly. "Then I woke up."

Rubbing the cleft in his chin, Jess stared into the air beyond Vernon as if an answer was written there. "You mean, you were sleepwalking?"

"Yep."

"How often do you sleepwalk?" Alonso asked.

Vernon shrugged. "Been doing it all my life. Keep thinking I've stopped, then I do it again. My pap tied me to the bed when I was a kid to stop me. Made me so ashamed." Vernon gave a sad smile. "Told you this had nothing to do with your murders."

Jess said nothing for a long moment. "Could you have been sleepwalking the night Doris was murdered?"

33

Sunday, June 11, 1944

"Why don't we park here, so we take him by surprise?" Jess said to Alonso.

They were on a narrow two-lane road in rural Silver Spring, Maryland. A breeze swayed the corn, its straight rows reaching across the field. From the surrounding woods, a cardinal sang.

Alonso pulled the Packard onto a tractor path and locked his camera in the trunk. They took their rumbled jackets from the backseat and adjusted their hats.

They walked the road's white dashes, both in good leather shoes from their father's closet. Shoes were Papa's weakness. He'd bought expensive pairs in Montgomery and Atlanta, not that his shoes fit either of them perfectly. Alonso put stretchers in his every night, so they didn't pinch, while Jess shoved cotton in the toes.

"This guy has it all, access to uniforms, a vehicle, and a history of violence against women," Alonso said.

Yesterday Eddie told Jess about Dan Wozniak, whose name had shown up on a list of men charged with assault in April. Unfortunately, the woman he had assaulted refused to press charges, so Wozniak was released before they ever questioned him.

"Two weeks from today will be the last Sunday of the month," Jess said.

"I was thinking the same thing."

Time pressed down on them. They felt it every waking moment. They had to find him before...

After the road curved, the corn fields ended. A long white building filled the horizon.

"That must be the uniform factory." Sounds of life drifted from it.

"He lives in the cottage closest to the factory." Jess pointed across a field blonde and stubbly with new mown hay. "He's a supervisor, even though he's only twenty-six."

Eddie had described Dan Wozniak and told him about the Rosens, their farm and factory. Jess imagined her voice with its hint of the mountains and her calm intelligence.

They left the road and cut through the field and a stand of pines, needles crunching under-foot. On the other side of a small muddy pond, they found a stone cottage. Cord wood was stacked floor to ceiling against the porch wall.

Beside the cottage, a car sat covered in a black tarp. The loose edge of the tarp flapped, teasing.

Alonso knocked on the door. No answer.

Jess put his ear to it. "Doesn't sound like he's home." He stooped and looked through a grimy window into a dim room.

Alonso went to the car, lifted the tarp, and let out a whistle. "A 1939 Ford Roadster convertible."

Jess didn't share his brother's passion for motor cars. "I'll go 'round back and check." He waded through knee-high weeds, passing more dark windows, no movement inside.

Beside the back stoop, a garbage bin lay knocked on its side giving off a terrible stench. Buzzing flies feasted. They had come to empty houses many times before. So why did this one feel different?

After the sun slid behind a cloud, he saw movement inside. The fingers of his left hand, his ghost hand, twitched. His ghost hand always felt danger. He reached into his jacket and pulled his gun from its holster.

With the gun heavy in his right jacket pocket, he knocked on the back door. "Mr. Wozniak. FBI. Open up." He hadn't intended on identifying themselves until they faced the man, but this was the safest way to do it.

No sound came from inside. He stepped off the stoop and headed around the other side of the cottage when a noise pierced the quiet: the pump of a shotgun. The sharp mechanical sound jolted through his body, nearly stopping his heart. The sound came from the front porch.

The last time Jess had seen Alonso he had been inspecting the roadster.

"No!" a voice screamed. The voice was Jess's own, all his police training out the window. A shot rang out. Glass exploded.

Jess ran around the side of the cottage.

The shooter came to the opposite end of the porch, his shadow flung across the grass.

"Put that gun down, or I'll blast you into eternity," called Dan Wozniak, shirtless and barefooted. He pointed the dark twin barrels of his shotgun at Jess.

"We're FBI, Mr. Wozniak," Jess yelled, his heart pounding on his sternum.

"Sure ya are. I'm gonna drop you if you don't put that gun down."

"All right." Jess took his time putting his gun in the weeds.

Dan Wozniak pumped the shotgun again and aimed, one eye closed as the other looked through the sight. Jess took a deep breath, figuring it was his last.

Before Wozniak could get the shot off, a rumbling came from behind him. An avalanche of wood hit him in the back and knocked him off the porch.

Alonso jumped from the porch and grabbed the shotgun. Jess picked up his own gun and ran to Dan Wozniak lying in the grass. They stood over him, pieces of wood scattered about.

Blood trickled down Alonso's forehead from his hairline. Other than that he appeared unhurt. For that, Jess wanted to shout hallelujah. "You all right?"

Alonso wiped the blood with his handkerchief. "Thanks for the warning. Gave me time to hit the dirt and roll partway under the automobile."

"That glass in your hair kinda looks like a halo."

"Saint Alonso. Been telling you that for years." He lowered his head and tried to shake the shards from his short tight curls. "He shot his car window out."

Alonso hated when machines suffered needless damage.

The man on the ground reached for a log.

"Not a good idea, Mr. Wozniak." Jess pressed his foot into the small of the man's back. "Let go of that and get up slow, hands in the air."

After Alonso set the shotgun on the other side of the porch, he ran his hands over the squirming man.

"Who the hell are you to touch me, jig?" Dan Wozniak's face was flushed, his bee-stung lips red and swollen.

"Like I said before you were about to shoot me, Mr. Wozniak, we're from the Bureau of Investigation."

Alonso showed Jess's badge while Jess held his gun on him. "We came here to question you, but now you're under arrest for the attempted murder of federal agents. Turn around."

Alonso snapped the handcuffs on.

"Follow my partner into your house. I'm behind you. Don't try anything."

Alonso grabbed the shotgun and led the way while Jess kept his gun aimed at Dan Wozniak's back. Walking across the porch, Jess took in the pungent smell of cordite from the fired shotgun. It was the smell of death.

They walked into the shadowy house.

"You know you're on private property, don't ya?" Dan yelled when they stood in his front room. It had wooden beams over head, a stone fireplace covering one wall, and reminded Jess of a hunting lodge. "You need a warrant to search here."

"After you shot at us, we don't need anything. Besides, your employer, Mr. Rosen, gave us permission to search your cottage last night."

Dan kicked at a chair leg. "Ah why'd ya have to bring him into this?" He sounded like a child caught in mischief.

"What is *this*?" Jess asked. "Tell us why you think we're here."

"Hell if I know," Dan Wozniak said, his voice less belligerent.

Over the telephone, Mr. Rosen hadn't sounded surprised when Jess told him they needed to question Dan. This made Jess think Mr. Rosen knew of his employee's history of violence. "If he's guilty of something, you'll let me know," he'd said, and Jess agreed.

Alonso righted the chair and set it by itself in the middle of the room. "Sit," he said. After Dan did, Alonso tied his legs to the chair.

Dan lifted his head, his face paler now. "Listen fellas, this has all been a terrible mistake. When I saw this one by my car," he nodded to Alonso, "I thought he was siphoning gas." Dan sounded like a different person, his tone conciliatory. "Sorry."

Jess handed Alonso his gun. "Keep that on him and move back here."

Jess stood on the fireplace's raised hearth and picked glass out of Alonso's hair, letting the shards fall on the floor.

After he finished he went to the kitchen, wet his handkerchief, and brought it back so Alonso could wipe the blood off his face.

"I keep bandages in the kitchen. Help yourself."

"Don't bother, Jess." Alonso touched the cut. "It's stopped bleeding."

"Look at it this way I shot out my Roadster's window, and I love that car." Wozniak gave a devilish grin.

"Shut up, Mr. Wozniak," Jess shouted, shaky from what had transpired. You never knew when a moment might be your last. It wasn't even 9:00 on a sunny Sunday, and Alonso could be dead and so could he.

Alonso kept a gun on Dan Wozniak while Jess searched the house. In the kitchen, flies nibbled on crusty dishes in the sink. Ashtrays overflowed and empty bottles of vodka, wine, beer were on every surface. The man lived in a state of siege.

In a cabinet over the sink, Jess found a prescription bottle. He got out his pad and wrote down the drug's name, a barbiturate, the drugstore, and the prescribing doctor.

"Why do your take this?" he asked Dan, showing him the bottle.

Dan groaned. "I work crazy hours, nights, days. Sometimes I need help going to sleep. What is it you think I did? Tell me."

Alonso made a check mark in the air. This guy was ringing their bells.

Jess went down the hall. In the bedroom, he opened an armoire and gasped. A girl crouched in the corner. Trembling, she fixed her large brown eyes on him. Other than the kerchief over her hair, she wore no clothes.

"Miss?" He grabbed a flannel bathrobe from the floor, turned his back to her and handed the robe in. "Miss, put this on and come out."

She spoke fast French, tears washing her face. He wished he understood what she was saying. She stepped out of the closet holding the robe around her.

He offered her his handkerchief and gestured to clothes on a chair near the bed. He assumed they were hers since they were folded. Dan's covered the floor.

"Get dressed and come out." He used sign language for this.

She nodded still trembling. Maybe she hadn't been in this country long. Eddie had said the Rosens managed to get refugees out of Europe. Did this poor girl think he was like the Gestapo?

He left the room for her to dress even though he really wanted to search it, wondering if he would find military uniforms. He had a feeling about Dan Wozniak. Maybe he was their man.

Dr. Kushner's list of characteristics sprang to mind. *The killer is fastidiously neat.* That didn't describe Dan Wozniak. Dr. K. had warned them that his template wasn't written in stone. *Mine is not an exact science.*

"Who's the young lady in your bedroom?" Jess asked Dan.

"Dominique. She works at the factory. It's best for both me and her if no one knows she's here."

Jess ignored this. "Are you her supervisor?"

"Yeah." Dan tilted his head, his eyes sizing Jess up. "I know that doesn't sound right, but these French dames are really something." He winked at Jess. "Hard to resist, know what I mean?"

Here was a young man who had too much power for his age. Certainly he'd abused his position, but was he their killer?

Dominique emerged from the bedroom dressed in a faded blouse and men's trousers, her arms folded over her chest. She let out a cry when she saw Dan handcuffed and tied to a chair. Jess blocked her from going to him, then showed her his badge.

She cradled it in her palm, her index finger tracing its words. "Justice," she said, pronouncing it *juice-tis,* sounding calmer. To Dan, she said something in French.

"What did she say?" Jess asked Dan.

"How should I know? I don't speak French."

Alonso drew Jess aside. "Why don't I drive the car closer? I'll bring in the fingerprint kit and my camera."

"Good idea." They were going to revisit all the victims' roommates and the workers at the dance hall downtown. Maybe one of them would remember Dan Wozniak from a photograph.

Jess took a small paper bag from his pocket. "I found a lipstick in his bathroom. Would you lock it in the trunk? I want the lab to check it for fingerprints."

"Is it azalea blossom?" Alonso whispered.

"It is."

Alonzo's face lifted. Jess read his mind. Maybe this was the break they'd been waiting for, the man they'd been looking for. And they owed finding him to Eddie.

While Alonso was gone, the telephone in the kitchen rang.

"That's the factory. I'm late for my shift." Dan nodded at Dominique. "So's she. Our watchman will come here to check on me."

Alonso returned and stood in front of Dan Wozniak with his camera. "Look up," Alonso told him.

Dan lifted his chin and Alonso snapped the picture, the dim room bathed in brightness.

"Hey, I didn't say you could do that."

34

Jess, Alonso, and Dan followed Dominique toward the gravel parking lot. Before them sat the factory, an immense two-story that hummed like a living thing.

Dominique went ahead, so she could punch in for her shift and take her place. When she almost reached the entrance, she ran back, threw her arm around Dan's neck, and pulled him down to her. With a quick kiss, she whispered something in his ear and hurried back.

"Dames," Dan said and wiped her kiss from his damp cheek.

Jess exchanged a wondering glance with Alonso. What was his appeal?

In Dan's bathroom, in addition to the pink lipstick, Jess had found bobby pins and a hair ribbon. Under his bed was a lace garter. Dan Wozniak appeared to be catnip to women, which didn't square with another of Dr. Kushner's descriptions. *This killer has difficulties with women, starting with his mother.*

The side of the factory nearest the road opened onto a loading dock. A man in overalls jumped from a truck, took hold of a strap, and closed its backdoor.

Jess and Alonso stopped in their tracks. The door's closing sounded like *soft thunder*, Vernon's description.

"Come," Jess said to Dan. The three walked over to the line of trucks and looked into the back of an empty one. The roomy inside was lined in gray canvas, floor, walls, and ceiling. Jess felt that tingling sensation and could tell Alonso was thinking what he was: the back of one of these could be the murder scene.

Jess wanted to search all of these trucks.

"You never seen a uniform truck before?" Dan asked and wedged a Lucky Strike in his mouth, produced a lighter, and flicked its flame at the cigarette's tip.

On the edge of the lot a gasoline pump shone in the sun. How convenient for Dan Wozniak. He could go anywhere he wanted with this setup.

On the other side of the gravel lot, in a stand of oaks, women sat at picnic tables, shucking corn, cutting vegetables. Others were setting fires in large stone grills.

When they passed, Dan greeted the women then said to Jess, "Since we're asking people to work on Sunday, we make it special by feeding everyone."

Dan struck Jess as an odd combination of maturity and adolescence.

"There's only one main entrance and exit," Dan said, "but the factory's lined with doors that open from the inside. Rose Clothing leads the way in fire safety."

Jess figured he'd said this because of the Triangle Shirtwaist Factory fire in New York at the turn of the century. More than a hundred young women, mostly recent Jewish and Italian immigrants, died because the owner had locked the exit doors.

With Dan between them, they stood at the window of a wire booth beside the entrance door. Inside the booth, a man with skin the color of milky tea got up from his desk. He had short graying hair, a smattering of brown freckles over a snub nose, and suspicion in his dark eyes.

"Good morning, Mr. Dan." The man offered a clipboard through the window. He'd been sewing buttons on a Navy pea coat. A silver thimble gleamed from his finger, incongruous with the man's muscular build. A brawny seamstress, but maybe all workers at Rose Clothing sewed.

"Morning, Abel. These two are with me." Dan tilted his head and handed the visitor sign-in to Jess. "From the Bureau of Investigation." Dan spoke as if they'd driven out here to ask for his help.

Abel's gaze slid over Jess and settled on Alonso, taking him in, one mulatto to another. Jess had seen this happen before. Their similar skin color gave them a common heritage. Alonso exchanged a look with the watchman that said: *I know about you, you know about me.*

Jess teased Alonso about being a member of the mulatto club, which had been an incredible help in catching the killer in New Orleans. In that city, more attention was paid to skin color than any place Jess had ever known.

They had come to check Dan's alibi against his time clock records and had agreed to take off his handcuffs so as not to put the workers in an uproar.

Last night Jess called Ray K. and asked him to look up the name and address of the woman Dan had been accused of assaulting, the one who'd refused to press charges. According to the police records, she worked here. They would question her.

They walked toward the noise of the shop floor.

Abel came out from his wire booth. Jess could feel the watchman's eyes on his back.

Rose Clothing had little in common with the southern cotton mills they'd known. It was a modern factory with white walls, a cement floor, and huge windows filled with sunlight. No lint clogged the air. Water stations were located in the room's corners, so workers could quench their thirst.

Yet it was still a factory in summer, noisy and warm with the fug of bodies at work, not that salty field hand smell, a lighter feminine blend of sweat, soap, and the delightful odor of new cloth. How Jess missed that smell. With rationing and making over old things, you seldom smelled new anything.

Women in kerchiefs, their heads bent, sat at row-upon-row of whirring sewing machines, their faces dewy with effort. Each pair of hands fed fabric beneath the machine's fast-moving needle, while a right foot kept time on the treadle. The machines going at once sounded like a squadron of air-planes advancing. On each machine was a pea coat like the one Abel had been working on.

Negro seamstresses filled the last row of sewing machines, as if this was a bus and they had to sit in back. Or had they wanted to sit with their own kind?

How easy would it be for Dan Wozniak to get his hands on a uniform? His closet and the armoire contained none. Still he could keep them in one of the trucks or in his office.

A quotation painted on the large expanse of wall the seamstresses faced read: *"Our powerful enemies must be out-fought and out-produced." President Roosevelt.* All the block letters were painted red, except for the word *produced* in blue. War posters of Rosie the Riveter along with no smoking signs decorated the other walls.

They passed tables of girls, silver thimbles on their fingers sewing buttons onto jackets. All these women wore their hair pulled back, faces bare of makeup, sleeves cut off, some in men's trousers. So different from the glamorous government girls in their sheer summer dresses and sandals.

None looked up as Jess, Alonso, and Dan passed.

Beyond the tables of women, older colored men operated pressing machines beside racks of revolving pea coats. Steam rose from the fabric when a man put the large press to cloth. How hot they must get in late afternoon when the temperature rose.

They climbed a metal staircase to a mezzanine overlooking the shop floor. "My office is on the other side." They followed Dan down a walkway past a large glass-walled office, MEYER ROSEN, President, painted on its door. From his office, you could see both sides of the factory floor.

Dan's office, next down, looked out on the back of the shop floor. Below men at large tables cut thick navy blue material. Beyond them more sewing machines, where women worked on sleeves or pockets. While Alonso searched Dan's office, Jess and Dan stood at the railing.

Dominique, head lowered, was among the women below. "Are those the workers you supervise?"

"Yeah. I started as a pattern cutter." Dan opened his right hand and showed Jess the scarred web between his thumb and index finger. "See my cutters badge."

Jess stared at Dan Wozniak's large rough hands, imagining them around a woman's neck. Yes, he could see that. He could imagine this man squeezing the life out of a young woman. What he couldn't imagine was Dan applying lipstick to a murdered girl or drawing those lines up her legs.

Jess returned to the moment. "I need to see your time cards since January. How often does Mr. Rosen work here?"

"Almost every day, when he's not going to meetings in the city with Senators or the President. He's an important man, you know." This said like a threat.

Eventually, Alonso knocked on the glass and gestured for them to come into the office. Standing over Wozniak's messy desk, Alonso handed Jess a matchbook from the Palace Royale Ballroom, the same kind Kaye Krieger had in her purse.

"Were you at the Palace Royale Ballroom on Sunday, May 24th?"

"I already told you." Dan pointed to the huge calendar on the wall. "That's a Sunday. I work Sundays." Belligerence in his voice. "And I never heard of the place. Whatever you think I did, you're wrong. Except to do some deliveries, I almost never leave here."

"So where did you get this matchbook?"

"Somebody must have given it to me." He reached in his pocket, pulled out his silver lighter, and held it up to them. "I always use this one my brother gave me unless it's low on lighter fluid. And if I have a free moment, I got better things to do than go to some dance place."

In the Personnel office off the main floor, Jess sat at a desk and went through Dan's time clock records. Just because he punched in and out ten hours later didn't mean he couldn't sneak away. He was a supervisor. And like he told them, all the doors opened from the inside.

This had been in Jess's mind on his way to Personnel. He opened one of the doors and in so doing, set off an alarm. Meaning Dan Wozniak could not leave undetected.

While Jess did this, Alonso was searching every truck in the lot for evidence.

Jess looked up at the personnel clerk, a matronly woman in her fifties, dressed like a waitress in a long white apron, eyeglasses hanging on a chain around her neck. "I also need to check that Velma Bonner still works here."

"She don't." The woman glared.

"Don't you need to check? There're a lot of workers here."

She thrust her big hip out and planted a palm on it. "Yeah, and I know 'em all. The Bonner woman left in April. Here one day, gone the next. Flighty."

Hurried footsteps sounded outside.

Dan came in, a young woman in pigtails, barely more than a girl, at his side. The girl's hand was wrapped in white cloth, blood seeping through. Her eyes shone with tears. She snuffled, but said nothing.

The matron sprang into action. "Set down here." She gestured to a chair next to a large industrial sink. So the personnel office doubled as a clinic.

The girl sat. The woman turned on the tap, took off the girl's makeshift bandage, and brought her hand under the water. The girl flinched when the water hit her cut, but made barely a snuffle.

Dan went to the tall medicine cabinet in the corner and brought out a roll of bandages and a bottle of mercurochrome. With his handkerchief, he dabbed the girl's runny nose. "You're a brave gal, Millie."

She gazed at Dan with adoration. He was the young man behind the window, the one who watched her work. That was Dan Wozniak's appeal. He was the man in power.

"Please, Mr. Dan. This is the first time I stitched my finger. Don't fire me."

"Millie, don't worry. Happens to all of us sometime."

Abel appeared. "Mr. Rosen wants to see you."

"All right," Dan said and was about to turn Millie over to the matron.

"No, not you, Mr. Dan. Mr. Rosen wants to speak to Special Agent Jessup Lindsay."

35

"What have you done?" Mr. Rosen asked Jess in his office. "Abel tells me he heard shots from Dan's. I gave you permission to search his cottage, not shoot at him!"

Jess sat and told the small gray-haired man behind the desk everything that had transpired this morning, except the name of the young woman he'd found in Dan's armoire.

During the telling, Mr. Rosen took off his spectacles, got up, and paced the room. "Is she one of the women he supervises?" Mr. Rosen hooked his thumbs in his braces and gazed out his window at the shop floor, his back to Jess.

Jess was determined to protect Dominique and said nothing. "She isn't involved in our investigation, so I don't want to get her in trouble."

Mr. Rosen swiveled, his brow pleated. "But you insist on locking up my hardest worker. This place won't run well without Danny." He gestured to the shop floor.

Jess followed his gaze. Dan was sitting at a sewing machine most likely taking Millie's place.

"Agent Lindsay, I answer to the War Production Board. Since our first uniform order, we've always met quota. Please don't throw a wrench in it for this month." He slumped into the chair beside Jess and lowered his voice.

"I know Dan is immature, especially when it comes to women. But he's devoted to our work here."

Did Mr. Rosen know about Dan's arrest for assault in April?

"My partner and I are investigating the government girl murders. Five girls have been found murdered since January."

Mr. Rosen covered his mouth. "I've read about these murders. They're terrible, terrible." He rotated in his chair, went to the window, and looked out at Dan. "But you couldn't suspect Dan, no." He turned and gazed at Jess. "Danny couldn't murder anyone. I've known the boy almost all his life. His mother was a widow working in our New Jersey factory when she died of influenza." Jess nodded. "His brother was old enough to join the military, but poor little Danny was only twelve and about to be sent to an orphanage when we took him in."

Jess had heard this from suspects' relatives. This child they loved could not have done what he was accused of.

"Dan shot at my partner and pumped his shotgun as if he was going to shoot me even after I identified myself." Dan was violent.

Still they had no physical evidence connecting Dan Wozniak to the murders. Even the lipstick, Kaye Krieger's shade, found in his medicine cabinet didn't prove anything yet. According to the lady at the People's cosmetics counter, the shade was popular, "our best seller."

Mr. Rosen shook his head. "He can be rash, I don't deny it." The two men looked at each other. "What if I give you my pledge Dan won't leave this property? I'll move him into our house, and he won't be allowed to drive any of the vehicles anywhere."

Jess gazed out the window. "I'll have to talk to my partner about this." If Alonso found anything in the trucks that tied Dan to the murders, Dan was going to jail.

But Alonso had found nothing in the trucks. So in the end, they agreed to let Dan stay at the factory and told him so in Mr. Rosen's office. "First we need to fingerprint you."

Dan's face darkened, but he gave a quick nod and sat in front of Mr. Rosen's desk.

Jess got the fingerprint kit out of his carryall. Alonso took Dan's right hand and pressed one fingertip at a time into ink and onto the card.

"You're wrong about me." Dan turned his head toward Jess. "I'm not perfect, but I sure as hell haven't..."

"Quiet, Danny." Mr. Rosen had paled so that a network of blue veins was visible in his temples. He took hold of the corner of the desk as if to steady himself.

Fingerprinting always drove home they meant business. They were looking for a killer and this man might be the one.

Abel knocked at the door. Mr. Rosen motioned for him to come in. Dan reddened as the other man entered and stood by the door. Mr. Rosen said, "I know we can count on you, Abel, to be discreet."

"Yes, Sir." Abel's face showed no emotion as if he witnessed a supervisor getting fingerprinted every day.

"Abel must call us every morning at seven with a report on Dan's whereabouts." Jess handed the watchman the card with their home number on it. "If we don't get a call from Abel, if we find Dan has left this property, we'll be out here to pick him up with the DC police. And the press will probably get hold of it." He looked from Dan to his employer.

"Agreed," Mr. Rosen said, nodded to Abel, and turned to Dan, who gave a meek nod, his sullenness gone.

Mr. Rosen walked them to the door. "You're welcome to have some dinner before you drive back to the city. Our picnic is ready under the trees, fresh corn, tomatoes, hamburgers and baked beans."

"That's kind of you, Sir, but we'll be getting on." Director Hoover had strict rules about accepting even as much as a cup of coffee while working. "And I need to look at one more time clock record."

"I'll phone down to Estelle, who's in the front booth now. She'll give you anything you need." Mr. Rosen offered his hand, and Jess shook it.

Jess felt sorry for Meyer Rosen. Even if Dan Wozniak wasn't their killer, he would eventually disappoint this man who'd invested his affection in him.

On their way out, Jess told Alonso about how he'd set off an alarm when he opened an exit door. They walked to the door under the metal staircase, almost hidden from view. When Dan sneaked out, and Jess was sure he did, this had to be the door he used.

Alonso lifted his index finger. Jess halted. Beside the exit was a trash barrel. Alonso reached behind the barrel and pulled out a small thin square of wood. He slipped the wood between the door's lock and frame and opened the door. No alarm sounded.

Jess said, "Handy piece of wood."

"I bet there's one hidden beside every door. See all the NO SMOKING signs?" Alonso pointed to the back of the building. "Workers aren't allowed to smoke in the building. So they have to go outside to those metal containers of sand."

Estelle, the woman from Personnel, was waiting for them inside the wire booth. She got up and came to its window.

Jess told her, "I need Dan Wozniak's time clock record for today."

She narrowed her eyes at him, walked out of the booth, and to the wall where the time sheets were filed in a metal rack on the wall.

She handed Jess the sheet. He read it and said, "I need a Photostat of this."

She huffed, went back into her booth, to the machine in the corner, and made the copy while Jess and Alonso watched.

"Don't seem right that a stranger from Washington can come in here and take whatever he wants," she said and handed the copy through the window.

Jess almost laughed at being accused of "being from Washington," but he took the copy, folded it one-handed, stuck it in his pocket, and walked out, Alonso behind him.

Smoke from the grills drifted across the parking lot. "Those hamburgers sure smell good."

Jess smiled and handed him a stick of gum.

They walked past picnic tables, where workers sat eating dinner. The leafy maples and oaks cast long shadows now.

Alonso asked, "Did his time clock records back up his alibi?"

"Yeah, but I doubt their accuracy. For instance, his time clock for today shows he has been working nonstop since 7:00 this morning."

"And that's odd," Alonso said, "since he was shooting at us from his porch around 8:10."

36

Voices were raised downstairs. Thad and Rachel were arguing.

"Uh-oh," Pearl said from across the room, where she lay propped on a pillow against the bed's headboard, flipping through a movie magazine. "Rachel doesn't know how to treat a man good."

"And you do?" Eddie stood at the window, ironing a blouse, her gaze on Jess's bungalow.

Jess and Alonso had left early this morning for the Rosen's. As the day progressed, dread crept up her spine. What was keeping them? No telling how Dan Wozniak would act when they turned up to question him. She had accused Pearl of sending them into harm, but what if she had done the same?

"I sure nuff do know." Pearl's smile went wide and satisfied. "I could teach you a thing or two about what men like."

"Stop being crude, Pearl. Continue those elocution exercises your instructor gave you."

Eddie needed to study her German for the Bureau's test tomorrow. Jess was taking her to dinner tonight at the China Doll, so she ought to study before he got home. But she was too worried about him to focus.

The weather was tense as well. All day a storm had been building. The rotating fan stirred the room's humid air but brought little relief.

"War Department," Pearl called out. "How may I direct yer call?"

"Your," Eddie corrected for the umpteenth time. "How may I direct your call?"

Pearl grimaced in the dressing table mirror. "Yo-or. How may I direct yo-or call?"

Rachel had trimmed Pearl's hair and given her bangs, which hid her bloody scalp, and her lip wasn't as swollen. She needed to look presentable enough to go to work tomorrow. If she didn't go, she might get fired.

Eddie said, "*Ubung macht den meister.* Practice makes perfect."

Fast footsteps on the stairs. Rachel stomped in. "Thad's being a jerk. He said he wouldn't be seen with me if I didn't wash the lines off the back of my legs. He said they look cheap."

"And I did a perfect job drawing 'em on." Pearl got up from the bed.

Eddie turned off the iron. "I'll wet a washrag to clean them off." She didn't say so, but she agreed with Thad. Lines up the backs of a girl's legs were meant to look as if she was wearing seamed hose, but they fooled no one and looked tacky.

In the bathroom, she reached for the faucet, when a hinge creaked out back. It was what she'd been waiting for all afternoon: the sound of Jess's door. She rushed to the tiny window and scanned the backyard.

Beneath a low plum-colored sky, a man stepped into the bungalow, a man who was not Jess or Alonso.

She rushed downstairs, through the empty house. Sunday afternoons, Bert took his mother to the movies. On the back porch, she slowed, closing the screen door behind her without a noise. Her bare feet moved silently down the stone path, her heart knocking against the cage of her chest.

Before she got to Jess's door, she heard papers being rustled.

She opened the door. "Get out of here," she shouted. "Now!"

The man rounded on her. Thad! Except for his tangle of curly hair, Thad was all angles, knife creases in his white linen suit, his shirt stiff with starch. A buttery tie rounded out his perfection. Rarely had she seen a man so well turned-out in this rumpled city.

Backlit by the window, he moved toward her.

She sensed menace and retreated. She could run back to the house, but that wouldn't stop him from going through Jess's things.

Outside, she stepped sideways onto the patch of lawn, grass prickly under her soles. She grabbed a hoe propped against the bungalow. The wooden handle's familiar feel comforted her.

Raising it like a weapon, she went back in the bungalow. "Out Thad!"

He had gone back to the desk and was reading the book she'd picked up for Jess from the library about sleepwalking.

"You and your garden tool don't scare me, Eddie." He didn't even look around.

"*Das ist nicht dein bier!*" she shouted this was none of his business and sent the hoe's sharp end down on Jess's desk, really a scarred table that she'd given one more scar. Whack!

Thad leapt away, tossing the book down. "Watch out. You could've hit me."

"If you don't get out of here, Thad, I'm going to pretend your curly mop is a patch of weeds and bury this hoe deep in your brain."

He faced her. "Your violence surprises me, Eddie." He walked to the door. "And you speak German like a female Hitler." He motioned at the door. "Ladies, first."

"Oh, no." She wanted to stay behind him. "Snoops before ladies, Thad."

"Eddie, you got the wrong idea about me." Still, he walked onto the path toward the back door. She followed. "I was looking for Jess," he said. "I need to speak to him about work."

"Stop imitating my mountain accent." Thad was a chameleon who could change colors to suit his audience. He might fool everyone else, but not her. At the back door, she almost left the hoe beside the steps, but changed her mind.

Thad stood on the porch, looking out the screen. "I'm curious about why he keeps that room over the garage padlocked."

"I'm curious about why you're curious. Keep moving, Thad. Don't stop until you're sitting on the sofa in the parlor, where you belong."

"You sound like the police, Eddie." Thad gave a hearty laugh, but obeyed.

"Something tells me you've had direct experience with the law." She was guessing.

"Of course I have, Eddie. The police are my friends. Remember I'm a crime reporter."

"What better person for that job than a criminal." Her confrontation with him had emboldened her. The back of his neck above his collar had turned beet red.

Sensing she'd hit a nerve, she wanted to see his face. But instead she saw her own in the mirror over the sink, still holding the hoe like an idiot. She left it in the pantry and followed him through the house.

When they faced each other in the parlor, she said, "So you made Rachel wash those lines off her legs, so you could sneak into Jess's."

"I find the heavy makeup *some* government girls wear disgusting, Eddie." Thad sounded outraged. "I suspect you feel as I do." He knew how to appeal to her. "Rachel's lucky to have you as a friend, but that other gal ya'll live with, the one who drew those lines on my lady, is white trash. Ya'll ought not associate with her."

"Who are you to judge Pearl or anyone else, Thad?" And who was she to accuse anyone of being judgmental? "I'm afraid you're using Rachel to get into this house, so that you can spy on Jess. Anything for a story, right?"

He folded his hands and sent her a look so meek she wondered how she could have found him threatening. "Eddie, I truly care about Rachel. She's beautiful, sweet, and…" he voice lowered, "right behind you."

"What's going on?" Rachel glanced from Eddie to Thad and back. "Looks like Eddie's giving you one of her lectures, which you deserve, Thad." Dimples creased her face. "I know why you made me clean off my leg makeup. You were afraid I might brush against you and smudge your white suit."

"I am a dandy." Thad straightened his perfectly straight tie. "I admit it. But I need to be to go out with someone as lovely as you, Miss Margolis." This, he spoke in his honeyed southern accent.

She giggled. "Stop, Thad. You're making me blush."

He offered her his arm, and she took it. "We're off to the Uptown to see *Laura.*" They walked to the door. He turned them to face Eddie. "How do we look?"

Rachel was wearing Eddie's white shirtwaist, a little long on her. She always wore clothes too big for her when she went out with Thad. Maybe she knew this appealed to Thad, a member of the morality police. Eddie counted herself as a member, too. She had been unable to leave her prudishness in Saltville.

They were waiting for her to say something. "You look like movie stars."

Rachel said, "That's good, since the theater owner asked us to come back this week and get our photo made standing in front of their ticket booth. Remember I told you?"

Eddie nodded. "I understand why he chose you two." They were a beautiful couple all in white as if they were going to be married.

"We're getting free movie tickets," Thad said. "Why don't you come with us?"

"Please," Rachel said. "You've been moping by the window all day."

From the alley, a car horn. Alonso often tooted to "his men" when they arrived back. Eddie wanted to run out there.

"Never mind," Thad said to Rachel. "I see on her face Jess Lindsay's come home."

On Monday, June 12th, Eddie pushed through the Justice Department's immense steel doors. Standing in the lobby, she lifted her face to the soaring ceiling and took in the art deco sconces.

"I have an appointment with Mr. Bauer," she told the man at security. When she showed him her Department of the Army Identification card, she noticed her hand shaking.

Last night over dinner Jess admitted he didn't know any translators at the Bureau who were women. If she got the job, she'd be the first.

"But times are changing," Jess had told her. "I showed Kurt the translation you did for me, and he was impressed."

The guard checked a list, found Eddie's name, and sent her to the third floor.

Eddie took the stairs, came to a hallway, and looked for room 309. At first, she passed the door because it was open. She backtracked and stood outside.

A heavyset young man with short blond hair sat behind a messy desk.

His head was bent, an egg sandwich in one hand, his eyes on what he was reading.

How did she know the sandwich was egg? The white peeked out between two slices of dark bread. Just as he lifted the sandwich to his mouth and took a bite, he noticed her, chewed, and swallowed too fast. He started to cough.

She stepped into his cramped office, came around the desk, and thumped him on the back.

"Miss, Miss!" He got out these words between coughs. "Thanks, thanks a lot, but you can't be on this floor. Restricted." He pointed to the sign in the hall. "See."

Embarrassed, Eddie went back in the hall. "But I was told to come here. I'm Eddie Smith, Mr. Bauer."

This time, he almost spewed his coffee. "Eddie? But I thought…"

"That I was a man?" She smiled. Obviously Jess had neglected to tell him her gender.

Kurt grinned, his cheek smeared with yolk. "I did, but hey Eddie, I have your security clearance right here from the Department of the Army." He thumped a file. "Would you mind waiting in the hall while I dress?"

She nodded, stepped out, and shut the door. What was he wearing behind his desk? She had acted so quickly she couldn't recall.

"You may come in now," he said.

She opened the door to find him in a shirt so wrinkled he must have picked it up from the floor.

"Please have a seat." He gestured to a folding chair.

She positioned it in front of him. His office was so small that her chair's legs were partly out in the hall.

The tiny space smelled of sweat and fried Spam, a smell she'd come to loathe. She noticed a hot plate on top of a filing cabinet and hoped he didn't cook in here.

"Don't worry," he said. "I'll get you a desk in the basement, where it's cooler."

"*Ich bin nicht besorgt*," she answered, feeling as if she was in class, showing off. Not that her accent was good. Her German professor told her she might pass for a German butcher's daughter and blamed her crude accent on her Appalachian roots.

"*Gut*, Eddie. *Sie sind der Deutsch abstieg?*"

He wanted to know if her family was originally German, and she told him in German about her great-grandmother.

They exchanged more conversation in German. Would she be speaking German if she got the job here?

"Your translation of this article by Ernst Gennat was impressive. Jess has already acted on it, getting himself a Dr. Freud."

"Thanks, Mr. Bauer." She wouldn't comment on Jess's investigation, which was secret, too.

"Please call me Kurt. I feel like I've aged thirty years since this war started, but I'm only twenty-eight." He got up from behind his desk for the first time. Eddie was relieved to see he wore trousers. Ironic that she'd worried about what to wear for her interview.

"So you are willing to leave the Department of the Army and work for us?" he said.

"Yes. I'd love to use my German." She offered him her hand.

"Welcome aboard, Miss Smith."

37

How quickly life could change in Washington. In a matter of days, Eddie had been hired by the Justice Department and sent for training at the Pentagon. Now she had her own office, if you could call it that, since it was no bigger than a broom closet.

On her desk were letters written in German she'd been assigned to translate into English. The writers, German Americans, wrote in their native language and may have been members of the German American Bund, a pro-Nazi group.

Before the Japanese bombed Pearl Harbor, pro-Nazi and anti-war groups flourished in the US. One of their rallies had filled Madison Square Garden, but after war was declared, these groups went underground. Part of Eddie's training had been to learn about them.

Someone higher up had determined these letters needed further scrutiny. Before Eddie got them, the letters had already gone through several processes to determine if they contained hidden messages. The paper had been scuffed and a special ink applied to look for invisible text.

She was supposed to use a small knife to cut out certain words or phrases that might pass on information important to the war effort. She'd been trained to look for phrases about the weather, a message to be given to a third party, criticism of any government, including complaining about rationing, which everyone did.

She read each letter at least five times, always using her German-English dictionary. She was scrupulous. Sometimes she cut out so much that when she finished, the letter fell apart. She had to glue a letter like that to another sheet of paper. She knew she was overzealous, but she vowed never to let anything slip through that might harm the Allies.

If the Axis powers conquered Great Britain, they would cross the Atlantic and bring the fight here. U-boats had been sighted off the eastern seaboard. And if the Nazis did invade, some of these German Americans would act as a fifth column, rise up, and help the enemy fight this country.

So she worked as if was a matter of life or death, because it was.

Kurt told her that once her security clearance was increased, she would be given letters from prisoners-of-war, mostly German seamen incarcerated at Fort Lincoln, North Dakota. They were allowed to write and send mail according to the Geneva Convention's rules.

"But could sailors locked up since before we entered the war have anything valuable to pass on?" she asked him yesterday after a translators meeting.

Kurt nodded. "Remember many are Nazi supporters. And the most devious at Fort Lincoln are the German nationals from South America that we rounded up."

Some South American countries like Argentina were friendly with the Nazis. President Roosevelt had assigned the entire Western Hemisphere to the Bureau in terms of tracking agents who hoped to carry out subversion, espionage, or sabotage. She was excited about being a small part of this offensive.

In addition to the letters, she also translated German magazines and newspapers smuggled out of Germany or occupied Europe. When she handled a copy of *Das Schwarze Korps,* the Black Corps, published by the SS, or *Ausland,* she sent out a prayer for the person who managed to smuggle it out. After she translated, she analyzed their system of lies, searching for any germ of truth. Often there was none. Truth was not important to Nazi Germany.

And all of this propaganda was virulently anti-Semitic. It made her sick.

How could anyone believe such disgusting lies? Rachel didn't know the half of it, nor would Eddie tell her. Her job really was secret and challenging. No more *blauer Montags,* blue Mondays.

She'd had no problem writing her Saltville High School principal that she wouldn't return to teach in the fall. Yet she put off telling her father. Mama had just come home from the asylum, which meant a period of adjustment for everyone. A time when the family wanted to believe she was all well again and would stay that way.

Eddie would wait until things settled down for them to write. And she was counting the days until she turned 21 on September 7th. After that her father had no legal hold over her.

That evening, she worked late, finishing her stack of letters. After she dropped them with Kurt, she ran for the streetcar and barely made it.

"Eddie," Jess called and signaled to the seat beside him. Her eyes dove into his.

"How are your blisters?" He took her hand and looked at her palm.

She'd gotten blisters from the weeding they'd done Sunday afternoon. She had never seen Jess as nervous as he had been that last Sunday in June. He weeded until dark, waiting for a telephone call that mercifully never came.

"They'll heal," she said.

He leaned toward her, and she filled up with his Jess smell, Old Spice, spearmint gum, and him. "Thank you for weeding with me," he said, "for sharing my anxiety, my fear."

"Jess, I would weed acres for you."

He brought his arm around her shoulder. "Oh Eddie, I…I"

She saw the word forming on his pink pebbly tongue and she wanted to capture it before he released it into the air. She brought her face to his and kissed him just as the streetcar jerked to a stop at 7th and G.

A woman sitting behind them said, "These government girls are wild as March hares."

This made Eddie laugh. They broke apart, red-faced and laughing.

They were on the long stretch between 7th and Florida Avenue when she whispered, "Two days have passed. Maybe *he's* stopped."

Because she worked for the Bureau now and had a security clearance, Jess had become freer with information about his case almost as if she was working on it with him. Last night he allowed her to read all his notes and study their case map.

"Or we just haven't found her body yet."

"It's for sure he's still out there. Is it possible he's changing his pattern?"

"Maybe or maybe he's not able to get out and kill this time." He spoke in a low voice so those around them couldn't hear.

She understood what he meant. "Dan?" Jess gave a quick nod and stood, holding to the pole above him. She moved down the car's aisle behind him.

Once they got off and waited to cross Georgia Avenue, she said, "But I believe the killer has to be charming to get a woman to go with him. And that doesn't fit Dan Wozniak. He couldn't charm a government girl."

"You mean he doesn't charm you, Eddie. But you're not the typical government girl." Jess's eyes brightened at this. "Is Pearl attracted to Dan?"

Eddie recalled the night they arrived, how Pearl had flirted with Dan. "Yes."

38

Tuesday, July 4, 1944

"So you only got one arm, and he's a colored fella, and both you work for that strange Mr. Hoover?" Velma Bonner had a raspy smoker's voice. Bringing her chipped coffee cup to her mouth, she downed the dark liquid. A dribble remained in the corner of her mouth after she set her cup on the table.

She was round-shouldered and looked worn-out or hung-over. The smell of alcohol wafted from her like perfume. She must have tied one on last night.

"Yes, Ma'am." Alonso pinched off an end of the fresh baked bread they'd just bought that sat warm and fragrant in a brown paper bag between them. They'd left Georgia Avenue early with the idea of stopping somewhere for breakfast, but hadn't found any place open.

Jess squinted at his brother. Sounded like Al was agreeing that their director was strange.

They sat at a small picnic table outside Velma Bonner's work place, a bakery on Lee Highway in Arlington, Virginia. It was almost eight in the morning. Overhead, two squirrels ran along a pine branch, bark crunching beneath them.

Miss Bonner tugged off her hairnet, her dull brown hair threaded with gray coming loose from its pins. "I know what you're thinking, Agent

Lindsay. What was handsome Dan doing in a hotel with this old gal." She rotated from the tabletop, dropped her head, and ran her fingers through her hair. Flour sifted from it like dandruff.

"No, Miss Bonner. Not at all." That was exactly what he'd been thinking, not that he saw Dan Wozniak as a matinee idol.

They had been tracing Velma Bonner's whereabouts for weeks. She changed addresses the way other women changed clothes.

"It's Mrs. Bonner. Corporal Vincent Bonner is in the US Marine Corps. Haven't heard from Vince since he shipped out for the Pacific in '42. If you ask me, them little Japs are tougher than the Heinies."

Jess gave an understanding smile. What else could he do? He needed rapport with this woman. "Please tell us about that night in April at the Roger Smith Hotel when you were with Dan Wozniak, Mrs. Bonner."

"Well, sure, long as I don't get Dan in trouble." She lifted her face, sun and shadow dappling her head and shoulders. "The Roger Smith is the nicest hotel I ever been to. It was real sweet of Danny to get us a room there. We was having a gas until the hooch got us. Brought our own since places like that'll charge you an arm and a leg for a cocktail."

She opened her compact on the table, tucked her head, and rearranged her hair, poking bobby pins in here and there.

In the morning light, he could see she was a good ten years older than Dan.

"I told them police I didn't want to press charges. Danny's done right by me ever since." Now she applied red lipstick and pressed her lips together.

So she was paid off.

Alonso set his briefcase on the table, opened it, and handed Jess the copy of Dan Wozniak's arrest record.

"The police report says a hotel guest heard a woman screaming." He looked into Velma Bonner's bloodshot eyes. "And called the front desk clerk, who sent a security guard to your room. When no one opened the door, he unlocked it and found you, Mrs. Bonner, on the floor with Daniel Wozniak straddling you." The report said both were naked, but Jess saw no reason to mention that. "Mr. Wozniak had a belt wrapped around your neck and didn't stop choking you until he was pulled off."

"Well, yeah, that's their version." She took a Camel from the pocket of her floury apron, struck a kitchen match against the bottom of the table, lit the cigarette, and inhaled, her nostrils flaring. She took smoke deep into her lungs.

He sighed. Some witnesses craved attention and loved to be questioned, in fact, tried to prolong their questioning, so they could soak up as much attention as possible. She was one of these. "So, Mrs. Bonner, tell us your version. Please."

"Look here, fellas, Danny and me was both drunk as coots." She extended the end of her pink tongue and picked shreds of tobacco off it. "When you know somebody real good, you know just how to get to him. I knew what to say to hurt Danny. See, he was trying to tell me it was over between us."

"That must have hurt your feelings. How long had you been together?"

"I never kidded myself about a handsome young buck like Dan. We wasn't really together. For a few months, I'd been slipping over to his place after my shift ended and he'd let me in, if you know what I mean." She gave Jess a coy glance.

"So Dan Wozniak was your supervisor?"

"Yeah, and the night in that fancy hotel, when he told me not to come 'round no more, he said he was going to transfer me to another department. But I'd had it with sewing uniforms, with old man Rosen always trying to get us to make more and more, faster and faster." Her lazy smoke ring drifted upward.

"So what did you say to Dan that got him so upset?"

"Called him a yellow-bellied coward." She laughed and flicked ash in the grass. "Told him he ought to be in the service like my Vince, instead of making uniforms, which was women's work...."

Jess recalled a line from Dr. Kushner's template: *The killer may feel deep guilt about not being in the military and, hence, he dresses in uniforms and pretends.*

"So that's when he started choking you?"

"Yep." She nodded. "I told you I had a mean streak."

"Mean streak or not, Dan Wozniak could have killed you, Mrs. Bonner. Why didn't you press charges?"

"See the police took me back to the house I shared with some other gals from Rose Clothing. God almighty, I was sick of being stuck way out in Maryland on that farm. If I'd wanted to live like that, I'd a stayed in Missoura." She leaned over and stubbed out her cigarette in the grass. "Anyhow, Abel came to me straight away that morning and offered me a place to live in the city and a hundred dollars if I'd forget about what happened at the Roger Smith." She shrugged. "So I called the police and told 'em to forget it, packed up, and moved down on H Street into my very own apartment. Beautiful little place."

Jess wondered why she'd left such a beautiful place, but asked, "Was Mr. Rosen behind this offer?" If so, he must know Dan had been arrested for assault.

"Maybe. I mean where would Abel get a hundred dollars? But Danny has money to burn, so it could of been his own money. He wouldn't like Mr. Rosen finding out. Oh, no, Danny's that old man's fair-haired boy."

"What shift did you and Dan work?"

"Seems like he was working all the time, but I was nights. Come on about 6:00 and work nine hours with breaks."

Jess straightened. "Did Dan ever disappear from work when he was supposed to be there?"

Pausing she crossed her arms over her chest, leaned back, and pursed her lips into a thin line. "Why you asking me all this? Exactly what do you think Dan has done?"

"We aren't sure what he's done. That's why we're asking you."

She tilted her head. "Okay, yeah. A lot of nights he went somewhere. If things were going smooth on the floor, he'd slip away, but who could blame him? He was working all the hours there was. He's a young fella. Who could blame him?"

"And when he left, he didn't clock out?"

"Why should he? It's not like any of us was going to tattle on him to Mr. Big, who isn't there at midnight. Oh, no, Mr. Big's tucked up in his comfy bed, isn't he?"

"Did Dan ever tell you where he went?"

"I teased him a little. Knew he had somebody on the side, probably several some bodies." She giggled. "He's a young man, with needs, if you know what I mean." At this, she winked.

Jess kept a straight face. "Did you ever see him leave? How he was dressed when he left?"

She shook her head and raised her palm to a large man with a handlebar moustache, standing in the bakery's doorway. The place did a steady business, customers coming in from the neighboring streets ever since they sat down.

"Gotta get back to work."

"One more thing. Did Dan ever say anything in general about government girls?"

"Oh, yeah." She laughed, got up, and smoothed out her skirt. "I reckon he got turned down by one. Said they was stuck up, snooty. Said he hated their guts, but I knew better."

"Well, June has come and gone, and he didn't kill again," Ray K. said. "You suppose he's shipped out or gone dormant or what?"

Jess and Alonso sat around Ray K.'s disaster of a desk, eating the honey donuts Velma Bonner had sold them from the bakery. They ate over their cups of coffee, so as not to waste any sweet crumbs.

Jess said, "Or we just haven't found her body yet." Nine days had passed since the last Sunday of the month.

They were going through missing reports of government girls with Ray. K.

Since Sunday, June 25th, they'd been on high alert. Every time the telephone rang, they were certain it was the summons to another girl's body. The 4th was truly Independence Day since Fred had insisted they take the afternoon off and come to his neighborhood picnic.

Alonso cleared his throat. "There's another way to look at this."

Ray K. spread his greasy fingers and licked each one. "Go 'head, Al."

Alonso sighed. "A chief suspect has almost been under house arrest for the last weeks."

"The guy out at Rose Clothing?" Ray K. swiveled in his chair and pointed to Dan Wozniak's photo thumb-tacked to his bulletin board along with a map of the area marked with the sites, where the bodies had been found.

"Right," Alonso said. "He couldn't get out to do what he's done before."

"Right," Ray K. said. "Too bad that tube of lipstick didn't have the Arlington Cemetery's girl's fingerprints on it."

"Kaye Krieger," Jess said. He disliked the way Ray K. always referred to the murdered women by the places their bodies were found. It dehumanized them. Jess repeated their names often to honor them. Catching their killer, of course, would honor them more.

Jess rose out of his slump. "Dan Wozniak is violent. I don't deny it, but I don't think he's our killer. The man we're looking for is someone women trust. Factory women are attracted to Dan, but I'm not sure government girls would be." Eddie had said this first, and he'd come to believe it.

"So the Rosies swoon for him?" Ray K. grinned.

"They're attracted to him because he's in a position of authority over them and because there aren't many men in their world."

"He tried to kill us." Alonso's voice rose. "He got fresh with Miss Margolis and tried to strangle her when she rebuffed him. He was strangling Velma Bonner until the hotel security man pulled him off her. He has a vehicle, access to military uniforms, and a prescription for barbiturates. We just need to tie him to one of the murders."

"I'm with you, Al. He's our prime suspect." Ray K. rubbed his hands with his handkerchief. "At last I see daylight between you two. I've been waiting for some disagreement."

39

Wednesday, July 5, 1944

Eddie stepped onto the back porch. Gray light in the eastern sky was replaced by a band of pink stretching across the horizon. Birdsong filled the air.

She ran to Jess's bungalow the garden rising high and shadowy around her crowding the path. Leaves brushed her skin. Movement in the green startled her. She flinched and looked around. It was just the chubby scarecrow, his empty shirt sleeves flapping in the breeze.

"Jess." She banged on his door.

Beyond the screen all was silent and still.

With his face rumpled with sleep, Jess appeared on the other side of the door. He wore only his pajama bottoms. How boyish he looked.

She swallowed hard. "Sorry to wake you, but Pearl never came home last night. We're worried. What should we do?"

Jess lowered his gaze to his pale stump. She knew he was concerned about her seeing him shirtless for the first time.

"I've got a bad feeling about her, Jess. Pearl always comes home, always."

He combed fingers through his thick hair. "Maybe she went to the room over the garage like she did the time she got beaten up. Wait for me, and we'll check."

Jess had let Eddie know that the room over the garage was off limits to everyone, including her. She could go up there only when Jess was with her. It seems Alonso had a policy of never being alone with a white woman. "It's part of his code," Jess explained.

Eddie didn't understand this code. In Saltville a Negro church abutted their property, and its preacher was one of their neighbors. Not that coloreds and whites socialized. Folks kept to themselves, but were neighborly.

Jess went into the tiny bathroom. She heard water running. He emerged in trousers and a shirt half buttoned. Slipping into shoes, he stepped out.

"Breakfast." Eddie showed him the basket she'd filled with ripe strawberries collected while she waited for him. She set the basket on the grass off the path.

He took her hand and kissed her palm. "You smell delicious," he said, and they hurried to the garage.

After Pearl broke in, Alonso put a padlock on the door, but the padlock hung open now. They clambered up the stairs. The place was dark, except for the red light behind the curtain where Alonso was developing negatives. No one else was here.

"Alonso, it's me," Jess called.

"Just drying some prints," Alonso called. "Be there in a minute."

Her eyes were drawn to the back wall, where Dr. Kushner's template had been posted. She didn't believe his guess work belonged with the facts of the case.

Okay, she resented the doctor, sight unseen. Because of her mother, she resented the whole field of psychiatry, more voodoo than science. And when she read Dr. Kushner's list, a person came to mind, a person who could not possibly be the killer. She resented that most of all.

Alonso, shirtless in overalls, appeared from behind the heavy curtain, small tongs in his hands.

"Have you seen Pearl?" Jess asked.

Alonso swallowed. "Forgot to tell you. I caught her up here yesterday." He gave Jess a pointed look. "It was my own fault. I was changing the Packard's oil and finishing up some developing at the same time. I didn't want to keep opening the padlock, so I left the door unlocked."

Pearl must have been watching for him to leave.

"What was she doing in here?" Eddie asked.

"Said she wanted me to take a photograph of her in her new hat, but I suspect there was more to it. She'd been writing something on a piece of paper."

"Pearl rarely picks up a pen," Eddie said. It sounded like she was spying, but why?

"Did you see where she went from here?" Jess asked.

"After I followed her downstairs, she took the alley toward Florida Avenue. Said she was meeting friends at Glen Echo Park in Maryland."

Eddie nodded with her whole body. "Yes. She was meeting her boy friend, Luca, out there, probably Tony, too."

"Maybe she went home with Luca?" Jess said.

"I doubt it. Pearl has work today. Luca doesn't have a telephone, so Rachel's waiting for the factory to open so she can call and find out."

"Ya'll don't have to wait." Alonso wiped his hands on a rag. "That plant runs on shifts. It never closes."

Eddie and Jess left for the house, as the sun broke over the houses on Georgia Avenue, turning the rooftops golden. The garden swayed in the breeze, not the least bit sinister in sunlight.

"Did you know Clarence is missing?" She stooped to pick up the straw-berries she'd picked. "Funny how I hated his crowing but now that he no longer crows, I miss him."

"Last night, Mrs. Friedlander told those of us sitting at the picnic table that Clarence had run away. I don't know how long she's been keeping chickens, but they don't wander off like cows."

The Friedlanders had a large Fourth of July picnic in their backyard and invited the entire neighborhood, white and colored. Everyone brought dishes to share. Agent Friedlander cooked wieners and sauerkraut on a big grill. According to Ruth, the Friedlanders' celebration was a neighborhood tradition.

In the kitchen, Bert stood at the sink washing his hands. "I put on coffee for everyone."

Alonso came in, having stopped at the bungalow to change into work clothes.

Rachel sat at the yellow Formica table going through the phone book. "This book's for Washington, but the factory is in Maryland. Their listing might not be in here." She sounded cranky. She'd awakened at 3:30, found Pearl not in the bed beside her, and hadn't been able to get back to sleep.

"We'll call the operator and get the number." Bert's voice was soothing.

Jess told them they ought to call now before night shift workers got off.

Rachel went to the telephone, Bert and Eddie in her wake. "Take the pot off once it starts percolating," Bert called.

The three stood around the telephone table in the narrow hall.

Once Rachel got the number from the operator, she dialed. "May I speak to Luca Marinelli?" She wrapped the telephone cord around her hand. "This is an emergency. My name? My name is Rachel Margolis, and I'm related to Mr. Rosen. Bring Luca Marinelli to the phone, please."

While they waited, Rachel, the telephone receiver wedged between her shoulder and cheek, snapped and unsnapped her locket. Bert cleaned his nails with his pocket knife, and Eddie tried to ward off evil thoughts about Pearl, who had them stirred up as usual.

"Luca. Hello, this is Rachel, Pearl's roommate. Pearl didn't come home last night and we wondered if…" Her knuckles tightened on the telephone receiver. "Listen Luca, you…" She held the receiver away from her face. "He hung up on me. Said he didn't know or care what happened to Pearl."

Bert took the receiver. "Where's that number?" He went through the same process Rachel had.

Luca came to the phone again. "Luca, this is Albert Trundle. Pearl lives here at my mother's house." Bert listened to the voice on the line a moment. "Luca, I don't care if you do get in trouble," Bert shouted. Eddie had never heard him so forceful. "Pearl never came back from Glen Echo Park last night. Have you seen her?"

Someone stirred down the hall. Eddie hoped they hadn't awakened Aunt Viola.

"Uh-huh." Bert sat on the telephone table's seat. "Uh-huh. But still…" Bert made a shooing motion with his hand for them to give him privacy.

Eddie and Rachel went back to the kitchen, where they sat and drank the coffee Jess poured. Alonso had capped the strawberries and set them in little bowls. He put a stack of toast on the table with a block of oleo, its color too yellow to be butter.

Rachel opened a jar of strawberry jam, a gift from Sarah Rosen. They ate strawberries and strawberry jam with their coffee, which was real and strong.

Coffee had stopped being rationed last year. While Eddie sipped and savored its rich taste, she tasted guilt as well. From their first night on Georgia Avenue, she'd wanted Pearl gone. And now she was. What if something had happened to her?

Eddie topped off everyone's cup, making sure she left plenty in the pot for Bert.

They sat around the table, all except Alonso, who leaned against the counter, his cup in his palms.

"Sit with us, Alonso." Eddie pulled out a chair for him.

Aunt Viola would be scandalized at the idea of white and colored sitting together, but so what? Last night at the Friedlanders', she had noticed how the races had segregated themselves at different picnic tables.

"Thanks." Alonso pulled the chair a little back from the table and sat.

Bert came in, an angry rash climbing his neck. "Luca and Pearl had an argument, so he left her in the woods near the amusement park." He slumped into the remaining chair.

"I can't believe he would do that," Rachel said. "What a schmuck."

"If that means he's no gentleman, I agree." Bert sipped his coffee.

"What else did he tell you?" Eddie asked.

Coffee in hand, Bert started to cough. Eddie patted him on the back. Eyes watering, face flushed, Bert said, "It's not something I could repeat in mixed company, Eddie." He could barely get his words out.

Eddie could tell that Luca had cared about Pearl, who was more interested in Tony. Eddie wasn't sure how Tony felt, but from the gossip he had spread about Pearl, he didn't respect her. So what had happened in the woods outside Glen Echo Park that would make Luca abandon Pearl?

"Maybe we ought to call the police and report her missing." Rachel rubbed her eyes.

"The police won't do anything for at least twenty-four hours," Jess said.

"And then they'll want to make sure she didn't pack up and go home, something they do whenever a government girl is reported missing."

"You mean they'll call her uncle in Saltville?" Eddie asked. Jess nodded. Eddie brought a hand to her mouth. "That's the last place she would go."

Jess sighed. "We're heading out to the Rosen's factory this morning on another matter. While we're out there, we'll try to talk to Luca about Pearl."

Alonso said, "Glen Echo Park is on our way. This morning, I developed the negatives from yesterday. I'll make a print of Pearl's, so we can take it with us and see if anyone there remembers her." He set his spoon in his empty bowl, his ripe strawberries leaving strawberry juice in the bottom.

Bert rubbed his forehead. "Yesterday morning I was coming from the Bond Bakery when I saw Pearl get into a taxicab on Florida Avenue."

Rachel's face lifted in a sunny smile. "I showed her how to hail a cab. Now she loves to do it, says it makes her feel like a real city woman. She took a cab all the way out MacArthur Boulevard after work the other day to look at a room for rent Thad had told me about."

"Is it possible she got a new place to live and moved out without telling us?" Eddie directed her question at Rachel. Pearl would love to have them worried about her.

"No, none of her things are gone," Rachel said. "She wouldn't leave them."

Bert stared at his chapped hands in his lap. "Last Saturday, I told Pearl she had a week to find a new place to live. I wished I hadn't been so…"

"Don't blame yourself." Eddie patted Bert's shoulder. "All of us wanted her to find a new place to live and for good reason."

Bert said, "You suppose her uncle or a man who worked for him could have come back and …"

40

Before Jess and Alonso left Georgia Avenue, Jess called Ray K., alerted him to Pearl's disappearance, and gave him a description of her.

On the drive out to Silver Spring, Alonso said, "You haven't asked me about the case of Clarence, the missing Rhode Island red."

Jess closed his notepad. "I noticed Mrs. Friedlander talking to you beside the barbecue pit. I figured it was about Clarence."

"I couldn't tell her this, but I suspect Clarence was the rooster left on Miss Minnie's porch two days ago. Someone had wrung his neck. Ruth told me about it."

"What did Miss Minnie do with Clarence?"

They were stopped at the traffic light on Colesville Road. With his arm out the window to signal a left, Alonso rotated his head to Jess, his smile so broad his eyes narrowed.

"You've been in the city too long, Brother. Alley folks aren't getting enough meat nowadays, probably never have gotten enough. Miss Minnie strung up old Clarence, plucked him, gutted him, and stewed him."

"Of course." Jess laughed from deep inside, savoring his brother at his most amused, a sunny expression that had all but disappeared with age and their occupation with murder.

"Clarence was meaty." The light went green. Alonso turned. "Made enough stew to feed everyone on the alley. Ruth said he was stringy, but delicious slow cooked with fresh dug potatoes, tomatoes and onions."

"So who killed Clarence?"

"No one on the alley wants to look a gift rooster in the mouth."

"Who do you think did it?" Jess offered him a stick of his favorite, Juicy Fruit gum.

"Well," Alonso rolled the gum into his mouth. "I doubt any alley folk would be crazy enough to sneak into an FBI agent's back yard and steal his wife's prize rooster."

The road became an asphalt ribbon lined with shade trees, the weather one of those July miracles, cooler with low humidity. A wind blew strong through the trees exposing the silver undersides of leaves.

"Something in Abel's words this morning made me wonder about Dan," Alonso said. "When I asked if he had left the property yesterday, Abel said, 'not to my knowledge.'"

"Like he was in the witness stand."

They heard the factory's fans whir before its boxy shape loomed over the cornfields.

"Something's going on." Alonso pulled into the lot, tires spewing gravel.

A crowd of seamstresses were gathered in a circle near the picnic tables, pointing and talking, their backs to the outside.

Jess and Alonso hurried from the Packard and waded into the crowd, the women making way. In the center, Luca and Tony rolled on the ground fighting, powdery dust rising around them. Tony clambered to his feet. Luca, almost a head shorter, knocked him to the ground again. Tony's nose gushed blood.

"I did it for you," Tony yelled, almost sounding drunk.

With Abel close behind, Dan charged into the crowd. "What the hell is going on here?" He tried to separate them, but Luca squirmed around Dan and punched Tony in his stomach.

Gasping, Tony folded forward.

"The last thing I need is for you two to get hurt and not be able to work." Dan brought his arms around the more determined fighter, Luca.

Abel helped Tony to his feet. The matron from the clinic led him inside.

The crowd dispersed. A shift was changing. People congregated at the entrance.

Luca, hands deep in his dungaree's back pockets, stood before Dan, who said, "I thought you two were best pals. What gives?"

Luca's eyes slid away from Dan's. "He's dead to me."

While Alonso went to the entrance to talk to Abel, Jess approached Dan, who shook a Lucky Strikes out and put it in his mouth. "I'm starting to think you like picking on me, Agent Lindsay." With a flick of his silver lighter, he lit the tip and sucked on it as if it was water and he was a thirsty man.

That's what Dan and Velma Bonner had in common: they smoked with the same desperation.

"Actually we're here to talk to Luca." Jess wanted to wait and hear what Abel said about Dan. If Dan had left the property, he was going to jail.

Dan gave a mean grin. "So now you think he's the government girl killer?"

They shifted their gazes to Luca, small as a child, standing between them. His head was bowed, the vulnerable white patch on the back of his neck visible, his despair palpable.

Alonso appeared, drew Jess aside, and whispered, "Luca didn't make it onto the company bus last night when it left Glen Echo Park."

So how had Luca gotten back here in time to work the midnight shift?

Jess showed Luca his badge.

"I know who you are. Everyone here knows."

Jess nodded. They had come out here enough to check on Dan.

Dan gestured to Luca. "Take him home and question away, but not too long. He needs to get some sleep so he can come back to work. No telling how Tony's going to do today."

Luca raised his head. "You don't give a damn about us, Dan. We're nothing but human scissors to you," he yelled. "All you care about is work."

Smirking, Dan pushed his cigarette into a bucket of sand. "You're right. The work *is* all I care about. And if we weren't in the middle of this war, I'd fire your Italian ass and your wop pal, Tony."

"Let's go," Jess said to Luca. They didn't need to hear anymore inspiring words from Dan.

Luca climbed into the Packard's back seat. "I know what this is about," Luca said. "It's Pearl, isn't it?"

Jess studied the man slumped in the backseat, fingers raking his carroty hair. "Pearl didn't come home last night. When was the last time you saw her?"

Luca raised his chin, his face old as the earth, purple arcs under his eyes from lack of sleep. "It was after 9:00 because the fireworks were going off at the park." His voice slowed and he stared as his hands, their nails bitten bloody at the quick. "I left her in the woods with Tony. I just ran off down the road. I ran and ran."

He leaned forward bringing both hands to the ridge of the seat. Three fingers on his left hand wore fresh white bandages. He'd had a tough night working. "She and Tony had been drinking whiskey all day."

This said like an excuse for his girl and his best friend. Both had hurt Luca. And Jess could imagine how. No wonder he felt betrayed.

They drove in silence until Luca leaned over the seat and told Alonso, "Turn right here."

A gravel road, little wider than a tractor path, divided the field of swaying corn. Someone had put up a makeshift street sign that read Victory Lane. Corn edged the road green as far as the eye could see, crackling in the breeze.

Alonso slowed to a crawl. Jess knew he hated gravel roads, where dust rose to coat the Packard, and where a rock might kick up and crack the windshield.

Soon they came to six small cottages facing each other.

"The last one's ours."

Jess recognized the houses built from a Sears and Roebuck plan.

Alonso parked in a weedy driveway, and Luca picked his way up the stone walkway barely visible through high weeds. At the front door he took a key from under the mat.

What would happen tonight when Tony returned? Would their fight resume?

The interior was open like Dan's with exposed beams, a big fireplace, and a kitchen, dining and living room combined. A squat table in front of the sagging sofa was strewn with overflowing ash trays and beer and soda pop bottles. Clothes and shoes lay everywhere, but the kitchen looked tidy.

Luca went to the refrigerator, took out a bottle of gin, and poured himself a glass at the counter. "Want some?" he asked them.

They told him no. He brought his glass to the table and sat.

"It's a little early for booze," Jess said and sat across from him.

Luca lifted the colorless liquid, swallowed, and coughed.

"Is it all right if I use your toilet?" Alonso asked. Asking permission was part of their Jim Crow rules. Many white folks would object.

"Go 'head." Luca set his glass down.

Alonso would snoop around while Jess questioned Luca.

"Why did you leave Pearl in the woods last night?" Jess asked.

Luca scrubbed at his eyes. "She-she-she let me know she preferred Tony to me." His eyes big and damp. He pinched the bridge of his nose to keep from crying.

"We know you didn't take the company bus back here last night. So how did you get to the factory for the midnight shift?"

Out the smeared front windows, a boy wearing goggles flew down the road on a bicycle, dust rising in his wake. The boy turned onto Luca's overgrown lawn and hopped off his bike. He pushed his goggles up into his wild blond hair, nudged the bike's kickstand down, made sure it was stable, and ran to the porch.

"Luca?" Jess said.

Luca stared at his bandaged hands. "Got a ride."

The boy knocked. "FBI, FBI men," he called. Alonso strode from the back room and opened the door.

"A message for Agent Jess Lindsay." The boy handed a paper to Alonso, who gave the boy a coin and took the folded paper.

After Jess read it, he tilted his head toward the door. Jess and Alonso went out on the porch. "Ray K. says we need to meet him at a place called Sycamore Island," Jess said. "A girl's body has been found."

41

Alonso stopped at a filling station. While the young attendant pumped gasoline for the Packard and cleaned the windshield, Alonso studied a map of Maryland to find Sycamore Island. Jess went to the telephone booth, called the Park Police, and got directions

With the camera in its case between them, they took off down winding Canal Road that paralleled the C&O Canal. Occasionally from a bluff, they got a view of the Potomac far below, its rocks silver in the sun. The breeze brushed sunlight into the treetops.

"According to this, Sycamore's the 73rd island downstream in the Potomac River." Jess read from the back of the map.

"It's next to the C&O and not far from the Georgetown Reservoir, the first murder site." Alonso lowered his visor and slowed behind a rattling laundry truck.

"That truck is from the laundry, where Bert and Miss Minnie work, Berman's," Jess said absently.

"Yeah, their plant's somewhere on MacArthur Boulevard." Alonso nodded at the truck ahead and pulled into a gravel lot and parked beside three DC black-and-whites. The only other vehicle was an ambulance.

At the sight of it, Jess swallowed hard. The ambulance would carry the dead girl away, not with its siren blaring, red light revolving, but silently.

There was no hurry for the dead. Their emergency was over.

At this, sadness enveloped him. He felt it in his step, dragging on the shoulder that held up his useless arm, making him feel more lopsided than usual.

From the parking lot, they crossed the canal on a mule bridge and followed the towpath east. The canal smelled briny, its water the color of clay. The land between the towpath and the river was heavily wooded, a gray soupy swamp. Tall river birches threw lacy shadows over them. Dense kudzu carpeted the ground.

After a quarter-mile, they came to a footpath through the woods. Jess looked at his notes and said, "This way."

The trees were so dense sunlight didn't penetrate. The path led down a steep hill that ended at a wide stream off the Potomac called a slough. A small dock jutted into the slough. Blue damselflies swooped low over the water.

They swatted at gnat swarms and dive-bombing mosquitoes.

Posted on the trunk of a spindly pine, a small sign that read: *Sycamore Island ferry, members only.* Near the sign was a rope. Alonso pulled it, and a bell tolled on the island.

Soon a Park Policeman appeared on the opposite dock and called, "Bureau of Investigation?" The silver shield on the man's hat flashed at them.

"Yes," Jess answered.

"Be right there." The policeman stepped onto a small barge at the island's dock and pulled on an overhead rope that connected the island to the shore. He tugged his way across the slough's tea-colored water on the hand-drawn ferry.

"Hold onto this, please." Alonso handed Jess his camera then grabbed the rope and helped the policeman dock the barge. Jess introduced himself and Alonso.

"They're expecting you," the Park Policeman said with a crisp salute.

Jess grinned at the young man. He must be a new recruit in his hat and jacket buttoned up as it was.

They got on the barge. While Alonso helped him pull to the other side, Jess held the beloved camera close to his chest, knowing how Al worried about it near water.

Jess asked the policeman, "Can anyone take this ferry anytime?"

"No, Sir. There's a caretaker who lives on the island. He locks the ferry at night."

The policeman tied up the barge. "Follow me."

Alonso took the camera back, and they went up a hill, their path surrounded by clumps of black-eyed susans and daisies, the smell of honeysuckle in the air.

From the second floor porch of the house, a large man, his hands and forehead flattened against the screen, watched them.

"That's the caretaker. He's the one who found the girl's body this morning. He's a little shaken by the whole thing."

The island was wooded with grassy sun-filled expanses, and weathered picnic tables scattered about. To their left, sheds held canoes, their hawk-like noses poking out.

Ray K. and other police were standing near the water's edge around a picnic table, where a small pale body lay as if on a funeral bier.

When they stepped back, the girl became more visible. The sight of her knocked the breath out of Jess. He swept off his hat and bowed his head. Beside him, Alonso stopped and let out a low groan.

Ray came to them. "She's the government girl you called about. I see it in your faces." He brought his hand to Jess' shoulder. "It's different when you...you know the person."

The three stood together a long moment until Alonso said, "Was she murdered?"

"Looks like she drowned." Ray K. glanced back at her. "The Potomac is a rough river. Even experienced swimmers drown in it."

Dr. Lee, who'd been examining Pearl, walked over. "I see no evidence of strangulation. Nor does she have the scrapes or contusions you would expect to find on a person who drowns in the Potomac's rapids. She has a few scratches, and her skull appears fractured from a single blow."

Ray was shaking his head. "Ever since I been with the Department, I've seen drowned folks pulled out of the Potomac." His wandering eye looked beyond them to the river. "Being knocked against one of those river rocks probably cracked her skull."

Dr. Lee pursed his lips and slapped at a mosquito on his neck. There was blood on his palm when he brought his hand away. "Two of the fingernails on her right hand are broken, as if she may have clawed at someone," he told Jess. "Did she keep her nails painted and filed?"

Jess closed his eyes, pulled himself together, and recalled Pearl. "Yes, she always had them painted." Eddie wore only clear varnish on hers, but Pearl and Rachel painted theirs.

Alonso took out his camera, put the case on another picnic table and screwed in a flashbulb. The island's deep shade required the flash. He went to Pearl and began doing what he always did, moving around her body, snapping photographs. How Jess envied him this. Alonso's camera buffered him from the world. When Al saw something he couldn't take in, he photographed it. That's why his pictures often seared the viewer.

"Where exactly was she found?" Jess asked.

"Follow me." Ray K. took him to a place in the shallows. Jess's shoes sank in the soft ground, but the water was clear enough to see a huge brown catfish flick between mossy rocks. A frog croaked nearby.

"The caretaker found her lying here, face up. She was fully dressed except for no shoes. I'm thinking she could have been wading somewhere upstream maybe around Great Falls, and got pulled out. The water looks calm there, but the current is especially strong."

"The problem is she was last seen at Glen Echo Amusement Park. So how did she get from the park to the river?"

Ray K. turned and looked up toward the bluff over the Potomac. "Glen Echo is close." He took out a cigarette and lit it with his lighter. "But too far for her to walk. Maybe she got a ride with someone."

"So why didn't that person call the police when Pearl got pulled into the river?" Jess asked.

Ray K. took a long drag, smoke coming out his nostrils like a dragon. "You got a point."

The ambulance crew loaded Pearl onto a stretcher. Jess went for a closer look. Pearl's makeup had washed off, and her long red hair lay curled on her shoulders. Her face was milky pale, her freckles almost faded.

"Dr. Lee?" Jess called. "Did you button her top buttons?" Pearl never did. She was wearing a pink flowered skirt and pink sweater, too warm for this time of year.

Dr. Lee stepped close. "No. That's exactly as I found her."

"Will you do a post-mortem to see if she drowned?" He wanted to know if her death had anything in common with the murdered government girls.

Ray K. appeared beside the doctor. "Jess, I know you knew her, but we got limited resources. There's a war on, remember? This was an accident."

"Let me worry about my resources, Ray K." Dr. Lee removed his rimless glasses and wiped them with a handkerchief. He hooked them back over his ears and blinked at them. "I will treat her death as suspicious and do a full post-mortem exam as well as test her blood."

Ray K. huffed and walked away.

42

On their way back to the car, Jess paused on the towpath and looked downhill through the trees to the water. "What if *he* brought Pearl here, hit her over the head with a rock, and put her in the slough? Which would explain why her body wasn't bruised or cut by the river. She was never in its rapids."

"If that's how it happened, then he must have parked where we did." Alonso rubbed the cleft in his chin. "It's the closest place."

They hurried to the dirt parking lot, empty now except for their Packard.

The ground was soft enough to leave tire tracks, but the police cars and ambulance parked here earlier had muddied any prints.

"If this is where he parked, he would have chosen the first space, right?" Alonso said.

"Yeah. He would have wanted to get her out of his car fast. And the first space is almost in the trees."

They squatted and combed the area. Part of a tire track remained. "Tire's almost bald." Alonso got out the camera and took a photograph of the tread.

Jess turned and looked up the hill. "Where's all that smoke coming from?"

"Looks like from MacArthur Boulevard. Let's go up there and see."

Once back in the Packard, Alonso hung a right onto the road then a left as they climbed through the wooded hillside.

"MacArthur Boulevard, huh?" Jess read the wooden street sign. "They were in a hurry to proclaim the General a war hero." They passed a small green grocer and a busy garage with cars lined up for gasoline.

"Used to be called Conduit Road, but folks out here didn't like that name." Alonso pulled into a parking lot full of white Berman Laundry trucks. The steam poured out the building's chimney.

"It's Berman's laundry plant," Jess said, his ghost arm twitching. "Bert works here."

"Bert?" Alonso whispered.

They looked at each other. "Nah," Jess said. Alonso gave his head a slow shake.

Still Bert fit Dr. Kushner's template. *The killer has trouble with women, starting with his mother. The killer feels guilt about not being in the service.*

"So where's that amusement park from here?" Jess asked.

Alonso turned left out of the parking back onto MacArthur. Soon they heard the streetcar's creak and saw its familiar colors, two shades of aquamarine whizzing through the trees. Alonso tilted his head toward it. "He's moving pretty good. Sure would be fun to drive one of them."

Above the woods, the amusement park's big three-story stone tower came into view.

They parked in a small lot and walked downhill, passing the entrance to a huge swimming pool called the Crystal Pool. Passengers were getting off the streetcar. Children swarmed the entrance, where the huge neon GLEN ECHO PARK sign was set high between red arches. Music from the carousel drifted out.

Beyond the entrance, an arcade curved off to one side. It was the nicest amusement park Jess had ever seen, everything done in the art deco style. But, at heart it was a children's paradise, and their excited squeals said they couldn't wait to get inside.

At a fast clip, a guard in a tan and red uniform waded through the children and their mothers waiting in line to pay the admission.

"You can't come in here," the guard said to Alonso.

Not until then did Jess notice that all the children and adults around them were white.

Jess pulled out his badge and ID. "We're from the Federal Bureau of Investigation." He emphasized the words *we* and *federal*.

Frowning, the guard took Jess's badge and studied it. After he handed it back, his frown went deeper as he looked at Alonso's identification without touching it.

"Negroes are not allowed in the park," he said to Jess, "no matter where they come from."

"I want to see the park manager." Jess crossed his arms over his chest.

"Wait and I'll see if he's here."

Once the guard left, Alonso said, "Jess, don't lose our focus. We aren't here to see the park, anyway. Luca told us they went into the woods near the streetcar stop." He pointed to a path across from the stop. "Let's check it out there."

They walked through the woods littered with empty beer and liquor bottles.

After almost a quarter of a mile, they came to a small clearing. "Look." Jess pointed to a spot where weeds were flattened. "Maybe they spread their blanket there."

They wandered around, heads lowered, their hands parting the weeds. Alonso picked up some cigarette butts beneath a tree across from where they imagined the blanket had been spread. "Chesterfields." He wrapped them in a piece of wax paper.

After they'd seen all there was, they took a path toward the road, where Jess noticed a grape soda bottle overturned in a clump of clover, thick with bees. He bent to pick it up when Alonso called, "Don't get stung."

"Looks like some of these bees have been drinking this grape Nehi." The bottle contained dead bees. Others lay lifeless in the clover. So as not to disturb any fingerprints, Jess picked it up with his handkerchief and dropped it into the evidence bag Alonso held open.

The clover lined another path, which they followed and found it opened onto a wide shoulder on the road, rutted from parked cars. "He could have parked here," Jess said. "Come in, subdued her, then put her in his car."

"Did he know Pearl or was she a random victim?" Alonso said.

"Good question. He could have been in the park or around its entrance, seen Pearl and Luca go into the woods with Tony close behind and followed."

They walked back along MacArthur Boulevard, discussing what they needed to ask Tony and Luca. From the road, they looked downhill to the park, where a stout man in a red tie stood with the guard who had confronted them earlier. Other guards in the tan uniforms clustered around them.

Alonso said, "Looks like I won't be swimming in their Crystal Pool today."

43

"If this is our killer," Jess said, "his pattern has changed radically." He was coming down off the high he'd gotten on Sycamore Island when Dr. Lee stood up to Ray K. "Pearl looks nothing like the other murdered government girls. Nor was she strangled…"

"But her body was found near where the others were, near the C&O, near the Georgetown Reservoir, near the Potomac."

As they drove back to Silver Spring, they were preparing for Fred's possible objections that Pearl's murder wasn't connected to the government girl killer, which would mean they couldn't investigate. They needed to do all they could today.

After they turned onto Victory Lane, a woman appeared on the dusty road, running toward them. Even though Alonso was driving slowly, he had to swerve not to hit her. The woman was Dominique, her hair long and loose under her kerchief.

Panting, she reached in Alonso's window and squeezed his shoulder. "Please, please." She spoke in a stream of French, all the while pointing toward the end of the lane. "Luca, Luca," the only word they understood.

"Get in." Alonso signaled to her.

She did. They sped down the lane and screeched to a halt in front of Luca's cottage. They ran through the high grass and opened the door.

The late afternoon sun spilled through west-facing windows. All was silent except for the steady drip of water. In the hall, Alonso slipped on water and caught himself before he fell.

Jess sloshed through water into the bathroom. Luca lay pale and motionless in the bathtub. Water overflowed the tub's rim, its color tinged with blood, seeping from his wrist.

Jess grabbed a tea towel from the cabinet, lifted Luca's arm out of the water, and wrapped the towel snug around his wrist. On the floor a straight razor glinted like a fish. Alonso picked it up by its ivory handle, closed it, and threw it into the sink.

Jess felt queasy imagining what had happened.

"*Mon Dieu,*" Dominique cried several times behind them and used the word, *mort,* which needed no translation.

Alonso brought his fingertips to Luca's neck. "He's got a pulse."

"Let's get him out of the water." Jess gave Alonso Luca's bandaged hand and went to the other side of the claw-footed bathtub in order to use his good arm. Together they lifted him, water sluicing from his body. Without a hint of embarrassment, Dominique dried him with another towel and managed to wrap him in his bathrobe.

Luca had cut only one wrist. What had stopped him from doing the other? Whatever the reason, Jess thanked God for it. Judging by his wrinkled fingertips, he'd been in the bathtub for hours. Maybe he got in soon after they left this morning.

Alonso carried him down the hall to the living room and laid him on the sofa. During this entire process, Jess kept Luca's hand in the air, so the blood flowed downward.

A step ahead of them, Dominique brought a quilt from one of the bedrooms and threw it over the ragged sofa. Alonso propped Luca's head up with pillows.

"I'll go to the factory and call an ambulance," Alonso said.

Luca's blood had begun to soak through the tea towel. Dominique started to remove it, when Jess pushed her hand away. "No. Another towel."

She went for one. Alonso ran out to the car and drove away.

After Dominique wrapped the new towel around the old one, Jess got her to hold Luca's hand up, bulky now with the towel bandages. Jess felt for his pulse in his neck and found it, faint but steady. Jess took Luca's hand again.

"You did well, Dominique." He nodded to her.

She returned a solemn nod, her eyes shiny with tears, and said something in soft French while stroking Luca's face. She went to the kitchen, came out with a mop and bucket, and sopped up the water on the floor.

Jess was struck at how Luca resembled Pearl, especially now with his freckles faded, and how he and Al had left Luca drinking gin before nine this morning. He'd sensed the young man's despair, yet he hadn't known it went this deep. With so many folks killing each other all over the globe, what had brought Luca to this?

Did he kill Pearl last night? Is that why he tried suicide?

The ticking clock divided the minutes. Jess was afraid Luca was slipping away, joining Pearl. At the sound of the Packard's engine approaching, he rejoiced.

Footsteps on the porch. Tony ran in and knelt beside his friend.

"Luca, Luca, what have you done?" He took Luca's other hand. "I'm so sorry, Luca. Forgive me." He bowed his head.

Unlike Luca, Tony looked Italian with his dark hair, high cheekbones, and Roman nose.

"Tony was in their break-room when I called for an ambulance," Alonso told Jess, who still held Luca's hand up. "He insisted on coming with me."

In the distance, they heard a siren. Soon the ambulance pulled up, red light revolving. The medics ran in and took over. Jess stepped back to the front window beside Alonso.

The medics made Tony do the same. He leaned against the wall and watched the medics, his face and hair slick with sweat. One eye had almost swollen shut from their fight. The skin around it had turned purple.

Dominique came out of the bathroom carrying a bucket.

At the sight of her, Tony's face contorted. "Get out." He pointed to the front door. "I don't want you here."

"Dominique found Luca," Jess said. "If not for her…"

"I don't give a damn. Thanks for your help, all of you, but time for you to go." He motioned to the door again.

Dominique set her bucket down and walked out.

"We need to talk to you, Tony." Jess showed him his badge.

"What the hell?" He knocked the badge out of Jess's hand. "You got nerve at a time like this."

Jess bent and picked it up.

"Could someone get this man something to wear?" the ambulance driver asked.

Tony went into Luca's room and came back with a stack of clothes.

After he gave the clothes to the medic, he stood next to Jess again.

"Pearl," Tony whispered to Jess. "She's why you're here, isn't she?" He reached back and thumped the wood paneled wall with his fist. "This is her doing." He gestured to Luca, whose arm was being bandaged.

"Could all of you take your business outside?" the ambulance driver asked without looking at them. The medic was giving Luca a drink of water. Luca coughed at first, but then swallowed, his eyes still closed.

"This way, Mr. Guarco." Jess tilted his head toward the back door.

Alonso tried to take Tony's arm, but he shook him off. The three walked to a stand of pines at the field's edge. A cow grazing nearby stared at them as she chewed grass, her long tail flicking at flies.

A picnic table, the same weathered wood as the ones at the factory, nestled under the trees. Jess sat on one side and Tony on the opposite bench, while Alonso took a chair at the end of the table. A breeze rustled the pine needles overhead.

The smell of pine always reminded Jess of the Lindsay plantation at timber cutting time. Loggers came with their giant saws, and the groans of the tall trees crashing to the forest floor echoed in Jess's dreams.

Tony shook out a Chesterfield and lit it. With long slender fingers, he brought the cigarette to his lips and inhaled. Jess recalled the cigarette butts they'd found earlier near Glen Echo.

"Okay. I'm grateful to you two for saving Luca." His tone softened.

"Dominique found him."

"And her, too." He tapped his cigarette ash over his shoulder. "What a crazy kid Luca is doing something dumb like this because of a whore like

Pearl."

Jess wanted to knock this guy on his ass.

"Wait a minute." Tony's face contorted into disgust. "You two are the G-men Pearl brags about. Anybody messes with her she'll sic the FBI on them." He looked from Jess to Alonso and back again. "And I see she has."

Jess took in his use of present tense. "What happened last night at Glen Echo Park?"

"Pearl." he made a dismissive click with his tongue. "First Luca had sex with her, then I did." He ran his fingers through his hair. "I did it to show him what a whore she is. If you knew how many times she rubbed up against me when Luca's back was turned." His voice broke. "But Luca loved her and had even bought her an engagement ring. I had no idea he would do what he did."

"How did you get back from Glen Echo Park last night?"

"Ran and caught the Rose Clothing bus. Barely made it." He shook out another cigarette and chewed the end without lighting it.

"Where was Pearl when you last saw her?"

"Left her buck naked in the woods and ran for the bus." He gave a harsh laugh.

"How did you get those scratches on your neck?"

He lifted his hand to them. "I don't know. Maybe on a tree limb…"

"Did Pearl scratch you?"

"I…I don't think so." His hands were trembling. "Why do you keep asking about Pearl?"

44

Jess heard the back door shut. It was close to 11:00, the night starless and dark as a cave, by the time he and Alonso got back from Suburban Hospital, where Luca had been taken.

Once inside their bungalow, exhausted he slumped at his desk. Before he wrote out the day's report, he ought to go to the house and tell Eddie and the rest about Pearl.

The back porch light came on. Eddie, her blonde hair visible through the corn, walked down the path. Full of dread, Jess stepped out to meet her.

"Hi," she said. "Pearl still isn't back yet, but I needed to tell you that I met Vernon Lanier tonight. He was coming to see you…"

"Eddie." Jess brought his hand to her bare arm. "Pearl was found this morning in the Potomac. She appears to have drowned last night."

"What?" Eddie searched his face. Jess repeated what he had said.

She let out a yelp and lowered her head. He drew her into the arch of his shoulder and held her. After a while he led her inside, where they sat close on the creaky wicker settee.

In a dreamy voice, she said, "I doubt Pearl can swim well. Sometimes she sneaks into the swimming pool in Saltville. Actually Saltville has two pools. One is filled with saltwater that's so warm on a summer day it feels awful, especially if you have any cuts on your body. The salt really stings, but it keeps you afloat..." Her voice broke into tears.

Jess stroked her shoulder. "The DC Police have contacted the sheriff in Saltville and asked that her next of kin, Alton Ballou, be notified."

Eddie straightened, her grape green eyes flashed. "That's rich, considering he sent that man who beat her up."

From the back porch, Rachel called, "Eddie, popcorn's ready. There's plenty for everyone."

"Do you want me to go in and tell them?" Jess asked.

"No." Eddie leaned closer, took hold of his chin, and kissed him. "I will."

Later, lying in bed, Jess traced his lips with his index finger, feeling her kiss. It was the only good that came out of his day. A sense of failure overwhelmed him. They were no closer to finding the killer than they'd been when they arrived here.

From the house, Jess heard shouts and cries. He ought to go and talk to Rachel, Bert, and Mrs. Trundle, who was sure to be dramatic. But he'd had his fill of sorrow. On the other side of the bungalow, Alonso and Ruth were sitting on the bench, talking in low voices.

Jess wished they would take their conversation elsewhere, but there were few private places. And the alley folks might see Ruth if she went to the room over the garage with Alonso.

To drown out their voices, he turned on the radio beside his bed.

Edward R. Morrow was reporting from London about Normandy. The Germans were holding the American and Canadian forces on the beaches. Although the Army's 7th Corps advanced only 200 meters inland in the last few days, they'd suffered staggering numbers of wounded and dead.

After D-Day, everyone had expected the Allies to push the Germans into France, where a big war-ending battle would be fought. No one foresaw that Allied troops wouldn't be able to get off the beaches. It had begun to feel like Dunkirk all over again.

Jess absorbed this bad news. While he was frustrated with these murders, he imagined how the troops felt. But eventually they would break out of Normandy, and eventually he and Alonso would have a breakthrough. They would find this man.

He cut the radio, lay in bed, and tried to clear his mind of the two pale faces that haunted him, Pearl and Luca's.

Just outside the window, Alonso said, "Tell me the truth now, Ruth. Who stole that rooster and wrung his neck?"

"Are you asking for the Bureau?"

Jess heard the smile in her voice. He shouldn't be eavesdropping. He was getting as bad as Mrs. Trundle.

Alonso said, "The Bureau doesn't investigate rooster murders."

She sighed. "I don't want him to get into trouble, but I expect it was Bert."

"Why do you say that?"

"Well, when Bert was young he gave funerals for animals. He got my brother Jasper and other alley kids to be pallbearers and mourners." She giggled. "Even had old black hats and such for them to wear."

"So how did these animals die?"

"I don't know. Bert was grown by the time I came along." She gave a low laugh. "Mama did say when they plowed the back yard for the victory garden, they found dozens of animal bones. Not that she minded. Says ground up bones make the soil richer."

Jess turned on the light and took out Dr. Kushner's template.

45

"How did Pearl know the lyrics to so many songs?" Rachel spoke from across the room. She was lying in the double bed that she and Pearl had once shared. "Ever wonder about that?"

It was after 1:00 AM, and Rachel had cried herself hoarse. "She never even owned a radio until she came here. She was smarter than we gave her credit."

When Rachel said *we,* she didn't mean herself, she meant that Eddie hadn't given Pearl credit. Eddie lay in her twin bed and listened to Pearl's Philco radio/ alarm clock combination ticking from the dresser top. Each tick brought dawn and the next work day closer.

"Remember when she bought that radio?" Rachel said. "She was so proud. She set the alarm over and over, so we could hear how it would ring when it woke us."

"I remember." Eddie hoped Rachel would exhaust her Pearl memories and go to sleep.

As Eddie's pulse came into synch with the clock's tick, she sensed Pearl's presence. Pearl's fan blew air over them, sending the sickly sweet scent of her Evening in Paris perfume she'd spilled into the floorboards, and her face looked out from snaps wedged into the dressing table mirror. In them, Pearl and Rachel mugged for the photography booth camera.

But most of all Pearl's voice lingered.

Eyes closed, Eddie could hear Pearl say, *how may I direct yer call?* Her rough mountain accent evident in every syllable. *How may I direct yer call?*

Pearl had never been part of their planned escape from Saltville. And since their first week in Washington, when Pearl and Rachel sang each other to sleep in the double bed they shared, Eddie had been jealous of their friendship, *grün vor neid,* green with envy

Why hadn't she admitted that before?

The bed's springs creaked. Rachel must have sat up again. "Pearl told me she couldn't swim, so I find it hard to believe she went wading in the Potomac River."

Jess had said it *appeared* Pearl drowned. Eddie had been so stunned at the news of Pearl's death she didn't question him about the circumstances, but she would tomorrow.

"Maybe Pearl was drinking," Eddie said.

Pearl had come back drunk from her date with Luca last weekend. So drunk Eddie and Rachel had to help her up the stairs.

"You never liked her, Eddie. So don't judge her now." Rachel's words were sharp.

Eddie said nothing. She wouldn't dispute it.

"Sorry," Rachel said. "I know you're upset, too."

"Don't apologize. You're wrong, though. I *did* like her, I just never trusted her and I wanted her to move out." Eddie lay still, blinking into the darkness, sensing Rachel doing the same. "I wanted her out of here as soon as she told me about the money she stole."

"We all wanted her to move." Rachel sobbed. "She told me she felt unwanted."

Not long after 3:00 a crash sounded downstairs. Rachel didn't stir. She must have fallen asleep at last.

Eddie slid her feet into shoes, grabbed her bathrobe, and crept downstairs. No one was in the kitchen. A ribbon of light glowed under Aunt Viola's door.

Eddie knocked. "Aunt Viola, are you all right?" She heard noise and opened the door.

Lamplight fell on her aunt still in her flowered housecoat stretched out on the brocade chaise lounge her white hair disheveled. She had knocked a glass over on the table and spilled whiskey. Eddie could smell it.

Last night after Eddie told them about Pearl, Bert got so upset he went back to MacArthur Boulevard to work, while Aunt Viola broke out a bottle of bourbon, which she and Rachel had shared.

Aunt Viola opened red-rimmed eyes. "Ed-die, Ed-die, what kind of chaperone lets one of her girls die. I'm so ashamed. What will Saltville folks say when they find out about Pearl?"

So that was it. Her concern was what people would think. "I doubt anyone in Saltville knows Pearl was living here with you."

They had never told Aunt Viola about Pearl's stolen money or that the man who broke in here was sent from her uncle Alton. Bert hadn't wanted to upset her.

"If your father knew about Pearl," Aunt Viola said, "he might make you come home."

Eddie drew in a breath. "I'm not going back to Saltville, Aunt Viola. My job with the Department of the Army was only for the summer, but when I accepted the translator position at the Bureau, I promised to stay for the duration of the war."

She had been working on a letter to her father explaining this. Rachel had begged her to wait in sending it. Rachel feared her father would find out about Eddie and insist Rachel come home early.

"Your position?" Aunt Viola rose from her stupor, nostrils flared. "Edwina, you think you're so high and mighty with your college degree. If my brother wants you home, girl, you will leave my house."

"Fine, Aunt Viola. I'm making enough money now that I can afford something nicer." She shouldn't have said this, but she couldn't help herself.

"You ungrateful…"The old lady managed to stand on the chaise, lean over, and slap Eddie.

Her face stinging, Eddie caught her aunt under the arms before she fell to the floor. In the process, the lamp turned over.

Aunt Viola collapsed back on the chaise. Her leg had hit the table hard. Tomorrow she'd be bruised.

When Eddie bent down for the lamp, she discovered a framed photograph under the bed. She pulled it out and held it to the light. In the photograph, a young woman, pudgy and dark-haired, wore a wedding dress, but the groom standing behind her had been cut out. Only his hand on her shoulder remained. It was bizarre to see the hand without a body. The bride was a young Aunt Viola.

The photograph gave Eddie goose-flesh, but she didn't know why.

She set it back on the table.

Bert threw open the door, the doorknob banging against the wall. "What's going on in here?" At the sight of him, Eddie shuddered.

He rushed to his mother and helped her to bed. "Mama, are you all right?" He knelt and patted her face.

Eddie strode to the door, ready to run. She wanted out of this room, out of this house. Young Aunt Viola's photograph would fit with the others on the wall above the garage. Aunt Viola had looked like the murdered government girls.

46

Friday, July 7, 1944

Jess held open the door to the morgue. Eddie took a deep breath as if diving under and stepped in. A blast of cold air met her.

"I should have warned you about the air conditioning, Eddie. Sorry. Would you like to wear my jacket?" He began to shrug it off.

"No thanks. The cold feels lovely," she lied. Cold reminded her of death. "In this heat I was wondering how they kept the dead..."

Not true. She couldn't stop thinking about Bert ever since she saw that old photograph of a young dark-haired Aunt Viola.

Last night upstairs in their bedroom, she calmed herself. Instead of waking Rachel so they could pack up and leave Georgia Avenue, she braced a chair under the doorknob. Then fully clothed, she got into bed and fell asleep. She could not believe she had been able to sleep under the same roof as someone she suspected of murder.

Dad always said things look different in the morning, and so they had this morning. Bert was her cousin, her blood kin. He couldn't be a killer. Since Pearl's death, Eddie couldn't trust her mind or her wild suspicions.

"Eddie, you're so pale," Jess said. They stood at the top of a staircase, surrounded by clam gray walls. "If you would rather, I can do this without you."

"I want to do it for Pearl. It's just that I've never been in a morgue before." A bubble of panic rose through her chest, *angst* at seeing the dead.

But she'd seen dead people before. In Saltville going to viewings and funerals was part of the town's social life. Since she was little, she'd been visiting the dead. Yet Pearl would be the first who'd been murdered. The word sent a shiver through her.

The medical examiner had determined Pearl died from a blow to the back of her head. That she was dead when she went into the water. She hadn't drowned. And the ME, as Jess called him, had found barbiturate traces in her stomach.

She and Jess took the stairs down to the basement, Jess in the lead.

At the bottom, a slender Chinese man in a white lab coat waited. On the glass door behind him was his title, Chief Medical Examiner, in black and gold lettering.

Jess introduced Dr. Lee to Eddie, who extended her hand. They shook. Dr. Lee's hand was ice cold. "I am sorry we meet under such circumstances, Miss Smith."

Dr. Lee bowed his head and ushered them into the large bright room nearby. Bulbs hung low from the ceiling over metal gurneys. On the first gurney was a form no bigger than a child covered in a sheet.

Gulping air, Eddie took in the room's formaldehyde smell and felt queasy. Drains sunk into the cement floor reminded her of mouths. Her legs went shaky.

Large labeled drawers filled one side of the room. When she realized what those drawers contained, she brought her arms over her chest. The dead pressed in from all sides.

"Are you all right, Miss Smith?" Doctor Lee asked. The light reflected in his glasses obscured his eyes.

"Yes," Eddie lied. *Mut*, she told herself, remembering how her grandmother had told her this. *Mut*.

With Jess on her left, his right hand gentle on her back, Dr. Lee lowered the sheet to Pearl's neck and stood back. Pearl's eyes were wide, her mouth a darkened circle, her tangled hair, falling almost to her shoulders. Eddie opened her hand over her hammering heart, as if to silence it. Jess tightened his grip on her shoulder.

Pearl's expression was one Eddie had never seen, certainly one she'd never seen when Pearl was her student. Pearl looked curious as if she was about to ask a question. Eddie closed her eyes.

Behind her lids, a dark-eyed handsome face appeared, Tony. Was this crazy speculation? Or had Tony killed Pearl? Eddie recalled the look Tony had given Pearl the evening she and Jess had seen the threesome, Pearl, Luca, and Tony, together in front of Peoples' Drugstore. When Pearl had stroked Tony's back, he recoiled from her touch, his expression hate-filled.

This morning, Jess had let Eddie read Dr. Lee's report. Two details stuck. That a few of Pearl's nails were broken and skin was found under others, meaning Pearl had fought back. Jess had shown her Tony's photograph with scratches on his face. Had Pearl scratched him?

The door whined behind them, and a deep male voice boomed, "Okay, sorry I'm late to this party." They turned to a large man in a snug suit, his pink scalp peeking through thinning brown hair glossy with hair oil.

"Eddie," Jess said. "This is Detective Kam…"

"Call me Ray K.," he told Eddie with a wink.

"I'm Eddie Smith." His cheerfulness offended her.

Ray K. grinned. "Now that we got that straight." His gaze went to the steel table, his left eyeball a little off center. "Is this your friend, Pearl Ballou?"

Eddie looked back at Pearl and thought how unfair life was. Pearl had just gotten out of Saltville and begun to live. "Yes," her voice broke. "This is the body of Pearl Ballou." Her words spoken like an oath.

"I wanted you to look at this, too." Jess turned her around to a tray that held Pearl's soggy clothing.

Eddie looked through the garments, realizing Pearl was naked under the sheet. "She was wearing a blouse when she left the house, but she always carried a sweater, a habit of us mountain girls. We're used to the weather getting much cooler at nightfall."

"We didn't find her blouse," Jess said and extended his hand. "She was wearing this skirt with this sweater buttoned all the way up to her neck."

She exchanged a glance with Jess. This didn't sound like Pearl. She filed his words away: *buttoned all the way up.*

When she turned back to the steel gurney, Dr. Lee had covered Pearl.

"Now we formalize the identification," he said. "This way."

Ray K. said, "Nothing happens in this town without a form filled out in triplicate."

Eddie and Jess followed Dr. Lee with Ray K. bringing up the rear.

In Dr. Lee's office, Eddie slumped into a worn leather chair. Jess and Ray K. took similar chairs on either side of her. Dr. Lee sat behind his large polished cherry desk and handed Eddie a form on a clipboard. The form required that she identify herself and her relationship to Pearl.

"Should I write that I was her high school teacher or her roommate?" she asked Dr. Lee.

"Put both, please. We like more information when the person identifying the body is not a blood relative."

Blood kin. That's what Eddie had been thinking about in connection to Bert. The blood that flowed through Bert was similar to her blood, and blood was thicker than water.

"Speaking of blood relatives," Ray K. said. "I need to talk to you about that, Eddie."

Once she had finished the form and signed it, Dr. Lee took it, stood, and said. "I'll be right back." Jess rose as if to leave.

"Please sit, stay." Dr. Lee waved his hand. "Enjoy the air conditioning, while I make some special tea for Miss Smith."

After he walked out, Ray K. said, "Nothing like getting the red carpet treatment at the morgue." With another grin, he unbuttoned his suit jacket to give his stomach more room and opened a file he'd taken from his briefcase.

"So here's the thing, Eddie." He shuffled through papers. "I'm having a hard time with the Saltville police. When I asked the sheriff to notify Miss Ballou's uncle that his niece died, the sheriff told me he wasn't sure where Alton Ballou lived, and if they did find his place, Mr. Ballou would shoot 'em." He sat back, closed the file, and crossed his arms over his chest. "Usually when we call another law enforcement agency, we get cooperation. Your town of Saltville, Virginia sounds like the wild west."

Ray K.'s insult made Eddie prickle with heat in this chilly room. Of course, she and Rachel joked about Saltville, but she resented when an outsider did the same.

She cleared her throat. "Mr. Ballou is a known bootlegger and feared by many."

"That's an understatement. And Mr. Ballou has no telephone, so since the sheriff wouldn't go to his door, we sent a telegram. At least Western Union had the guts to deliver it. The delivery woman, a woman mind you, said Mr. Ballou came to the door, opened the envelope, and appeared to read the telegram then tore it up in her face."

Eddie slipped down in her chair, her hand over her mouth.

"See Eddie," Jess said. "Dr. Lee is ready to release Pearl's body, but there's no family member to accept it."

"For an unclaimed person," Ray K.'s right eye focused on her, "the city will cremate them and ship their remains to a contracting cemetery in Virginia or Maryland, land being at a premium inside Washington City. No headstone, no service, just a name in the cemetery's logbook."

Eddie dropped her head. She couldn't let that happen. This was her chance to do right by Pearl. "Can you release her body to me as her friend?"

"Yep, happens all the time, but are you sure you can handle this?"

"I'll pay the funeral expenses." Jess covered her hand with his. "Don't worry about that."

"Thanks Jess," she whispered.

To Ray K., she said, "My cousin, Bert, works on weekends for a funeral home on 16th Street. I'll talk to him about the arrangements. But I won't see him until tonight."

"That's fine," Ray K. said. "Just have your cousin call this number to arrange for the funeral home to pick up Miss Ballou's body." Ray K. handed her a card.

Dr. Lee brought in a black lacquered tray that held a large china pot and small matching cups. He set the tray on his desk, poured a cup, and gave it to Eddie. The handle-less cup warmed her palm. When all of them had a cup, they raised them.

"To Pearl," Jess said.

Eddie felt the pull of tears, but wouldn't allow herself to cry. *Mut.* "What is this, Dr. Lee?" She sipped the strong tea. "It's delicious."

Ray K. had already gulped his down and held his cup out for more.

"It's oolong." Dr. Lee poured for Ray K. "Difficult to obtain right now because of the war." He set the teapot down and smiled at Eddie. "I've been saving it for a special occasion." He offered her a plate of cookies.

"Thank you," Eddie told him. "For everything…" She took an almond cookie and sipped. "I love the tea's woody flavor."

Dr. Lee pointed to a jar of dark leaves wedged on a shelf between his anatomy texts. "It is said a tea picker named Wu Long was gathering tea leaves in the woods when he saw a beautiful deer. He left the leaves he had gathered and followed the deer. When he got back at nightfall, his leaves had darkened and curled in the sun. Still he took the leaves home, brewed them, and Wu Long or oolong tea was discovered."

"A happy accident." Eddie forced a smile, her thoughts with Pearl. Did her uncle have her murdered? How would Jess investigate Alton Ballou from Washington? Pearl deserved justice.

"And I thought that jar of yours contained some lab specimen," Ray K. said.

For half an hour they talked tea, coffee, and their favorite Washington bakeries and tea rooms. "We're lucky to live near the Bond Bread factory," Jess said. "Our neighborhood always smells delicious."

Eddie savored his pronoun *we*. At the same time she hoped Dr. Lee and Ray K. understood that she and Jess lived close, but not together.

Out on the street, beneath a darkening sky, Ray K. said to Jess, "Hey, where's Tonto today?"

"Alonso's following up on a tip from a waiter at the Florida Grill."

"The Florida Grill, huh?" Ray K. nodded at this. "Good place to get information. Gotta hand it to you two Bamas. You managed to get your ears to the ground fast." Ray K. gave Jess a mock salute. "Want a ride back to Hoover-ville?"

Jess and Eddie laughed. Everyone teased about their boss. "I think we'll walk." Jess looked at Eddie, who nodded.

"All right, lovebirds. Don't get wet." Thunder rumbled from the Potomac.

Eddie felt her own blush and noticed that Jess' face had become rosy as well. They set off, matching each other stride for stride. "Ray K.'s a real character."

"Oh, yeah," Jess said. "He grows on you."

"Jess, do you think Pearl's uncle did this to her?"

"I can't rule him out. We've contacted our field office in Bristol. Two agents are going to question to Mr. Ballou."

"I hope they go armed and prepared for a fight."

"They will. They've been warned." Jess took her hand. "But because of the barbiturates found in Pearl's stomach, I doubt she was murdered by one of Ballou's thugs." He let out a deep sigh. "I think Pearl was a victim of the government girl killer."

A fine drizzle began to fall. On North Capitol Street near Union Station, a young boy selling *The Washington Herald* called, "Another government girl murdered."

Eddie stopped on the street corner. Tears came. Jess brought his arm around her, then stepped away to flag a taxicab and opened its door.

They slid in. "Could you take us to the Parrot Room?" he said.

"Thanks, Jess," she whispered in the taxi's big backseat, rain speckling the windows. Over lunch she would tell him her suspicions about Bert, and he would tell her she was wrong.

47

Eddie fried big slices of fresh potatoes in the huge wrought iron skillet. She put the slices that she'd cooked in a baking pan and slipped it into the oven to stay warm while she cooked more. She longed to fill her stomach and go to bed.

"You look like you're a million miles away," Rachel said from the counter, where she sliced juicy beefsteak tomatoes.

Eddie nodded her head wooly with fatigue. "Do you realize how many German words there are for secretive?"

"*Geheimnisvoll, verschlossen, heimlich*," Rachel said with a fluency Eddie admired.

Like Eddie, Rachel's maternal grandmother had spoken German in addition to French. Rachel could probably do the Bureau's translating job better than Eddie. But Eddie had the certification, her degree from Emory and Henry.

"Don't forget *sekretorisch*."

Eddie had been secretive with Jess when they sat across from each other at a table in the charming Parrot Tea Room. There he had told her about his visit to the Rosen's farm and Luca's suicide attempt. And she'd told him about the image of Tony Guarco that had come to her when she stood over Pearl in the morgue. But she never mentioned Bert.

She couldn't, not yet and not just because Bert was blood kin, but because he was a good and kind man, who loved his unlovable mother.

As if summoned, a bedraggled Aunt Viola shuffled into the kitchen still in her bathrobe. She held an ice pack to her head, her feet in bedroom shoes.

"Hello Mrs. Trundle," Rachel said in a careful voice. That morning on the streetcar, Eddie had recounted her conversation with drunken Aunt Viola. "Are you hungry?"

"Not so much, Rachel, honey. Feels like someone's hammering inside my head."

Eddie turned from the skillet, spatula in hand and waited for her aunt to repeat her threat to make her move out.

Instead, Aunt Viola gave her a weak smile. "Edwina, I ought to be cooking for ya'll, not the other way round. You girls worked all day."

Eddie searched Aunt Viola's pale saggy face and said, "About last night…"

Her aunt waved stubby fingers in the air. "Death brings out the worse in folks, Edwina. No need for you to apologize." With that, she sank into a kitchen chair.

Eddie exchanged a gleeful glance with Rachel. Leave it to Aunt Viola to think she deserved the apology.

Someone knocked on the back porch screen. "I'll get it." Rachel came back leading Miss Minnie, who carried a long pan of cornbread between crocheted potholders.

"This is for ya'll," Miss Minnie said. "Careful, it's hot."

Eddie thanked her, took the pan with the pot holders, and set it on the stove.

Miss Minnie looked around at all of them. Her right eyelid fluttered a semaphore of distress. "I'm awful sorry about Miss Pearl."

Aunt Viola got up, brought her arms around Miss Minnie, buried her face in the colored woman's neck, and sobbed.

Eddie watched, surprised at the affection between them. Miss Minnie had worked for her aunt for years before getting the job at Berman's Laundry. They had a shared history Eddie didn't understand.

The two were about the same height, both a little under five feet. Miss

Minnie was the tidier of the two in a dazzling white apron and starched shirtwaist dress.

She hugged Aunt Viola back, patting her and saying, "there, there, Miss Viola."

The front door opened and shut.

"Your cornbread smells delicious, Miss Minnie," Rachel said at last. "We'll eat it with our supper."

The two women broke apart, and Miss Minnie left.

"Evenin' ladies." Bert came in, went to the sink, and washed his hands. "Something smells so good."

Eddie searched his familiar face. *Familiar*: a word taken from family. Bert had her father's smoke colored eyes and his large pink ears, flattened against the sides of his head. Bert was blood. He could not have murdered those girls.

A detective should not think like this. Jess often said everyone was a suspect until they had an ironclad alibi.

Eddie piled the golden corn on a platter and set it on the table. They bowed their head as was their custom and each said a private grace. As they ate, Eddie told them how Pearl's uncle Alton didn't want her body to be returned to Saltville. Even dead, Pearl was unwanted. "He wants nothing to do with her funeral."

"Well funerals cost a purty penny in Washington City." Aunt Viola sounded like her old self. "Don't think Bert nor I can pay for that gal's funeral."

"Hush, Mama," Bert said, his eyes darkened with anger. Aunt Viola shot him a fierce look but stayed silent. "I would help ya'll if I had the money."

"Jess and I will pay for it," Eddie told them. "We already decided."

Rachel patted her lips with a napkin. "I will pay, too. Pearl was my friend."

"I'll talk to Jim, the funeral director at Jones," Bert said. "We'll put on the nicest funeral you ever seen at a reasonable price."

"I just remembered something." Rachel rose from her seat. "Let me show you something." She went out to the porch.

Curious, Eddie and Bert followed. Rachel walked down the path along the garden and turned into the row of staked tomatoes.

She went to the scarecrow, lifted his shirt, and took out a roll wrapped in a small piece of tarp. "This is the money Pearl stole from her uncle."

"Well, I'll be," Bert said. "So that's where she hid it."

The rest of the evening Rachel and Eddie talked about what to do with the money.

48

Friday, July 14, 1944

In Saltville, depending on the prominence of the deceased, the body would be on display for several nights at the funeral parlor. Mourners came by to pay their respects to the dead and comfort the family. This was called the viewing. On a subsequent morning, the casket would be taken to church for the funeral service then driven in a hearse to the cemetery for the burial service. More prayers were said over the casket before somber men in dark suits using ropes lowered the casket into the ground. Mourners threw handfuls of dirt on top. *Ashes to ashes, dust to dust.* Afterwards, a reception would be held either in the church basement or at the deceased's home.

But in war-time funerals were accelerated stripped-down affairs. Pearl's would take place this Saturday.

"Thanks to Pearl's obituary you wrote and placed in newspapers, the word is out," Jess told Eddie on Friday night over dinner at Hot Shoppes. "It's possible the killer will show up tomorrow. We'll have plenty of police there watching everyone who attends."

Eddie swallowed hard. One man certain to be there: Bert. Since Jess was sharing more about the investigation, she wanted to reciprocate and had planned on telling him tonight her suspicions about Bert. But she couldn't.

After dinner, Alonso pulled up beside the curb, and Jess got in beside him. They were going to a taxi stand to talk to a driver about something he saw near the river on the Fourth of July. She watched them drive away.

She had more than blood in common with Bert, who was described by family members as "a little odd," the same way they described her. Anyone who didn't fit the Smith pattern of dropping out of school early, marrying young, and going to work for the mine was considered odd. But what if Bert was the killer?

Bert hadn't liked Pearl. After the night Pearl went to his bedroom and offered to rub his back, he had avoided her. While he was kind to her when the thug from Saltville beat her up, he'd recently insisted she move out. And Eddie had been glad for that. Poor Pearl had felt unwanted, unloved.

Back on Georgia Avenue, Eddie went to her bedroom, took out her secret notebook, and went over her notes about the case. From memory she'd listed the psychiatrist's template about the killer's personality. One characteristic gave her pause: *the killer has troubled relationships with women, especially with his mother.*

Bert certainly had an unusual one with Aunt Viola. He was more attached to his mother than a grown man ought to be. And he appeared to have no sexual interest in women, something Eddie hadn't noticed until her suspicions about him were aroused.

Downstairs, the phone began to ring. Eddie looked at her watch. "The Green Hornet" was on the radio, meaning Aunt Viola wouldn't stir from her chair. Eddie went down and answered it.

"Hello Eddie," her father said. "I got your letter."

"Dad, hello, how are you?" Her heart began to drum. Although she'd told herself she wasn't going back to Saltville no matter what, disobeying her father would not be easy. Unlike her wild twin sisters, she'd always been the good daughter. In that regard she was like Bert, too attached to a parent. Because of Mama's illness, they'd lived in a state of siege. As a ten-year-old, she was on guard while her father worked, watching over her sisters, making sure they got fed and Mama didn't burn the house down. School had felt restful to Eddie.

Her father cleared his throat. She knew he was afraid of losing her. "Eddie, you promised me your work in Washington was only for the summer. You're going back on your word."

And a person was only as good as his word.

"But I didn't know the Bureau of Investigation would need my translation skills. I'm doing important work now, Dad." This was true. She was working on a project called "The White Rose," preparing German leaflets the Allies would drop over German cities.

Her father sighed, a signal of his resignation.

She wanted to tell him she was making more money than she had as a high school teacher, but this would make him feel bad because it meant she made more than he did. She wanted to tell him she would help the twins with their education. Dot wanted to go to beauty school, and Irene hoped to take a secretarial course to learn shorthand, but this might backfire, too. Her father was a proud mountain man, who believed he ought to be the one to help his daughters.

"Well, you'll be twenty-one in September," he said at last. "But could you come home to see your mother? As much as she loves the twins, you've always been her favorite."

"I will if I can get away." If she visited Saltville, she was certain to get mired in their troubles, but she could put this off for a while. He had accepted that she was staying in Washington. That was enough for now. "Would you like to speak to Aunt Viola?"

"Heavens, no," he almost shouted. "Remember I'm paying for this call. One more thing, I need to ask you. It's about this murdered girl, Pearl Ballou. I recall you mentioned her name before. Did you know her?"

Eddie had sent Pearl's brief obituary to all the Washington newspapers as well as to the *Saltville Daily News*. She knew Dad, who devoured the newspaper, would read it.

Eddie swallowed hard. Until now, their call had gone well. "I taught her last year." The less said about Pearl the better. "How are my sisters? Has Irene heard from Elmer?"

"They can tell you about their boyfriends in a letter, Edwina." With that, they said good-bye.

When Eddie got up from the telephone bench, her own eyes met her in the dusty hall mirror. "You haven't grown up yet," she whispered to her reflection. While she hadn't lied to her father about Pearl, she hadn't told him the truth, either. When he found out Pearl had lived here at Aunt Viola's, which he was sure to, he would be furious.

She went upstairs, sat on her bed and wrote him a letter, telling him how Pearl had become part of her life.

Saturday arrived cloudy and hot with fierce humidity. She looked forward to Washington in winter when your breath turned to clouds, and a cool wind blew around corners and down the broad avenues.

An hour before the funeral ceremony, Alonso drove Jess, Eddie, and Rachel to Jones Funeral Parlor. Alonso would stay outside with the car, his camera handy to photograph mourners.

Air conditioning met them in the lobby. Eddie and Rachel signed the guest book beneath Aunt Viola's signature. A solemn Bert opened the door to the small chapel, icebox cold, and whispered, "Mama's up front."

The chapel was small and windowless except for a large stained glass window behind the altar. Its deep greens and blues made the room dark. Wall sconces gave off an eerie yellow light.

Pearl's coffin was set on a dais before the altar, its lid open.

From the first row of chairs, Aunt Viola in a little black hat, veil and dress looked over her shoulder and waved a white-gloved hand at them. No one else was here. "I hope other people come," Eddie whispered to Rachel. What if no one showed up? That would be awful.

"Do you want to go and and…look at her?" Rachel's words quivered.

Because Pearl had been murdered, Eddie thought an open casket would be inappropriate, but Bert changed her mind. "Don't worry," he'd said. "I'll hide her wound. You know Pearl. She would have wanted the works."

Eddie took Rachel's hand. Together, they walked to the casket and looked inside. Rachel gasped. Astonished, Eddie covered her mouth. "She's so beautiful, isn't she?" Tears in Rachel's voice.

"Yes." Eddie took in the pale red-haired girl on a bed of white satin. Bert had rolled Pearl's long hair into a blue net snood that matched her flowered dress. He let her freckles show, colored her lashes lightly with mascara, and painted her lips with the pink lipstick Pearl always wore. "Bert's an artist with makeup. She looks so alive."

"I can't stand that she's gone." Rachel sobbed and went to sit beside Aunt Viola, who comforted her.

Eddie couldn't afford to get weepy. She needed her wits about her to help Jess watch for the killer.

"She's wearing that same lipstick color, azalea blossom," Jess said over Eddie's shoulder. He stared down at Pearl. "I wonder why Bert put her lipstick on a little above her lip line."

Jess's comment made her skin prickle. It signaled that Jess suspected Bert, too.

"That's the way his mother wears it," she whispered and looked into Jess's baby blue eyes. "When women get older, their lips become thin."

A large spray of yellow roses stood behind the coffin. Jess read the card attached to them and handed the card to Eddie. *Forgive me, Pearl. I'll love you forever. Luca.*

"Forgive him for what?" Eddie whispered. Maybe Luca killed her. "Is it possible Luca…?"

"I'm not ruling him out."

A tall thin man in a limp beige linen suit came in the small side door, sat at the organ, and played "Amazing Grace." Deep resonant chords filled the chapel.

"Time to take our places." Jess went to the chapel's back corner, where he could survey the crowd.

Eddie extended an arm to Rachel, who dried her eyes and got up.

A woman's sharp voice in the lobby made them hurry to the chapel doors. They would act as Pearl's next of kin and greet mourners as they entered. Rachel squeezed Eddie's hand. "Maybe that's her cousin."

Eddie had sent a telegram to Pearl's cousin, Mae, in Chilhowie, Virginia, informing her of the time and place of Pearl's funeral and encouraging her to come. Mae was the cousin who'd adopted Pearl's son, Billy. If Mae showed up for the funeral, she would be richly rewarded. They would give her the money Pearl had stolen. They wanted Billy to have the money and knew of no other way to give it to a baby.

A slender woman in a cloche hat, her silver hair streaked with gray, ushered in three young women. "Hello, I'm Mrs. Shelton, Pearl's supervisor."

She took Eddie's hand, then Rachel's. "These young ladies trained and worked with Pearl on the switchboard." She said each girl's name. "We're so sorry about Pearl."

Eddie said Rachel's name and her own, hoping Mrs. Shelton wouldn't remember she was the one who had given Pearl an excellent job reference.

The government girls shook hands and hurried to Pearl's casket. Were they here because they cared about Pearl or had they come out of curiosity?

The organist moved on to a vigorous "Leaning on the Everlasting Arms," his shoulders rolling over the organ's keys, his foot pumping its pedals.

Mrs. Shelton sat in the back row of chairs. Maybe they would need to slip out before the ceremony was over. After all, who was manning the switchboard while they were gone?

"I hope Mae comes," Rachel whispered, hugging her shawl around her bare shoulders.

Three men entered.

"Hello there," said Dan Wozniak in a dark tie and stiff suit. He gave off the scent of mothballs and Old Spice aftershave. He nodded to Eddie then took Rachel's hand, which he held longer than necessary. "It's a crying shame about Pearl. I didn't know her so well, but she…" At a loss for words, he tugged at his collar and stepped aside.

Tony, his hair slicked back, eyes darting away from theirs even as he took their hands. His mumbled *condolence* was negated by his lips that curved into a slight grin. Blushing, he covered his mouth.

He wasn't sorry Pearl was dead. Eddie wished she had a camera to photograph him. If ever a man looked guilty, it was Tony. He scurried away to join Dan on the back row, which was getting crowded.

Luca, pale and drawn, stood before them, gazing from Eddie to Rachel and back again. His Adam's apple bobbed when he swallowed. "Sorry for being so rude when you called my work that day to ask about Pearl… I…"

He raked his fingers through unruly red hair, and Eddie noticed the white bandage on his wrist. She brought a hand to his shoulder, remembering how she'd thought he was Pearl's doppelganger the night they first met. Since then, Luca had aged. Now he looked a decade older than the girl in the coffin.

"Eddie, would you please go with me up there?" Luca asked. "I have to see her one more time, but I don't want to go alone."

She nodded and whispered to Rachel, "Be right back."

Eddie walked beside Luca to the coffin. The government girls stepped aside for them.

"She's, she's so lovely," he said, reached his hand in, and brought his palm to the side of Pearl's face.

Eddie stepped back. "I'm right behind you, Luca." She had viewed Pearl once. That was enough.

"You're Madge, aren't you?" Eddie said to the pudgy brunette from Pearl's office. "Pearl said you helped her work on her diction. Thank you for being kind to her."

Madge grinned. "Pearl was quite a gal. Our office isn't as much fun without her." She looked toward the coffin and Luca, who was openly weeping. "I reckon that's one of her fellas."

This surprised Eddie. How many fellows did Pearl have? Tony had come to Luca's side and was whispering to him, so Eddie drew Madge aside. "The red-headed man is Luca, Pearl's boy friend. I think Pearl also had a crush on Tony, the dark-haired man with him."

"Oh, yeah, Pearl carried a torch for a lot of 'em. Her latest was the curly-headed one over there." Madge turned to the front row of chairs, where Thad Graham in a dark suit and tie sat talking to Aunt Viola, his hand around her shoulder.

Eddie hadn't noticed him come in. "Are you sure Pearl liked Thad?"

"He's the reporter, right?"

"Yes."

"Pearl told me he was Rachel's boy friend first," Madge said. "Pearl felt real bad about that because Rachel was her friend." Madge shrugged. "But, like I told Pearl, all's fair in love and war."

Eddie recalled Pearl using that phrase and had wondered where she'd gotten it.

Rachel had joined Aunt Viola and Thad on the front row. Thad sat between the women, an arm around both.

Had Pearl only imagined a romance with Thad? Pearl believed she had only one thing to offer a man. And she hadn't recognized or appreciated Luca, who really cared about her. Did that mean Luca didn't kill her? Or that he had?

Bert came to the front, gazed into the casket a long moment, and closed it, a signal the ceremony was about to begin. The minister, who was affiliated with the funeral home, entered in a black robe and put a Bible and some papers on the lectern.

"I'd like to talk to you some more about Pearl," Eddie whispered to Madge.

"Pearl told me you're with the FBI." Madge's was gaze full of admiration.

Eddie nodded, not bothering to say she was a mere translator.

"Call me at the War Department," Madge said. "I'm on the switchboard. I'll do anything to help you catch Pearl's killer." Madge squeezed her hand and joined her supervisor and the other government girls on the back row.

Jess was talking with a small man in a dark jacket. Eddie recognized him as the owner of Florida Avenue Radio and Electronics, Pearl's favorite shop.

Eddie sat beside Rachel. Thad had his arm snug around Rachel's, his palm cupped on the ridge of her shoulder. When he sent Eddie a concerned look, she nodded to him, glad he had come.

The minister stood behind the lectern and cleared his throat. "Brothers and sisters, so will it be with the resurrection of the dead. The body that is sown is perishable, it is raised imperishable; it is sown in dishonor, it is raised in glory, it is sown in weakness, it is raised in power, it is sown a natural body, it is raised a spiritual body. First Corinthians, chapter fifteen."

The minister said he didn't know the deceased. Eddie was afraid he would mention something about Pearl's murder, but his talk focused on how hard it is for people to accept the death of a young person. The smooth flow of his words told Eddie he gave this sermon often. Young American men were dying all over the globe.

Rachel lowered her head and sobbed. Would her grief be lessened if she knew Pearl had a crush on Thad? Out the corner of her eye, Eddie watched Thad, wondering about him and Pearl. Eddie couldn't believe Thad had been interested in Pearl.

After the minister gave a final prayer, and the mourners sang "O God,

Our Help in Ages Past," Bert and other Jones Funeral Home men carried the casket out of the chapel. The mourners followed in the procession.

Outside, a bruised sky greeted them. Ray K. and a uniformed policeman waited beside a police car. The casket was loaded into the back of the hearse.

From two directions, flashes of light went off. Alonso took photos from behind the Packard, while another photographer, a badge hung around his neck, stood on the grass snapping shots of them exiting the church. Thad was standing beside the other photographer.

Furious, Eddie brought her purse up to cover her face.

Rachel said to Eddie, "Aunt Viola and I will ride with Thad out to the Rosen's."

"Do you really want to take Thad out there? He's using you and the rest of us for a story about Pearl's funeral."

Rachel went pale. "I'd like to slap you, Eddie. Jess wants to keep Pearl's name in the news so people might come forward with information. Thad is doing Jess a favor."

49

Eddie rode beside Alonso in silence. Her argument with Rachel had left her feeling hollow and sad. Aunt Viola was right. Death brought out the worst in people.

But at least Alonso trusted her enough now to be alone with her.

Jess was riding with Ray K., so the detectives could talk.

When they crossed over streetcar tracks, Alonso steadied his camera between them on the Packard's big front seat.

"Oh, by the way, I've been meaning to congratulate you," Eddie said to him. "Jess told me your photographs were selected for the show at the Phillips Gallery."

"Thanks." Alonso smiled into the rain-flecked windshield. "When the museum director called me with the news, I had to sit down to catch my breath. I could hardly believe it."

"You shouldn't be surprised. Your photographs are unforgettable."

"Thanks, Eddie. That means a lot. I didn't think they would choose me because well, because I'm a Negro. When I reminded the director of this, the man laughed." The funeral cortege had stopped for the light on Colesville Road. Alonso looked over at her. "He actually laughed and said he had figured that out. See, I sent him my photograph, but sometimes in black and white, folks aren't sure about me."

"In a better world a person's color won't matter."

"Uh-huh, sure," Alonso said with a hint of sarcasm.

"Which photographs did they choose?" Eddie was glad to talk about something other than Pearl.

Later Eddie remembered what Rachel had told her. "Did Jess ask Thad to write about Pearl's funeral?"

"No. The Bureau still believes the less people know about the government girl murders the better. Clay told me Thad was here for Rachel's sake."

"Clay?"

"Thad's photographer. We got to talking outside during the funeral. Turns out, he was a freelancer until the government girl murders, when Thad got him a job with *The Herald.* "

"Odd how something as awful as murder can be good for someone's career."

"If folks didn't kill each other, Jess and I would still be in Alabama, trying to wrestle a living from those tired acres outside Abbeville. Not that I'll ever be grateful for murder."

Rain lashed the Packard as they turned onto a narrow road that cut through a cornfield on the Rosen's farm. Wind whipped the corn into a green frenzy. "This is all we need, to bury Pearl in a rainstorm."

The Rosens had offered a burial plot in their small family cemetery.

Alonso pulled up beside the tall wrought iron fence that enclosed eleven headstones and a freshly dug grave. Pearl would lie for eternity with strangers, but in her case strangers had been kinder than kin. Not even her cousin Mae had shown up for her funeral.

"Wait right there, Eddie." Alonso jumped out, opened the trunk, and appeared at Eddie's door, a huge umbrella opened over her. She stepped out beside him.

"You take the umbrella," he said. "I've got a rain slicker in the back big enough for me and my camera."

Yes, Eddie thought. This lonely graveyard in the rain surrounded by waves of swaying corn would make for dramatic photographs. The mourners, all under black umbrellas provided by the funeral parlor, had dwindled. Neither the switchboard operators from the War Department nor the

Florida Avenue shop owner had come here.

Aunt Viola and Rachel stood huddled around Thad, who held their umbrella with one hand, his other snug around Rachel.

Bert and the funeral home men carried the coffin to the grave with the rest of them following. The girl named Dominique walked among the mourners, giving out long-stemmed red roses.

At the head of Pearl's grave was a tall thick cross, its wood grain varnished to a gloss that shone even in the rain. Where the two pieces of wood met, a flat board was attached. There her name had been burned into the wood in block letters: PEARL BALLOU. Beneath her name were the words GOVERNMENT GIRL in flowing script.

Eddie choked at this.

Luca wiped raindrops off the cross with the end of his sleeve. Tony stood behind him, sheltering him with an umbrella. Luca's touch said so much. He must have made the cross, varnished the wood, and burned her name into it.

The words he had chosen to describe Pearl showed he knew her heart. Being a government girl was her highest ambition. Eddie felt the pull of tears.

After the coffin was lowered into the dark rectangle in the ground, the minister read the Twenty-third Psalm. *The Lord is my shepherd, I shall not want...* When he got to the part about walking through *the valley of the shadow of death,* Luca's sob could be heard above the crackling rain.

One by one, they dropped their roses into the grave. Eddie liked this symbolism better than Saltville's custom of throwing a handful of dirt on the coffin.

Sara Rosen appeared in a belted trench coat beside the cemetery gate. "Lunch will be served at the house. Everyone is invited." She pointed to her house, its tin roof visible over the sea of corn.

Eddie turned back to the cemetery and found Rachel standing in the rain alone. Eddie ran to her and brought the umbrella over her. Rachel, her hair plastered to her head, stood at the foot of another grave. The stone read: *Barbara Bendix Margolis.* Below her name were the dates 1908-1939.

She had been thirty-one. At one time, Eddie thought thirty was old, but not anymore.

"I've never seen her grave before." Rachel's voice a scrape. She brought her arm around Eddie. "Papa never even told me where she was buried. What kind of a family are we?"

"I've always thought the Sunday afternoon grave-visiting people do in Saltville is depressing." Eddie brought her hand to the side to Rachel's face. "Remember what you loved about your mother, like the way she read you fairytales in German. Forget weeding her grave or putting flowers on it and remember."

"You're right, dear Eddie." Rachel's eyes crinkled above a brilliant smile. "Forgive me for what I said earlier at the funeral home."

"You were just upset about Pearl. We both are."

"Rachel?" Thad strode toward them from the cemetery gate.

On the way to the Rosens' house, Jess rode with them. Ray K. and his driver had to go back to town. Bert, the minister, and the other men from the funeral home left as well. Bert had two more funerals to put on today.

Jess said, "Ray K. and I want to have a meeting with both of you. We're going to pool everything we know and see where it takes us."

"I'm included?" Eddie tried to hide her excitement.

"Absolutely," Jess said. "I let Ray K. know you're helping us out in an unofficial capacity."

Sara Rosen greeted them at the front door. "Welcome. Leave your umbrellas and slickers on the porch, and come in." Eddie introduced Jess and Alonso to her. "I've heard a lot about you two from my husband. Thank you for coming. Go into the dining room and help yourself to lunch."

When Alonso turned toward the kitchen, Sara took his arm. "No, Mr. Crooms. We eat together here. No segregation."

A buffet of cold turkey, cheese, thick crusty bread, potato salad, tomato slices, pickles, and many desserts were laid out on the table in the dining room. On a drinks trolley were bottles of wine. Beside the trolley sat a tub of ice filled with soft drinks and beer.

All of the men got wine or beer, except Jess and Alonso, who went for the grape sodas. After a long sip, they exchanged a look that made her imagine them as little boys at a general store, digging in an ice chest for cold grape Nehis.

They ate in chairs along the windows, plates on their laps, the gauzy curtains blowing about. Thunder grumbled in the distance, before a bolt of lightning lit the sky.

A storm brewed inside as well. Dan's dark eyes stayed on Thad, who was charming the ladies, Rachel, Aunt Viola, and Sara Rosen. A brooding Tony sat alone in a corner watching Dominique coaxing Luca to eat. Chubby Clay, the photographer, ate standing by the food table, filling his plate and emptying it as if he was starved.

A door shut, and Meyer Rosen appeared from the front porch.

Dan went to him and helped him off with his raincoat. Jess and Alonso stood and greeted him. "May I speak with you in private, Agent Lindsay?" Mr. Rosen said.

Jess followed him away, while Alonso went around the dining room looking at the photographs of the Rosens with famous people. Clay, carrying a thick turkey sandwich, joined Alonso.

In the parlor, a young man began to play "The Chattanooga Choo-Choo" on the grand piano. Rachel clapped. "That's Pearl's favorite." She led Thad out of the dining room, followed by a delighted Aunt Viola, who was enjoying this funeral so much. Dominique and Luca went to the music as well. Sara Rosen knew how to lift people's spirits.

"Who's the Goldie Locks hanging on Rachel?" Dan asked Eddie, still sitting, uneaten food on her plate. She had no appetite.

"His name is Thad Graham. He's a reporter for the *Herald*."

"Seems pretty full of himself." Dan finished off a bottle of beer in one swig.

"Oh, yeah," Eddie said. "I'm afraid he might be here under false pretenses." In saying this she was throwing gasoline on Dan's fire, but she wanted to see how Thad would react if confronted by Dan Wozniak.

"What do ya mean?" Dan sat beside her, elbows on his knees, his face flushed. Eddie hadn't seen Dan eat anything. His only consumption was beer.

"I mean he's gathering information to write a story about Pearl's funeral. He even brought his photographer along." Eddie nodded across the room to

Clay, admiring a photograph of the Rosen's with President Roosevelt.

"Meyer doesn't want publicity about this." Dan got up and strode to the parlor.

Tony was watching her across the room. Eddie saw her chance and went to him.

"Buzz off," Tony told her. "I know you're with the Bureau. Pearl must of bragged about the great Eddie Smith a hundred times. To hear her tell it, you're Hoover's right hand."

Eddie warmed inside, so happy Pearl had been proud of her. "Tony, you were the last person to see Pearl alive."

"Listen Nosey Parker, whoever killed her was the last person." His features contorted into the hateful look Eddie had seen him give Pearl.

When she was younger, Tony's rebuke would have silenced, but not anymore. "Did you kill her? I know you despised her."

An evil smile opened his face. "For your information, I didn't kill her even though I'm not sorry she's dead."

Eddie kept her expression neutral. Outside the sky became dark as night. When Luca showed up on Georgia Avenue, Pearl had often asked her to come along with them and be Tony's date, but Eddie refused. Tony gave her the creeps.

"Why did you leave Pearl alone in the woods?"

"Because she's a disgusting slut. First, Luca did the deed with her then me. I wanted to show him how low she was. Then she goes and gets herself killed, and he swears he'll never love anyone again." He slumped in his chair. "He's my best friend even if he is an idiot."

Eddie felt embarrassed, imagining this scene on a blanket in the woods. But a detective couldn't be a prude. "So you just walked away and left her there alone in the woods?"

"Yeah." His laugh was wicked. "Old Pearl was drunk and naked, but still very much alive." He shrugged. "And when they found her, she had her clothes on."

The sound of a scuffle came from the parlor. The music stopped. Rachel shrieked.

"Stop it, Dan," Sara called.

Eddie jumped up and ran into the other room behind Clay and Alonso. "You don't know who you're messing with," Thad shouted.

Dan was straddling Thad on the floor, waving a broken beer bottle near his face.

Clay grabbed Dan's arm and brought it behind his back, forcing Dan to drop the broken bottle. Alonso picked it up.

"Danny, what are you doing?" Mr. Rosen called from the doorway, Jess at his side. "This young man is our guest."

Dan got up, went to his benefactor, and whispered something to him. "I'll handle that," Mr. Meyer said. "Get some coffee in the kitchen and go back to work."

Dan walked out, his head low like a chastised child.

Clay helped Thad up.

"Are you all right?" Mr. Rosen asked.

After Thad assured him that he was, Mr. Rosen said, "We were happy to provide a burial place for this poor girl, but we'd prefer not to see our names in the newspaper in connection with these awful murders."

"I understand, Sir." Thad straightened his tie. "I assure you neither your name nor your home will be mentioned in my story. I'm so impressed with the work you do for the war..." Thad launched his charm offense, but Meyer Rosen might be a little tougher than the ladies who fell so easily for him.

The pianist played a familiar song. Rachel and Eddie joined in. *I'll be seeing you in all those old familiar places.* Rachel, her eyes bright with tears, brought her arm around Eddie.

"I'm feeling low about Pearl." Rachel wiped at her eyes.

"I know," Eddie said. She wanted to ask Rachel if she knew about Thad and Pearl, but she didn't want to rock the boat of their friendship right now. Not until she had the facts.

When they got ready to leave, Rachel took Eddie aside. "The room we three shared feels haunted to me. I'm not sleeping well there, so I'm going to stay out here with Sara and Meyer a while and ride with Sara into the city to work."

"I understand," Eddie said, sensing this was a kind of ending.

She went to sit in the Packard's backseat. As Alonso drove away, she got on her knees and looked out the rear windshield at Rachel on the Rosen's porch until she faded from view.

50

Tuesday, July 18, 1944

Eddie ran down the marble steps of the gorgeous Beaux-Arts building. She was late. On Seventh Street, a streetcar passed so full it didn't stop. She blinked hard. Her eyes burned from the strain of reading the blurry print of archived newspapers for hours, but she had to go prepared to this meeting.

When the next streetcar stopped, she got aboard, her document case under her arm. This streetcar was filled with women shoppers carrying Hecht Company and Woodward and Lothrop bags. They must be in the same club because they talked to each other across the aisle about children and what they intended to make for dinner. All wore white gloves and hats, so similar in dress they could have been in uniform.

Eddie always believed she wanted to be a wife and mother, but now she wasn't sure. She knew she was doing the most important work she would probably ever do. Not just translating, but helping with the investigation of the government girl murders. She was using everything she'd ever learned and was learning more every day. All this made her feel fully alive. She sensed nothing in her future would ever be as challenging. She dreaded the present becoming past.

And her happiness seemed wrong considering Pearl's murder.

Holding tight to the strap above, she closed her eyes, her pulse drumming in her throat. She'd uncovered information that might lead to the killer. She couldn't wait to tell Jess. Of course, it was also possible her information might lead nowhere.

Only last month she had run along this street, fleeing from Austin at the Hay-Adams Hotel. That day felt like a decade ago. She barely recognized the frightened young woman who had wanted to go home to her father. She belonged here now. When had that happened?

The smell of baking bread signaled her stop. At the aroma, her stomach gurgled. She'd skipped lunch, so she could leave the Bureau early for the Carnegie library.

After crossing on V Street, she took the alley. Two women on a stoop snapping string beans went silent. Their eyes narrowed at her. White women didn't go down the alley. From the stoop next door, one of Miss Minnie's friends waved at Eddie, and Eddie waved back. The bean snappers returned to snapping and gossiping.

She opened the gate, ran under the honeysuckle arch, and knocked on the garage door. Beyond her, Miss Minnie and Ruth deep in the garden's green were watering, while Aunt Viola watched from the porch, directing them like an overseer.

Eddie vowed to weed tomorrow. She needed the exercise.

No one answered her knock. She heard male voices in the room above and pushed open the door.

Jess met her on the steps wearing his lopsided grin. He lowered his head to give her a quick kiss when she took hold of his tie, brought him closer, and kissed him deeply.

"No lovey dovey stuff you two," Ray K. called.

Jess broke away, whispered her name, and let her go first up the steps, his hand on her back.

"There she is," Ray K. said. "You want sugar in your iced tea, Sugar?" Glasses of tea were set on the large scarred desk placed in front of the case map that covered the entire back wall.

"No sugar needed. It looks delicious." She sat with Ray K. behind the desk, accepted the tea, and sipped. But her delight was short lived.

Bert's photo had been added to the wall along with Luca and Tony's.

In his photograph, Bert wore his black suit, shiny at the seams. Alonso must have taken it during the funeral.

"Why is Bert up there?" she asked.

"Before we get to Bert, Eddie," Jess said, "let's talk about what we need to do here. How this will work." His eyes lingered a moment.

"You were saying?" Ray K. said.

"Our meeting is for the free exchange of ideas." Jess took the chair closest to her. "All of us need to say whatever comes into our heads, no matter how crazy. No censorship, not from ourselves or each other. Agreed?"

Alonso nodded.

"Yes," Eddie said, but she doubted this would produce good results. She had never played well with others.

"Do we have to cut our fingers and become blood brothers?" Ray K. squinted with delight, and Eddie wondered if Detective Ray K. had detected that Jess and Alonso were brothers.

"Speaking of blood, why is Bert's photo up there?" She persisted.

"That's what I mean, Eddie. Just because Bert's your cousin, doesn't mean he isn't the killer. We can't rule anyone out. Alonso and I decided to include any man who knew Pearl and had access to a vehicle."

"So that would include you and Alonso?"

"Okay," Jess said. "You want our photos up there? We'll put 'em up. And I'll admit I didn't like Pearl."

"Me, either." Alonso sat beside the case map, twirling a grease pencil.

"How come?" Ray K. asked, his feet up on a small stepstool.

Jess blushed. "She was a little wild."

"You're censoring yourself, Jess," Eddie said. His word *wild* snagged on something in her memory, but she couldn't recall what, so she wrote it in her notebook to be considered later.

Jess told Ray K. about the night Pearl came to their bungalow and offered herself to them in thanks for sending her uncle's thug back to Saltville.

Eddie had known about this because Pearl got locked out of the house, and Eddie had to sneak downstairs and let her in. Jess described the incident in a factual way, only his flushed face showed how he felt.

Ray K. covered his mouth. "Guess that surprised you."

"There's more," Jess went onto to tell him about the night Pearl died.

Eddie could not believe she was sitting among men who were talking so explicitly about sex.

Alonso, clearly uncomfortable, poured everyone more tea from a sweating pitcher.

"And Pearl was your roommate?" Ray K. asked Eddie.

Refusing to be embarrassed, Eddie said, "Yes. I don't think I ever told you Jess, but Pearl went to Bert's room a week after we arrived and offered him a back rub."

"Did he take her up on it?" Ray K. asked.

"No." If he knew Bert, he wouldn't ask. Now she was censoring herself, protecting her cousin. "After that Bert walked a wide path around her, not that he was ever unkind to her."

"We questioned Bert today at Berman's Laundry." Jess got up and went to the map. "Its plant is located here on MacArthur Boulevard, near Glen Echo Park and not far from all the murder scenes." Alonso got up and marked it on the map.

Eddie set her glass down. "He must have been upset when you showed up there."

"He has no alibi for the night Pearl was murdered. He told us he got drunk and slept it off on a cot in the laundry's break-room, but the plant was closed, so no one can verify this."

"Drunk? That doesn't sound like him."

Jess shrugged. "He says he does that every now and then to let off steam away from home."

Alonso turned from the wall. "A taxi driver told us a laundry truck pulled in front of him on Canal Road the night of the Fourth right here. He said the truck was weaving like the driver was drunk."

Eddie got up and went to the map. "So the truck pulled out near Sycamore Island?"

"Right here." Alonso pointed to an x on the map. "It's the closest parking area to the C&O Canal and Sycamore Island."

"Did Bert say he drove anywhere that night?" Eddie asked.

"No. He swore he would never do that."

"Well, my boys uncovered something interesting," Ray K. said. "Tony

Guarco has a nice little roadster that's in a garage for repair on Colesville Road." He got up and brought his thumb to the place on the map. Alonso marked it.

Jess said. "Maybe he lied because the Philadelphia Department of Motor Vehicles says he has no driver's license. We'll go out to Rosen's and talk to him tomorrow." Jess picked up his glass. "If he doesn't come clean about all this maybe a few days in the DC jail will jog his memory."

From her new leather document case, Eddie took Photostat copies from the library. "Thad Graham's photograph ought to be in your gallery. He knew Pearl, and he has a car. He was working as a proofreader for *The Herald,* writing only a few "Society Page" articles until he broke the government girl murders in May."

Ray K. groaned. "I knew Thad before those stories broke. He's a Princeton grad, working his way up. *The Herald* starts all their cub reporters out proofing. The kid got lucky that Sunday night in May. He happened to be watching the police station when I left for Arlington Cemetery."

Eddie slumped. All her research for naught. "Thad lives in a house on the Palisades owned by Mr. Berman. The house isn't far from the laundry plant. Bert said Thad sometimes borrowed a truck when he was low on gas."

"She's good," Ray K. made a gun with his finger and shot it at her. "Get's the bit between her teeth and won't let go."

Jess wrote in his notebook. "On our way out to see Tony, we'll stop at that plant and ask the manager about Thad borrowing their trucks."

Eddie looked up from her notebook. "I want to talk to Pearl's friends from the War Department switchboard about the men in Pearl's life. Also Thad told Rachel he had a lead on a place out his way that Pearl could rent. She went there not long before she was killed."

"Eddie will be able to get more out of those gals than we could," Ray K. said. "Girl talk, right? Maybe on Saturdays you ought to take her around to all the roommates of the murdered girls. Interview them again."

Eddie wasn't sure this was a compliment, but she would do it. "Sure. Good idea."

"Alonso, you haven't opened your mouth. What's your contribution to all this?"

Alonso crossed his arms. "Okay. So we've interviewed a lot of service-men and fellows working here, but what if our suspect is none of these guys? What if he's someone out of the blue, a total stranger?"

Ray K. shrugged. "So where should we look?"

"We believe he's in uniform, right?" Alonso raked them with a glance. They nodded.

Alonso said, "What if he's a policeman?"

At this, Ray K. took his feet off the stool and straightened. "Now wait a minute."

Jess nodded. "Good possibility. It would explain how he got into all these parks and other places with the woman. In a police uniform, no one would question him."

"And the women would trust him," Eddie said.

"Most DC police have had their backgrounds checked seven ways to Sunday."

"But Ray K., you told me how you lost a lot of men to the war and had to hire some you didn't think were up to the job."

"I meant they're too old. We took back some guys who'd retired."

"Could you look at men who were let go from the force?" Jess leaned forward. "Or men who've been disciplined for using too much force?"

The idea of looking at the bad apples mollified Ray K. He tilted his chair back. "Okay," he said. "I'll do the same for the Park Police, and the forces in Arlington and Silver Spring."

"Could the killer be a woman?" Eddie asked.

Ray K. gave his wide wolfish grin. "See what you started, Al."

Jess said, "She'd have to be a large strong woman. Would a government girl go off with such a woman?"

"In your notes about finding Kaye Krieger's body," Eddie told Jess, "you wrote that two vehicles were parked near the gates to Arlington Cemetery, Thad's car and his photographer's truck. Why did they come separately?"

"I already told Jess that Thad followed me there," Ray K. said. "Then he found a telephone booth and called Clay, his pal, who's a photographer. They were both there waiting for these two to find their way through the city." He sent two fingers at Jess and Alonso.

"The nearest telephone booth is in the cemetery's visitor's center, which closes at dark." Eddie said. "Thad couldn't have called from there."

Jess was writing in his notebook. "I'll look into this."

"Stop chasing your tail, Jess," Ray K. rolled his eyes with exasperation as if Jess was humoring her. "Arlington, Virginia is the civilized world, Eddie. They have plenty of telephone booths over there. Thad could have driven up Wilson Boulevard and called Clay."

Someone knocked downstairs. Alonso grabbed a wad of money from his wallet and answered the door. "Hey there, Macy," he said. "Sure smells good."

Eddie and Ray K. looked at each other, while Jess got out plates.

Alonso came up with a bag of fried chicken and biscuits. "Dinner from the Florida Grill."

Eddie understood why they'd ordered out. It was hard to find a place where coloreds and whites could eat together. They dug into the crispy chicken and fluffy hot biscuits.

Late that night Jess walked Eddie to the front door on Georgia Avenue. "You and Rachel, be careful around Bert." Jess held her.

Eddie didn't have the heart to tell him Rachel hadn't slept on Georgia Avenue since Pearl's funeral. Eddie had been sleeping fine in her twin bed by the window, but that night her suspicions went wild. Maybe because Bert's photograph was up on the wall now.

She tiptoed downstairs to the kitchen and got a butcher knife from the block.

On the cabinet over the sink was a calendar that listed Bert's Civil Defense meetings. She took it down from the wall and looked through the months. Every meeting was around the time a government girl's body had been found, except for Pearl's.

Her heart thumped as she took the stairs back to bed, her hand around the knife handle. She wedged a chair under the door handle and got into bed, the knife under her pillow.

She was certain she wouldn't be able to sleep, but she drifted off as if she had no cares.

51

Thursday, July 27, 1944

"Eddie," Rachel called and waved from across Constitution Avenue. In her fitted gabardine suit from her first day as a government girl, and her hair rolled into a wreath around her head, she looked older, less glamorous, a quiet beauty.

Eddie ran across with the walk light and hugged her. She hadn't seen Rachel since the funeral almost two weeks ago.

"I've missed you so much, *Bubala*," Rachel whispered.

Eddie got teary. "Me, too, Schatzi."

Pet names they'd dispensed with once they arrived here. Being here in Washington among so many young women their age and living with Pearl had diluted the friendship they'd had in Saltville. For that moment, holding Rachel, she longed for their shared past, their friendship, the deepest Eddie had ever known.

"Where can we go and have a long talk and a decent dinner?" Rachel asked.

"Saltville," Eddie said.

Rachel threw her head back and laughed so hard her face pinked. "I'd forgotten what a nut you can be."

Eddie walked to the curb and hailed a taxi, which stopped with a screech of brakes.

"Be still my beating heart." Rachel's dimples deepened with glee. "Eddie Smith hailed a cab."

"Okay, I'm a little less of a penny pincher than I used to be." Eddie slid into the back, Rachel at her side. The friends exchanged a glance. Rachel had changed in some basic way, and Eddie couldn't put her finger on how.

Lemony light filtered in the taxi's back window, the breeze lifted their hair, and their light teasing would remain with Eddie like a beautiful souvenir of their friendship. Not that she knew then what was ahead. Later, she would go over every word Rachel said to her that evening, wishing she had questioned her friend further because in hindsight a lot of what Rachel said made no sense.

At the Parrot Tea Room, a rambling old mansion on Connecticut Avenue, they took a table in a corner of a cool room, sheltered on one side by a leafy potted palm, fans whirring from the ceiling. Most diners sat outside in the shade since the day was milder and less humid than usual. A pianist in the adjoining room played a soft Chopin "Nocturne."

"This is nice." Rachel looked around. "And calm. Who knew a warehouse full of girls banging on typewriters all day could give me such a headache."

"Alone in my basement closet, I actually miss all those typewriter carriages ringing. That sound tells me we're winning this war."

"I'm glad you think so. I've missed your optimism, Eddie. I want to be like you, I want to do more than be a cog in wartime Washington's wheel." Rachel took a cigarette from a silver case and lit it with a lighter.

Eddie nodded that she understood. "When did you start smoking?"

"You mean when did I start smoking in public?" Rachel had sneaked cigarettes for as long as Eddie had known her.

"Okay, let me have one, too." Eddie took a cigarette, and Rachel lit it for her. One puff, and Eddie began to cough. Rachel laughed, releasing smoke through her nostrils like a dragon, which made Eddie laugh, too.

"What can I get you young ladies?" the gray-haired waitress asked.

"Two gin fizzes, please," Rachel told her.

"Maybe you two have had enough strong drink?" Her look kind, but firm.

"We were just acting silly." Eddie stubbed out her cigarette. "Sorry,

Ma'am."

"Nothing wrong with silly, honey. Just don't need any rowdy government girls breaking up the place. Now how about some hot bread right out of the oven with your cocktails?" She handed them small menus from her apron pocket.

"Yes, thank you," Eddie said. The waitress left.

Rachel crossed her eyes at the waitress's back. "She makes me want to throw a potted plant through their fancy French doors, Ma'am."

This was the irreverent Rachel she'd known.

"You're just another rowdy government girl wanting to break up the place." Eddie put on the waitress's Southern accent.

Rachel hooked a pair of wire-rimmed glasses behind her ears and read the menu.

Eddie studied her. "Your glasses make you look scholarly." They also hid Rachel's good looks and aged her further. "How long have you worn them?"

"Not long." Rachel winked. "Men don't make passes at girls wearing glasses."

After the waitress brought their gin and bread, they ordered dinner.

"We could get our palms read here," Eddie said. "A Madame Sofia will come to our table and tell us our future. I watched her at work when Jess brought me here for lunch."

"Palms read among the palms, eh?" Rachel's face clouded. "But I don't want to know the future."

"You already know it. More than half the summer is gone," Eddie said. "You'll be going back to Saltville and starting at Emory and Henry." Rachel would live on campus, unlike Eddie, who hadn't been able to afford it. "You'll love it, Schatzi."

"I'm not going back." Rachel's face emptied of emotion.

Eddy leaned forward. "Is it Thad? Are you in love with him?"

Rachel put down her fork and lit another cigarette. "No, I'm going to break up with him the next time I see him."

Now this was a surprise. "Why?"

She twirled the end of her cigarette in the ashtray, her eyes cast down. "You were right about him. He's a *dummkopf*. In his article about Pearl's funeral, he didn't mention my cousins, but he named you and me, and wrote that we had said Pearl was wild and boy-crazy."

Eddie's spine straightened. That's where the word *wild* had come from: Thad's articles. "He's a liar." Eddie slapped the table making their cutlery and glasses rattle. "He writes fiction."

"Precisely. Along with the story, there was a photograph of us leaving the funeral home, but you were covering your face with your purse. My mug looked straight at the camera for all the world to recognize. Papa saw the paper and called me yelling."

Eddie leaned back and sighed. "Rachel, I'm so sorry."

"It's okay." She stared out the French windows into the graying twilight and said, *"Es ist ein boser Wind, der niemand etwas Gutes blast."* It's an ill wind that blows nobody any good.

"What do you mean by that?"

Wearing her mysterious smile, she shook her head. Eddie couldn't read her expression, but Rachel had a secret that made her almost glow.

"Remember when Pearl went to look at a room Thad told her about?" Eddie asked.

"Yeah, which made no sense since Thad lives out MacArthur, and Pearl was going to be working at the Pentagon." Rachel sprawled in her chair, not her usual proper posture. She had eaten little and had drunk three gin fizzes fast. "Still Pearl met him out there. She must have been pretty desperate to move away from us."

Eddie sat back and sipped her gin. "Madge, one of Pearl's switchboard operator friends, told me Pearl had a crush on Thad. Is it possible he liked her as well?"

"I doubt it." Rachel tilted her head. "Pearl disgusted him. He was always going on about how he couldn't stand the thought of me sharing a bed with her." She bent her head low and whispered, "But you know what, Eddie? You were right about people. You can't trust them."

"You're just feeling *weltschmerz*."

"The world is not what I hoped." She gave a harsh laugh. "You can say that again."

"If anyone listened in on us speaking German, they'd report us for being

Nazi spies."

Rachel didn't smile at this. "I'm a Jew, Eddie, which exempts me from suspicion."

When the waitress appeared with the bill, Eddie insisted on paying. "Do you know how many tabs you've picked up? It's my turn."

"I can see in your face how happy you are here, aren't you, Eddie?" Rachel said.

"I am." Yet she didn't want to jinx her happiness.

Because of Mama's downward spiral, she had never trusted happiness, but she knew when she felt it and she felt it now. She had fallen for Jess and for this city. She felt sorry for Rachel having to return home and start college. No matter what Rachel said to the contrary, Eddie was sure that's what she would do.

On Connecticut Avenue, Rachel said, "I'm meeting Sara at their apartment at the Cairo. It's not far from here."

"Will you ever come back to Georgia Avenue? Aunt Viola misses you and keeps asking. She'll be leaving for Saltville soon for her vacation, so I'll be alone in the house with Bert." Eddy heard her dread, but wasn't sure why.

Ever since Jess and Alonso went to Bert's work-place and questioned him, Bert had avoided her. He got home from work late and left before dawn. Eddie sensed he was ashamed of being questioned in connection with the government girl murders and didn't want to face her.

Rachel patted her wreath of hair. "Sure. I'll come back after this weekend."

They hugged. Eddie crossed Connecticut Avenue and waited at the streetcar stop, watching Rachel walk up the steep hill, her reflection moving across a bakery window, a leather goods shop window, and a branch of Riggs Bank before she gave a backward wave and disappeared around the corner.

"See you soon," she had whispered to Eddie before they separated, but that wasn't true.

52

Thursday, August 3, 1944

Kurt knocked on her door. His mustard smeared mouth turned down, unusual for her cheerful boss. "There's a reporter in the lobby asking for you."

Eddie stood and realized she was barefooted. Like the other translators, she followed Kurt's lead and relaxed as she worked. And she understood why Kurt was upset. The Bureau strictly forbade employees from talking to the press. Besides everything about their translation division was secret. If a higher up discovered a reporter had come asking for her, she could get fired.

"Don't worry, Kurt. He's probably the reporter my roommate dates. I'm furious he came here while I'm working."

"Go up and tell him so." Kurt crossed his arms over his chest.

Eddie slipped on her cork sandals, one of them held together with tape, and took the stairs to the lobby.

Thad was standing hunched in front of the bank of elevators, expecting her to come from on high. He wore a dark suit she'd never seen before. Where did he get all his well-made suits? And he had on Clark Kent glasses, which he seldom wore.

"Thad." Eddie took his arm and led him toward the big double front doors. The sharp smell of Bay Rum cologne wafted from him. "Never come here and ask for me, understand?"

His face was rumpled, eyes bloodshot. "Please tell me you know where Rachel is."

"Isn't she with the Rosens?"

"No, Eddie." He squeezed her hand, sending a tremor through her. "The Rosens don't know where she is. Sara's out in their car, waiting for me. Rachel hasn't been to work this week, and her boss hasn't heard from her."

Rachel would never miss work without calling in.

"I can't believe it." She became light-headed and leaned against the marble wall, cool against her skin. "I assumed when she didn't come back to Georgia Avenue, she was with the Rosens."

Thad offered her a handkerchief. "You look like you're going to faint."

Eddie took it and dabbed her damp face.

"Will you come with us now to police headquarters? We need to find her."

"Wait here. I'll be right back." She ran down to the basement, first to Jess's office. Neither he nor Alonso was there. Theirs was not a desk job. They often went out to check leads.

She left Jess a hurried note then found Kurt and told him what was going on.

Kurt said, "You better go with them, but come back as soon as you can."

"I will."

He nodded. "We need all hands on deck to finish. We've got to get that translation done. I'll probably be here all night."

"I'll stay until we finish." They had to send a final translation of the first White Rose pamphlet to the Department of the Army by tomorrow morning.

Eddie got into the back of the big car beside Sara Rosen, who reached across the seat and squeezed Eddie's hand. Sara, dressed stylishly in a light-weight blouse and cotton skirt, slumped in the opposite corner. Fine lines fanned from the corners of her eyes and mouth. She looked older than Eddie remembered.

Thad sat in the front beside the driver, the young pianist from the Rosen farm, in a chauffeur's uniform. He had a map of the city opened over the steering wheel.

"It's on a short block of Indiana between 4th and 5th," Thad told him. "Two blocks north of Pennsylvania."

His quick directions to police headquarters reminded her of how he first broke the story of the government girls' murders.

"When did you last see Rachel?" Sara asked Eddie.

Her question pulled Eddie back to their dinner at the Parrot Room. She could almost taste the sweet gin fizzes and feel the tickle of leaves from the potted palms that surrounded them.

"We went out together on a Thursday." Eddie opened the little calendar she kept in her purse. "It was the 20th of July after work."

In the chaotic precinct lobby, telephones jangling and uniformed officers moving in and out, they were met by a chubby red-faced Detective Flynn, who ushered them upstairs through a room of typists into a small office.

The detective plopped behind his desk. "So how long has your government girl been missing?" His head down, he dated a form on a clipboard.

Eddie didn't like his tone. It was routine, while this was an emergency. Rachel was gone. The detective's untidy desk made her think he was a paper pusher, who wanted to appear busier than he was.

"May we speak with Detective Kaminski?" Eddie came to the edge of her chair. "Rachel Margolis' disappearance could be connected to the government girl murders."

Sara let out a sharp cry and buried her face in her hands.

Thad punched the detective's metal desk. "You don't know that, Eddie. Let's deal in facts here."

Detective Flynn brought his hands up as if in surrender. "You said the magic words, young lady. Ray K. wants to know about every government girl who disappears under suspicious circumstances."

Thad leaned over and whispered something to Sara.

Glad to pass them on, Detective Flynn went out in the hall and returned with Ray K., who was buttoning his wrinkled linen blazer over his wrinkled shirt.

Eddie, Sara, and Thad rose to greet him.

He brought an arm around her. "Eddie." His jacket smelled of sweat.

"We meet again."

Eddie introduced him to Mrs. Rosen, who extended her hand. They shook.

He clapped Thad on the shoulder as if they were old friends, then led them further down the hall to a corner office. The graying sky pressed at the windows, where raindrops flowed like quick silver.

Ray K. insisted Sara Rosen sit in the leather easy chair, the best in the office. "What can I get you? Iced tea, coffee?" he asked.

Sara refused, but took a cigarette from a silver case much like Rachel's. "May I?' she asked, waving a filtered cigarette.

"Be my guest." Ray K. smiled, got one of his own from a pack, and lit hers with a match. He pushed a huge filthy ashtray toward her. Sara leaned back in the chair and took a deep drag, her face smoothing with the comfort of nicotine.

Eddie wished she smoked.

"Okay, first of all give me the young lady's name and your relationship to her." He started his own form.

"I'm her boy friend." Thad planted his elbows on the end of the desk, his eyes shiny with tears. "Almost her fiancé."

Eddie wanted to contradict him, but that would slow this process.

"So when was the last time any of you saw Rachel?"

"We went to the Uptown last Saturday night to see *Gaslight.*"

"Did you like it?" Ray K. asked, looking up from his notepad.

"Not much," Thad said.

When Eddie's turn came, she told him about her dinner with Rachel. "We had a wonderful time. She said she was tired of typing. I think she wants to do more for the war effort." Eddie turned to Thad and softened her tone. "She also told me she was going to break up with you."

"Eddie, Eddie," Thad cooed. "You're so jealous of Rachel you almost glow green at times. You were even jealous of poor Pearl's friendship with Rachel. You've got a lot going for yourself, young lady, if only you could see it."

His condescension made her want to throttle him. Worse, he was right about Pearl.

"But did Rachel break up with you?" Ray K. asked, patting the desk in front of Thad.

Eddie could have hugged the detective for staying on track.

"We had an argument, but we made up." Thad leaned toward Ray K. "Rachel told me she was tired of acting like Eddie's protégé and dreaded rooming with her because..."

Eddie flushed at this, because it might be true.

"Stop, Thad. Let's deal in facts here." Sara put her hand on his shoulder. "Rachel was with us Friday night for Shabbat, the 28th of July. After dinner, I found her packing up most of her clothes. She said she was moving back to Georgia Avenue to live with Eddie. Saturday morning, Meyer, my husband, gave her a ride to our apartment at the Cairo."

Ray K. nodded. "Tallest building in the city."

"Yes. Meyer had a meeting on Capitol Hill, so he dropped her off at the door and left. He returned to Silver Spring in the afternoon. We haven't seen her or heard from her since."

"So none of you has seen her since the 29th of July, five days ago?" His gaze, one eye slightly off center, focused on each of them. He whistled. "That's a long time to go missing." He took a drag on his cigarette. "So Eddie, you thought she was with the Rosens, and Mrs. Rosen thought she was with you."

They agreed. Eddie was beginning to see that this was what Rachel had intended for them to think. She hadn't been definite about when she would return to Georgia Avenue.

"Have you called her parents in Saltville?" Ray K. asked.

Sara explained that Rachel's mother was dead. "Her father is very protective of his only child. He will be on the next train up here when he find out she's missing."

She was right. Eddie dreaded facing Mr. Margolis, but face him she must.

"Is it possible she got fed up with Washington and went home to Saltville?"

"No," Eddie said. "She would never leave her job without giving notice. But she did tell me that once summer ended, she wasn't going back to

Saltville. I didn't believe her. I thought she was just being rebellious."

"Yes, she told me the same thing," Sara told Ray K. "And, like Eddie, I thought she was blowing off steam."

Thad nodded as if she had told him this as well.

"Aha. Is it possible her father was going to make her go home, so she ran off?"

We discussed this. Thad said, "She wouldn't go without telling me. We were… well in love. Sara knows." Sara nodded at this, which puzzled Eddie. Why hadn't Rachel told Sara how angry she was with Thad about the article he wrote after Pearl's funeral?

Eddie realized Rachel's story about breaking up with Thad made no sense. Thad's article came out right after Pearl's funeral on July 15th. Why had Rachel waited more than a week to tell Thad she was angry and wanted to break up?

Eddie had been so glad Rachel had finally seen what an opportunist Thad was that she hadn't questioned her further.

"She wouldn't have run away without telling me," Thad said. "She told me everything." With that, he bowed his head and covered his mouth. Sara leaned over and held him.

"I'll put out an all-points bulletin for her with a description and send it to neighboring jurisdictions. Do any of you have a photo of her?"

They all did and gave them to Ray K. But none of the photographs showed Rachel's new look, the wire-rimmed glasses and severe hairdo. She had disguised her good looks, but why?

When they went over a description of her, Eddie included these.

"She dresses better than most government girls," Thad added. "I mean she's a lady and dresses like one."

What a pompous ass he was. Government girls were doing more for the war effort than Thad. Why wasn't he in the military, anyway? But none of this mattered now. Rachel was missing.

Ray K. stood up as they were about to leave. "I've dealt with a lot of these cases, so I get a sense about these girls. All that packing of clothes and mystery leads me to believe she was making her get-away. I'm going to send my boys to check the trains, buses, and National Airport."

He wanted this news to comfort them, but Eddie wasn't comforted. The end of July had passed without the police finding a government girl's body. Had Rachel been murdered then and her body not found yet?

Rain was falling in silver strands when they ran down the slick stone steps of police headquarters to the car.

Once in the backseat, Sara looked at Eddie. "Someone's going to have to call Moses."

"I know I need to do that, but I'll be at work until midnight tonight if not later," Eddie said. It was her duty to call Mr. Margolis. She had promised him she would watch out for Rachel, and she had failed. She needed to tell him his daughter was missing.

Sara sighed. "I'll have Meyer call him. He's his cousin. They're close."

When Thad got out, Eddie did, too. "I can walk from here." Sara insisted she take her umbrella.

"Wait up," Eddie called to Thad and followed him into the *Herald's* lobby. Every woman they passed greeted Thad, their eyes sliding over him with delight. He really was catnip to women.

"You wear the worst looking shoes, Eddie." He was staring at her taped sandals.

Eddie waved away his comment. She didn't care what he thought of her or her shoes. "You told Ray K. Rachel changed in an evening. That she was different."

"Yeah?" He dabbed raindrops off his jacket with a handkerchief. "Not long after Pearl's funeral, I took her to the Willard Hotel for dinner. She went to the ladies, and when she returned, she was distant, distracted yet excited about something. I asked if she'd seen someone she knew and she gave me her Mona Lisa smile and said not really."

What had distracted her? Or maybe a better question was: who had distracted her?

53

Friday, August 4, 1944

"You're riding home with us," Jess told Eddie in the Justice Department's lobby. He took her arm and felt her lean against him. He had never seen her look so exhausted with a purple arc under each eye. Her blouse and skirt looked as if she'd slept in them.

She had worked through the night at the Bureau on some hush-hush translation project and had stayed and worked all day. And on top of all this, Rachel had disappeared.

At the glass doors, brilliant sunlight streamed in. "I can't see." She reached into her purse for dark glasses and put them on. "I'm a blind mouse."

Jess grinned. The rest of the Bureau referred to the strange band of translators as "the Kraut mice," because they worked in a tiny basement warren and scurried around, whispering to each other in German.

In the car, Jess said, "We have an appointment to talk to Rachel's boss tomorrow. I made it for lunchtime, so maybe you could get away and come with me."

Eddie nodded. "He supervises about a zillion typists, so I hope he remembers Rachel."

"Actually our appointment is with her immediate supervisor, a Miss Strother. Did Rachel ever mention her?"

"Oh, yeah. Good idea. Miss Strother's in charge of keeping Rachel's section of government girls in line. I'm wondering why it took the Department of the Army four days to notify anyone that Rachel hadn't come to work."

When they pulled up in front of the house on Georgia Avenue, a short wide man stood on the porch facing them. He wore a hat, starched shirt, braces, and pleated trousers. His hands were anchored on his hips, his face a scowl.

"Oh no. That's Mr. Margolis."

"Could you tell him you worked all night and ask him to come back later?"

"No. I should have been the one to call him in the first place. I have to talk to him."

"Then I'm coming with you." Jess put on his hat and turned to Alonso.

"I'll go through all my photographs, crop out other people, and enlarge the ones of Rachel," Alonso said. "Ray K. said he could use more."

Jess nodded, opened Eddie's door, and helped her out. They went down the sidewalk arm-in-arm to face Moses Margolis.

"Tell me what happened, Eddie." Mr. Margolis sat at the kitchen table, his chin anchored in his hands. His bald head was beaded in sweat. Pouches under his eyes told of his sleepless nights.

Jess stood behind them, pouring the last of the sweet tea into glasses. He was clumsy in a kitchen, but could manage.

Around them, the house stood silent and still. The familiar drone of the radio was gone. A few days ago, Mrs. Trundle left for Saltville, her annual pilgrimage to get out of Washington's August steam. Jess would have insisted Eddie move out rather than be alone here with Bert, but Mrs. Trundle had seen to that. She'd rented Pearl's space to another government girl who worked for the War Department.

"After Pearl died," Eddie said carefully as if she were picking her way across a stream on slippery rocks, "Rachel began staying at the Rosen's farm on the weekends and at their apartment in the Cairo during the week."

Jess set a glass of cold tea in front of the man and one for Eddie, too. He took some water out for himself and sat across from this man with the gravelly voice.

"I know about Pearl Ballou," Mr. Margolis said, shaking an index finger at Eddie. "I had to see my own daughter's photograph in a Washington newspaper to find out that her roommate had been murdered." His voice broke over this. He dabbed his brow with a square of handkerchief. "Has the same thing happened to my Rachel?" He released a deep sob and dropped his head almost to the table.

Eddie slumped in her chair, her usual erect posture gone, her hand over her mouth. She cried without making a sound.

"Tell me what you think, Miss Valedictorian," Mr. Margolis shouted at her, his eyes fiery.

Jess patted the table with his palm. "Pull yourself together, Mr. Margolis. I don't think Rachel was murdered."

Mr. Margolis raised blazing eyes to Jess. "Who the hell are you?"

Eddie had introduced them earlier, but Mr. Margolis must have been so frightened or tired, he didn't remember.

Jess took a card from his shirt pocket and pushed it across the table. "My name is Jessup Lindsay and I'm a special agent with the Federal Bureau of Investigation."

The man took his card and studied it. "Special Agent? What's so special about you?"

Jess told him why he'd been brought to Washington.

"So you're in charge of this murder investigation, and you don't think this killer got Rachel?" The light of hope came into his eyes. Jess had seen it before when a loved one was given a bit of good news, no matter how small.

"No. And I'm going to do everything in my power to find her." Jess paused to sip his water. "Tell me about Rachel. What was she like growing up?" To Mr. Margolis' puzzled expression, he said, "The more I know about her, the better."

This gave the father time to talk about his daughter, which he clearly loved to do.

"When did her mother die?"

"Four years ago. She came here to Washington for a checkup and never returned. It was her heart." His eyes left Jess's and rested on the table.

Either this was too painful for him to talk about or he was lying about something. Jess believed everyone lied about something.

Eddie raised her head, stared at Mr. Margolis a moment, and said, "Your wife is buried at the small cemetery on your cousin's land in Silver Spring."

He nodded without looking at either of them.

"How good was Rachel's German?" Jess asked him.

"You'd have to ask Eddie. I never promoted her learning German. That was her mother's doing." Anger in his voice. "Barbara's mother lived with us until Barbara died, always speaking German to my wife and daughter, so I couldn't understand what they were saying. I taught Rachel a little Yiddish, so my daughter and I could have a secret language, too. And just when Rachel needed her grandmother most, the old crow flies off to her sister in New York City."

Jess wrote something in his notebook.

"Rachel's grandmother left Germany in 1933, the year Hitler came to power," Eddie said. "She had read *Mein Kampf* and decided that…"

"Please no more talk about the old crow. She wasn't as brilliant as Barbara or Rachel imagined."

"And Rachel's German?" Jess asked Eddie.

Eddie sat straighter. "She's as fluent as I am, meaning she can speak it, while her reading and writing are not as strong." She shook her head as if she had water in her ears.

Distant voices from the backyard, probably Miss Minnie and another woman from the alley working in the garden.

Jess said, "Mr. Margolis, I'm coordinating efforts with Detective Kaminski of the DC Police. At this moment, my assistant is making copies of Rachel's photographs to be given to every ticket agent in this city. We'll do all that's possible to locate your daughter."

Mr. Margolis studied him. "*Locate*, I like that word, Jess," he said. "Thank you. And my Rachel is beautiful. Someone will remember her." The light of hope grew brighter in his eyes.

They heard footsteps in the hall.

The young man who drove the Rosens' car appeared in his chauffeur's uniform, shiny double-breasted buttons catching the afternoon light, his cap under his arm. "Sorry. I knocked, but no one answered. The Rosens sent me to pick you up, Mr. Margolis. I'll be waiting outside."

"All right." Mr. Margolis pushed himself up from the table. Eddie and Jess walked him through the house to the front porch.

Before he went down the steps, he turned back and took something from his pocket. "The maid found this in Rachel's room at the Cairo." He handed a silver necklace to Eddie. "I want you to have it."

It was Rachel's locket. Jess had never seen Rachel when she wasn't wearing it. So why had she taken it off?

The driver opened the door for Mr. Margolis.

Jess said, "That locket's a clue and needs to go to the police."

Eddie opened it then handed it to Jess.

The photograph of Eddie was still on one side of the locket. "Her mother's picture used to be in there, too." She pointed to the empty heart. "Rachel must have taken it with her, but she left me behind."

54

Saturday, August 5, 1944

"Hey, Rip Van Winkle," Inez, Eddie's new roommate, said, shaking her. "I have some wake up java juice for you." She handed Eddie a cup of coffee.

Eddie sat up, sipped, and looked at the clock. She'd slept for twelve hours, her dreams full of wild images. In them, she was barefoot and kept finding one nice shoe but not its mate, which in the light of day didn't sound so scary. But it was a clue in the murders, which Jess referred to as the killer's souvenir.

"I'm so groggy." Eddie thanked Inez for the coffee and sipped. "What day is it?"

In her thirties, Inez was a brunette with short curly hair, a mouth of crowded white teeth, and an easy-going manner. "It's Saturday, honey, August 5th, just another working day for us government girls. I'm finished with the bathroom, so be my guest."

As Eddie sank in the hot water, she was grateful for Inez, who was older and quiet. Considering Aunt Viola chose this woman, Eddie knew she'd gotten lucky.

Once dressed, she went downstairs and found Inez reading *The Washington Herald.*

"Isn't this the other girl who lives here?" Inez turned the newspaper to Eddie, who was spreading oleo on toast. Rachel's face looked out at Eddie.

It was her photograph from Pearl's funeral.

Thad had used Rachel for another story, but this time Eddie was glad. The more people who saw Rachel's photograph the better. Maybe a witness would come forward, someone who had seen her at Union Station or National Airport.

"Yes. You may decide it's dangerous to be my roommate." Eddie sat and ate.

Although her tone sounded light, Rachel's disappearance cast a shadow over Eddie. Still Rachel hadn't lived here on Georgia Avenue in so long that even now Eddie imagined her looking out over the city from the Rosens' swanky penthouse in the Cairo.

"Eddie, you couldn't get me out of here with a stick of dynamite." Inez let out a hearty laugh. "The last place I lived I had to share a bathroom with four other women and an elderly man."

"Wait a minute, Inez. How do you know what Rachel looks like?"

Rachel hadn't been here since Pearl's funeral. Inez only moved in ten days ago.

"She came by one afternoon when I was off. As a supervisor, sometimes I work swing shifts, so I have..."

Eddie leapt to her feet. "What did she do while she was here?"

"She went through the closet and packed up some things."

Eddie ran up the stairs. She had to find out what Rachel had taken.

At noon Miss Strother, Rachel's supervisor, met with Eddie and Jess in a small conference room on the first floor of a tempo on the Mall. A rotating fan blew at them from the center of the table.

Miss Strother held an employee card in her hand. "Yes, I remember Rachel, a satisfactory worker, if a little distracted recently."

Distracted: there was that word again.

"Why was she distracted?" Jess asked.

Miss Strother wasn't much older than Eddie. Rachel had said the woman's supervisory position had gone to her head. She certainly dressed like a supervisor in a neat blue suit with a pen on a chain around her neck, but her suit was too warm for today. Damp arcs appeared under her arms.

"Well, she had special permissions to leave work, not once or twice, mind you, but several times for interviews." She raised her pale palms, showing dirt beneath her long red fingernails. Miss Strother was dramatic and would be picayune about the work of those under her, no wonder Rachel hadn't liked working here. "Not that I was privy to where she was interviewing, but it had to be in some office of the Department of the Army."

Why hadn't Rachel told Eddie about these interviews? They really had drifted apart.

On their walk back to the Bureau, Jess said, "Who else knew Rachel spoke German?"

"The Department of the Army applications asked what other languages you know, how fluent you are. Rachel and I debated about writing German because we were afraid they might think we were spies, but in the end we put it down."

Before the Justice Department came into sight, Jess pulled her behind a wide broad-leafed oak, the rough bark at her back, and kissed her. Eddie could feel him through her dress, and she liked her effect on him.

For a long time to come, she would remember this kiss, the way Jess closed his eyes, his thick wavy hair between her fingers, his one arm holding her closer than any two arms could.

Late that afternoon, Eddie in old clothes was in the garden whacking at knotweed, mallow, and purslane, the same weeds that grew in Saltville. Maybe the exercise would help with her terrible angst about Rachel. She felt as if she walking across Saltville's marshes, about to be pulled under.

From the house, the phone was ringing. She ignored it until it rang in Jess's bungalow. Maybe someone was calling with news about Rachel.

She set the hoe against the fence and ran to Jess's door. Sliding her hand along the ledge above it, she found the key, unlocked the door, and answered the telephone, "Jessup Lindsay's residence."

"Eddie." Jess sounded breathless, excited. "You and Inez need to leave the house right now."

"Why?"

"Alonso and I are out at the laundry plant. A blouse covered in blood was found hidden in the truck Bert usually drives. The blouse fits the description you gave of the one Pearl was wearing on the night... We're going to arrest Bert as soon as he gets back here. But in case he goes home first, I don't want you to be there. Leave now, Eddie." Jess hung up.

Eddie placed the telephone back in its cradle, her body trembling as if she were cold. Still something gnawed at her. She returned to the garden and looked up at the third floor. From down here, she could see the part of the flat roof off Bert's bedroom.

She and Rachel had always wanted to sunbathe on that roof, but Bert told them never to go out there. He said its boards were rotten.

What she hadn't noticed before was the small shed at the end of the roof. Its weathered wooden doors made the shed look more like a closet. What did Bert keep in there? She had to see. She went into the house.

From the bottom of the stairs, she called, "Inez?"

No one answered.

She waited a moment. The house stood silent. No one was here.

She ran up the stairs, but this time she didn't stop at the second floor. She went up to the third, where she'd never been before, to Bert's bedroom. All was neat and plain, a narrow twin bed in a metal frame beside the open window, a bare wood floor, a fan on a little table at the end of his bed. It could have been a monk's cell.

What made her cousin tick? She sensed he was a man of secrets, but what they were she didn't know.

On top of his chest of drawers was a photograph of a family, a wide fleshy man in a suit and hat, a woman who had to be Aunt Viola, and a chubby little boy with sad downcast eyes, Bert.

Bert's father died of a heart attack. None of the Smiths ever spoke of him. Eddie didn't know how Aunt Viola had met him, since Mr. Trundle was not from Saltville. He'd worked on the railroad, a conductor, maybe. Eddie sensed there was a scandal surrounding him, but to her family not being from Saltville was scandal enough.

Behind the photograph was a tube of lipstick, azalea blossom, Pearl's lipstick. Not that finding her lipstick here proved anything. Bert had used it when he got her body ready for the viewing. But why had he kept it?

The front door opened below. Maybe it was Inez. Eddie prayed it was

Inez.

Someone was coming up the stairs quickly, someone with big feet. Her heart began to pound. She didn't want Bert to find her in his room. She imagined him filling the doorway.

She tiptoed to the landing and opened the screen door that led to the flat part of the roof. The door whined loudly, its hinges rusty.

"Eddie," Bert called from the second floor. "Don't go out there!" He thundered up the steps.

She ran out on the flat roof and felt as if she'd stepped on stage. Her inky shadow stretched across the roof, a white tablecloth of sky overhead. She had to see what was in that shed.

"Eddie, stop," Bert called behind her. "Don't go any further."

In front of the shed, she flung open its doors, releasing a fug of mold and mildew. Her eyes watered, and she coughed. Men's clothes hung inside, clothes from an earlier era that had been worn by a man heavier and shorter than Bert. Maybe they belonged to his father. Why had he kept them here?

"Eddie," Bert called from the screen door. "Come back from there. I told you the roof..."

He squinted at her. His hair was matted, his face slick with sweat. He unbuckled his belt and slid it out through the loops of his pants.

She gasped, and her knees went weak. Without a conscious decision to do so, she walked backward from him toward the roof's edge. Most of the government girls had been strangled with a belt.

"Bert, stay right where you are." Her voice a scrape. How she wished she'd done what Jess told her and gotten out of here. "Don't move, Bert."

Still walking backward, she heard a creaking. A board crunched under her. The roof was rotten. She sensed the boards might give at any moment, and she would fall through.

She couldn't go forward toward him and one more step back and she'd fall.

Bert came out on the roof, holding his belt by its buckle. He put one foot in front of the other as if he was walking a tightrope. "Stay where you are. I'll get you."

He was almost arm's length from her now.

"Bert," she whispered. "Don't strangle me, please."

"What?" Bert grabbed her arm. "I've got you now."

Eddie took hold of the end of his belt, wrapping it around her palm.

"Bert, let her go," Jess called from the garden.

Eddie looked over her shoulder. Jess stood below in the corn, his gun aimed at them. "Get down, Eddie, get down now."

"Don't shoot him, Jess," she yelled, too late.

Jess fired just as Eddie yanked on the belt, sending Bert off the roof into the corn.

55

Eddie went with Bert in the ambulance. All that had happened felt like a nightmare.

"Make sure you tell 'em his condition," Miss Minnie had instructed Eddie.

"My cousin is a hemophiliac," Eddie told the medics in the ambulance and the nurse, who met the ambulance. "It means his blood doesn't clot right."

Later, she told the young doctor. She searched each face for a sign that they knew what she was talking about. Eddie watched the nurse write the word on Bert's chart.

It was a miracle Bert was alive. Jess hadn't shot him. She was the one who had hurt Bert. She had pulled on the belt, sending him forward so that he fell three stories.

She had stood on the edge of the roof, looking down at Bert lying in the smashed rows of corn. She would never forget that sight. In a moment, she knew she'd made a terrible mistake. Her cousin had not been trying to strangle her.

"Praise the Lord for the corn," Miss Minnie had said kneeling beside Bert, her fingertip pressed beneath his chin. "He's still here." She patted his face.

At the hospital, a medic came out and asked Eddie her blood type. "A negative," she said, which turned out to be Bert's as well. She gave her blood so he could be transfused.

Time rushed forward and stood still. Bert was still unconscious, and night had come when she took a stack of change to one of a row of telephone booths outside the hospital. She sat on the little bench seat and called relatives in Saltville, everyone except her father. She was trying to find Aunt Viola.

Finally she located her at her cousin's house in Marion, Virginia not far from Saltville. "Aunt Viola, this is Eddie. Bert has been..."

"Say no more. I already know, Eddie." She sounded angry. "We just heard on the radio that Albert Trundle is a suspect in the government girl murders. I'm so ashamed I don't know what to do. He's brought shame on all of us."

"Aunt Viola, Bert fell off the roof. He's here at George Washington Hospital. He needs you. You've got to come back to Washington tonight or tomorrow."

"Don't tell me what to do, missy. Bert got his self into this, and he's going to have to get himself out."

"You don't understand, Aunt Viola. Bert could die. You must...."

Aunt Viola hung up.

Eddie sat there stunned, unable to move from her seat, the dial tone sounded in her ear until the operator came on. "Would you like to place another call, ma'am?"

"Yes, yes I would." She needed to get upstairs to Bert, but first she asked to be put through to the train station. She took a pen from her purse, a scrap of paper, and wrote down the schedule of trains to New Jersey.

Once she hung up, she went back into the hospital and ran up the stairs. A policeman sat on a chair beside the door to Bert's room.

"I'm his cousin," she told the policeman and reached for the door handle.

The policeman leapt to his feet and blocked her way. "No visitors allowed."

Eddie heard Jess's voice and turned. He came around the corner from the nurse's station, Ray K. at his side.

She rushed to them. "I need to be with Bert," she said. "I called Aunt Viola." She directed her gaze at Jess. "She refused to come. Can you believe it?" Her voice broke over these words. "She refuses to come, and the doctor says he could die tonight from internal bleeding."

"Sorry, Eddie." Ray K. crossed his arms over his chest. "No one can go in and talk to him until we do."

"I don't want to talk to him. I just want to be with him. I don't want him to be alone. Can't you understand?" She was crying now. "He could…"

"Come with me, Eddie," Jess took her arm. "Let me get you a taxi to take you home."

"Maybe you didn't hear me. Bert, he could die tonight. " She stomped her foot even though she could tell it was useless. They weren't going to let her in to see him.

Bert lay dying, and at the same time they were going to charge him with the government girl murders.

She followed Jess to the elevator. They got on a crowded car.

On the way down to the lobby, she said, "Don't you think it's strange that Bert didn't throw Pearl's blouse away or burn it? I think he's being set up, framed."

"Eddie." Jess shook his head, letting her know she shouldn't discuss this in front of others in the elevator.

When they were alone in the lobby he said, "Eddie, you're the one who pointed out that all the murders happened around Bert's Civil Defense meetings. And, guess what? I checked with the local Warden. Bert stopped going to Civil Defense last year."

"Don't hold that against him. Right after Pearl Harbor, everyone was afraid we were going to be invaded by the Japanese, remember? But as the war went on, people relaxed about it."

Jess raised his palm. "Bottom line, Bert lied about where he was. He has no alibi for the times the women were murdered."

He tried to draw her close, but she pushed him away. "You haven't paid any attention to the information I found at the library about Thad."

"That's because I already knew most of it. Thad wrote feature stories until he broke the story of these murders, so he got promoted. He's a young ambitious Southerner."

"Didn't you read how he described almost all the murdered government girls as *wild*, and when I talked to those same roommates they claimed they never used that word? They never called their friend *wild*. He made it up." She sounded hysterical even to herself.

Jess shook his head slightly. "That's sloppy journalism, but it doesn't prove anything."

They sat on a bench in front of the hospital.

Jess took her hand. "Standing in the garden looking up at you on the roof." He closed his eyes tightly as if to conjure the image. "When I saw Bert with his belt in his hand, I was so afraid he was going to strangle you. I fired in the air, thinking that would distract him and give Alonso enough time to get upstairs and stop him."

She sandwiched his face between her hands. "That's what I thought at first, too. But he took his belt off to help me. That roof really is rotten, and he wanted me to take the end of the belt, so I wouldn't fall."

"Eddie, you're letting family ties color your judgment. If Bert wasn't your cousin, you would see it the way we do. Ray K. and I have a meeting with the prosecutor first thing in the morning. We have more than enough evidence to indict Bert for Pearl's murder."

She sat stunned.

He walked to the curb, where a taxi idled. He opened its back door for her.

She got up from the bench and walked to him. "Maybe you're right." She sank into the cab's backseat and could have sunk further. She had never felt so low.

"Get some sleep, Eddie. I'll see you tomorrow." He leaned in and touched the side of her face. She put her hand over his, but they did not kiss.

56

Eddie went up the front steps in the dark. No one had left the front porch light on. Inez must have packed her things and moved out. Who could blame her after hearing the news that her landlady's son had been arrested for being the government girl killer?

Eddie took her key out of her purse, squatted, and was feeling around for the opening in the lock when a man cleared his throat behind her.

She let out a cry and turned toward a dark figure on the swing, readying to sprint to the street, her pulse revving.

"Miss Smith? Sorry to startle you." A willowy man got up, making the swing creak behind him. "I've been waiting for you."

She opened the door, reached in, and turned on the porch light, but it was out. She sighed. Nothing around here worked these days.

"That's all right," she said. In the light from street lamp, she studied the man, who looked vaguely familiar. "I'm a little on edge right now. Have we met?"

"I'm Owen Wheeler, Bert's friend. I play the organ at Jones Funeral Home."

"Yes. That's where I've seen you, Pearl's funeral."

"How is Bert? I heard about it on the radio…" The fabric of his suit made a swishing sound as he crossed his arms over his chest. "I even went to the hospital, but they…" His voice broke.

"I know. They wouldn't let me see him, either."

She invited Owen Wheeler into the house. "Come on back to the kitchen." Her voice quivered. She didn't know this man and here she was taking him into the empty house.

Organist, she told herself. He was an organist, and organs were in churches. Still the word didn't calm her fears. She needed *mut,* lots of it.

She sensed him behind her as she led him through the dark silent house. He could be taking off his belt right now, ready to wrap it around her neck, and…

She turned on the kitchen light and swirled around, then felt foolish for her fears. She gestured to a chair at the table. "Have a seat."

He was tall and lean in his forties with a thin creased face and weariness in his shoulders. His dark brown linen suit, the same one he'd worn at Pearl's funeral, looked as tired as he did.

"Things have been pretty disorganized around here for a while, so I doubt I have anything to offer you except ice water." When she opened the refrigerator, she was pleasantly surprised. "I can offer you a glass of cold tea." Inez must have made it.

"That sounds delightful. Thanks, Miss Smith."

Owen Wheeler had a soft Southern accent. Had the entire South come north to Washington?

"Please call me Eddie." She poured him a glass of tea and one for herself. She took the chair across from him, where they sipped their tea.

"Right, Eddie," he said and did something odd. He put his hands on the table, palms down. His fingers were impossibly long as if they had an extra joint in them. "Bert talks about his amazing cousin, Eddie, all the time."

She smiled. "He's been so kind to me." But why hadn't Bert mentioned Owen to her? "I'm glad someone else cares about him the way I do." She felt the pull of tears. "And tonight he's fighting for his life."

"I know." Tom lowered his head, his palms still flat on the table as if it were a keyboard he could play. "I care about Bert very much." His hazel eyes met hers. "I hope that doesn't shock you, Eddie."

She understood at last. Owen and Bert were more than friends. Owen was Bert's big secret. He held her gaze. Behind him, the noisy refrigerator hummed.

She pushed her hand across the table and touched her index finger to his. "Love is never wrong."

He gasped as if he'd been holding his breath. "Thank you, Eddie. You're everything Bert said you were."

They sat and drank their tea, united in their concern for Bert. Eddie relaxed, maybe for the first time today. The cricket choir rose from the garden, and Miss Minnie's radio droned in the alley. Laughter from the radio joined laughter from the folks listening on Miss Minnie's porch.

"Bert's going to be charged with Pearl's murder, and they're working on indicting him for the other government girl murders. I'm sure Bert didn't kill anyone."

Was she really? She had only known her cousin since May. All she knew was Bert was blood.

"No, he wouldn't hurt anyone. Least of all, a woman."

Eddie took a notebook out of her shoulder bag. "They found Pearl's bloody blouse in the laundry truck Bert usually drives. And they've discovered Bert wasn't at his Civil Defense meetings, which coincided with the nights of the murders."

Owen leaned toward her and let out a low sigh, as sad a sound as she had ever heard. "He was with me. The only way he could get away from his mother was to say he was going to the Civil Defense meetings."

"Where did you two meet?"

"Usually at the funeral parlor. Sometimes at a park off P Street."

"Would you be willing to tell the police?"

He sat straighter. "Bert doesn't want me to. He called me earlier today and told me someone had put a woman's bloody shirt in his truck. I told him I would vouch for him the nights we got together, but he didn't want me..."

"They don't need to know about you two. All you have to say is that you and Bert met on those nights as friends."

"Eddie, the police aren't stupid." He tilted his head, the corners of his mouth lifting in a slight smile. And Eddie could see his charm. "They'll know." He swallowed hard. "They may not believe me. Because we're different, Bert and me. Still I'll go in and tell them. Anything to help Bert." Owen stood, and she walked him through the house to the front door, where they said goodnight.

Eddie went back to the kitchen to wash up. She was hanging the tea towel on its rack when she saw a shadowy figure in the backyard near Jess's bungalow. Had Thad come back to snoop? If so, she was going to get him.

Without turning on a light, she went down the back steps and grabbed the hoe still leaning beside the porch wall. She had left it there this afternoon, which felt like a century ago.

She tiptoed through the garden's leafy shadows, blood pulsing in her ears.

"Who's there?" she called and raised the hoe over her head.

A tall broad man in overalls unfolded from Jess's front stoop and raised his hands as if to surrender.

"Vernon Lanier, Ma'am. Came by to see Jess and tell him something, but he's not here. I've been waiting a while and now I best be getting on."

"Sorry, Vernon." She set down the hoe. "It's been a long awful day. I'm feeling jumpy." She walked him to the gate.

From the alley, the radio was silent now. *Amos and Andy* had ended.

He turned to her and raked his fingers through long coarse hair. "Are you going to Alonso's photography show?" He dug in his pocket and produced an embossed invitation like the one she had received.

"Yes, of course." Alonso's work would appear in a photography show at the Phillips Memorial Art Gallery. "That's Monday night, isn't it?"

"Yes, Ma'am. Alonso told me the museum man chose a photograph of me for the exhibit." He pushed his thumbs under his overall straps and stood straighter. "I'm proud as punch about it."

"I don't blame you." Eddie plucked a honeysuckle trumpet, pulled off its tip, and sucked the end, tasting its sweetness, something she had done since childhood.

Vernon stepped through the gate.

"Vernon, what did you want to tell Jess? I'll pass on a message to him."

"It's about this fella they arrested." He threw his sack over his shoulder and turned to the alley.

"Wait," Eddie almost shouted, opened the gate and stood before Vernon, studying his angular face in the dim light. "What about the man they arrested?"

The key to this whole thing had always been Vernon. He knew something or at least the killer thought he did.

"I hate to tell Jess, but I don't reckon they got the right fella."

Eddie threw her arms around him and hugged him hard. "Oh Vernon, you don't know how happy that makes me." Tears in her voice. "Why do you say that?"

He patted her back softly. "It's about the man who tried to run me over. Could be wrong but I seen enough of his face behind the steering wheel that I don't figure this man is the one."

57

Monday, August 6, 1944

"The Phillips Memorial Art Gallery," Eddie told the taxi driver. She was reading from her engraved invitation.

"The Phillips is closed at night, Miss." He pulled out of the hospital's shadow and took Washington Circle onto New Hampshire Avenue.

"I know, but tonight they're having a new photography exhibit. A friend of mine had his photographs chosen for it." Eddie heard excitement in her voice.

An art opening: this was the wonderful life she had dreamed of when she stood on her lawn in Saltville and watched trains go north. Rachel came to mind, and Eddie pinched the bridge of her nose to hold back tears. How she wished Rachel was here to enjoy this with her, but tonight she would set aside her grief and enjoy it for both of them.

Before the taxi turned onto 21st Street, she saw the gallery's lights blazing. The flat-roofed town house was partially covered in ivy that fluttered in the breeze like ruffles on a dress.

The taxi driver swung around to let her off at its front steps. She reached over the front seat and paid him.

Jess, handsome in a beige suit and tie, opened her door. "Eddie, I've been waiting here, hoping you would come." He took her hand. "I knew you wouldn't miss this."

At the sight of him, she felt herself unfurl. Ever since Bert had fallen off the roof, she had been like a clenched fist, angry with the world and with herself.

She stepped onto the sidewalk, her small suitcase in hand, and drank in his cornflower blue eyes. "It's wonderful to see you, too, Jess."

The need to kiss him was a living thing inside her chest, but she suppressed the urge. She felt as if she'd been gone a year, but it had only been a day, a long one in which she'd left and returned in darkness and had a lot of time to think.

"Where have you been?" He brought his arm around her and held her close. "I've been worried about you."

As well he should be. She came here with two roommates and now she was the only one left, the last government girl from Saltville.

She set her suitcase down and kissed him, her tongue entering his mouth. How bold she'd become. He returned her kiss, closing his eyes tight, pressing his chest to hers. She pressed back.

When they broke apart, she said, "On my way from Union Station tonight, I stopped at the hospital. Bert has regained consciousness. The nurse said he ate some dinner tonight."

"I know. I talked to him earlier." He brought his hand to the side of her face and gave her a look that emptied out the world. "You didn't come to work today. You called in sick. And I couldn't get anything out of Inez except that you had to make a quick trip out of town. Where did you go?"

"Princeton, New Jersey."

"Where Thad went to college," he said.

"Yes." She didn't want to say more, not yet. She picked up her suitcase. She had washed up and changed clothes in the train's untidy bathroom. "I have some information for you, but it can wait."

"I have something to tell you, too," he said.

"Let's set aside all that, go in, and see this photography show."

The banner over the front entrance read: *The City and Its People at War, a Photographic Perspective.*

They took the winding stone stairs to the door and presented their invitations to a young man in a tuxedo. In the vestibule, a gray-haired lady in a white evening gown, a rose corsage on her shoulder, handed them a program. Eddie turned to the page that contained Alonso's face, his biography below.

I remember you, you're the one who made my dreams... A piano played the tune softly in the music room, its notes light and silvery. Eddie hummed along. Guests milled around the piano, sipping an orange-colored punch. Voices and laughter carried from upstairs.

The photography exhibit took up most of the second floor. Alonso's portraits and cityscapes filled a large room with a rectangular bay window. Alonso stood in the middle of the hardwood floor in a double-breasted pinstriped suit Eddie had never seen before.

"In that suit he's the spitting image of our father," Jess whispered.

Alonso was talking to a white couple who gestured to the huge photograph on the opposite wall. In its foreground, a barefoot colored boy stood in a shadow-filled alley behind a high wooden fence. The boy's face was tilted as if to see over the fence to the gleaming white Capitol dome filling the night sky. The picture showed the American dream versus its reality.

A crowd, including Miss Minnie and Ruth in hats and white gloves, stood in front of the photograph. When Miss Minnie saw Eddie, she came over and asked about Bert. Ruth went to Alonso, who in his excitement leaned down and kissed her on the mouth. This was a night of kisses and joy.

Reserved Ruth took a step back from Alonso, her mouth opened in a circle of surprise.

Closer to the staircase, Vernon, a head taller than those around him, stood in front of his own photograph, shaking his head and grinning. A pretty strawberry blonde on his arm drew him closer, whispering to him.

"I'm going to say hello to Vernon," Jess told Eddie.

When Eddie saw a break in the group around Alonso, she went and congratulated him. "Your photographs are windows into a world some people never see."

"Thanks, Eddie. This city has been good to me, giving me powerful subjects and people to appreciate how I see them. I love Washington."

A voice she recognized drew Eddie's attention to the doorway, where Jess's smile had gone stale. Thad stood at Jess's side, a press badge around his neck. She threaded her way through the crowd to them, the pump of her heart speeding up.

"Eddie," Thad said. "I've been in touch with your aunt Viola in Marion, Virginia. You can't imagine how upset she is at what her son has done. I'd like to hear your thoughts…"

Eddie raised her hand to slap him, but Jess took her arm before she could.

"This isn't the time or place, Thad." Jess steered Eddie to the stairs. "Let's get some refreshments," he said. But in the foyer, he turned her to the door.

On the sidewalk he said, "Want to take a ride out MacArthur Boulevard?"

58

In the taxi, Jess leaned forward and told the driver, "521 MacArthur Boulevard."

He sat back and brought his palm to her shoulder. "Alonso and I spent today talking to workers at the laundry. They said Thad often borrowed trucks. The Bermans are away in Maine for the summer. Living in their basement, Thad has keys to everything at the laundry." His eyes flashed. "I accused you of being blind to Bert because he was your kin when I was worse. I felt kinship with Thad because we're Southerners and I admired his Ivy League education and his profession. Can you forgive me?"

"So while Thad is at the opening, we're going to search his house. Is that legal?"

"It is with this search warrant." Jess patted his pocket. His open suit jacket showed the handle of his gun in its armpit holster.

Eddie brought her index finger to his holster ties. "What made you come armed?"

Jess shrugged. "I don't know. I put it on tonight without thinking."

Soon they stood in the parking lot behind the laundry. All was dark and still, the air soap-scented. A fleet of battered trucks filled the lot. The clink and slam of metal came from deep inside the laundry. Someone was working the pressers, cooler to do at night.

"Where do we go from here?" Eddie asked.

"This way," Jess said.

Hand-in-hand, they walked through a stand of pines, needles crunching underfoot to a gravel street on a high ridge overlooking the C&O Canal and the river. How quickly city became country here. Night birds called overhead. Shards of moonlight through the treetops illuminated the Potomac, a silver ribbon shining below.

Not far along the gravel road sat a dark three-story house, its lawn overgrown as if abandoned. Odd that in a city so crowded, a huge house could sit empty.

They went up the gravel horseshoe driveway and took steps to the front door, which was locked.

"I made a mistake in bringing you here, Eddie." He rubbed his half arm. "Let's call a taxi and get back to the opening. Alonso and I will come out here first thing tomorrow."

"Please let's just have a quick look. Once Thad realizes he's under suspicion, he'll get rid of any evidence. He's clever. I think he got away with murder before." That's what she had learned in Princeton today.

"You're right about, Thad." He paused still rubbing the place where his arm ended. "Well, let's see, where do people hide a spare key?"

Eddie held the bottom of a wicker chair so it wouldn't tip while Jess stood on the chair and felt along the lintel. "No," he said.

She lifted the doormat, but the key wasn't there either. While Jess tried the front windows, Eddie went to a wicker table at the end of the porch. Potted begonias and African violets were set out to catch some sun. She checked under each pot. No key.

"I'm going to look around back," she said.

"No, stay with me. Thad could show up. I don't want him to find us doing this."

"He has to go to *the Herald* to file his story about the opening. He won't be home for hours." She went down the steps, took her white gloves out of her purse, and put them on. "If I find anything, I'll be careful not to touch."

"All right, but don't be long."

The overgrown grass brushed her ankles. From the mottled limb of a river birch, a hooting owl made her jump. Halfway around the house, she heard the groan of a window. Jess must have found one unlocked and had gotten inside.

In the back, so close to the laundry she could see their lights through the pines, she found a door to the basement. This must be where he lived. The door was locked, so again she looked in the usual places. Under a rock, she found a key that fit, opened the door, and went in.

She ought to go and get Jess, but she wanted to see this for herself.

She turned on a wall switch and took in his room, neater than her own with its bed made and floor swept. In the little kitchenette, a glass had been washed and set to dry on a dish drainer.

The nightstand beside the bed showed a photograph of Thad and Rachel, their arms around each other's waists. It had been taken on the Rosen's front porch. Thad faced Rachel, his eyes fierce, while Rachel looked out at the camera. Eddie had never seen the photograph. When was it taken?

In the nightstand drawer behind paper and receipts was a small brown bag, soft with age that contained two eyebrow pencils and a lipstick, azalea blossom, Pearl's shade. Eddie gasped.

The German policeman Ernst Gennat had said that the *serienmorder* often marked his victim. Her hand shook as she put the bag back where she found it.

She ran to an armoire and found his handsome summer suits and starched shirts hanging inside. At the end of the rack were clothes beneath Berman Laundry's paper covers.

She hung these over the mirrored door, lifted the paper, and found Marine Corps dress blues and two summer khaki-colored service uniforms that looked to be Thad's size. The name tag in the back of the summer shirt read Captain GC Graham.

That's right. Rachel had told her Thad had a brother, who'd been killed in December in the Pacific. The first government girl was murdered in January. Was his brother's death the reason Thad started killing women here in Washington?

Hearing a scrape on the other side of the wall, she froze. "Jess?" she called.

No answer. She listened but heard nothing.

So Thad had a reason to have the uniforms. They were his brother's. Eddie could imagine him saying this in court.

A small desk in front of the window well held a typewriter. Beside the desk was a wastepaper basket. She went through it and found pieces of paper in Pearl's handwriting, which Eddie would recognize anywhere. She put the pieces together on his desk. Pearl had drawn the case map on Jess's wall, labeling the clues. Was that why she was killed? Had she discovered Thad was the killer or had he gotten rid of her because she was no longer useful?

She slipped the pieces of paper into her purse.

Among his books on a bookshelf was a scrapbook. She sat at his desk and opened it. Thad had clipped and glued all his newspaper articles, including the ones from his time in Princeton about the woman strangled there. Under one of these articles, he'd written: I'M ON MY WAY!

Jess had told her that in murder investigations there are no coincidences. She hoped he would feel the same about Thad's career. She closed the scrapbook, put it back, and turned off the lights.

Outside, she looked at the house and noticed Jess had turned on lights upstairs. Maybe he'd found some evidence against Thad. She hoped so, since she hadn't found anything conclusive. Nothing a smarty like Thad couldn't explain even the eyebrow pencils and lipstick. He could say he wanted Pearl's case map diagram for a story.

On the other side of the basement was a garage, its door closed and locked. The garage appeared little-used with weeds growing up through the gravel track that led to it, but some of the ryegrass weeds had been flattened recently.

The garage door wouldn't budge, so she knelt and peeked under. All was dark. There must be a way into the garage from the house. She would go in the way Jess had and check.

Around the corner of the house, she found a root cellar. Its double doors were closed with a rusty padlock, but the padlock hung open.

She took off the padlock and opened the doors. The smell of mold and damp earth wafted from the dark opening. Their house in Saltville had a root cellar accessible through the kitchen. How she'd hated going down there to get a can of tomatoes or peas for dinner.

She ought to go and get Jess, but instead she set her purse beside the opened doors, took a deep breath and stepped down on the first cinderblock step. A flashlight had been left on the end of the second step. She picked it up and turned it on. Nothing happened. Its batteries must be dead. She shook it and got enough light to eat a tiny circle of light in the darkness, enough for her to see the steps.

Once she was at the bottom and surrounded by dirt, she remembered why she hated root cellars. It was as close as the living got to being buried. She shone her light on a wall and saw cans of corn, string beans, then something red. Blood!

She stepped closer, put a white-gloved finger on the red, and smelled. A can of beets had exploded. If air got under the wax seal during the canning process, the can would explode. Why the cans always exploded at night when everyone was in bed she didn't know.

As she turned in the narrow space, something soft brushed her cheek. She shone the weak beam up. The light caught a row of shoes hanging across the ceiling like a necklace. She dropped the flashlight. The last shoe in the strand was Pearl's canvas sandal. Pearl had been wearing it when...

She bent to pick up the flashlight when something came around her neck. She pulled at the belt but it only tightened. She gasped and tried to straighten. He was going to strangle her here in the root cellar. With all her strength, she sent her hand holding the flashlight behind her and hit his leg.

"Ow. Don't, Eddie." Thad's voice was low and soft. He loosened the belt a little. "Please behave so I don't have to kill you down here and drag your long bony body up those steps. I already hurt my back getting Jess into the trunk of my car."

"Jess?" Her pulse exploded in her ears. Her heart pounded so hard she felt as if it would break out of her chest.

"Yeah. I knew you'd want to be together in the end so go on up those steps. Just remember I'm behind you, and I have his gun." He picked up the flashlight and shone it on the steps.

She took the steps slowly trying to calm. Nearing the top she thought about kicking backward, hoping to send him down into darkness and close the doors on him, but he was too close, the end of the gun pressed against her spine.

Light from the garage threw a golden rectangle over the weedy backyard. Thad's Oldsmobile was parked inside. Through the swaying pines came sounds from the laundry. Would anyone working there hear her if she screamed?

"Go over to my car, Eddie." His voice was so calm. "Don't even think about running away or making noise. If you do, I'll shoot you on the spot."

Her legs trembled but somehow she managed to put one foot in front of the other.

When she and Thad stood behind the Oldsmobile, he moved the gun to his other hand and took a set of keys from his pocket. He aimed the gun at her and raised it so that she looked into the barrel's dark eye.

The gun shook in his hand, a fact that didn't fill her with confidence. He could shoot her by accident.

He threw the keys on the ground. "Pick 'em up and unlock the trunk." She did.

Inside the trunk, Jess lay on his back, his eyes closed. Thad had tied his hand behind him.

"Poor old Jess went down like a sack of bricks when I hit him on the back of the head. You know it's hard to tie one arm behind someone's back." Thad nudged her with the gun barrel. "Your turn now, Eddie. Get in the trunk beside Jess. This is going to be real peaceful for you two."

She sensed what Thad was planning. If he closed that lid on them, they were goners. He could gas them with carbon monoxide from the exhaust.

"Do what I told you." Thad stepped closer to Eddie, who stepped back against the garage wall.

In the trunk, Jess opened his eyes and sent his gaze to the wall behind her. She felt a hoe hanging within reach, but would need more distance between her and Thad in order to hit him.

Using his half arm, Jess swung his legs out, kicking at Thad, throwing him off balance. The gun went off in Thad's hand, the recoil jerking his arm back. The gun fell on the ground, a burned smell in the air.

She yanked the hoe off the wall and swung it, catching Thad under his chin. He went down on his knees. Lifting the hoe, she sunk it into his scalp. His head spurted blood, and he fell forward.

Out of the car now, Jess stood in front of Eddie, who untied his hand.

Thad managed to struggle to his feet. Blood dripped down his face. He lunged at Eddie, twisting an arm behind her.

"Take your hands off her." Alonso ran up and grabbed the gun from the ground. He had come from the laundry.

Thad turned. "Give me the gun, Alonso. A colored man won't shoot a white man. You know that." Thad's voice was soft as if he was speaking to a child. "You'd sure feel the rope around your neck if you did."

Letting go of Eddie, Thad stumbled toward Alonso, holding out his hand for the gun.

Alonso watched him a moment, aimed, and fired. Thad went down and stayed down.

Three colored men emerged from the trees.

Jess handed Alonso his handkerchief. "Wipe your prints off it."

Jess turned to the men, who'd come closer. "Could one of you fellas call the police? I'm an agent with the Bureau of Investigation, and I just shot this man." He pointed to Thad, sprawled in the weeds, moaning.

Using the handkerchief, Alonso gave the gun back to Jess. Jess made sure his prints were on the handle before he holstered it.

Although the men must have seen what really happened, they nodded agreement at Jess's words.

One of them ran back to the laundry. "Better call an ambulance, too," Alonso yelled after him.

Using Thad's belt, the one Thad had put around her throat, Alonso make a tourniquet for Thad's arm.

Later Thad Graham would tell the police that Alonso Crooms, a Negro, had shot him, but no one believed him because Thad was the government girl killer.

59

Thursday, August 10, 1944

Eddie heard the knock and slipped the worn copy of *Signal,* a Nazi war magazine, into an envelope. A reader would never know the war was going badly for Germany by reading this magazine's propaganda.

Kurt stood at her door as disheveled as ever. Their department was under a lot of pressure, but Eddie had learned that Kurt saw crisis and deadlines in everything they did. Kurt had no life other than work.

"Agent Friedlander wants to see us in his office," he said. "Whatever you've done to upset his apple cart, I hope I don't get blamed."

"I'll make sure you don't." Was she in trouble? Getting up she smoothed her hair, glad she'd worn her new green dress. Jess said it matched her eyes. If she was going to be reprimanded, she might as well look her best.

She and Kurt took the stairs to the first floor then wound their way down hallways to the agent's office. When they arrived, Agent Friedlander sat behind his desk. Jess and Alonso got up from their chairs, insisting that Kurt and Eddie take them.

Agent Friedlander cleared his throat. "Eddie, Jess told me how you solved the case. How you suspected Thad Graham when no one else did. We feel it's unfair that you haven't gotten the credit you deserve."

Eddie took a deep breath to hold back tears. "I understand why my part can't be…known." Just as no one could know Alonso shot Thad, her part in the case was secret.

She had watched the Bureau's press conference and read the newspaper stories about Thad's arrest. None had mentioned her. After all, she was a translator, not an agent. But she knew what she'd done, and that was enough for her.

The newspapers gave Ray K. credit for assisting Jess. Which was ironic since Ray had been cozy with Thad.

"I've called you here along with your supervisor," he nodded at Kurt, "to let you know formally that the Bureau appreciates your efforts, Edwina Smith." Agent Friedlander stood, so Eddie did, too. "I present you with this commendation signed by the Director."

With trembling hands, Eddie took the paper and read the signature at the bottom: J. Edgar Hoover. She would treasure it always.

"Thank you," she said and straightened.

Alonso picked up his camera. "Eddie, would you shake Agent Friedlander's hand for this one?"

Jess said to his boss. "Eddie would make a fine agent for the Bureau. Why don't you promote her?"

Fred Friedlander's mouth dropped open in shock just as Eddie shook his hand, and Alonso snapped their photograph.

60

Sunday, September 3, 1944

A little after daybreak, Eddie and Ruth, their hair in kerchiefs, aprons covering their clothes, filled clean Mason jars with cooked string beans fresh from the garden. They made sure not to fill all the way to the jar's brim, but left "head space," as Miss Minnie called it.

Jess and Bert sat at the table putting lids and bands on each jar.

"Don't screw them bands too tight," Aunt Minnie said. She was supervising the process, so none of their cans would be wasted by not sealing properly.

Alonso arranged the quart jars in the big pressure cooker. From the pressure cooker, he and Bert, wearing thick oven mitts, carried each jar to the porch to cool, setting them on an old door balanced between two sawhorses. Twenty-four quarts of beans were arranged in rows. These fruits of their labor would be eaten in the winter ahead, another winter of war and rationing.

A gray sunless sky looked in at them. And the cool wind carried a hint of fall. Yet the kitchen pulsed with heat. Sweat beaded their faces. All the while they worked happy. Bert was back among them and on the mend. Soon he would return to work at the laundry.

And Thad Graham would remain in jail until his trial for killing six women or "six government girls" as the newspapers called his victims. Eddie was tired of being called *a girl*. In four days she would turn twenty-one.

With the "The Boogie Woogie Bugle Boy" playing on the radio, Inez danced across the floor, managing not to spill the pitcher of cold tea. Bert had brought the radio in from the parlor. His mother wasn't here to object to it being moved.

After Bert had been vindicated in the newspapers, his mother came back to Washington for a few days to pack up her clothes. She was returning to Saltville.

"Folks won't ever look at you the same," she told Bert in the parlor her first afternoon home.

Eddie, sitting beside Bert on the sofa, said, "Don't be ridiculous, Aunt Viola. Bert is a good man and anyone who knows him knows that."

Aunt Viola sighed. "But no woman will want to marry him now. He'll never find himself a wife." She got up and waddled out of the parlor, slamming the door.

Eddie and Bert exchanged a look and laughed. Last night, Bert's friend Owen came to dinner for the first time. Eddie enjoyed seeing Bert relax and have fun.

The radio's music stopped. "We interrupt this regularly scheduled program for a news bulletin." They paused to listen. "Today American forces have turned over the government of France to the free French under General Charles de Gaulle."

They cheered and cried and hugged each other. Eddie wasn't exactly sure why. Certainly there was still more war to go in Europe and in the Pacific.

"I think I hear the telephone," Inez said.

Eddie ran and answered it.

"Eddie?"

"Hello, Mr. Margolis. Did you get my letter?"

She'd written him after Thad confessed to murdering the women. In her letter, she said that Thad never confessed to murdering Rachel. In fact Thad insisted he knew nothing about Rachel's disappearance, and Eddie believed him. *I feel certain she is alive,* Eddie had written Mr. Margolis.

"I did. Thank you, Eddie. Detective Kaminski called and told me the same thing. He still believes Rachel ran away. Do you think she knew this reporter was the killer?"

Eddie had wondered about that. "No. I'm sure she didn't. He had us all fooled."

Why did Thad kill those women? His mother drank and had died in a fire. Thad had been commended by the police for trying to rescue her. Eddie suspected he might have also set the fire.

Dr. Kushner said Thad wanted to cleanse the world of women he deemed immoral like his mother. But Eddie saw Thad another way. In this city of ambitious people, Thad had been willing to do anything to get ahead. In order to get the scoop, he made news. But of course, his reasons weren't as simple as that. Perhaps they would never know.

Mr. Margolis said, "I read about Jess Lindsay in the newspaper. He's a remarkable detective."

"Oh, yes." She was more in love with Jess than ever.

"The newspaper said Jess will be leaving the Bureau soon and will set up his own detective agency." His voice was choked with tears. "I want to be his first client. Do you think he can find my Rachel?"

"I do." Eddie knew her own life would never be right until she knew what had happened to Rachel. "Hold on, Mr. Margolis. I'll bring him to the telephone."

She set the receiver down and ran to the kitchen.

The End

Acknowledgements

I have lived this story through my mother's memories as a government girl. My research material includes David Brinkley's memoir, *Washington Goes to War, Alley Life in Washington* by James Borchet, *Historic Restaurants of Washington, D.C.* by John DeFarrari, Scott Hart's *Washington At War: 1941-1945*, the *World War II* series published by Time-Life books, and the Martin Luther King Center. Rebecca Kyle read early drafts of this and was my fantastic copyeditor. Writer Phyllis Rozman shared her experiences of living in Washington at this time. I thank my friends at the Writer's Center and The Maryland Writers Association. I could not have written anything without the support of my husband, John Henry Herbert, and my son, John Joseph Herbert.

For book discussion questions and more, see my website http://ellen-herbert.info.

About The Author

Ellen Herbert's short fiction has won a PEN Fiction, a Virginia Fiction Fellowship, and other prizes and has been published in literary magazines, women's magazines, and read on NPR. Her short story collection, *Falling Women and Other Stories*, was published by Shelfstealers Press in 2012. Her nonfiction won *The Flint Hills Review Prize for Creative Nonfiction* and has been published in *The Washington Post*. She teaches creative writing at The Writer's Center, Bethesda, Maryland and leads a mystery book club at One More Page Books in Arlington, Virginia.

Maryland Writers Association Acknowledgments

Primary Judges

Holly Morse-Ellington has published essays and photographs with *Wanderlust and Lipstick, Matador Network, Three Quarter Review, Baltimore Fishbowl, Outside In Literary & Travel Magazine, Urbanite, The Journal of Homeland Security, The Washington Times*, and elsewhere. She is an editor for *Baltimore Review* and the publicist for award-winning singer-songwriter, Victoria Vox. Holly is also the State Vice President of the Maryland Writers' Association. Holly and Jason Tinney co-authored the play, *Fifty Miles Away*, winner of the Frostburg State University Center for Creative Writing One-Act Play Festival 2015. They write and perform music as Limestone Connection.

Born in India, **Lalita Noronha** is a research scientist, science teacher, poet, author, and a fiction editor for *The Baltimore Review*. Her literary work has appeared in numerous journals and anthologies such as *Crab Orchard Review, The Cortland Review, The Baltimore Sun, The Christian Science Monitor, Get Well Wishes (Harper Collins)* among others, in the US, India, Canada and Australia. She is the author of a short story collection, *Where Monsoons Cry (BlackWords Press)* which won the Maryland Literary Arts Award and a poetry chapbook, *Her Skin Phyllo-thin (Finishing Line Press)*. Other credits include a Maryland Individual Artist Award in fiction and awards from *Arlington Literary Journal*, Dorothy Daniels National League of American Pen Women, Maryland Writers' Association (fiction, creative nonfiction and poetry) and two Pushcart nominations in poetry and creative nonfiction. She has also been featured a few times on National Public Radio, WYPR, *The Signal*, and currently serves as the State President of the Maryland Writers' Association.

Brandi Dawn Henderson is a traveling writer, on regular journeys that prove truths to be no strangers to fictions. She co-created and edited *Outside In Literary & Travel Magazine*, a resource dedicated to promoting cross-cultural understanding through global storytelling. She wrote a relatively successful expat column and an utter failure of an advice column for a year in New Delhi, is the editor of the travel anthologies *Whereabouts: Stepping Out of Place* (2Leaf Press) and *(T)here: Writings on Returnings* (Martlet & Mare Books), and has had work published in a variety of journals. She now resides near Portland with a red-bearded outdoorsman and two dogs, Lola and Cormac McArfy. www.outsideinmagazine.com

Shenan Prestwich is a writer, poet, editor, and Washington, DC native recently transplanted to Portland, OR. Publishing in a wide variety of venues both in print and online, Shenan holds a Master of Arts degree in writing (with a concentration in poetry) from Johns Hopkins University and her first full-length collection of poetry, *In the Wake*, was recently released from White Violet Press. She has served in an editorial capacity for publications such as *Magic Lantern Review, Outside In Literary and Travel Magazine,* and *Prompt & Circumstance.* You can follow her at http://shenanprestwich.com.

Born and raised in Baltimore, **Dean Bartoli Smith** is the author of *NEVER EASY, NEVER PRETTY: A Fan. A City. A Championship Season* (Temple University Press, 2013) and a contributor to the 2nd Edition of Ted Patterson's *FOOTBALL IN BALTIMORE* (Johns Hopkins University Press, 2013). His poetry has appeared in *Poetry East, Open City, Beltway, The Pearl, The Charlotte Review, Gulf Stream,* and *upstreet* among others. His book of poems, *American Boy,* won the 2000 Washington Writer's Prize and was also awarded the Maryland Prize for Literature in 2001 for the best book published by a Maryland writer over the past three years. He writes sports for *Press Box* and *Baltimore Brew.* He attended Loyola High School and graduated from Loyola Academy in Wilmette, Illinois. He majored in English at the University of Virginia and received an MFA in Poetry from Columbia University. He was the director of Project MUSE at The Johns Hopkins University, a leading provider of digital humanities and social science content for the scholarly community, and is currently the director of Cornell University Press.

Apprentice House is the country's only campus-based, student-staffed book publishing company. Directed by professors and industry professionals, it is a nonprofit activity of the Communication Department at Loyola University Maryland.

Using state-of-the-art technology and an experiential learning model of education, Apprentice House publishes books in untraditional ways. This dual responsibility as publishers and educators creates an unprecedented collaborative environment among faculty and students, while teaching tomorrow's editors, designers, and marketers.

Outside of class, progress on book projects is carried forth by the AH Book Publishing Club, a co-curricular campus organization supported by Loyola University Maryland's Office of Student Activities.

Eclectic and provocative, Apprentice House titles intend to entertain as well as spark dialogue on a variety of topics. Financial contributions to sustain the press's work are welcomed. Contributions are tax deductible to the fullest extent allowed by the IRS.

To learn more about Apprentice House books or to obtain submission guidelines, please visit www.apprenticehouse.com.

Apprentice House
Communication Department
Loyola University Maryland
4501 N. Charles Street
Baltimore, MD 21210
Ph: 410-617-5265 • Fax: 410-617-2198
info@apprenticehouse.com • www.apprenticehouse.com

CPSIA information can be obtained at www.ICGtesting.com
Printed in the USA
BVOW06s2055220915

419234BV00009B/98/P